LAWRENCE SANDERS

"A masterful storyteller!"
—*King Features Syndicate*

"A writer who has matured into one of our great ones."
—*Pittsburgh Press*

"One of the most consistently satisfying 'entertainment' novelists in America today!"
—*Washington Post*

"A master!"
—*New Yorker*

**Don't miss
his other explosive bestsellers—
Available from Berkley Books**

Lawrence SANDERS

The Timothy FILES

BERKLEY BOOKS, NEW YORK

This Berkley book contains the complete
text of the original hardcover edition.
It has been completely reset in a typeface
designed for easy reading, and was printed
from new film.

THE TIMOTHY FILES

A Berkley Book/published by arrangement with
the author

PRINTING HISTORY
G. P. Putnam's Sons edition/June 1987
Berkley international edition/November 1987

ISBN: 0-425-10676-4

A BERKLEY BOOK ® TM 757,375
Berkley Books are published by The Berkley Publishing Group,
200 Madison Avenue, New York, New York 10016.
The name "BERKLEY" and the "B" logo
are trademarks belonging to Berkley Publishing Corporation.

PRINTED IN THE UNITED STATES OF AMERICA

BOOK ONE

The Wall Street Dick

1

AN ELEGANT YOUNG man, plumpish but dapper, bounces down the stairs into the Union Square subway station. He is wearing a three-piece suit of pin-striped gray flannel, a fawn fedora cocked at a rakish angle. He swings an attaché case of black alligator. It is empty. Just a prop.

On the uptown express platform, he stands well back from the tracks and looks about casually. Spots the target he has been following by leading: the first at the coin booth, the first through the turnstiles. He is sure of the subject, knows the route, knows the destination. Why run the chance of being recognized as a shadow when you can go ahead?

The target leans against a pillar, starts flipping through the pages of the *New York Post*. But then the rumble of an approaching train is heard, the newspaper is closed and folded. People move closer to the edge of the platform. The elegant young man saunters up, too, and positions himself so he can get on the same car as the subject. Everyone stands patiently, waiting.

The train rounds the curve, headlight gleaming. Experienced passengers congregate in the areas where they know the doors will open when the train halts. The young man inches closer to the edge of the platform, keeping an eye on the target, ready to hold back or even jump off the train at the last minute if his quarry decides to bolt.

3

The train roars into the station, slowing, clattering. The dandy smiles faintly, clamps the empty attaché case under his arm.

Suddenly he is pushed from behind. A powerful thrust in the middle of his back. It propels him forward, off the edge of the platform. Hat and alligator case go flying. Arms and legs stretching, he falls directly in front of the train.

Yells, screams, the shriek of brakes. But he is hit, hurled down the track. The first car passes over him before the train can be brought to a stop. There is shouting, confusion, everyone running, peering. One old man goes down on his knees, praying, crossing himself.

The target moves back, disengages slowly from the mob. Walks up into the sunlight and takes out a cigarette. A moment later the assassin arrives.

"Beautiful," the subject says.

And they stroll off together to the nearest bar where both have martinis, very dry, straight up, with a twist of lemon.

Haldering & Co. is not as large or prestigious as Kroll Associates, Intertel, or Bishop's Service, Inc., but has a good and growing reputation as one of Wall Street's dependable "specialists in corporate intelligence." None of the firms engaged in this unique activity approve of the terms "private detective" or "private eye." But regardless of nomenclature, they are all involved in confidential investigations.

When a buyout, merger, or unfriendly takeover is in the works, inevitably the companies involved seek the advice of attorneys or investment counselors. And they more often than not turn to Wall Street's financial dicks to provide information on corporations and, more important, their owners, chairmen of the board, directors, presidents, chief executive officers, and anyone else whose probity or lack thereof might affect the deal.

Haldering & Co. has been in existence only four years, and as new boy on the block, the boss, Hiram Haldering, an ex-FBI man, does not expect to be called in on multibillion-dollar oil, steel, or chemical takeovers, friendly or otherwise. But as H. H. is fond of remarking, "You've got to walk before you can fly"—which makes little sense to anyone but him.

So Haldering & Co. contents itself, temporarily, with financial deals of modest proportions or with jobs that do not involve the activities of the better-known corporate raiders. H. H. is satisfied with assignments to investigate the principals in mergers, buyouts, and takeovers in the seven- and eight-figure range. As he likes to say, "There's enough lettuce around for all us rabbits."

The offices of Haldering & Co. are located in a dilapidated, turn-of-the-century building on John Street that is scheduled for the wrecker's ball as soon as a hotshot developer succeeds in completing a real estate parcel that will level another entire city block and fill it with a steel, concrete, and glass skyscraper that will have windows that can't be opened and high-speed elevators chronically marked Out of Service.

Haldering's offices look as if the demolition has already started. It is a floor-through of individual cubbyholes divided by painted plywood partitions. The pitted wood floor has been covered with peach-colored tiles, and the plants in the reception area are plastic.

Hiram Haldering, with a passion for chains of command and tables of organization, has divided his work force into three divisions: attorneys, accountants, and investigators. Each division is headed by a supervisor. Samantha Whatley oversees the detectives.

News of G. Edward Griffon's death at the Union Square subway station reaches the offices of Haldering & Co. at about three-thirty in the afternoon. Two New York Police Department detectives show up and inform H. H. that one of his investigators has fallen to his death under circumstances that are being investigated.

H. H. calls in Samantha Whatley, and the two offer what

assistance they can. The city detectives want whatever is in the victim's employment file, and are given photocopies. Then they ask for information on the cases currently assigned to G. Edward Griffon. Hiram Haldering balks, his muttony face reddening.

"Look," he tells the detectives, "you know what we do. All our jobs are hush-hush. I mean, news of an investigation gets out, and someone could make a fortune trading on insider information. The reputation of the company would go down the drain. If we can't guarantee our clients confidentiality, we've got nothing to sell."

One of the city detectives sighs. "Do we have to get a court order?" he asks. "We've cooperated with your people in the past. Do you want to play hardball and end all that?"

Mr. Haldering is a puffy man who thinks walking upstairs to his second-floor office keeps him in splendid condition.

Running a hand over his balding pate, he looks at the NYPD detectives. "You think Griffon was scragged?" he demands.

The detective shrugs. "He fell, jumped, or was pushed. Who the hell knows? No one saw anything. No one wants to get involved. You know how these things go, but we've got to go through the drill. Now do we find out what he was working on or don't we?"

Haldering makes his decision; he can't afford to alienate the local police. "All right," he says, "as long as you abide by the SEC regulations on insider information, I'll give you photocopies of Griffon's current files. See how I cooperate? And I suppose you'll want to talk to everyone who works here. Sam, will you arrange things? I've got a meeting with a client."

Samantha Whatley nods, knowing that the "meeting with a client" is Hiram Haldering's weekly session with a doxy who services many executives in the financial community. In addition to her renown as a mattress acrobat, she is reputed to be one of the most knowledgeable and successful commodity traders on the Street, specializing in pork belly futures.

All Haldering & Co. employees on the premises are told to stand by for questioning, and the two NYPD cops get to work. Meanwhile, Samantha Whatley calls her staff into her office. Ordinarily she honchos seven investigators, but one is on sick leave and two on out-of-town assignments.

"You've all heard about Ed Griffon," she says tonelessly when the remaining four have crowded into her office. "I know how you feel. The police have notified his mother and sister. When the body is released we'll all attend the funeral. That's not a suggestion, it's an order."

They all look down at the floor, shuffling their feet. Griffon's death is an unwelcome reminder of the hazards of their profession. They are all licensed to carry handguns, but a shooter hadn't helped Ed any, had it? Recognition of their own mortality has the sound of muffled drums and the taste of bile.

"What in God's name happened, Sam?" Ernie Waters asks finally. "Do the cops know?"

"Not yet. They say he fell, jumped, or was pushed."

"He was pushed," says Timothy Cone, who has remained standing at the open office door.

Samantha looks up at him sharply. "How the hell do you know that?"

"Ed wouldn't go down in the subway unless he was tailing someone. The guy owned a Jaguar, and when he wasn't driving that, he took cabs. Take a look at his expense account chits, and you'll see."

"He could have fallen," Fred Burgess says. "Accidentally."

"No way," Cone says. "Ed didn't have accidents; he was a careful man. And he wouldn't jump. He enjoyed life too much for that. I tell you he was pushed."

"You know so much," Samantha says angrily, "tell the cops about it."

"I intend to. It may have been a crazy. Or it may have been the subject he was tailing."

"Jesus Christ, Tim," says Samantha, "I wish I could be as sure about anything as you are about everything."

"I'm sure about this," Cone says coolly. "Ed was killed. What was he working on, Sam?"

"That's why I called you all in," she says, slapping a stack of file folders on her desk. "I'm going to divide Ed's cases—one or two to each of you. Until Joe gets back from sick leave or we hire another warm body."

"My God," Sol Faber says. "Sam, we've all got more than we can handle right now."

"Tell me about it," she says bitterly. "You think I haven't been bugging H. H. for help? Maybe Ed's death will convince him we need more working eyes. But until that happens, you'll just have to forget the two-hour lunches and work harder."

"Two-hour lunches?" Cone says incredulously. "How can you spend two hours on a cheeseburger and Coke? You're spinning your wheels, Sam."

She glares at him. "If you're trying to be a pain in the ass," she says, "you're succeeding admirably."

Samantha Whatley is a tall drink of water, with the stretched body of a swimmer and the muscles of a gymnast. She is a sharp-featured woman with a lot of jaw and blue-green eyes with all the warmth of licked stones. A flattish chest and practically no ass at all. Even her long auburn hair is worn up, tightly coiled, and looks like a russet beehive.

Her background includes four years in the US Army, three in the NYPD, and two working as a private investigator for a bondsman on Hester Street. She may not be feminine, but no one doubts her competence.

"All right," she says, "let's cut the shit and get back to work." She begins to hand out the folders. "Ernie, here's yours. Fred, yours. Sol, you take these. Tim, there's one left for you."

"Gee, boss," he says, "why are you so good to me?"

"Up yours," she says. "All you guys hang around until the cops have a chance to talk to you."

"Do they have copies of these files?" Sol Faber asks.

"They do," Samantha says. "And if you find anything in them that you think may have something to do with Ed's death, don't be shy about telling them. Another thing: You're all falling behind in your weekly progress reports. Will you, for Christ's sake, get on the goddamned ball? That's all. Take off."

The four investigators wander down the corridor to their own broom closet offices.

"There is one tough cookie," Ernie Waters says, sighing.

"An iron fist in an iron glove," Tim Cone says.

"The woman's a fucking barracuda," Fred Burgess says.

"I don't think so," Sol Faber says. "Just a barracuda."

They all laugh.

Timothy Cone takes Griffon's file folder to his office and slips it into a manila envelope, so tattered that he's patched the seams with Scotch tape. Then he leaves the building, figuring the NYPD detectives will catch up with him eventually; he's not about to sit around waiting.

Cone lives in a loft on the top floor of one of the few cast-iron buildings on lower Broadway, between Spring and Broome Streets. On good days he walks to and from work. It's a nice hike and gives him the chance to get some of the cigarette smoke out of his lungs and observe the changing profile of Little Old New York.

This particular evening is not all that great: a warm September mist in the air, a clotted sky, and humidity thick enough to skim his face. But he plods uptown anyway, reacting automatically to traffic signs and construction sites, and thinking about G. Edward Griffon.

Ed was no particular pal of his—but neither is anyone else. The other dicks at Haldering think him sometimes sullen, sometimes manic. Generally, they leave him alone. But Griffon really tried to be a friend. He didn't succeed, but Tim Cone appreciated the effort. Maybe Ed saw that behind Cone's love of solitude was an innate shyness.

Griffon constantly tried to get Timothy to spruce up.

"Look," he'd say, "I know you've got the money, but you live in a dump and dress like a bum. What's *with* you?"

"I don't like to go shopping," Cone would say, not admitting that department stores and salesclerks intimidated him. "Besides, I've got no interest in style or fashion."

"Tim, if I go with you, will you at least buy a decent suit?"

"No. I've got enough clothes."

In a way, Cone decides, slogging uptown, he admired G. Edward Griffon, and envied him. The guy always looked so fresh and smartly dressed. Now he is a clunk on a stainless steel table in the morgue, and some butcher in a bloody apron is carving him up to find out how he died.

"It isn't right," Timothy Cone says aloud, and passersby glance at him nervously.

The Wall Street dick is a scrawny, hawkish man who has never learned to shave close enough, so his coffin jaw always has a bluish tinge. He is tall and stooped, with a shambling gait that reminds people of a hardscrabble farmer, although he was born in Brooklyn. His nose is a hatchet and his big ears flop.

No one has ever accused him of being handsome, but when he smiles (infrequently), his ugliness has a quirky charm. Few have heard him laugh. He moves through life, shoulders bowed, carrying a burden he cannot define. But morosity is his nature, and he is continually shocked when good things happen. He expects the end of the world at any minute.

On this day he wears a black, flapping raincoat, so ancient that the wrinkles are grayish, and the collar and cuffs greasy. Atop his spiky, ginger-colored hair is a limp black leather cap, an ebony omelet. Beneath the raincoat is a worn corduroy suit, so old that the pants no longer whistle as he walks. On his big, splayed feet are heavy yellow work shoes laced high.

When he reaches his loft building, he sees the lock on the street door has been jimmied again, the third time in as many months. He stoops swiftly, slides his Smith & Wesson .357 Magnum with a short barrel from the ankle holster and transfers it to the pocket of his raincoat.

There are commercial tenants on the first four floors, but the big freight elevator stops operating at six P.M. Cone climbs the iron stairs, gripping his handgun, carrying the manila envelope and listening to the sounds of conversation from some of the offices he passes. On the sixth floor, he pauses to catch his breath and examine the lock on his door. It looks all right to him. His place has been broken into twice. But that was months ago, and they've never come back. Why should they? He's got nothing worth stealing.

Griffon was right: It *is* a dump: one big room with cracked plaster walls. Sink, stove, and bathtub are exposed; only the toilet is hidden in a closet. Overhead are the bare pipes of a sprinkler system. There is a skylight, so filthy that it might as well be a steel shutter for all the sunshine it transmits. One of the glass panes is broken and stuffed with an old undershirt.

There is a mattress on the floor; Cone has never gotten around to buying a bedstead. A rickety desk doubles as a dining table. A few nothing chairs. A chest of drawers he found in the street and lugged home. The only decoration on the walls is a framed lithograph: *Washington Crossing the Delaware*. It was there when Cone leased the place, and he's never removed it.

When he enters, Cleo, his cat, comes up and rubs against his leg, meowing piteously.

"Shut your mouth," Timothy says. "You eat when I do." But he bends to scratch the animal behind its ears.

The cat looks like it's been in many fights and lost all of them. Cone found it one winter night in the gutter, bruised and torn, and brought it home to thaw out, lick its wounds, and gobble a slice of salami. It was originally a tom, but Cone had it neutered and declawed, and then named the castrated tom Cleo, for Cleopatra, it being the ugliest, least seductive cat he has ever seen in his life.

He inspects the contents of his obsolete waist-high refrigerator. There's a cold fried pork chop, hard as a rock; a jar of instant coffee; a chunk of cheddar covered with green mold; an unopened package of turkey pastrami. Also, four cans of Budweiser, a bottle of Gallo Hearty Burgundy, one soft tomato, and a browned head of iceberg lettuce. Not too encouraging.

But in the freezer section are two pizzas, individual size, both sausage, and a bottle of vodka with about four slugs left. That's better. He gives the old pork chop to Cleo, who grabs it and runs away under the tub where no one can take the feast away.

Cone pours himself a healthy jolt of vodka in an empty jelly jar and sits down on one of the spindly kitchen chairs to wait. He's good at that.

He's halfway through his drink when there's a knock on the door. The familiar signal: two short raps, pause, one more knock. He rises, goes over to unbolt and unlock. Samantha Whatley is standing there, wearing a belted trenchcoat.

"Hello, asshole," she says.

"Hello, shithead," he says.

Ten minutes later they're naked on his mattress, fucking their brains out.

Samantha Whatley wakes first, a little before seven A.M., rises from the mattress, relieves herself in the closet, and washes, as best she can, at the kitchen sink. She makes a grimace of distaste at the condition of the only towel she can find. It is clean enough, but fragile as Belgian lace. She puts up her hair, using rubber bands, pins, and two barrettes.

She dresses swiftly, then digs a heavy brogue into the ribs of the still-sleeping Timothy Cone.

"Get up, you monster," she says loudly. "I'm going home, but I want a cup of coffee first."

He rouses slowly, groaning, then scrubs his face with his palms. His hair sticks up like a fright wig. Cleo wanders over to sniff at his bare toes, but he kicks the cat away.

"Put the water on," he says in a growly voice, "while I shower. I smell like a goat."

"Tell me about it," she says.

She puts the kettle on to boil, searches his cupboard for two cups and saucers that match, gives up in disgust.

"You live like a gypsy," she tells him.

"I am a gypsy," he says. "And if you keep complaining, I'll put the curse on you."

"I had the curse," she says. "But not since I got spayed."

She watches him take the enameled lid off the bathtub. There is no shower, but he has a long rubber tube and spray head that attaches to the faucet. He has to hold it in one hand while he soaps with the other, standing up in the corroded tub. Water splashes onto the linoleum floor.

He has a splintery body, all sharp bones, stretched tendons, hard muscles. His fair skin is freckled across the shoulders and on his upper arms. Stomach flat, buttocks tight. He is hung like a donkey—which is okay with Samantha.

He climbs out of the tub and picks up the towel.

"This is damp," he says accusingly.

"Tough shitski," she says. "If you remembered to pick up your laundry occasionally, we'd have dry towels and clean sheets. Also, we finished the vodka last night, so you need another jug. Also, you might get some white wine; I'm getting tired of red."

"Yes, sir," he says, knocking off a mock salute. "And how about some champagne and caviar?"

"That'll be the day," she says. "You're the bologna sandwich and beer type. I knew that the first time I saw you."

They sit at his desk and sip their steaming cups of black coffee.

"Sam," he says, "did you go over Ed Griffon's weekly progress reports for the past few months?"

"Give me credit for a little sense," she says indignantly. "Of course I went over them. The first thing I did after I heard how he died. They're strictly routine. Not a word hints of any trouble. You want to see them?"

"No," he says. "If you say they're clean, then they're clean."

She looks at him. "I get suspicious when you start acting like Mr. Nice. What do you want?"

"I may be a little late getting to the office this morning."

"So what else is new?"

"I brought that Griffon file home with me," he tells her.

"You took a file out of the office? You schmuck! If H. H. ever finds out, it means your ass. You know that, don't you?"

"Yeah, well, I'll worry about that when it happens. Anyway, I want to go over the file without the phone ringing and the cops asking questions. I'll be in later."

"Tim, you're not going to neglect your own caseload because of this, are you?"

"Yes," he says, "I am. Any objections?"

"Would it do any good if I had?" Then she covers one of his bony hands with a warm palm. "Ed's death really hit you hard, didn't it?"

He swirls what's left of his coffee around in the cup, then gulps it down. "It's just not right," he says stubbornly.

She gathers up her shoulder bag and trenchcoat, then leans to scratch Cleo's ribs. The cat purrs with delight.

"Don't forget to feed her," she says.

"It's not a her," Cone says crossly. "I keep telling you: It's a deballed he."

"He, she, it," Samantha says. "I couldn't care less."

At the door, she turns her face up to him. "Knock us a kiss," she says.

"Sentimental slush," he mutters. But he kisses her.

The moment she's gone, the door locked and bolted, he

rummages around frantically for a package of cigarettes. Nothing. All gone. But he finds two long butts in the ashtray, and one more in the garbage can. He salvages them all, straightens them out, lights his first of the day. He inhales deeply, closes his eyes, and coughs, coughs, coughs.

Soothed, he fills Cleo's water bowl and gives the cat a chunk of moldy cheddar and a slice of turkey salami. That beast will eat anything. Then Cone makes himself another cup of black coffee and sits down at the desk with Ed Griffon's case file open before him.

He flips through it swiftly to see what he's got. Mostly it's a sheaf of documents Haldering & Co. call PIEs— Preliminary Intelligence Estimates. These are prepared by the company's accountants and attorneys, then handed over to the detectives for further investigation into the private lives of the individuals involved, if the facts seem to warrant it.

In addition to the PIEs, there are a few rough notes by Griffon. It gives Cone a queasy feeling to see the dead man's handwriting. Almost as bad as hearing a message left on your answering machine by someone suddenly deceased. A voice from the grave. Cone lights his second cigarette butt of the morning and starts reading the file slowly.

The case seems innocent enough. The client is Samuel Evanchat & Sons, an old and respected developer-builder of Manhattan East Side properties. The firm has the reputation of putting up elegant townhouses with a Stanford White look about them. Isaac Evanchat, the last of the clan, is now in his late sixties and has decided to retire to his Mizner-designed Palm Beach home and spend the rest of his days trying to hook a world-class sailfish.

Isaac is contemplating selling out to Clovis & Clovis, Inc., a miniconglomerate which, if you believe New York newspapers and magazines, seems to own or manage half the real estate in midtown Manhattan. The selling price is projected at $175 million. But Evanchat, proud and cautious, wants to make sure his family business will be in good hands, and the 175 mil will be forthcoming. So he has hired Haldering & Co., asking for a complete intelligence rundown on Clovis & Clovis.

Both principals in the proposed deal are privately held companies, and it's been difficult for Haldering's attorneys and accountants to assemble an accurate balance sheet on Clovis & Clovis. But they've done what they can, using the few public records that exist, confidential sources, and talking to ex-employees, particularly the disgruntled ones. They've produced a report in which Clovis & Clovis comes up smelling like roses.

Their summary notes that the parent company, with assets of more than one billion, owns controlling interest in four other companies involved in general contracting, plumbing and electrical supplies, foundations and underpinning, and an outfit called New World Enterprises, Inc., only fourteen months old, organized, according to its corporate charter, "for purposes of building and renovating commercial and residential real estate properties."

It all seems cut-and-dried to Timothy Cone, lighting his third and final cigarette butt. Here's this big real estate corporation with four subsidiaries. Nothing sinister there. Apparently all the divisions are profitable.

Cone turns to Griffon's personal notes and reads them carefully. Mostly they're short biogs on the owners of Clovis & Clovis. That would be Stanley Clovis, forty-three, and his sister Lucinda, forty-one, each of whom owns 50 percent of the parent company. Stanley is married and has two children. Lucinda is unmarried and has no children.

Brother and sister are very active in civic affairs, Manhattan politics, and charities. They are generous donors to libraries, museums, ballet groups, and symphony orchestras. They are on the society pages frequently, and recently Clovis & Clovis hosted a big bash to celebrate the opening of a park and playground in the South Bronx that they built and gave to the City of New York.

Both Stanley and Lucinda Clovis sound like fine, upstanding citizens. With their gelt, Cone reflects sourly, they can afford to be. There seems to be little in the file that indicates further investigation into Clovis & Clovis would be justified.

But then, the last item in Ed Griffon's personal notes, there is a torn sheet of green scratch paper. On it Ed had scrawled, DUM? Cone stares at the capital letters. DUM? What the hell could that mean. Initials maybe? Department of Underwear Manufacturers? Division of Undertaker Matrons?

He closes the folder and ruminates in his stolid, methodical way. If this particular file has no connection with the death of G. Edward Griffon, then perhaps the other cases Ed was handling do—the ones that were inherited by Ernie Waters, Fred Burgess, and Sol Faber. And if those files show nothing that isn't kosher, then maybe Ed really did fall or jump to his death.

Cone doesn't believe it for a minute. The guy was wasted. Deliberately.

But what the hell does DUM? mean?

Sighing, he rises, slips the Clovis & Clovis folder back into the shabby manila envelope, prepares to go to the office. He's still wearing his sleazy corduroy suit, yellow work shoes, the black leather cap. As he goes out the door, he pauses to raise an admonishing forefinger at the watching Cleo.

"Guard!" he orders the astonished cat. Then locks up and clatters down the iron stairs.

He stops first to buy two packs of Camels, then continues his amble downtown. The air has cleared, there's a sun up there, and the streets are bustling. Guys are tearing up Broadway, dancing around the steelwork on new buildings, and sidewalk vendors are heating up their franks and sauerkraut. Everyone hustling to make a buck.

When he gets to his office, he finds a NYPD dick waiting outside, sitting on a folding chair and placidly chewing on a wad of something. The detective is big and overweight. He doesn't exactly spring to his feet; he levers himself slowly upward as if he isn't sure he'll make it. The conversation goes like this:

"You Timothy Cone?"

"That's right."

"You're an investigator here?"

"Yep."

"You were told to stick around last night. How come you took off?"

"My cat was sick. The vet wasn't sure he could save her."

"That's a new one. Usually it's a wife in Intensive Care. Let's talk."

"Sure."

In Cone's minuscule office, the detective shows his ID. Neal K. Davenport. He's a ruddy-faced man with plump hands and a habit of cocking his head to one side while waiting for his questions to be answered. Cone isn't fooled by the laid-back manner. This guy, he decides, is one shrewd apple.

"You want a cigarette?" he asks.

"No, thanks. I swore off. Now I chew Juicy Fruit." He takes out a package, extracts a stick, shoves it into his mouth. He crumples the wrapper, stuffs it into his jacket pocket. "You and the deceased buddy-buddy?" he asks Cone.

"Not really."

"No, I guess not. From what I hear you're a loner."

"That's right."

"Nothing wrong with that," Davenport says, shifting his bulk in the uncomfortable chair, "if it gets results." He chews his gum steadily. "You know anything about Griffon's private life?"

"Very little. I know he lived with his mother and sister. Somewhere in the Gramercy Park area."

"Yeah. He ever talk about any girlfriends?"

"No."

"Friends? Enemies?"

"No, nothing like that. I told you, we weren't close."

"Yeah," the fat detective says, sighing. "I understand you think he was pushed."

"I think so. He'd never jump, and he was too smart to fall. Maybe it was a crazy who gave him a shove."

"Maybe." The gumshoe climbs laboriously to his feet. "He was carrying an empty attaché case. You know why he'd do that?"

"No."

"You got the file on one of his cases?"

Cone nods.

"Anything interesting in it?"

"Strictly routine."

The detective slides a personal card across the desk. "If you come up with anything," he says, "give me a call."

"I'll do that," Cone says.

"Sure you will," Davenport says with a bleak smile. "We're both on the same side—right?"

After he's gone, Cone walks around the corridors to the section inhabited by accountants and attorneys. He stops at an office twice as large as his, with a rug on the floor and two windows. The brass sign on the desk reads: MR. SIDNEY APICELLA. Cone likes the "Mr."

Apicella is a sweet man, but the poor fellow suffers from rosacea of the proboscis. Although a nondrinker, he's got the schnoz of an alcoholic moose. The big, lumpy nose is the first thing you see when you look at him, and even the politest visitor has trouble tearing his fascinated stare away from that rosy balloon.

He looks up when Cone enters. "I haven't got time," he says.

"Sure you do, Sid," Cone says, slumping into the chair alongside Apicella's desk.

The chief accountant sighs. "I'm sorry about Ed," he says.

"Yeah, he was an okay guy. Listen, Sid, you signed that PIE on the proposed buyout of Samuel Evanchat and Sons by Clovis and Clovis."

"That's right, I did. Anything wrong with it?"

"Not that I can see, but I've got a question. Clovis and Clovis is in the business of brokering or developing properties. So why did they start a subsidiary, New World Enterprises, Inc., to do exactly the same thing?"

"I caught that and asked Stanley Clovis himself. He says the parent company handles megabuck deals: skyscrapers and luxury co-ops and industrial parks. Stuff like that. New World was organized to develop smaller parcels, like renovating old brownstones or abandoned tenements."

"Yeah," Cone says. "It makes sense." He gets up to leave, then pauses at the doorway. "One more thing, Sid: In your business does DUM mean something special?"

"Sure: 'stupid.'"

"Not d-u-m-b," Cone says patiently. "This is spelled d-u-m, all in capital letters followed by a question mark."

"You mean like in dum-di-dum-dum? Nope, it doesn't mean a thing to me."

"Me neither."

Cone's next stop is Samantha's office.

"So glad you could make it," she says, glaring at him.

He ignores the sarcasm. "Did you talk to the other guys about Griffon's cases?"

She slams a palm down on her desk top in frustration. "When the hell are you going to give me credit for having brains? Of course I talked to them. They all say they found nothing suspicious."

"Okay," he says equably. "Just asking. See you around."

He waves, goes back to his office to pick up his cap, and starts out. He takes an uptown bus, knowing it's going to be a long trip, but relishing the opportunity to look out the windows at the crazy city he loves, for reasons he cannot define. Also, the ride will give him time to think.

Cone knows very well there are cubbyhole offices on Wall Street where one honest man sits alone and shuffles billions of dollars in pension funds by telephone. There are also glitzy offices, with ankle-deep rugs and abstract and impressionist paintings on the walls, that are no better than bucket shops and will be down the tube as soon as the SEC gets wise to their shenanigans.

Despite all that, he still believes in making on-the-site inspections when working a case. Appearances may be deceiving—but not always. Sometimes you can get an accurate impression of a company's probity just by seeing where they're headquartered.

After getting off the bus at Fifty-seventh Street, Cone walks over to the main offices of Clovis & Clovis, just west of Lexington Avenue. They're in a building that seems to be all glass, sloping inward with a graceful swoop. You hit that façade in the right place, Cone figures, and the whole thing will come tumbling down, filling the street with broken glass, like a gigantic shattered windshield.

Clovis & Clovis occupies nine floors, and the reception room seems just a little smaller than Grand Central Terminal. There are plenty of people sitting and standing around, waiting, so Cone has no worries about wandering about to inspect the big blowups of color photographs, propped on easels, showing Clovis & Clovis properties.

He stands before one labeled HEADQUARTERS OF NEW WORLD ENTERPRISES, INC. It looks like a waterfront warehouse, two stories high, and appears to be the size of a football field. No address is given on the photo label, but Cone reckons that won't be hard to find.

"May I be of service, sir?" a chirpy voice says at his elbow.

He turns. A flashy blonde is giving him a beamy smile. She's wearing an office uniform of purple jacket and heliotrope skirt. Cone takes off his leather cap.

"Why, I hope so, ma'am," he says. "I've got a

brownstone on West Seventy-third I want to sell, and I was hoping to talk to someone here about making a deal.''

"Oh, my," she says in her girlish voice, "I do think you'd do better to write us a letter. Or go through a broker."

He nods gravely. "Very good advice, ma'am. I guess I'll do just that."

"'Bye now," she says, and sashays away.

He stops at the receptionist's desk on the way out. It is occupied by another flashy blonde in purple and heliotrope.

"Ma'am," he says, "do you have a business card for New World Enterprises? I'd like to write them a letter."

"Certainly, sir," she chirps, handing him one. "It's in Brooklyn. That's across the river, you know."

"Yes'm," he says. "Always has been."

He takes a final look around. If the reception room is any indication, the offices of Clovis & Clovis are nothing less than sumptuous. The place is all buttery rugs, vanilla Swedish furniture, soft lighting, and wallpaper music. It could serve as a stage set for "Corporate America 1980s style." Cone wonders if the whole thing is struck at nightfall and carted off to a theatrical warehouse.

He takes the subway to Brooklyn, standing well back from the tracks while waiting for the train.

It takes him almost two hours to find the headquarters of New World Enterprises, Inc. By that time the day has soured; the sky is filled with an ocher light and the air smells of sulfur. Rain clouds are beating in from New Jersey, and Cone's corduroy suit is beginning to feel like a damp blanket.

He stands across West Street, studying New World. It really is a warehouse, set well back on a black tarmac and surrounded by a high chain fence topped with barbed wire. There's a small guard shed at the double gates. Two bulldozers and three heavy-duty trucks are neatly lined up just inside. They all look clean, polished.

There are no signs of human activity. No lights in the

warehouse. It looks like it's been abandoned. Something is twisted in that scene, and Cone can't figure out what it is.

He crosses the street and strides briskly up to the gate. It's locked, but on closer examination Cone knows it would be a piece of cake to break in. He bangs on the gate and an old geezer comes limping out of the guard hut.

"Yeah?" he says.

"Anyone around?" Cone says cheerfully. "I'd like to talk to one of the officers."

"Nobody here," the guard says. "They all gone home. Come back tomorrow."

"Shit," Cone says. "Another trip. Oh, well. Say, does Vic Spagnola still work here?"

"Who?"

"Vic Spagnola. A friend of mine. He used to work night guard on the gate."

"Mister," the gaffer says, "you got your wires crossed. There's no night guard. Never has been as long as I been working, and I been here since the place opened."

"Son of a gun," Cone says. "I guess I am mixed up. Thanks for your help. I'll be back tomorrow. Better get back in your shack. Looks like rain."

"Yeah," the guard says grumpily, "that's what my hip tells me."

Cone has a long walk back to the subway through littered streets lined with grimy industrial buildings. But it's worth it; he realizes what's been bugging him about the New World premises. That tarmac in front of the warehouse looked like it had been poured yesterday. No oil stains. No tire marks. No pits or bald spots. The whole place was spotless. New and unused.

It is just beginning to sprinkle when he gets on the subway, and when he gets off at Prince Street about an hour later, the rain has stopped. Cone takes it as a good omen. He opens his second pack of Camels and does some chores.

He picks up his laundry, buys a bottle of Popov and a jug of California chablis. Then he stops at a deli and selects a frozen package of two short ribs of beef, planning to give one to Cleo. He also buys some cheese with jalapeño peppers, a can of hot chili, a kielbasa sausage—and wonders how long his stomach is going to endure these assaults before ulcering in protest.

After he and Cleo dine, they both have a nice, long nap. Cone wakes shortly before midnight. He straps on the ankle holster after checking the action of the Magnum. Dons his ratty black raincoat and leather cap. Puts a small flashlight in his pocket and adds a set of lockpicks in a suede pouch.

"Wish me luck, baby," he says to Cleo, and sets out.

He does have luck, because by the time he gets back to the New World Enterprises, Inc., headquarters in Brooklyn, there's a thick pelt of clouds masking the moonglow, and even the streetlights are dimmed by night mist. He's the only one abroad at that hour in that neighborhood, and he feels for his .357 to make certain it's there.

It takes him less than a minute to pick the lock, and then he's inside, closing the gate carefully behind him. He walks swiftly across the tarmac, still glistening from the day's rain.

He makes a complete circuit of the warehouse, not using his flashlight but peering for electronic alarms. He sees nothing.

All the windows are barred, but, shining his light inside he can see enough to make out a small office. One room with two desks, a file cabinet, a phone, and what appears to be a computer on a separate table. Then he moves slowly around the building again, peering in every window. The warehouse is huge. It looks like an airplane hangar. Steel trusses overhead but no pillars.

The place is completely empty.

"You know," Samantha Whatley says, "if you were a really wealthy man, people would call you eccentric. But you don't have all that much money, so you're just plain goofy. What if you set off an alarm or a squad car picked you up for B and E? Nice headlines. Great publicity for Haldering. The company would go right down the drain.''

"No great loss," Timothy Cone says, shrugging.

"You're really a turd," she says. "You know that?"

It is a sparkling Saturday afternoon, and they could have been in Central Park, up at the Cloisters, or down at the South Street Seaport. But she won't be seen with him in public. She's afraid someone from the office will see them together.

That's okay with him; he plays according to her rules. So on that super afternoon they're holed up in his loft, drinking white wine and talking shop.

"Will you let me finish my story?" he asks her. "Yesterday I went back to Sid Apicella. He says New World Enterprises, Inc., was capitalized for one-three-five million when it was incorporated fourteen months ago. So far they've bought and renovated that Brooklyn warehouse, and they've got some office equipment and some dozers and trucks parked outside. How much could all that cost? A mil maybe—if that much. So what are they doing with their money?"

"What they were set up to do," Sam says. "Developing and building residential and commercial properties."

Cone shakes his head. "No record of it. Sid checked. I checked. No building permits in their name, and none applied for. So Sid called Stanley Clovis and asked him what New World is doing. Clovis says they have several projects in the planning stage—whatever that means. I called New World in Brooklyn and pretended I was the owner of several West Side brownstones and looking for a renovator. I talked to a dese, dem and doze guy who said New World is too busy to take on any new work at this time. *Bullshit!*"

Sam is silent a moment. Then: "Pour me some more wine, Tim. Please."

She is wearing tight denim jeans and a black turtleneck sweater. Her hair is down and her long feet are bare. She's got a wide leather belt cinched tight, and it makes her waist look about the size of Cone's thigh. He thinks her stretched-out body is really neat and hopes that, later, she'll be willing to Indian-wrestle on the mattress.

"So," she says, taking a sip of her wine, "how do you figure it?"

"Let me show you something," he says. "I took the Evanchat file back to the office, but I kept something out. It was in with Ed Griffon's personal notes."

She inspects the scrap of green scratch paper. "DUM?" she says. "What the hell does that mean?"

"I didn't know, and neither did Sid Apicella. But now I can guess. DUM? is Ed's shorthand for 'dummy.' He thought New World was probably a dummy corporation, and I think so too. The goddamn thing is a front."

"For what?"

"I have no idea. But it's been in business fourteen months and hasn't done a lick of work. Those bulldozers and trucks have never moved a yard of dirt. The tarmac outside is squeaky clean. The warehouse itself is empty. But Clovis and Clovis put a hundred and thirty-five million into the business. Why? I don't know, but I think Ed Griffon found out and got wasted for being smart."

"Holy Christ, Tim, do you know what you're saying?"

"Sure I know. Clovis and Clovis are involved in some dirty scam big enough to kill for."

She shakes her head. "I can't believe it. A big outfit like that. Passing out bucks to every charity drive in town. Openings at the Met, building free parks in the Bronx. And they're killers? How can you be sure?"

"I'm sure," he says.

She sighs. "Okay, assuming you're right—what do we do next?"

"The first thing you do, Monday morning, is talk to H. H. Tell him to stall Evanchat. Tell him to convince Isaac to hold off on the deal with Clovis until we complete our investigation. Next thing you do is this: Joe is coming back from sick leave on Monday. He'll have nothing on his plate.

Give him my whole caseload, except for the Evanchat-Clovis deal. Let me zero in on it.''

"And get yourself murdered," she says.

"Probably," he says cheerfully.

When she arrived at his loft at noon, she brought two Rock Cornish hens and a big container of salad she had made herself. They eat at about three P.M., sitting at Cone's desk and feeding tidbits to the attentive Cleo. They even roll the cat a cherry tomato and watch the chase across the linoleum floor.

"That's one crazy animal," Cone says.

"Takes after you," Samantha says.

They're both tight, private people, and they'd rather be sautéed in oil than say, "I love you." But, grudgingly, each acknowledges an attraction, a comfort with each other. It's a no-horseshit relationship with feelings masked by cold profanity, and intimacy shielded away. Like two old soldiers cursing each other and ready to be the first to leap on the live grenade.

But they cannot deny their bodies' appetites, and when their hormones take over, they go berserk. On that lumpy mattress with clean sheets—thank God!—and Cleo watching with wise eyes.

"What are we doing?" she whispers wonderingly. "What *are* we doing?"

"You tell me," he says. "You're the boss."

They're two stick figures, all bony knobs and hard muscle. Their mating is a furious battle, not against each other so much as the emptiness and lunacy of their lives. When they strain, it is not to punish but to break out into another world. Oh, look at the meadows and the daffodils! The lawn they seek is bliss.

It's such a sweaty wrestle, not quite hysterical but frantic enough. And when they're done, staring at each other with dulled eyes, reality comes seeping back, the real world takes over again. But something remains . . .

"Tim," she says, touching his cheek softly, "be careful."

He puts his face to her little breasts. "I always am," he says.

"Jesus," she says, "don't you ever shave?"

The first thing Timothy Cone does on Monday morning is stop by the office of Hiram Haldering's secretary. He asks for the keys to one of the two company cars.

"What do you want it for?" she says sharply.

"I'd like to take a drive in the country and see if the leaves are turning."

The old biddy sniffs. "You can't have the Impala; Mr. Haldering is using it today. You can have the Toyota, but only till noon."

He frowns, considering a long moment as if he has a choice. "Well . . . all right," he says finally, "I'll take the Toyota."

"Just make sure you have it back by twelve," she snaps, handing him the keys.

"And if I don't?" he asks. "It turns into a pumpkin?"

His next stop is at Sol Faber's office. He borrows Sol's binoculars, promising to return them in good condition. Then he walks around to the garage on Dey Street and signs out the Toyota.

It takes him more than an hour to get to the New World warehouse, but when he arrives, it looks exactly as it had before: same number of bulldozers and trucks, no human activity. Cone figures he hasn't missed a thing. He parks across West Street, scrunches down, and focuses the binoculars on the New World gates. Then he puts the glasses aside and begins reading the morning *Times*, looking up frequently to make sure nothing's going on.

About eleven-fifteen, a woman walks up to New World's gates. Cone grabs up the binocs and watches as the guard lets her in. She walks across the tarmac, unlocks the office door, and enters. Cone makes her to be 5'3", 120, about thirty-eight years old, black hair, olive-skinned, poorly dressed, and carrying a brown paper bag that could contain her lunch.

About ten minutes later, a silver Chrysler LeBaron GTS pulls up at the gate, and Cone again grabs the binoculars. He can't see who's driving, but he gets a good make on the license number and repeats it aloud so he won't forget. The LeBaron crosses the tarmac and pulls up close to the office door. The driver gets out and whisks inside. Cone gets a fleeting impression of a big, husky guy—but that's all he gets.

He drives back to Manhattan and returns the Toyota's keys to Haldering's secretary.

"You're more than an hour late," she says accusingly.

He looks at her in astonishment. "You mean we're still on daylight saving time?" he says. "I could have sworn we switched back."

He gives Sol Faber his binoculars, then goes to his office, puts his feet up on the desk, and ponders his next move. He's still in the same position, smoking his fifth cigarette of the day, when Samantha Whatley appears in the doorway. She's carrying a small white envelope that she flaps at him.

"Guess what I've got," she says.

"Your draft notice?" he says sullenly. "How the hell do I know what you've got."

"What a nice mood," she says. "No wonder they call you Mr. Congeniality. This happens to be an invitation to a press conference and cocktail party being hosted by Clovis and Clovis to announce a grand plan to tear down those decaying West Side piers and create a fairy wonderland on the river. The invitation came to H. H., but he doesn't want to go. He gave it to me, and I don't want to go. So I'm giving it to you. All the Clovis bigshots will be there."

He realizes she's trying to help, but he doesn't know how to be grateful. "I'll think about it," he says.

She tosses the invitation onto his desk and stalks away, making him feel like a crumb. He doesn't touch the envelope, but searches through the mess in his top desk drawer until he finds the card of Neal K. Davenport, the NYPD detective. He calls. It rings eight times before the phone is picked up.

"Davenport."

"Yeah. This is Timothy Cone. I'm the investigator with Haldering and Company. You talked to me about the death of G. Edward Griffon."

"Oh, sure, I remember you. How're you doing?"

"Okay. Anything new on Ed's death?"

"No, nothing. These things take time; you should know that. You got something for me?"

"Not a thing. I called to ask a favor."

"Oh? What's that?"

"I got a license number I was hoping you'd trace for me. Find out who the car is registered to."

"Now why should I do that?"

"Just as a professional courtesy," Cone says, grinning at the phone.

Davenport laughs. "Kid, you've got chutzpah. Has it got anything to do with Griffon's death?"

"It might have."

Pause. "All right, give me the number; I'll see what I can do."

Cone recites the license number twice, to make certain Davenport has it right.

"I'll get back to you," the city dick says, and hangs up.

He spends the remainder of the day with Joe Washington, who has returned from sick leave and inherited Cone's caseload. Washington has a mordant sense of humor. He once said, "I am not a black, I am a person of the colored persuasion."

"Joe," Tim says, "I hope you won't take this as a personal insult, but you look a little washed-out to me."

"Still a bit puffy about the gills," Washington admits, "but I can function. I've been handed your crap."

"To ease you back into the real world. But there's nothing heavy in it."

They go through the cases: a merger, a buyout, an unfriendly takeover. They spend hours, and send out for cheeseburgers, fries, and Cokes. When they finish, Joe Washington acknowledges he can't see any great problems.

"About Ed Griffon . . ." he says, troubled. "Tim, what the hell happened?"

"No one knows," Cone says.

"A sweet guy," Joe says. "About a year ago I was in a bind and borrowed five bills from him. He handed it over without even asking what for. I paid it back, and he just said, 'Thanks,' and stuck it in his pocket. Like it didn't surprise him at all that I had paid him back. Tim, you working one of the cases? That's what I hear."

Cone nods.

"You think it's got something to do with Ed's death?"

"Maybe."

"You need a field hand," Washington says, "an experienced cotton picker, you know where to find me."

"I may take you up on that."

Cone goes back to his office and is opening his second pack of cigarettes of the day when his phone rings.

"Timothy Cone?"

"Yes."

"Davenport here. That license plate you gave me . . ."

"Yeah?"

"I think we better talk about it. Not on the phone."

"Okay," Tim says. "Where? A bar, restaurant?"

"I don't think so," Davenport says.

"Oh-ho, it's like that, is it? Well, I live in a loft on Broadway between Spring and Broome. Wanna come up for a drink?"

"That sounds more like it. I've got your address."

"How did you get that?"

"Your personnel file at Haldering. I'll be there about six. Okay?"

"Fine."

"If I'm late," Davenport says, "don't get your balls in an uproar; I'll be along."

"I'll wait," Cone promises.

He walks home, pausing occasionally to look in store windows at things he doesn't need and doesn't want. He's got a lot of vices, he knows, but vanity isn't one of them. Maybe it should be, he thinks. A little vanity wouldn't hurt him.

He stops in front of a jewelry shop and sees a heavy necklace of chunky beads, alternating ebony and crystal, that would look great on Samantha. But he's never bought her a gift and is disturbed about starting now. Somehow, he feels, it would upset their special relationship. Maybe change it for the worse, maybe for the better. But he's afraid to take the chance.

At home, he gives Cleo fresh water and a wing left over from Saturday's dinner with Sam. Cleo eats the whole wing: skin, meat, and bones. That cat could eat a steel anchor, Tim figures, and then belch delicately and groom its whiskers.

Davenport is only twenty minutes late. When Cone lets him in, the detective stands in the doorway and looks around.

"Be it ever so humble," he says. "Is this place available for weddings and bar mitzvahs? What's that thing under the bathtub?"

"That's Cleo, my cat."

"You're kidding. It looks like a cheetah to me."

Cone gets him seated on one of the plain wooden chairs drawn up to the battered desk.

"I have white wine, vodka, or beer," he says. "What's your pleasure?"

"Pussy," Davenport says. "But I'll have vodka on the rocks, providing you don't have to send out for the ice."

They both have heavy Popovs, sipping and talking about the weather, air pollution, the water shortage, traffic jams, and the high cost of a good corned beef sandwich.

"Enough of this idle chitchat," Davenport says finally. He's still wearing his snap-brimmed fedora because there's no place to put it that would be safe from the prowling Cleo. "Where did you get that license number?"

"Who's it registered to?" Cone counters.

They stare at each other.

Cone sees a porky guy who can chew Juicy Fruit and drink vodka at the same time. But beneath the suet, he reckons, is hard muscle. Davenport has the face of a dedicated drinker—the spider web of red capillaries and the swollen beezer. But the eyes are clear and shrewd. Cone believes he could take him, if necessary, but he doesn't want to find out.

"Look," he says to the cop, "you and I could play games forever. Why don't we level with each other? I don't mean all the way. I'm going to hold back, and you're going to hold back. We both understand that."

"Keep going," Davenport says. "You're making sense."

"Haldering isn't in the law-enforcement business," Cone continues. "We're not interested in putting anyone in the slammer. We get paid fees by clients who want other people investigated. Should I let this guy buy me out? Is he good for the dough he promises? What about this company that wants to merge? Are they legit? And what about this raider who's buying up our stock like mad? Is he a gonnif or what? We try to provide the information that lets our clients make their decision. Sometimes we give them bad news, but they go ahead anyway. You understand?"

"Sure," Davenport says, "I'm keeping up."

"What I'm trying to tell you," Cone says, "is that you and I aren't competitors. Most of the stuff I deal with is confidential. It has to be if we want to stay inside SEC regulations. But then a lot of your stuff is confidential, too. Has to be if you want to make a case."

"You're so right," Davenport says. "How about another shot from the wonderful pot? Keep your booze in the freezer, do you? I do, too."

"So," Cone says, topping off their jelly jars, "I inherited one file from the late G. Edward Griffon. It concerns a planned buyout.''

Then he describes the proposed deal between Evanchat and Clovis & Clovis. He mentions nothing about Griffon's DUM note, or that New World Enterprises, Inc., might be a dummy corporation. He just says that in the course of checking out Clovis' subsidiaries, he inspected New World's Brooklyn headquarters and got suspicious.

"Why's that?" Davenport asks.

"Because the place is so clean," Cone says earnestly, avoiding the story of his break-in. "Trucks and bulldozers that have never been used. And no record of their doing any business even though they were organized fourteen months ago for a hefty one-three-five million. So, of course, I staked out the place. And eventually this big, heavy guy drives up in a silver LeBaron. I glom the license plate. And that's it."

The city dick looks at him thoughtfully. "Uh-huh," he says, "that listens. I think you're telling me the truth. Not *all* the truth, but we both agreed we're going to hold back a little. Since it's trade-off time, here's what I've got: That LeBaron you saw at New World is registered to Anthony Bonadventure. Ever hear of him?"

"No, I can't say that I have."

"He's had some publicity, off and on. None of it good. I can't say the guy is with the Families. He's not Sicilian. Not even Italian, for God's sake. Corsican, as far as we can make out. Anyway, he's been in this and that. Nothing heavy. I mean it's not prostitution, armed robbery, hijacking, or anything like that. Our Anthony is too smart. The guy's a university graduate, got an MBA. What he's into mostly is fraud, extortion, and misrepresentation with the intent to commit a felony. Like peddling fake oil leases or rigging phony tax shelters.''

"Those are Federal offenses," Cone observes.

"Sure they are," Davenport agrees, "and the Feds have had him up twice, but they've never been able to pin him. I told you, the guy is smart, can afford the best legal eagles.''

"So what's the interest of the NYPD? It's white-collar crime, isn't it?"

"Yeah, in a way. But some of the scams this Bonadventure has pulled, well, he could never have started them without the cooperation of the Families. I mean, he doesn't *belong* to the mob, but when necessary, he works *with* them. Which means he pays his dues—right? Which brings our Organized Crime unit into the picture."

"What kind of scams does he do with the bentnoses?"

"Well, like for instance, he's suspected of forging green cards for aliens. Now you know he's got to be working with the locals to provide a steady stream of immigrants to make that profitable. That's how the NYPD got interested in him—his local ties. He's out of the green-card business now—the Feds got too close—and we haven't heard hide nor hair about him for almost a year. Now you come up with his license plate."

"A year?" Cone says, frowning. "New World was incorporated fourteen months ago. That's interesting."

"Yeah," Davenport says, grinning, "ain't it? I'll call you tomorrow and give you his last known address. They're running it through Records for me. Look, Cone, right now the Department has absolutely nothing we can charge Anthony Bonadventure with. But we'd love to nail that shtarker; it would really put the Feds' noses out. If you can come up with something, we'd be as happy as hogs in the mud. Why don't you take a close look at this guy? Maybe he's up to something."

"You're using me," the Wall Street dick says.

"You bet your sweet ass we're using you. But it's your job, isn't it? I mean, you're working for your client, this Evanchat, aren't you? So just do your job, and we'll provide all the cooperation we can, as long as you keep us in the picture. That's fair enough, isn't it?"

"Sure," Cone says, "that's fair."

Davenport drains off his vodka and rises to leave. "Thanks for the belt. I'll call you tomorrow with Bonadventure's home address, and I'll also try to dig up a mug shot of the guy so you can make him. By the way, he's known to pack a popgun on occasion, so watch your back. You carry?''

"Yeah," Cone says. "A short-barreled Magnum in an ankle holster.''

Davenport laughs. "You been reading too many detective novels. What are you going to do in a shoot-out— pretend you're bending down to tie your shoelace?" He pauses at the door for a final look around. "I love this place," he says. "The Garden of Sleaze. It looks like my old YMCA locker room back in Topeka. Invite me again.''

"Anytime you can make it," Cone says. "You're always welcome.''

"Oh," the detective says, "about Griffon's death. . . . We got a halfass witness who *thinks* he saw your buddy pushed. But he can't be sure, he won't swear to it, and he doesn't want to get involved.''

"What else?" Cone says.

Davenport doesn't call the next morning, but he sends over a manila envelope, heavily sealed, with Anthony Bonadventure's last known address, a photo—taken outside, seemingly by surprise; the guy looks startled—and a copy of Bonadventure's sheet.

Timothy Cone—a cheapskate, and he knows it—carefully peels off the tape; it's a good, clean envelope; he can use it again. He puts the sheet away to read later, but he studies Bonadventure's photograph. It could be the man he saw get out of the LeBaron. Same build, same bulk.

He's a heavy guy with grossly handsome features. Plenty of brow and jaw. A massive face that's going to get jowly with age. Shadowed bedroom eyes and a full mouth: sculpted lips below a strong nose. He's really attractive in an animal kind of way, and Cone figures he does all right with the ladies.

He locks up everything and leaves the office. He takes an uptown bus, heading for the Clovis & Clovis press conference. During the trip, he wonders why Davenport has been so generous with the photo, address, copy of Bonadventure's record. Because the NYPD wants this guy real bad, Cone reckons, or Davenport's trying to establish an obligation. "I scratch your back, you scratch mine."

Timothy Cone is wearing his "good" suit. It's an old, thready Harris Tweed jacket with greasy suede patches on the elbows. The pants are unpressed gray flannel, dark enough—he hopes—to hide the spaghetti stains. When he put on a white button-down shirt that morning, one of the buttons popped, so a flap of his collar swings free. His tie is a knitted black wool with several slubs where Cleo has bitten at it while dragging it across the linoleum, shaking it like a snake.

The press conference and cocktail party are being held in the mammoth reception room of Clovis & Clovis headquarters on Fifty-seventh Street. There's a uniformed security guard at the door collecting invitations.

"Thank you, sir," he says to Cone in a bored voice. "Please pass down the receiving line. Then the bar's on your left, buffet on your right."

Cone gets on the receiving line and is gratified to see several men as grungy looking as he, and supposes they're reporters. The file moves swiftly. The one man and two women shaking hands seem to be practiced. They clasp a guest's hand, give it one firm shake, and gently tug the owner along.

"Hi! I'm Stanley Clovis," the host beams, moving Cone to his right.

"Timothy Cone from Haldering and Company."

"So glad you could make it, Mr. Haldering."

"Hello. I'm Mrs. Grace Clovis."

"Timothy Cone from Haldering and Company."

"So glad you could make it, Mr. Timothy."

"Good morning! I'm Lucinda Clovis."

"Timothy Cone from Haldering and Company."

"So glad you could make it, Mr. Company."

He turns toward the bar, wondering who the hell he is. He asks the mess-jacketed bartender for a vodka rocks, and gets it with a slab of lime he didn't order and doesn't like.

He takes his drink and moves to a position where he can observe the Clovis family.

Stanley is a surprisingly small man, lean, dapper, and dark. He's wearing a raw gray silk suit with a mirror sheen. His wife, Grace, is almost a head taller: a statuesque blonde who looks like she might have been a model or showgirl. She's weaving slightly and Cone wonders if she might be bombed.

Lucinda Clovis, the sister, is as short and swarthy as her brother. She looks like a hard one, with a hatchet face and a jerky way of moving. She's flashing a spray of diamonds on the lapel of her black gabardine suit.

They make quite a trio, and Timothy Cone studies them, noting their frozen smiles, the smooth way they're greeting their guests, the public-relations performance they're putting on. They've done it a hundred times, he's sure, and wonders what happens when their public masks drop and they take off their jewelry and expensive clothes. Private masks?

But then the receiving line bunches up, and he can't get a good look at them. He wanders over to the buffet table and asks the toque-topped chef to make him a rare roast beef sandwich on those little slices of cocktail rye. He's munching on that when he notices a couple standing near the entrance, holding glasses of what appears to be white wine. They're bending toward each other in whispered conversation.

The man is Anthony Bonadventure; Cone is sure of it. That big, rugged build, heavy head, porcine features. He's wearing a pinkie ring that's got to be good for two or three carats. No doubt about it; the guy has presence. He looks assured, confident, and ready to wrestle the world.

The woman he's talking to is small, olive-skinned, poorly dressed: the one Cone saw entering the New World office.

"Hello there!" he says softly.

He finishes his tiny sandwich, licks his fingertips, and gets another vodka, without fruit. Then he positions himself where he can observe Bonadventure and his companion. They don't seem to be arguing, but they're having a very intense discussion, gesturing like mad.

The reception room has filled up, the receiving line has dribbled away. Cone, looking around, spots Mrs. Grace Clovis standing alone at the bar, working on what seems to be a beaker of scotch. He pushes his way to her side and gives her a smile.

"Lovely party," he says.

"Is it?" she says, staring at him. "Who you?"

"Mr. Haldering, Mr. Timothy, or Mr. Company. I'm not sure who I am."

"Welcome to the club," she says indifferently, taking a gulp of her drink. She looks around. "This thing sucks," she says.

He'd like to hear more, but Stanley Clovis mounts a small dais and taps a glass with a spoon. Gradually the room quiets.

"Sorry, folks," he yells, giving everyone a flash of his California caps, "you got exactly two minutes to replenish your drinks, and then we're going to close down the bar and buffet for a short presentation. And I promise you it will be short—and exciting! Then, after I make my pitch and answer questions, the bar and buffet will reopen. Okay?"

Laughter and applause. The guy handles himself well, Cone acknowledges. A real manipulator. As people crowd the bar, Tim moves away in the direction of Anthony Bonadventure and his lady. They seem to be inching closer to the exit. Cone inches right along with them.

Assistants set up easels, charts, enlarged architectural drawings on the dais. A public address system is plugged in and tested. Stanley Clovis takes his place behind the lectern. Immediately Bonadventure and the olive-skinned woman move to the door. Cone leaves his empty glass on the rug near the exit and follows.

They ride down together in the same elevator, but it's crowded and there's no conversation. If they take the LeBaron, Cone thinks, or hop a cab, I've got problems. But no, Bonadventure and the woman walk west on Fifty-seventh Street. The man moves to the outside and takes her arm. A gentleman.

Cone tails them for two blocks. The sidewalks are jammed; there's no way they're going to spot him. He moves closer, and when they go into a corner branch of the Merchants International Bank, he's right behind them. He stands at one of the glass counters and diddles with a deposit slip and a pen on a chain while he watches them.

Bonadventure stands aside, leaning negligently against a marble pillar as the woman goes up to one of the tellers' windows and pushes some papers under the brass gate. She gets a slip of paper and rejoins Bonadventure.

They leave, Cone on their heels. A cab stops in front of the bank, a woman gets out, and Bonadventure and his partner pop in and are whisked away. Cone gives up.

Back at Haldering & Co., he goes directly to the office of the chief accountant.

"You again?" Sidney Apicella says.

"Yeah, me. Sid, can you get the current bank balance of New World Enterprises? It's a subsidiary of Clovis and Clovis."

"And would you also like the mean temperature of the planet Jupiter during the month of April?"

"Cut the crap, Sid. This is important. I need to know how much New World has got in the till."

"Why do you need to know?"

"Because New World started out with a capitalization of a hundred and thirty-five million. That was fourteen months ago. Maybe they've spent a million or so on their warehouse and equipment. But they've done no jobs. There's no record of income. I'll bet my left nut that someone is looting that outfit."

Apicella sighs. "I'll see what I can do, Tim. Things like this aren't easy. But we have our contacts."

"Guys we bribe, you mean."

"Not exactly," Sid says, frowning. "We do favors for them, they do favors for us."

"You mean one hand washes the other?" Cone says. "That's an original concept. I'll be in my office. Let me know as soon as possible, will you? It really is important."

He goes back to his desk, digs out the NYPD sheet on Anthony Bonadventure, and starts reading. It's a long record, and Cone shakes his head in amazement at how many times the guy has been arrested, charged, indicted, tried, and has waltzed away whistling a merry tune.

He's still studying the transcript when Apicella comes to the door of his office, carrying a little piece of scratch paper.

"You said you'd bet your left nut that someone is looting that outfit," he says, looking down at his notes. "Well, New World Enterprises, Inc., was incorporated fourteen months ago with an initial capitalization of one hundred and thirty-five million provided by Clovis and Clovis."

"I told you all that, Sid," Cone says, sighing. "Get to the bottom line. How much is left?"

"As of yesterday," Apicella says, "their bank balance was one hundred and eighty-eight million."

"There goes my left nut."

2

He doesn't enjoy getting jerked around, and that's exactly what he thinks is happening.

"Look here," he says angrily to Samantha Whatley, "that outfit has made more than fifty million. And with no record of developing or building, which is what they were set up to do. I tell you something kinky is going down."

"Drugs?" Sam suggests.

"Nah," he says, shaking his head. "Stanley and Lucinda have to protect their reputation as public-spirited citizens and world-class partygoers. No, it's not something as heavy as drugs, but it's a scam, no doubt about it. And Clovis and Clovis must be aware of it."

They're in Samantha's gentrified apartment in the East Village. You'd think, wouldn't you—considering the woman's hard, edgy personality—that her home would be high-tech, with white walls and furniture of stainless steel and glass.

But no, her studio is one big bouquet. Lots of bright, flowered chintz, ruffles, a French doll in lace on the bed. The walls are covered with paper in a trellis and vine design, oval rag rugs scatter the polished wood floor, and there, over a fake marble mantelpiece in a place of honor, is a big, framed reproduction of Wyeth's "Christina's World."

They've had supper—grilled knockwurst, baked beans,

and cold sauerkraut with caraway seeds—and are now
working on chilled bottles of Heineken dark. They're lying
on one of the rag rugs, mostly because Samantha's chairs
are so bloody uncomfortable. "Designed for midgets,"
Tim once growled, and Sam had to agree. But she likes
them; they're so *pretty*.

"Did you read the paper today?" she asks him.

"Of course I read the paper. I keep up."

"Sure you do," she says. "The front page and the financial section."

"Don't forget the obituaries. I always turn to that first,
looking for my name."

"You should read the society pages occasionally. Maybe
you'd learn something."

She takes a folded newspaper clipping from the breast
pocket of her blue denim shirt and hands it to him. He reads
swiftly. It's a short account of a charity bash held at the
Parker Meridien. The article lists several well-known
guests.

"'Also present,'" Cone reads aloud, "'were the socially
active Lucinda and Stanley Clovis, dressed to the nines and
holding hands as usual. And where was the beauteous Mrs.
Grace Clovis'?"

He looks at Sam. "What the hell does that mean?"

She shrugs. "Beats the shit out of me. I just thought
you'd be interested."

"Yeah," he says, "thanks. Can I keep it?"

She nods, and he stuffs the clipping into his hip pocket.

"Getting anywhere?" she asks him.

"This guy Anthony Bonadventure . . ." he says. "I told
you about his record. Well, I checked with our legal department, and they found out he's listed as treasurer of New
World Enterprises, Inc. Now you know that anything he's
connected with has got to be dirty."

"Who are the other officers of the corporation?"

"Stanley Clovis is president, Lucinda is vice-president,
and in addition to Bonadventure being treasurer, there's a

secretary, Constance Figlia. I just feel in my bones she's the short, dumpy broad I saw at New World and then later with Bonadventure at the press conference. They're all in it together."

"In what?"

"How the hell do I know?" he yells at her, then calms. "I'm sorry," he says contritely. "I just feel I'm getting the runaround, and I don't like it. Tomorrow I'm going to call Neal Davenport, the city dick, and ask him to run a trace on Constance Figlia. Maybe the computers can turn up something."

"And you want something from me, too, don't you?" Samantha asks.

"How can you tell?"

"You're acting so fierce."

"Fierce?" he says with his quirky smile. "I haven't been fierce since the age of eight when a kid tried to steal my best aggie. Well, yeah, Sam, I want something from you. I need wheels. Trying to requisition the company Toyota a few hours at a time just won't do. I need a car so I can run the job. I mean I've got to get around, and subways and buses and even cabs just won't do."

"H. H. won't approve."

"Sure he will. Tell him I'm on to something hot. Tell him it's going to make him King Jesus on Wall Street. Tell him anything. But also tell him it's not going to cost him a cent; he can always charge Evanchat for the expenses."

"I'll try," she says.

"That's my own dear shithead," he says, patting her cheek.

"Okay," she says, "enough shoptalk. Were you planning to spend the night?"

"I was planning," he admits. "All right with you?"

"All right," she says, "you smooth, sweet-talking son of a bitch."

"You want me to take a shower first?" he asks her.

"Every time I walk into this perfumed boudoir of yours, I figure you want me to be squeaky clean."

"Fuck you," she says.

"I hope so," he says.

He gets his wheels—a little black Honda that he wouldn't select for a high-speed chase but does just fine in city traffic. What's on his mind—something he didn't mention to Samantha—is the role being played by Mrs. Grace Clovis. He figures that wobbly lady is on the sauce, or stoned, and might be willing to gabble if the time is right.

So, in the morning, he drives to the residence of Stanley Clovis. It's a triplex penthouse atop one of the Clovis & Clovis properties on Third Avenue near Eighty-fifth Street. Cone has to drive around the block three times before he finds a parking space that gives him a good view of the entrance. Then he settles down with the *Times,* a container of hot coffee, and a pumpernickel bagel.

He looks when a long blue Mercedes pulls up on the curved driveway. He watches as Stanley and Lucinda Clovis come out, both carrying attaché cases, and step into the chauffeured limousine. So Lucinda lives with her brother and sister-in-law, does she? That's interesting. Cone stays right where he is, crossing his fingers because he's a superstitious man.

His luck pays off in about a half hour. Grace Clovis comes out alone, wearing a sheath of something that sparkles and carrying a silver fox stole carelessly looped over one arm. The doorman moves out into the street to whistle up a cab, and Timothy Cone drops his newspaper and starts up the Honda. Half of the bagel is still clamped between his teeth.

Eventually a taxi stops and Mrs. Clovis climbs in, with a flash of thigh Cone can see, and appreciate, from across the street. He follows the cab downtown, almost bumper to bumper because traffic is so jammed up; there's no way Grace or the hack driver is going to spot a tail.

When they get below Forty-second Street, Cone guesses where Grace is going. Sure enough, the cab pulls up in front of a handsome converted brownstone on East Thirty-seventh Street, just off Park Avenue: the last known home address of Anthony Bonadventure.

"Well, well," Cone says aloud.

He drives by, then double-parks just long enough to watch Grace stalk across the sidewalk and enter the brownstone. Then Cone pulls away and heads for Brooklyn. Traffic is murder, but he doesn't mind; he's got a lot to think about.

He parks in front of the New World warehouse and gets out of his car. The same guard comes limping from the hut.

"Me again," Cone says cheerfully. "Is Constance Figlia in?"

"She's in," the guard says grudgingly, "but you gotta have an appointment. You got an appointment?"

"Well, no, but I'm sure she'll see me."

"No appointment, no see," the guard says. "Them's my orders."

"Okay," Cone says breezily, "I'll give her a call. If you happen to see her, will you tell her Mr. Javert was asking for her."

"Javert?"

"That's right. J-a-v-e-r-t. Thank you very much."

Cone drives back to Manhattan, satisfied with the long journey. He's a methodical man, and he's established, to his satisfaction, the presence of Constance Figlia at New World headquarters. Now he's got the cast identified; he can concentrate on the plot.

In his office, it takes three calls to locate Detective Davenport.

"Thanks for sending that stuff over," Cone says. "It's been a big help."

"Glad to hear it. Now it's your turn."

"How about this . . ." the Wall Street dick says. "Anthony Bonadventure is treasurer of New World Enterprises,

Inc. In the past year or so, the company has made a profit of more than fifty million with absolutely no record of any business activity. No building, no renovation, nothing.''

"Oh-ho," Davenport says, "the worms are squirming, are they?"

"I'd say so. Something is going down, but I haven't a clue—yet. Can you do something for me?"

"Depends."

"The secretary of New World is a woman named Constance Figlia. F-i-g-l-i-a. She's dark-haired, olive-skinned. I make her as five-three, one-twenty, maybe around thirty-eight years old. She dresses like she buys her clothes at a thrift shop."

"It takes one to know one," the Department man says.

"Could you see if you've got anything on her?"

Silence.

"Davenport?" Cone says. "Are you there?"

"I'm here. You think this Figlia dame is mixed up in whatever's going on?"

"Oh, yeah. Has to be."

"All right. I'll see if we've got anything on her and get back to you."

"Great. I may not be at the office. Do you have my home phone number? It's unlisted."

"I've got it," Davenport says. "I know a lot about you. Why didn't you tell me you have all those medals from the Marine Corps?"

"I hocked them," Cone says.

The detective laughs. "You're a flake, you know that?"

They hang up and then, just because he feels he's on a roll, Cone calls Clovis & Clovis and asks to speak to Miss Constance Figlia.

"Just a moment, please," the receptionist chirps, "I'll connect you with her department."

Click, click, click. Another operator comes on.

"Comptroller's office," she says.

"May I speak to Miss Figlia, please."

"I'm sorry, sir, she isn't in today. Would you care to leave a message?"

"Just tell her Mr. Javert called," Cone says. "I'll try her tomorrow."

He sits for almost an hour in his cramped office, smokes three Camels, stares at the wall, and runs scenarios through his mind like videocassettes in living color. But nothing makes sense. He just doesn't know enough.

Sighing, he pulls a yellow legal pad toward him and starts working on his weekly progress report. Progress, he thinks dourly—it is to laugh. He puts nothing in his report that Samantha Whatley doesn't already know.

He's home, he and Cleo have dined royally on pastrami sandwiches and cole slaw, and he's still running those videos through his mind and still coming up with zilch. It's past eleven o'clock when his phone rings.

"Did I wake you up?" Neal K. Davenport asks.

"No, but you woke up Cleo."

"Tough shit," the detective says. "I need sleep more than that cat. As soon as I hang up, I'm packing it in and going home for eighteen straight hours of shuteye."

"Where do you live?"

"Staten Island. You know the place?"

"No."

"There's nothing to know. About that lady of yours, Constance Figlia, we got nothing on her, she's got no record. But I talked to a pal of mine in the Organized Crime Unit, and he made her. She's a niece of Vincent Figlia. You know who he is?"

"Never heard of him."

"A lower-echelon mafioso who works out of Long Island," Davenport says, giving it the correct pronunciation: "Longuyland." "This Vincent is small-time stuff: some minor loan-sharking, bookmaking, shakedowns—things like that. But he's got connections with Brooklyn Families. And, like I say, that Constance is his niece."

"Well," Cone says, "that's something. But not much."

"Uh-huh, but here's what makes the cheese more binding: Remember my telling you that Anthony Bonadventure was mixed up in a counterfeit green-card scam? The Feds got close and broke it up, but were never able to put the thumb on Bonadventure. Well, it turns out that Vincent Figlia was one of the guys supplying the illegal aliens. Figlia and Bonadventure did business together. So your lady, the niece, Constance Figlia, probably knew Bonadventure before this New World deal, and knows he isn't a straight arrow. That's interesting—don't you think?"

"Yeah," Cone says slowly, "interesting."

"One more thing," Davenport says. "My pal at Organized Crime tells me that Constance is supposed to be a computer whiz. Good night and pleasant dreams."

They hang up. Cone starts playing more videocassettes through his mind. New ones, as senseless as the old. Finally he gets undressed, turns out the lights, and lies down on the mattress. After a while Cleo comes padding up and curls into the bend of his knees.

"What's it all about, you stupid cat?" he asks.

Cleo growls and nuzzles closer.

"Something screwy happened this afternoon," Samantha Whatley says. "Stanley Clovis himself called H. H. and asked if we have someone named Javert working for us."

"Javert?" Cone says. "Who he?"

"That's what H. H. wanted to know. Clovis said a guy named Javert has been harassing one of his execs, and he thought it might be a Haldering employee. So H. H. got huffy—you know how he can be—and said Haldering people do not, repeat *not*, harass anyone. He said there is no one named Javert working here and never has been. That seemed to satisfy Clovis, and he apologized."

Sam is in her office, heavy brogues parked atop her desk, denim skirt pulled demurely down over her knees. Cone lounges in the doorway, leaning against the jamb. As usual, he is sucking on a cigarette, tilting his head to keep the smoke out of his eyes.

"You know who Javert was, don't you?" she asks, looking at him closely.

"Nope. Never heard of the guy."

"He was the policeman in *Les Misérables*."

"*Les Misérables?*" Cone says. "Is that French for 'lousy fuck'?"

"You know," she says, "when you get that innocent look on your ugly mug, I know you've been up to something. Anyway, the reason I called you in is this: After Clovis and H. H. got over their little squabble, Clovis invited him or his representative to an open house tonight in the ballroom of the Hotel Bedlington on Madison Avenue. Stanley and Lucinda are having a cocktail party so a friend of theirs can announce his candidacy for Congress. Free booze and Swedish meatballs. From five till seven. I thought you might want to stop by."

"I might," Cone says. "The free booze doesn't interest me, but I go ape for Swedish meatballs."

"Get the hell out of here," Sam says roughly.

Cone stops at Joe Washington's office and sticks his head in.

"How you coming with my stuff?" he asks.

"Bore-*ring*," Joe says. "Nothing but phone calls and visits to the public library."

"How would you like to go to a cocktail party tonight? From five to seven. Free booze and meatballs."

"I can live with that," Washington says. "What'll I be—the token spade?"

"Nah," Cone says. "This is a political shindig. East Side liberals. They'll be delighted to see you there. You may even get two meatballs."

"I could use them," Joe says. "According to my wife."

"I'll brief you on the way up."

"Ah-ha. So this isn't purely a social occasion?"

"Not exactly."

"Got something to do with Ed Griffon's death?"

"Maybe."

"Let's go," Joe Washington says.

In addition to being cantankerous and superstitious, Timothy Cone is also secretive. He isn't about to tell anyone anything they don't need to know. When he has it all wrapped up in a package, he'll deliver it.

So on the long, stop-and-go ride uptown, all he tells Joe is that there are probably going to be five people at the party he'd like to keep an eye on. Since he can't cover them all, Joe can take two of them: the brother-and-sister act—Stanley and Lucinda.

"I'll point them out," Cone says, "but they're the host and hostess; you won't be able to miss them. Both short, dark, expensively dressed. Charm kids."

"What am I supposed to look for?" Joe asks.

"I just want your take on them. How they act in public towards each other. If you get a chance, try to talk to both of them."

"Should I tell them I'm with Haldering?"

"Don't volunteer it, but if they ask where you're from, tell them."

The ballroom is already crowded when they get there, and jammed elevators keep bringing up new mobs. The room is filled with flags, balloons, streamers, confetti; it already looks like a victory celebration. A big banner over the dais proclaims: A NEW BEGINNING!

Cone and Washington push their way to the bar where two sweating bartenders are doing their best to quench the freeloaders' thirst.

"There," Timothy says, "over in the corner; the short couple talking to the tall guy in the seersucker suit."

"I got them," Joe says. "Now I'll get me a drink and I'll be all set."

"I'll see if I can find the others. You stay as long as you like, then take off. I'll see you in the office tomorrow and we'll compare notes."

He drifts away, sliding through the crowd. A lot of young, noisy yuppies are wearing big badges that also proclaim: A NEW BEGINNING! That slogan doesn't cut much ice with Cone. He prefers TIPPECANOE AND TYLER, TOO.

Timothy doesn't like people much, and he dislikes them most in crowds.

He moves through the happy crush with an idiot grin donned for protective coloration. But his sharp eyes are searching for a target. He spots one: Grace Clovis, standing erect in a short cocktail gown that seems to have been chiseled from one enormous rhinestone. She's not speaking, but listening to a man with three chins, two stomachs, and thighs that threaten to pop the seams of his designer jeans.

Cone watches as Grace finally staggers away, leaving the guy in the middle of a gesture with his mouth open. She moves to the bank of elevators. Cone follows. He doubts very much that she'll remember him from the press conference, but just to play it safe, he doesn't get on the Down elevator with her but waits for the next, hoping he's not going to lose her.

He doesn't. When he gets to the lobby, she's standing, looking about vaguely. She's not tottering now, but appears almost catatonic.

She wanders, with little-girl steps, into the cocktail lounge. Cone waits a few minutes, then follows. It's a dim room, almost empty. He sits at the bar, orders a vodka, and inspects the room via the back mirror. Grace is sitting by herself at a small corner table. A waiter is serving her a tall drink with a lot of fruit in it, topped with a little paper parasol.

Cone watches, and can't figure her out. She's sitting like a statue. Not smoking a cigarette, not sipping her drink, not looking around. He figures if someone touched her with a fingertip she'd topple sideways.

Finally Anthony Bonadventure comes striding into the cocktail lounge. Cone watches the action. Bonadventure looks around, walks smiling to her table. He's carrying a folded newspaper under his arm. Cone thinks it's *The Wall Street Journal*.

Anthony sits down at her table, takes one of her hands, turns it over, kisses the palm. Then he leans toward her and whispers rapidly. A waiter comes over. Anthony straightens up, gives his order. The waiter moves away. Grace gets up and walks to the lobby, carrying the folded newspaper. Bonadventure sits down again, and when his drink is served—something in a stemmed glass—sips it quietly.

Cone glances at his watch and waits for this little melodrama to be played out. In less than ten minutes, Mrs. Grace Clovis returns. No newspaper. She's practically bouncing, bopping to a tune no one else can hear. She's snapping her fingers as she walks, and kisses Bonadventure's ear before sliding onto her chair in a lithe, sexy glide.

The two chatter, heads close together again. Then they finish their drinks, Bonadventure pays the tab, and they leave together. The waiter cleans off their table and brings a small tray with their empties and crumpled cocktail napkins back to the bar. Cone reaches for the discarded paper parasol.

"May I have this?" he asks.

"Sure," the waiter says, "help yourself. Afraid it might rain tonight?"

Cone smiles dutifully. He turns the wee parasol in his fingers, opening and closing it. Made in Taiwan, probably. And here it is in Manhattan, decorating a drink in a fashionable Madison Avenue cocktail lounge.

"Go figure it," he says to the bartender.

That worthy, experienced at humoring nutty patrons, nods and says, "You're telling me."

Cone drives home, figuring Joe Washington will get back to Queens one way or another. He finds a parking space only two blocks from his loft, but he'll have to get up early to move the Honda to the other side of the street or risk it being towed away. He puts a sign inside the windshield. It came with the rented car. NO VALUABLES, DRUGS, OR RADIO. THIS CAR WIRED WITH ELECTRONIC ALARM. Lots of luck.

He isn't hungry, but Cleo is. He gives the cat a treat: a can of tuna. Topped with the tiny paper parasol. Cleo sniffs at the fish, then looks up at him, suspicious of this largesse. But starts gobbling. Half the tuna disappears. The cat strolls away, licking its chops. Then sits down to groom its whiskers.

"Not even a thank you?" Cone asks, then, suddenly famished, eats the remainder of the tuna, spooning it directly from the can. He also eats a chunk of kielbasa and a piece of moldy cheddar. He belches—which is understandable. The sudden eruption startles Cleo, who darts under the bathtub.

It is almost midnight before he calls Samantha Whatley.

"I didn't wake you up, did I?" he asks her.

"No. I'm watching *The Johnny Carson Show*."

"Good?"

"A repeat. What do you want?"

"Not a thing. How are you?"

"I'm fine. Just the way I was this afternoon. Did you go to the party?"

"Yeah, I stopped by. Had one drink. A drag."

"Find out anything?"

He considers what he might tell her. "Lucinda Clovis, the sister, lives in the same apartment with her brother and sister-in-law. Well, in the same building, anyway."

"So?"

"Don't you think that's a little unusual?"

"Maybe," Sam says.

"What did you do tonight?" he asks. "After you got home."

"Washed my hair. Did some laundry."

"What did you eat?"

"Chicken chow mein. With fried noodles. It was pretty good. What did you have?"

"A tuna fish salad."

"You liar," she says. "You ate it right out of the can."

"Well, yes," he admits. "Cleo's leftovers. You're feeling okay?"

She sighs. "What's *with* you? Yes, for the second time, I'm feeling okay. May I go to sleep now?"

After they hang up, he wonders why he called. How are you feeling? What did you do tonight? What did you eat? A real nothing conversation—and so comforting.

He has a nagging suspicion that he's being recruited as a living, breathing, dues-paying member of the human race.

"How did you make out?" Cone asks Washington the next morning.

"Like a thief. I practically OD'd on those meatballs. Dee-licious. Then I get home, and guess what the little wifey has for dinner? Spaghetti and meatballs. Wouldn't you know?"

"Screw the meatballs. Did you get a chance to talk to Stanley and Lucinda?"

"Oh, yeah. I had a nice little chat with both of them, and I kept them in sight all the time I was there. They didn't ask me where I was from, and I didn't say."

"What's your take?"

Washington looks down at his desk and fiddles with a pencil. Then he looks up at Cone. "You think there's something kinky there, don't you?"

Timothy nods.

"I think you're right," Joe says, "but don't expect me to swear to it in a court of law. Look, I got a sister I dearly love. We meet, hug and kiss each other's cheek. Maybe I'll put my arm around her. All casual-like—you know? But Stanley and Lucinda—they're something else again. If you hadn't told me they were brother and sister, I'd have figured them for a happily married couple, or maybe lovers. I've never seen so much hand-holding, and little pats, and strokings. I really don't think they're aware of what the hell they're doing, or how it looks to other people. I spotted a few smirks and raised eyebrows, so other people probably have the same dirty, disgusting suspicions you and I have."

"Yeah," Cone says. "You got a Manhattan telephone directory?"

"Of course I've got a telephone directory. You think I'm a second-class citizen, honky?"

"Do me a favor, will you? Look up the home phone number of Stanley Clovis, then see if Lucinda has a different listing."

He waits patiently, lighting another Camel while Joe flips pages. Finally the black looks up, his face twisted into a strained grin.

"Yeah," he says, "you're right. Lucinda's number is the same as Stanley's."

"It figures," Cone says. "I know Lucinda lives in the same apartment house. I just wanted to make sure she lives in Stanley's penthouse, along with wife Grace and their two kids."

They stare at each other.

"The family that plays together stays together," Washington says.

"Maybe," Cone says. "But how are you going to nail down something like that?"

"You're not," Joe says. "Unless you're in the bedroom with a Polaroid and flash."

"Oh, I don't know," Tim says slowly. "There may be ways. Did you eyeball Stanley's haircut?"

"Oh, yeah, man. All those ringlets. Real spiffy. The Blow-dry Kid. And Lucinda has the same style. His-and-hers."

"Uh-huh," Cone says. "I think I need a haircut."

"I thought you did it yourself," Joe Washington says. "With a salad bowl and an electric shaver."

Cone grunts and goes back to his office. He spends almost a half hour with the Manhattan Consumer Yellow Pages, going through the section on Barbershops. He's happy to find a special Guide included that groups businesses according to the locations they serve. So he concentrates on the East Side, Fifty-ninth to Ninetieth streets.

He makes the same pitch to each barbershop he calls.

"Hello there! I wonder if you might help me. I met Mr. Stanley Clovis at a party the other night, and I so admired his hair styling. I'd like a do just like his, but I neglected to ask him where he goes. Is he a customer of yours?"

He strikes pay dirt on his eighth call: Venus-Adonis Hair Styling, Inc., a unisex barbershop on East Eighty-sixth Street.

"Is he a customer of yours?" Cone asks.

"Not a customer," the receptionist says coldly. "Both Stanley and Lucinda Clovis are clients of ours."

"And could I get a haircut like Stanley's?"

"Just a moment, sir. I'll have to talk to Luis. He created Mr. Clovis's styling."

Cone waits patiently. Finally the receptionist comes back on the phone.

"If you're able to get here by eleven o'clock," she says, "Luis can fit you in."

Cone suppresses an obscene reply to that. "I'll be there," he says. "Thank you, and thank Luis."

"Name, please?"

"Javert. J-a-v-e-r-t."

He leaves his black leather cap in the office and drives up to East Eighty-sixth Street. The Venus-Adonis salon is as bright and bewildering as a discotheque, with garish colors, crackled pink mirrors, and hard rock blasting from ceiling speakers.

Cone identifies himself as Javert, and the receptionist, who's wearing a black leather jumpsuit and a purple wig, looks at his spiky, ginger-colored hair in amazement.

"You *do* need help, don't you?" she says.

But she gets him into a chair and swathes him up to the chin in a Ralph Lauren sheet.

"Luis will be with you presently."

Cone waits, and waits. He's not the only client; four of the six chairs are occupied: three women and a man, all swaddled in sheets. He remembers when barbershops had copies of the *Police Gazette* available for customers. This hair-styling salon has *Elle* and *Town & Country*.

Luis shows up, looking like an anorexic basketball player. He's got to be six-eight, at least, and so thin a strong wind might blow him across to Queens, where he belongs. He's wearing white painters' overalls, with apparently nothing on underneath, and he's doused with a cologne that reminds Cone of a visit to a geisha house.

Luis claps a palm to his cheek in horror after viewing Cone's hair. "Oh, my God, my God," he groans. "Who did this to you?"

"A butcher."

"A sadistic butcher," Luis says. "There is no way, *no* way, I am going to re-create Stanley Clovis's styling with what you have. It will take at least three consultations. And meanwhile you must let the hair grow and grow to give me something to work with. The color isn't bad," he admits. "I can live with the color, but it needs brightening. And also a protein thickener and conditioner. I will start with the preliminary shaping, but you must promise to come back again in a month."

"I promise," Cone says humbly.

Luis sets to work, snipping gently, and frequently standing back to observe his handiwork through narrowed eyes.

"Stanley and Lucinda are wonderful people," Cone offers.

"Beautiful people," Luis says, clipping a bit here, a bit there. "So chic. So soigné."

Cone isn't sure what soigné means, but it sounds like a compliment. "Definitely soigné," he says. "And so devoted to each other."

Luis giggles. "Oh, you've heard those stories, too, have you? My lips are sealed."

"Everyone's heard those stories," Cone says. "With Lucinda living in the same apartment."

"Well, they do say that bro and sis are just a little *too*

close, if you get my meaning. But *Que sera, sera* is my motto.''

"Live and let live," Cone adds. "If they're happy, that's all that counts."

"You couldn't be more right, dearie," Luis says.

"It's the wife I feel sorry for."

Luis laughs. "Don't waste your sympathy. She gave him two pups, didn't she? Now she wants to spread her wings and fly. And I do mean fly, if you catch my drift."

"So I've heard," Cone says. "That magic white powder."

"You better believe it," Luis says. "Now upsadaisy and over to the sink, and we'll see what we can do with your wild mop."

Sitting on a stool, head bent into a stainless steel basin, Cone feels Luis' surprisingly strong fingers massaging shampoo in his scalp, and says, "They could be a little more discreet about it—Stanley and Lucinda."

"With their money?" Luis says. "Who needs to be discreet? It just makes their reputation a little more piquant—wouldn't you say?"

"Definitely piquant."

Luis leans close, whispering in Cone's ear. "The last time they were here together, I did her first, and when I started on him, she stood by his chair, and she was definitely groping him under the sheet. Can you believe it?"

"I can believe it," Cone says.

He has some glop rubbed in his hair. Then Luis rinses away the soapsuds and other junk, and dries Cone's hair with a big, thick towel.

"Back in the chair, ducky," he says.

When Cone is seated and sheeted again, Luis says, "I can't give you a perm; the hair is too short. But I can give you a little frizz, a little panache."

"Soigné?" Cone asks.

"Absolutely," Luis says, setting to work with blow-dryer and brush.

When, finally, Cone inspects himself in the crackled pink mirror, his heart quails. His hair looks like a Brillo pad.

"I like it," he says bravely.

"But of course," Luis says.

Cone pays everyone and tips everyone—enough money to buy Cleo a year's supply of Norwegian sardines. He wonders how he's going to get that tab approved on his expense account, but convinces himself it was solid investigative work. He wanted knowledgeable gossip, and he went to the most authoritative source.

He drives back to the office, all the Honda's windows open because he can't stand the miasma emanating from his scalp. As luck will have it, the first person he meets in the office is Samantha Whatley. She takes one look at his coiffure and collapses with laughter, leaning against the wall and holding her ribs.

In a few moments he's surrounded—four or five people—all pointing at his hair and spluttering to get out their comments: "A demented porcupine!" "Sue them, Cone, sue!" "Did you fall asleep in the chair?"

"Fuck all of you," he growls. "It happens to be soigné. With panache." Then he stalks into his office and slams the door. Runs a palm over his frizz and tells himself, "It's not *that* bad," knowing it is. He lights a cigarette and then, after a while, lights another. It takes him a moment to realize he's got two cigarettes going. He curses and stubs out both of them. Then, minutes later, rescues the long butts from the ashtray and straightens them out.

He thinks he's getting a good handle on the people involved: Stanley and Lucinda Clovis, Mrs. Grace Clovis, Constance Figlia, and Anthony Bonadventure. He's beginning to grasp the interaction there, but he's no closer to what's going down. And no closer to why, or by whom, G. Edward Griffon was pushed in front of a subway train. That, he tells himself angrily, is all that matters.

He digs out the Clovis-Evanchat file and goes over it again. He has an aching suspicion that there are questions he should be asking, and isn't. Somewhere, in all those PIEs and Griffon's reports and his own notes, is something of real import. He's convinced of it. But what?

He goes through the Preliminary Intelligence Estimates again and spots something he thinks is freaky. Clovis & Clovis do their banking at Manhattan Central, the Madison Avenue branch. But when he tailed Bonadventure and Constance Figlia from the press conference, they went into the Merchants International Bank, and seemed right at home. Of course either of them might have a personal account there.

"Oh, my God," Sidney Apicella groans, "you again? What happened to your hair?"

"Forget it," Cone says angrily. "Your PIE on Clovis-Evanchat says that Clovis banks at Manhattan Central, but no bank is listed for New World Enterprises. How come?"

Apicella sighs. "I've got it somewhere," he says. He goes to one of his many steel file cabinets, digs out a folder, flips through it rapidly. "New World banks at Merchants International. Satisfied?"

"Isn't that a little weird, Sid? The parent company banks at one place and a subsidiary banks at another."

"Nothing weird about it. When you're dealing with that much money, you like to spread the risks. It's done all the time. I mean, Clovis and Clovis is always making very heavy cash deposits and withdrawals. It makes sense to have more than one bank. Then you can shuffle funds in case of an emergency."

"Yeah," Cone says, "I can see that. Thanks, Sid. The place is Venus-Adonis Hair Styling on East Eighty-sixth. Ask for Luis."

Apicella, who wears a rug, says, "Go to hell."

Timothy spends another couple of hours on the Clovis-Evanchat file, smoking up a storm and pondering his next move. He decides he better dig into Constance Figlia, the mystery woman. He's got some good skinny on the other characters, but that Constance is a cipher.

He locks his desk and prepares to leave. When he dons his leather cap, it slides down to his ears. "Shit!" he says aloud, and sneaks out of the office.

He spends three days on the track of Constance Figlia. It's a frustrating penetration because he can't get a firm handle on that short, dumpy broad with the posture and stride of a sergeant major. But at the same time it's fascinating just because he can't pin down her time-habit pattern, and the secrets of her daily activities remain secrets.

He starts by visiting Louis Kiernan in the attorneys' section. Lou is a paralegal and custodian of Haldering & Co.'s collection of out-of-town telephone directories. Cone can't find a Vincent Figlia in Suffolk County, but finds a listing in Nassau. Lou, who lives on Long Island, tells him the address is east of Hicksville.

"Some swanky homes out that way," he observes.

"So?" Cone says. "I can do swanky. Just keep your fly zipped up—right?"

He goes back to his office and calls the Figlias' residence.

"Yeah?" A man's voice answers, sounding like a laryngitic frog.

"Could I speak to Miss Constance Figlia, please."

"Who's this?" the frog demands.

Cone decides he can keep the Javert scam going a little longer, and also get Haldering & Co. off the hook.

"My name is Javert," he says. "J-a-v-e-r-t. I'm with the Old Glory Insurance Company, and I was hoping to interest Miss Figlia in our single-premium annuity plan, with interest compounded monthly and tax-deferred until the time of withdrawal."

"Forget it. She ain't interested."

The phone is slammed down, connection broken. But Cone is satisfied; now he knows where she lives. He digs out an old, scuffed briefcase and stuffs it with outdated office memos and other junk to give it bulk. Then he sets out for Long Island, wondering how many insurance sales-men wear corduroy suits and black leather caps.

Traffic is murder, and it's almost noon before he locates Figlia's home. As Louis Kiernan said: swanky. The place looks like a Virginia horse farm, with a wide lawn and shrubs that appear to have been trimmed with manicure scissors.

There's a white picket fence around the property, with an unlocked gate leading to a flagged path to the portico. When Cone gets to the steps, carrying his bulging briefcase, the front door opens, a man steps out, closes the door behind him.

"Yeah?" he says—the frog himself.

Judging by the voice, Cone had envisioned a short, squat guy with no neck, plenty of suet, and the appearance of a thug with maybe a bent nose and a wet cigar stuck in his kisser.

But this man could be a mortician or an economist. He's tall, skinny as a rapier, wearing a black silk suit, white shirt, narrow black tie. His jacket is beautifully tailored. Cone thinks maybe he's just imagining the slight bulge under the left arm.

"Good morning!" he says brightly. "Is Miss Constance Figlia at home?"

The guy looks down with stony contempt.

"You the guy who called earlier this morning?"

Cone nods. "That's me."

"I told you she ain't home, and even if she was, she wouldn't want to talk to you. Now beat it."

Cone shrugs apologetically. "You know how it is: I get a list of insurance prospects from my supervisor, and I've got to check out each one personally and file a report. You can understand that, can't you?"

"I couldn't care less," the tall one says. "All I can understand is that you're trespassing on private property. So take a walk, sonny, while you can still walk—which might be hard to do with busted kneecaps."

"You know," Timothy says pleasantly, "it's been my experience that tough guys don't threaten. Tough guys *do* it, fast, and take advantage of surprise. I don't think you're as tough as you think."

"Want to try me?" the guy says, but something changes in his face, a shadow of doubt appears.

"What are you going to do?" Cone says. "Kill me? I honestly don't think you've got the balls for it. That hunk you're carrying under your left arm is all bluff; it's going to stay right there. And just to prove it, I'm going to turn my back to you and walk slowly down the path to my car. You want to plug me in the back, be my guest. It would be your style."

The tall man is trembling now, not just his hands but his entire body. Cone wonders if he's pushed it too far, but he can't stop now. He turns and begins to stroll toward the gate. The frog shouts something after him, two words, and not Happy Birthday.

In the Honda, Cone looks at his own hands. No shakes—which pleases him. He drives back to Manhattan, listening to the news on the radio. Something about a tropical depression north of Bermuda that might develop into a full-fledged hurricane and strike New York. Cone couldn't care less.

Back in the office, he phones out for a cheeseburger, fries, and a Coke. While munching, he calls New World headquarters. No answer. Then he tries Constance Figlia at Clovis & Clovis. She isn't in, the receptionist in the comptroller's section tells him, but is expected within an hour.

Cone spends fifty minutes finishing his lunch, smoking two cigarettes, and leaning on Sidney Apicella again.

"Tim," Apicella says, groaning. "Can't you leave me alone? I've got my own work to do, you know."

"I know, Sid. I know. But this will only take a minute. Have you got a snitch at Merchants International Bank?"

"Well . . ." Apicella says cautiously, "we've got a contact there who owes us one."

"Very simple request," Cone says. "Try to find out if

Constance Figlia—that's F-i-g-l-i-a—has a personal account at the bank. That's all. Give me a call when you get the answer, will you? I'll be in my office.''

He's lighting another Camel when his phone rings, and he grabs it up.

"Yeah?" he says.

"Tim? This is Sid. Merchants International has no customer named Constance Figlia.''

So now Cone knows that Constance Figlia's visit to Merchants International was not to make a deposit or withdrawal from a personal account. It's a fair assumption that she was depositing or withdrawing funds for New World.

He tries her at Clovis & Clovis again; she's still out. But a second call gets through, and suddenly he's talking to the lady herself.

"Miss Figlia?"

"Yes. Who is this speaking?" Her voice is husky and unexpectedly stirring.

"Miss Figlia, my name is Jeffrey B. Robbins, and I've recently been assigned to the Madison Avenue branch of the Manhattan Central Bank—with a promotion to assistant vice-president, I might add in all modesty.''

"Congratulations.''

"Thank you. Anyway, I've been here less than a week, and am just getting my feet wet, so to speak. One of the accounts handed to me for supervision is Clovis and Clovis.''

"What happened to Fred Hartle?" Constance Figlia asks.

"Oh, onward and upward," Cone says smoothly. "He's been transferred to our trust department. Miss Figlia, the reason I'm calling is that there seems to be a discrepancy in your last deposit. Quite frankly I think it's our teller's error, but the amount involved is so large, I'd like to get it straightened out. Would it be too great an imposition to ask you to stop by in the next day or so? I'm sure we can get the whole thing resolved in a few minutes.''

"A discrepancy?" she says. "How much?"

"A six-figure number," Cone says. "I suspect it's a matter of inverted digits, but I would like to get it cleared up."

"I would too," she says sharply. "Suppose I come over right now? I can be there in fifteen minutes."

"Excellent," Cone says. "I'm looking forward to meeting you personally. Clovis and Clovis are *very* valued clients. Please ask for Jeffrey B. Robbins."

"I'll be there," she says and hangs up abruptly.

"Lots of luck," Cone says softly, replacing his phone.

So now he knows Constance Figlia is handling funds for both Clovis & Clovis and its subsidiary, New World Enterprises. But whether that's significant or not Cone hasn't the slightest idea.

That's the first day. He spends the next two trying to tail the damned woman and making, he admits, a miserable job of it. She's either at Clovis & Clovis in Manhattan or at New World in Brooklyn. But she's hard to locate, seems to have no set schedule, and he still hasn't figured out how she gets from her Long Island home to the city. Train? Bus? Car? He doesn't know.

He sees her with Anthony Bonadventure several times. The two of them go to the banks together, but as far as Cone can tell, there's nothing personal to their relationship. Bonadventure treats her with respect, opening doors, assisting her down curbs, helping her get a speck out of her eye. But neither appears to have an overwhelming passion for the other.

It's business, Cone decides. Strictly business.

On the third day, something odd happens. He is lurking around the Clovis building on East Fifty-seventh Street when Constance Figlia gets out of the elevator, talking animatedly with Stanley and Lucinda. Cone dodges behind a pillar like Inspector Clouseau, peering out now and then to watch them. They're obviously waiting for someone and lo and behold, who should finally arrive but Grace Clovis with Anthony Bonadventure. Noisy greetings, hugs, and cheek kisses. Then the group, laughing and chattering, moves out onto Fifty-seventh Street. A stretch limousine is waiting, a white Cadillac, and away they go.

Cone, who has parked his Honda on Fifty-fifth Street and can't possibly get to it in time, searches about desperately for a cab. No luck. So he has to watch the white Cadillac disappear into traffic, traveling westward, and wonder where the five little elves are heading. Cocktails? A dinner? Maybe a party. Birthday? Anniversary? Or perhaps just to celebrate the frustration of Cone-Javert-Robbins.

He finds the nearest bar, on Lexington, bellies up and treats himself to a double Absolut on the rocks, figuring he can continue fiddling his expense account until Samantha Whatley lowers the boom.

He stands there, foot up on a genuine brass rail, and tries to make sense out of what he's just seen. All five exchanging hugs, kisses, giggles. A merry crew. Which probably means that whatever's coming off, they're all involved—or have guilty knowledge.

Maybe it's the vodka, maybe it's his misanthropy, but he gets some wild ideas. Perhaps the precious five are engaged in an orgy-type activity: the men stripped down to black socks and shoes, the women flaunting garter belts and mesh stockings, and all of them wearing masks—like those old blue movies.

Or they're in the counterfeiting game, with some good plates churning out quality twenties or fifties or hundreds, laundered by cash deposits at Merchants International and Manhattan Central.

Or maybe Grace Clovis isn't the only one hooked on nose candy. It's possible all five are sniffing up a storm, snickering while they soar up into the wild blue yonder. It's possible.

Anything is possible, Timothy Cone grumpily admits, and he's no closer to discovering what these people are up to than he was the day G. Edward Griffon died.

That, he decides, is what he's got to keep in mind and

never forget. Ed got scratched, and it had something to do with those ha-haing, hugging, ain't-we-got-fun people. But it isn't a romp; it's the deliberate killing of a guy who tried to be a friend. And if Cone lets that slide, he doesn't want to think of what the rest of his life will be like . . . remembering . . .

"It's all shit," he says to the bartender, paying his tab.

"You're telling me?" the guy says, scooping up his tip. "Have a nice day."

"I'm going to make a feast for you," he tells Samantha Whatley on the phone Friday night.

"Oh, God," she says despairingly. "The last time you made a feast for me, I had the runs for two days."

"Not this time," he promises. "You'll love this feast."

He spends Saturday morning buying this and that: peeled shrimp, hot Italian sausage, mushrooms as big as yarmulkes, a small filet mignon, green pepper, scallions, a crown of garlic. And a jug of California zinfandel.

It's a blustery day. That approaching storm never did develop into a hurricane, but it's still strong enough to kick up forty-knot winds with the prediction of three to five inches of rain over the metropolitan area by nightfall. The sky already has a phlegmy look, and clouds are scudding.

He gets home with his treasures and sets to work making what he calls a "hunters' stew." It's sautéed chunks of filet and sausage, cooked up with the garlic, green pepper, mushrooms, and scallions. The shrimp will be added when he's reheating this concoction just before serving.

As he labors, helped along by a jar of zinfandel, he tosses Cleo bits of beef fat, a raw shrimp, a slice of sausage, even a nibble of garlic. That crazy cat eats everything. Afraid his creation might prove too bland, Cone adds salt, pepper, Italian seasoning, Worcestershire sauce, a dollop of wine, a dash of Tabasco and, just for fun, a couple of chopped-up jalapeños. Everything smells good.

Samantha shows up a little before five o'clock. Her

trench coat is soaked, umbrella dripping. She brings a small frozen Sara Lee cheesecake for dessert.

"What a night this is going to be," she says. "Lightning to the east. Did you hear the thunder?"

"I wasn't listening," Cone says.

"No," Sam says, "you never do. Something smells good."

"Cleo likes it. When we're ready to eat, I'll pop in the shrimp for a few minutes."

"What are we having?"

"A kind of stew. I learned to make it in Nam. But with different ingredients. I won't tell you what we put in over there."

"Please don't. Will you, for God's sake, offer me a drink?"

"Sorry," he says. "Wine, beer, or vodka. And some brandy I'm saving for later."

"Wine'll be fine. Wow, listen to the thunder. You heard *that,* didn't you?"

"I heard it," he says. "Sounds like one-oh-fives. But we're in a dry, warm place with a hot meal coming up. What more can life offer?"

"Not a whole hell of a lot," she admits. "Can we eat soon? I'm famished."

They sit on the wooden kitchen chairs pulled up to Cone's desk. He serves the meal, with a baguette of French bread to be torn into chunks and used for the gravy. Cleo perches on a third chair, waiting patiently for scraps.

Samantha samples her bowl. "Jesus," she says, exhaling, mouth open, "do you think you put enough pepper in it?"

"Too much?"

"Not if you've got a flannel tongue. But I can live with it. How about a couple of ice cubes in my wine?"

All in all, the feast is a success. Even Cleo seems satisfied. Then they pile the emptied bowls into the sink and start on Sam's cheesecake.

"How was it?" Cone asks.

"It tasted just fine after my tonsils got numbed. How you coming with the Clovis-Evanchat buyout?"

"Okay," he says. "I think. Something very unkosher is in the works, so you better tell H. H. to keep stalling Isaac Evanchat."

"But you haven't pinned it down?"

"Not yet."

"How long?"

He shrugs. "Another couple of weeks maybe. Of course I could be whistling 'Dixie.'"

She looks at him thoughtfully. "You really think something stinks, don't you?"

"To high heaven."

"Want to tell me about it?"

"No," he says. "Not till I've got it wrapped up."

She accepts that. "Do it your way," she tells him. "Just don't take too long. I'm not sure Evanchat is going to stand still for the expenses you're running up."

"Screw him," Cone says, pouring them more brandy.

Samantha inspects him. He's wearing blue jeans that have been washed so often, they're a frayed pearly gray and a T-shirt that says SAVE THE WHALES.

"God," she says, "you're such a scruffy character. I can't for the life of me understand what I see in you."

"Oh, I don't know. I have my virtues."

"Yeah?" she says. "Like what?"

He stares at her. "I'm faithful," he says. "Since we've been rubbing the bacon, I haven't looked at another woman."

She takes up his hand, kisses the knuckles, then looks up at him. "Talking about sleeping together . . ."

"Yes?"

"Lock Cleo in the john, will you? The last time she kept biting my toes."

"*He,*" Cone says. "Or *it.*"

The storm really hits: thunder, lightning, a driving rain.

They cuddle on the mattress, as if the flashy sky were a performance just for their benefit.

"Let's talk about us," Samantha says.

"Do we have to?"

"Yes," she says firmly, "we do."

"Later," he promises.

She's as bony as he, but Cone can't get enough of her long, elegant back. Her shoulder blades jut and her spine is a rope of stones, but there's a rhythm and delicacy there, all subtle curves and sly shadows.

"I want to eat you up," he tells her.

"Do," she says.

They're like two rough hawsers, braided, rasping against each other and welcoming the scratch. In no way are they gentle or tender, because they are both hard, hurt people, wanting to get out. And this is the only way they know.

So there are no proclamations of love or undying passion. Instead there is a gritty intenseness, both of them serious and hoping. Their coupling is a partnership of two bank- rupts, as if all their liabilities combined might show up in black ink and make them wealthy.

"I've asked you a hundred times," she says, touching a fingertip lightly to a pink seam running along the back of his left thigh. "How did you get this scar?"

"I was born with it."

"Liar. I told you about my scars. This one was from an appendectomy, and this one I got when I was a kid. I fell against an iron railing while I was playing volleyball in the school gym. Come on, tell me: How did you get it?"

"I zigged when I should have zagged."

"My poor, wounded hero," she says, kissing the pink seam. "And all the time you were trying to make the world safe for democracy—right?"

"Something like that."

She lies back, and they both stretch out, apart but holding hands. The thunder has rumbled off, but they still hear the drumfire of hard rain, and occasionally the darkened loft is set ablaze by a distant lightning flash.

"About us . . ." she says. "How long do you think we've got?"

"Together? As long as you want. You're the boss."

"In the office maybe. Not in this dump."

"When we started," he reminds her, "we agreed: no strings and no connections."

She stirs restlessly. "Aren't you ever going to buy a bed?"

"Sure," he says. "Someday. But not while I know you."

"Why not?"

"Because you'll put ruffles on it."

They both laugh, turn to each other, embrace.

"Okay," she says, "I won't lean on you."

"You haven't," he says. "So far. And I haven't leaned on you, have I?"

"No, you haven't, you bastard. Because you just don't care."

"Oh, I care," he assures her. "In my own way."

"And what way is that?"

"I don't know. I haven't figured it out."

"Thanks a lot," she says. "That makes a girl feel very secure."

"Is that what you want—security? Forget it, babe. There ain't no such animal."

She snuggles closer to him. "All right," she says, "now I'll tell you the truth. Big confession—but you might as well know. All you are to me is a sex object. A good lay, and nothing more. I worked my evil way with you. All I want is your damp, white body—covered with freckles. I'll get tired of you eventually, I know, and trade you in for a new model."

He shakes with silent laughter. "You're as nutty as I am," he tells her. "The only thing we have in common."

"Oh, I don't know," she says, moving his hand between her legs. "Surely we have other things in common."

"Uncommon," he says, squeezing. "Damned uncommon."

"I'm ready," she says. "Has the hunters' stew given you enough strength for an encore?"

"It's the garlic," he says.

"You could have fooled me," she says. "I thought you've been gargling with Arpège."

And that's the extent of their intimate discussion of their relationship. They've done it before, never taking it too far, never digging too deeply. Because both are afraid of what they might find, what they may admit. So it's a hard, surface thing with these two invalids, neither willing to be the first to cry, "Nurse!"

They really do get out with each other, as attuned as a duo of violinists, bowing and scraping in unison and losing themselves in mutual harmonies. Carried away and lost with closed eyes and seraphic smiles, loving life and its surprises.

"You're not going home in this shit," he says later.

"No," she agrees, "I'm not going home in this shit. Let Cleo out of the john."

And, still later, she says, "I suppose we should shower."

"I suppose," he says. "Go ahead if you want. I'm too lazy."

"Tomorrow morning," she says. "Right now I like the way I smell—all garlicky and peppery and sexy. I'll keep till morning."

So they slump at the desk, bare feet up, their nakedness minimally covered with grungy T-shirts and Jockey shorts. They sit in silence, replete, sip a little brandy, and have no desire to talk, amazed that they can be content with each other's silent presence.

Cleo chases a ball of aluminum foil across the linoleum, and they watch the cat fondly, amused by its leaps and gallops. Cleo slaps the toy here and there, whacking it, chasing it, never biting but just playing, then suddenly collapses to lie quietly, breathing heavily.

"Just like us," Samantha says. "It's a game."

"Is it?" Timothy Cone says.

*   *   *

Without telling Sam about it or getting permission from H. H., Cone enlists Joe Washington in the investigation of the Clovis-Evanchat deal. Joe is easy to persuade; the guy is bored with the routine cases he's handling, and he's just as anxious as Timothy to nail the person or persons responsible for the death of Griffon.

Cone doesn't tell Washington everything—just enough to hook him. He gives Joe short biogs of the characters involved.

"Crazy people," the black says, shaking his head.

"And greedy," the Wall Street dick says. "Anthony Bonadventure seems to be the only heavy, but that Constance Figlia comes from a family who play rough, so it makes sense to figure she's not in it just for laughs. The others—the Clovises—I can't figure their motive. They seem to have all the money they need—but that doesn't mean they don't want more."

Washington brings in his own beat-up Plymouth with rusted fenders, and between Joe in his clunker and Cone in his Honda, they begin to get a better idea of Constance Figlia's daily routine.

She usually takes the train at the Hicksville station. Sometimes she goes to Brooklyn and cabs over to the New World warehouse, but always gets out of the cab a few blocks away. Sometimes she rides the train into Penn Station, and takes a taxi to the Clovis & Clovis office on East Fifty-seventh, again getting out of the cab a few blocks away.

"Now why in hell is she doing that?" Joe Washington says.

"Standard operating procedure," Cone says. "Someone's taught her. If you think there's a possibility of your being tailed, you never lead the hunter directly to your home base. Walking the last few blocks away gives her a chance to look around and maybe spot a shadow. She's playing it cozy."

"She went to the bank again today," Joe reports. "Merchants International. Bonadventure was with her. That's the third time this week."

"And on Monday," Cone says, "she and Bonadventure went to the Manhattan Central branch on Madison Avenue. If they're making deposits, I'd sure as hell like to know where the loot is coming from. Listen, Joe, you stay on Constance for another couple of days. I'm going to switch over to Bonadventure and see if I can find out where that gonzo spends his idle hours."

He doesn't discover a whole hell of a lot. Anthony seems to rise late, usually has a leisurely lunch at an expensive East Side restaurant (twice with Grace Clovis), and then frequently makes his way to the Clovis & Clovis office where he accompanies Constance Figlia to the bank.

"Goddammit it!" Cone explodes to Joe. "What's he up to?"

In the evening, Bonadventure usually meets with a bunch of pals at an uptown steak house or a downtown spaghetti joint. All the chums are heavy, florid-faced, middle-aged gents, well-dressed, with French cuffs and pinkie rings. Their gatherings look to Cone like a reunion of the Class of '65, Attica College—or maybe Leavenworth U.

One afternoon Anthony has lunch with Grace and the two of them go back to Bonadventure's brownstone. So they're shacking up. So what else is new? Cone goes back to Haldering & Co., almost convinced he's wasting his time. He finds Detective Davenport waiting for him.

"You keep lousy office hours," the city dick says, chomping on his Juicy Fruit. "I didn't snoop into anything. Besides, your desk is locked. Let's you and me have a talk."

"Why not?" Cone says, flopping into his battered swivel chair. "I wish I had something big to tell you, but I don't. Just a lot of little bits and pieces."

"Let's have them," Davenport says. "Something is better than nothing."

Cone tells him most of what he's learned, holding back a few items as bargaining chips. For instance, he doesn't tell the detective about the Anthony-Grace connection or the more than brother-sister relationship between Stanley and Lucinda.

The cop listens intently, his fingers laced over his belly.

"My, my," he says when the Wall Street dick finishes, "you've been a busy little boy, haven't you? How do you figure all those trips to the bank?"

"I don't," Timothy says miserably. "I don't know what's going on. I can understand retailers wanting to make frequent deposits if they have a heavy cash flow. What the hell, you want your money to be working for you. So naturally you deposit your cash as soon as possible. But New World isn't a retailer, and has no cash flow."

"All right," Davenport says, "now let me give you some food for thought. New World was started and capitalized by Clovis and Clovis for one-three-five million—right?"

"Right."

"Who owns the stock?"

"The four officers of the corporation: Stanley and Lucinda Clovis, Constance Figlia, and Anthony Bonadventure. They each own twenty-five percent. I got that from our resident CPA."

"Okay. And supposedly the purpose of New World is to renovate brownstones and maybe develop and build small residential and commercial properties—right?"

"Right again."

"So why do they need a hundred and thirty-five million? My God, you can fix up a brownstone for a couple of mil— at the most. And what can a small commercial parcel cost? Nowhere near what Clovis and Clovis put into New World. That outfit is overcapitalized. They were given far, far too much cash to do what they allegedly were set up to do."

Cone can feel his face reddening, and he slaps his desk wrathfully. "God*damm*it!" he shouts. "Why didn't I see that? I've been closer to this than you have, and it slid right by me."

"Take it easy," Davenport says soothingly. "Maybe you've been too close to it. Sometimes that happens. But what I said makes sense, doesn't it?"

"Of course it makes sense. I could kick myself for having missed it."

"But what does it add up to?" Davenport goes on. "New World was given too much loot by its parent company. So what? That's no crime."

Cone takes a deep breath and blows it out. "Yeah, it doesn't tell us anything. But thanks anyway. It might turn out to be something—you never know."

"All right," the detective says, "now I'm going to give you another gift. Maybe it'll convince you to open up with me."

They stare at each other a moment, two poker players not wanting to reveal their hand.

"A couple of days ago the narcs busted the biggest dealer on Wall Street," Davenport says. "You know how the kiddies down there like to snort a line of coke on their lunch hour. This guy who got busted was King Shit in the dope biz on Wall Street. They said he was actually operating in the Trinity graveyard. Anyway, the narcs grabbed his little black book of customers and credit accounts. Most listings were just initials or abbreviations. One was 'Ant.B.'"

"Bonadventure?"

"Who else? Now do you want to tell me anything?"

Cone is silent a moment, swinging back and forth in his swivel chair, considering.

"Yeah," he says finally. "I've got a trade-off for you."

"Jesus," Davenport says, "I've got to pry things out of you with a crowbar. What have you got?"

"Mrs. Grace Clovis is snorting. Bonadventure is her candyman."

"That's interesting. The Department wants that guy bad, and maybe we can nail him for dealing. What else have you got?"

Cone doesn't respond.

"Look, sonny," Davenport says patiently, unwrapping another stick of chewing gum, "I'm not one of your glory-boys. I'm never going to make lieutenant or captain; I know it. All I want is to do my job and make a good bust. But you, you're all screwed up with ideas of revenge. You're the Lone Ranger gunning for the villain who knocked off your pal—right?"

"Something like that," Cone mutters. "Griffon tried to be a friend. I just can't let it slide."

"I can understand that. But don't get so involved or you'll find your brain turning to gravel. Now I've given you two choice items, so you still owe me another. Let's have it."

Cone looks at him with admiration. "You really know how to deal, don't you? All right, here's something. The gossip around town is that Stanley and Lucinda Clovis are more than brother and sister; they're making it together."

Davenport stares at him. "You believe that?"

Cone nods.

"But the guy is married."

"I know. With two kids. But the sister lives in the same apartment. And the wife is hooked on happy dust and playing bed games with Bonadventure. Go figure it."

The city detective sighs and heaves himself to his feet. "Sometimes I think I'm getting too old for this business." He starts out, then stops at the doorway and turns back. "You gave me two for two. Fair enough. Now I'm going to give you a bonus. You remember my telling you we had a halfass witness to the murder of Griffon?"

"Sure, I remember. A guy who doesn't want to get involved."

"That's right. He was hazy about everything, said he just couldn't remember. But we talked him into going under hypnosis—and guess what? While he's in a trance, he says it was a woman who pushed your friend off the subway platform. How does that grab you?"

3

In that hot and humid climate, he developed a rash in his armpits and around his scrotum, and a fungus infection of his fingers, palms, and between his toes. His fair, freckled skin was in a cruddy condition, and the docs' wonder drugs didn't help a bit. Then an old Marine gunnery sergeant told him what to do.

He was to scrub his entire body with one of those stiff-bristled brushes used on barracks floors. The soap was yellow carbolic stuff that stung like hell. After he scoured every inch of his hide and rinsed, he dried thoroughly, then rubbed on cornstarch. Crazy remedy, but it got rid of the prickly heat.

After he got home, it took two years for the fungus infection to disappear in a more temperate climate. But once a month he still gave himself the brush-yellow soap-cornstarch treatment. Samantha Whatley watched him do it once, him standing up in the tub, brushing away furiously, and shook her head in disbelief.

"Why don't you wear a hair shirt?" she suggested. "Or whip yourself with barbed wire?"

On the night after he talked to Detective Neal Davenport, Cone goes through the ceremony once again, with Cleo staring in bemused puzzlement. Scrubbing away religiously, not neglecting the places where the sun don't shine, Timothy reflects on what he's learned and what it might mean.

He ponders the possibility of a woman having pushed G. Edward Griffon to his death from the Union Square subway platform. But it's not until he's carefully dried and is rubbing cornstarch on his raw pelt, as if he's thickening himself for wonton soup, that he asks the question he should have asked weeks ago:

What was Griffon doing in Union Square?

It's obvious Ed knew New World was a dummy corporation. But Clovis headquarters are on East Fifty-seventh, and New World is in Brooklyn. So how come the guy got chilled on Fourteenth Street? What in God's name was he doing there, with his snappy three-piece suit, fedora, and empty attaché case?

Cone is still wrestling with that puzzle the next day when Sidney Apicella clumps into his office. The CPA is pulling worriedly at his swollen, roseate nose.

"Oh-ho," Timothy says, "the mountain comes to Muhammad."

"Yeah," Sid says, frowning, "something like that. Listen, Tim, you keep asking me questions about this Clovis-Evanchat deal, so I've got to figure you think there's something there that smells. Correct?"

"Correct," Cone says.

"I more or less gave the buyout a clean bill of health in my PIE, and I don't want to get my balls caught in the wringer. You can understand that, can't you?"

"Sure. Very painful."

"So I took the file home last night and spent a couple of hours going through it line by line. There's something there I didn't see before, and it bothers me."

"Yeah? Like what?"

"Well, you know that in addition to New World, Clovis and Clovis owns three other companies. They're in general contracting, plumbing and electrical supplies, and foundations and underpinning. All those three corporations are headquartered in the New York area. But one of them banks in Newark, one in Chicago, and the third in San Diego."

The two men stare at each other.

"What does that mean, Sid?" Cone asks finally.

"Beats the hell out of me," Apicella says angrily. "You can bank wherever you like. But I'd call this situation highly unusual."

"Highly unusual," Cone repeats. "You accountants do have a way with words. So what happens now?"

"Let me look into it. I'd like to find out if those three corporations have been banking out of state since they were formed or if they switched banks recently. This may take some time, Tim."

"I can understand that. Let me know as soon as you get something."

"Of course."

"I love you, Sid," Cone says solemnly.

"And I love you, too," Apicella says, "you miserable bastard. I spent two hours last night doing your work when I could have been watching *Dallas*."

Cone stays in his cramped office, feet up on the desk, and smokes up a storm while he reviews what he knows and what he doesn't know. He's still brooding when Joe Washington slouches in and slumps into the extra chair.

"Enough already," Joe says.

Cone pushes his pack of Camels across the desk, but Washington shakes his head and lights up one of his own lowest-tar, lowest-nicotine cigarettes.

"I'll live longer with these," he says.

"Lots of luck," Cone says. "What's with the 'Enough already' crack?"

"How many times can I tail that Constance Figlia to the bank?" Washington says. "Now she's there two or three times a day."

"With Anthony Bonadventure?"

"Sometimes with, sometimes without."

"Any pattern to her bank visits?"

"Not that I can spot. Tim, am I doing any good?"

"Sure you are," Cone says. "Joe, you know where Griffon got whacked, don't you?"

Washington stares at him. "Of course I know. On the Union Square subway platform."

"Yeah. Now tell me this: What was he doing on Fourteenth Street?"

"He was investigating the Clovis-Evanchat deal at the time?"

"I think he was. The other stuff he was handling was just routine research and phone calls."

"Then I don't know what the hell he was doing in Union Square. Not eating a brown-bag lunch on a park bench, that's for sure."

Cone nods. "I think he was tailing someone. Griffon was the kind of man who'd never go below Twenty-third Street except to come into the office or do a job. I mean he was an *uptown* kind of guy."

"Right."

"So it was the job that took him to Union Square. Joe, drop Constance Figlia for the time being. I'd like you to concentrate on the Fourteenth Street area. Check all the banks around there. Try to find out about applications for new accounts in the last couple of months. Especially if Clovis and Clovis or New World Enterprises, Inc., tried to open one."

"Holy Christ," Joe Washington says, "how do I do that? A black walks in, flashes the ivories, and says, 'May I look at your new account applications, please?' They'll call the blues. You know that, Tim."

"Yeah, well, maybe you're right. But try it anyway. Show them your credentials and come on strong. If that doesn't work, here's another possibility: Go to Sid Apicella and get him to tell you the names of his contacts at all the big credit agencies. You know banks use those outfits just like department stores. Maybe you can find out if some bank in the Union Square area asked for a credit check on Clovis or New World."

Washington considers that. "It might work," he says, "but I doubt it."

"Maybe. But then, on the other hand, we could be doing something right. Do you believe in Divine Retribution?"

"Oh, hell yes," Joe Washington says. "My wife."

Timothy doesn't laugh. "Well, I think we got a kind of retribution going here. These are not nice people. They got money and reputation and social status—and all that shit. But they don't play by the rules."

"You believe in the rules, Tim?"

"Sure, I believe in the rules. If you don't, then you've got no game at all, do you? It's just a mess. I spent three years of my life with no rules, and I didn't like it. I want rules. Standards. If you can't measure up, get off the world. That's what we're dealing with: people who won't follow the rules. Fuck 'em!"

"If you say so," Washington says, looking at him queerly.

After Joe leaves, Cone wanders down the corridor to the office of Louis Kiernan. Cone lounges in the doorway, leaning against the jamb, until the paralegal looks up from the papers he's working on.

"Hi," he says.

"Lou," Cone says, "what exactly is a dummy corporation?"

Kiernan sits back and peers at the Wall Street dick over the tops of his reading glasses. "A dummy corporation? A legal entity, usually chartered by a state. But it's a fake corporation. It doesn't do any legitimate business."

"Why do people set them up?"

"A lot of reasons. To avoid personal liability. For tax purposes. Maybe even to register a name."

"But they're legal?"

"They're legal as long as the proper fees and taxes are paid, and the proper reports filed. That's all the state and federal government are interested in."

"When do they become illegal?"

"When they're caught. There are innocent dummy corporations, I suppose, but generally they're set up for fast wheeling and dealing, like hiding profits from the IRS or claiming a tax loss—stuff like that."

"But if a dummy corporation shows a profit, it has to pay taxes, doesn't it?"

"You better believe it. Unless the owners want to go to the clink."

"And anyone can set up a dummy corporation?" Cone persists.

"Anyone," Kiernan assures him. "I shouldn't tell you this, but you don't even need a lawyer. If you get the proper applications and all the other bumf, you can do it yourself. Thinking of setting up one?"

"Not today. Thanks, Lou."

The whole thing exploded so suddenly that, thinking it over later, Cone decides there was no way he could have avoided the confrontation. It's true he's a guy with a short fuse and a radioactive temper, but in this case he was goaded into it, he tells himself.

Like all experienced cops and private investigators, he knows that when you have multiple suspects, you zero in on the one with the criminal record. Christian charity has nothing to do with it; the recidivist rate does. The guy with the sheet is odds-on to be the perpetrator because that's all he knows how to do.

So Timothy sticks to Anthony Bonadventure like a leech, picking him up at his brownstone late in the morning, tailing him to lunch with Grace, following him to the banks with Constance Figlia, and then shadowing him in the evening when he meets with his coven of bentnoses who, for all Cone knows, might be plotting to kidnap the Statue of Liberty and hold her for ransom.

He's sitting in his rented Honda outside a snazzy French restaurant on East Fifty-second Street. Inside, Bonadventure and Grace Clovis are probably lunching on snails and brains and sipping a fine chablis. Cone is eating a Coney Island red-hot piled high with mustard, relish, sauerkraut, and peppers. He bought it from a sidewalk vendor, along with a can of cherry cola.

He's finished this repast and is trying to get the mess off his fingers and the stains off his lap with a paper napkin, when his two targets come out of the restaurant. Cone is double-parked across the street and watches. He sees immediately that there's trouble in paradise.

Grace is staggering, flopping around like a marionette with broken strings. Bonadventure is trying to support her, practically dragging her toward his silver Chrysler, standing in a No Parking zone. But Mrs. Clovis will have none of it. She struggles, twists away, breaks free, starts wobbling down the street. Anthony catches up with her, swings her around, and slaps her jaw, a heavy blow with all his shoulder behind it. She almost falls, but he grabs her.

Cone gets out of the car and runs across the street. When he comes up to them, they're waltzing around like a couple of drunken sumo wrestlers. By this time a dozen pedestrians have stopped to watch the action—from a distance. No one is interfering.

"May I be of help?" Cone asks pleasantly.

"Fuck off," Bonadventure snarls at him. "It's none of your goddamn business."

"But it is my business, sir. I am a paid-up member of the Society for the Prevention of Cruelty to Women, and if you attempt to strike this lady again, I shall have to restrain you."

"What?" Anthony says, astonished. "You some kind of a nut or something? This is a private matter, so butt out. She's had a little too much to drink, that's all."

Meanwhile he is holding on to Grace tightly, both arms wrapped around her. Cone sees her eyes are dulled, her head lolling on a limp neck.

"Ma'am," Timothy says in a loud voice, "would you like to get away from this man? I can drive you home."

"Yes," she says in a faint voice. "Please."

"Turn her loose," Cone orders Bonadventure. "I'll take her home."

"Who the fuck are you?" Anthony demands loudly. "Let's see your credentials."

"Certainly, sir," Cone says. He pulls up his right trouser leg, showing the ankle holster with the short-barreled Magnum. "Will that be satisfactory?"

Bonadventure looks down. His eyes widen. Slowly he loosens his grasp on Grace. Cone steps in quickly, puts an arm about the woman's waist, begins to move her gently toward the Honda.

"I'll get you, you prick," Bonadventure yells after him. "I'll find out who you are and demolish you, you no-good shit."

Cone stops and turns back. "Want to start now?" he asks. "You think you can take me? Be my guest."

The two men stare at each other, eyes locked. Then Anthony turns away.

"He's crazy!" he yells at the small mob of rubbernecks who have gathered to watch this incident. "The guy's a weirdo! Someone call the cops."

Then he runs to his LeBaron. Cone gets Grace across the street and into the Honda. She is dopey but functioning, remembers her home address, mumbles her thanks.

By the time he gets to the tower on Third Avenue near Eighty-fifth Street, she's revived enough to sit up straight, look at her face in the rearview mirror, feel cautiously along the line of her chin.

"He clipped you a good one," Cone says. "It'll probably be discolored tomorrow. You can cover the bruise with makeup."

She turns sideways on the passenger seat to stare at him. "Who *are* you?" she asks.

"Sir Galahad," he says. "Looking for the Holy Grail. Why don't you dump that miserable crud?"

"I've got no one else," she says dully. "Thanks for the lift."

She leans forward suddenly to give him a peck on the cheek, then gets out of the car and clacks across the street on her high heels. Cone watches her go, thinking that if he ever smacked Samantha on the jaw, she'd cut his balls off. But Sam isn't a victim and never will be.

He figures that little set-to with Bonadventure ends his, Cone's, effectiveness as a shadow. With Joe Washington canvassing banks in the Union Square area, Timothy reckons his best bet is to concentrate on Constance Figlia and Stanley and Lucinda Clovis, and try to discover what those tykes are up to.

The prospect doesn't set his blood atingle. He's depressed at how *small* all these people are, despite the big money involved. They have no quality. The cash is strong, but the people are weak. The guy out at Vincent Figlia's home backed off. Anthony Bonadventure backed off. Grace Clovis said helplessly, "I've got no one else."

Stanley and Lucinda Clovis seem to be prisoners of their own selfish wants, and who the hell knows what drives Constance Figlia? Greed, probably. What disturbs Timothy Cone most is that none of these characters have any spine. He'd prefer staunch opponents willing to stake their lives on their sins, go down in a blaze of gunfire because no matter how rotten they might be, their pride demands they stand up for their evil.

The cheapness, the flimsiness of these people diminishes his own role. It's one thing to have the job of defusing a horrendous bomb, when the slightest, tiniest miscalculation could be your last. It's another thing to be required to quench a wee firecracker. Even if it went off, it would go "Pop."

Sometimes Cone feels like an old-fashioned whitewing, sweeping up the world's garbage and droppings. Nothing exciting, glamorous, or rewarding there. But still, it's a job that must be done—by someone. Why it should be him, and how he got to where he is now, he cannot understand.

Brought low by these mournful reflections, he still has the self-discipline to drive down to Clovis headquarters on

East Fifty-seventh, hoping to get a line on Constance Figlia or Stanley and Lucinda. They may be worthless people, but he's convinced they're breaking the rules, and that's sufficient reason for this essentially puritan man to keep working.

"You didn't!" Samantha Whatley wails.

"I did," Cone says, after telling her of his run-in with Anthony Bonadventure. "First of all, I didn't want to sit there and watch the woman get bounced around. And also, I wanted to try the guy, to see what I'm up against. I found out. He's got no moxie. All mouth."

"And if he hadn't backed down?"

"Then I probably would have."

"Oh, sure," Sam says, staring at him. "You really are an asshole—you know that? Anyway, I'm glad it went no farther than it did."

"Well," Cone says uncomfortably, "we may have a little problem there."

They're drinking dark Michelob in Samantha's chintzed and ruffled apartment after a dinner of beef stew—to which Sam added a strong dose of chili.

"All right," she says, sighing, "let's have it. What's our little problem?"

"After Bonadventure made a dash for his car, I'd bet he grabbed a pen and made a note of the Honda's license number. No trick at all to see it's a rental car, and with his bucks and contacts he can bribe the right people to find out that it's rented to Haldering and Company."

"Oh, Jesus!" Sam says despairingly.

"Not to worry," Cone reassures her. "If Clovis complains, Hiram can fuzz it over by saying the employee who was driving the car was not authorized to be in that area, and he's been reprimanded or canned. No problem."

"That's what you say," Sam says bitterly. "You're really a world-class troublemaker."

"But you love me," he says with his quirky smile.

"Yeah," she says, "like a cobra loves a mongoose. What other nasty surprises have you got for me?"

He tells her what he's learned from Davenport, and how Sid is checking the out-of-state banks used by Clovis & Clovis subsidiaries.

"And what has Joe Washington found out?" Sam asks, looking at him narrowly.

"Oh," he says, flummoxed, "you know Joe's been working with me?"

"Will you give me credit for some brains?" she yells. "Of course I know it. Don't ever get the idea that I don't know what's going on in that office, buster, because I do. But I can't keep covering your ass if you don't play straight with me. So no more secrets—okay?"

"Okay."

"Liar," she says. "Tell me something—honestly now: Why did you try that *High Noon* face off with Bonadventure? He could have pounded you to a pulp. You never would have drawn your gun on him."

"Maybe, maybe not. Listen, I just don't like people who think they own the world. Bonadventure, the Clovises— they all figure their money entitles them to shoulder everyone else out of the way. All their ego comes from *things:* bucks, new cars, expensive homes. But I tell you they're hollow people. Breathe on them hard and they blow away. Like Bonadventure. That lad will have a few scars before I get through with him, I promise you that."

She sighs. "Tim, you scare me when you talk like that."

"Look," he says earnestly, "as far as I'm concerned, those people are evil. The only way to beat them is to prove to them that they can feel pain like ordinary mortals, maybe even die if they don't straighten up and fly right."

"Who the hell are you—an avenging angel?"

"No, I'm just an ex-grunt who's eaten enough dirt to last me a lifetime. Dying isn't so bad; everyone's got to do it. And once you realize that, it gives you a big edge on those scumbags, because they think they're going to live forever."

"You really believe that, don't you?"

"You bet your sweet ass I do. And speaking of your sweet ass . . . ?"

"What if I say no?"

"I'll accept that. Are you going to?"

"Are you out of your mind? Let's go!"

She's in a wild mood, and he takes his cue from her frenzy. It's a fight to a draw: no winner, no loser, but both satisfied with their private combat, convinced it's something special that neither will ever find again with anyone else.

After, he becomes suddenly subdued and tender, kissing her ribs, stroking her hard thighs.

"Christ!" she gasps. "I swear to God you're mellowing out."

"Maybe I am," he admits. "Want me to stop?"

"Hell, no! But after all that shit you were giving me, this is a new Timothy Cone I'm seeing. Just keep it up, kiddo; I love it."

So they lie quietly, not speaking, just touching, feeling, embracing sweetly: a new kind of intimacy for them, and something both find wondrous, though neither would admit it.

He imagines what his life would be like if he spent the rest of his days with this splenetic woman. She ponders if she might dare a lifetime with this violent, crabbed man who may be a loner—but not entirely from choice.

Finally, ignited again, they come together in a different mood: all murmurings and soft twistings. They couple in a drugged tempo, slow and lazy, as if this night might last forever.

Later, drowsy and satiated, they lie entwined, peering at each other with dazed eyes. They say nothing of what has happened, not wanting the moment to slip away—as it inevitably does.

"It's late," he says. "I've got to go."

"I suppose," she says. "I've got something for you. I

wasn't sure I should give it to you, but I think I will. It may help on the Clovis-Evanchat case.''

"What is it?"

"I told you that you should read the society pages occasionally. You know what a house tour is? Well, every now and then a charity will arrange a tour of rich people's homes, usually on the East Side. You buy a ticket and the money goes to the charity. In the *Times* today, it listed a tour that included the Clovis triplex. Wanna go?''

"Why not? Give me a chance to see how the other half lives.''

"I'll get a ticket for you.''

She pulls on a flannel robe and they each have another beer while he dresses. She watches him strap the holster to his shin.

"You really need that thing?'' she says.

"It's just for show. Besides, I'd feel naked without it.''

"You ever use it?'' she asks.

"It impressed Bonadventure,'' he says, not answering her question.

Their farewell is strained. Something has changed, but neither can define it nor understand. So they keep their parting short and light. A quick kiss. A hurried embrace.

He drives home through deserted streets to his empty loft. Cleo comes growling up to rub against his legs, but it doesn't help.

Wakes up with a hacking cough. Decides, for the 1974th time, that he'll cut down on the coffin nails. Gives Cleo fresh water and the remains of a can of tomato herring. Has a cup of instant coffee and his first cigarette of the day, proud of himself for waiting so long.

Gets to work on time—a miracle. Joe Washington, waiting in his office, is amazed.

"What happened?'' he asks. "Insomnia?''

"Very funny,'' Cone growls. "What have you got?''

"*Nada*,'' Joe says. "I braced every bank within ten

blocks of Union Square. They all kicked my ebony ass onto the street. Applications for new accounts are confidential, and I can't get a look at them without a court order. That's the way I thought it would go."

"Yeah," Cone says, "you're right, but it had to be done."

"So I figured to try Sid. To get the names of his contacts at the credit agencies, like you said. But he was busy. I'll hit him again, but I don't think this is going to work, Tim. We just don't have the muscle to get that kind of information."

"I guess," Cone says, then slams the top of his desk angrily. "Goddammit, I know Griffon was tailing someone involved in the Clovis-Evanchat deal because he found that Clovis's dummy corporation was up to its ass in banks."

"Someone mention banks?" Sidney Apicella asks, standing in the doorway and rubbing his big schnozzola furiously. "I'll tell you about banks!"

He seems so distraught, they look up at him in astonishment. His face is flushed, and his swollen nose is flashing like a lighthouse.

"Those three other subsidiaries of Clovis," he says. "They're all headquartered in New York, and they were all banking here up to about a year ago. Then they switched to Newark, Chicago, and San Diego."

"Oh, boy," Cone says.

"Yeah—oh, boy," Apicella says. "I'm no detective, but even I can see that a month or two after New World Enterprises was organized the other Clovis subsidiaries switched their banks. Coincidence?"

"You don't really believe that, do you, Sid?" Cone asks.

"Of course I don't believe it. Three New York corporations suddenly switching to out-of-state banks—there's something going on there that's not kosher. You going to follow up on this, Tim?"

"Sure."

"Anything I can do to help? I okayed the deal in my PIE, and I don't enjoy being played for a patsy."

"Yeah," Joe Washington says, standing up. "You can help. I'll go back to your office with you, and you can give me the names of your contacts at the credit agencies."

"What for?"

Cone answers: "We're trying to find out if Clovis or any of its subsidiaries tried to open a new account at a bank in the Union Square area."

Apicella nods gloomily. "Where Griffon was killed. Come on, Joe; I'll give you what I've got, but don't expect too much. Those guys are closemouthed. You ask them how they're feeling and they want to know why you're asking."

Alone in his office, Cone opens a fresh pack of cigarettes, forgetting his morning resolution. He blows a plume of smoke at the dingy ceiling and reflects ruefully that's what he's good at—blowing smoke. When the phone rings, he lets it shrill five times before he picks it up.

"Yeah?" he says.

"Must you say, 'Yeah'?" Samantha Whatley barks. "Can't you say, 'Timothy Cone's office' or something half-way respectable?"

"I'm not a respectable guy," he says. "You know that. What's got you in a snit? You sound ready to chew spikes."

"Get your ass in here," she commands.

"Oh-oh," he says. "Bad news?"

She doesn't answer; just slams down the phone. So he shambles along the corridor to her office. She's sitting erect behind her desk and gives him what he once called her top-sergeant stare: cold, stony, and completely without mercy.

"What's up?" he asks.

"Close the door and sit down," she orders, and he does.

"You're off the Clovis-Evanchat deal," she says.

"Oh? Why is that?"

"Because there is no deal. Isaac Evanchat got a registered letter this morning; Clovis and Clovis have decided not to go ahead with the buyout. So Evanchat called Haldering and told him to drop the investigation."

"Good," Cone says.

"Good?" Samantha cries. "Good? We lose a profitable client, and all you can say is good?"

"Bonadventure traced the Honda, like I told you he would. So he knows he's being tailed. Also, they're nervous about a guy named Javert who's been asking too many questions."

She glares at him. "You son of a bitch, that was you."

"It was me," he admits. "Don't you see what's happening? We're getting close to the jugular, and Clovis figures the best thing to do is pull out of the deal. So we stop poking into their private affairs."

"Well, they've succeeded," Sam says. "H. H. told me to drop the whole thing and reassign personnel."

"And you're going to do it?"

"Tim, for God's sake, it's my neck if I don't do as he says. So just forget it."

They stare at each other, knowing something important is happening. Not so much about the Clovis-Evanchat deal as between themselves.

"I'm not going to forget it," Cone says. "If you want to can me, then can me. I couldn't care less. But Griffon got wasted, and he was a guy who tried to be a friend. And he worked for this outfit; that counts for something. So I'm going to push it. On my own if I have to."

"Jesus," she says, groaning, "what a hard-on you are."

"Not so much," he says. "But I know what's right. I'm going to keep digging. Am I bounced?"

She takes a deep breath, blows it out. Swings back and forth in her swivel chair. Fiddles with a ballpoint pen on her desk. Rubs her forehead worriedly. Pulls at her jaw. Scratches her scalp. Finally she looks up at him.

"The Honda is leased until the end of the month," she says. "That gives you another ten days. I can cover that. And I can diddle the reports to give you some wiggle room. Can you clear it up in a week?"

"I'll try," he says. "No guarantees."

"If you blow it, we're both out on our ass."

"I know. Do I still get the ticket to the house tour?"

She takes another deep breath. "All right, idiot boy," she says, "you'll get it. I'll scam it—somehow. But I'll have to start Joe on some new assignments. You can understand that, can't you?"

"Sure."

"Okay," she says, "you've got a week. Then it's back to the salt mines for you, sonny."

"I've been there before," he says.

"I like the way you express appreciation for what I'm doing for you," she says. "Get the hell out of here. You're disgusting."

"First I'm a hard-on and now I'm disgusting. This is my lucky day."

"Out!" she says, jerking a thumb toward the door.

He goes back to his office and calls Davenport. The city detective is out, so Cone leaves a message. He works on his weekly report—a great work of fiction—for almost an hour before Davenport calls back.

"I hear Haldering is out of the picture," the NYPD man says. "The Clovis-Evanchat deal is kaput."

"My God," Cone says, "bad news travels fast. Yeah, the buyout has been canceled. But that doesn't change anything as far as I'm concerned."

"This is a goddamned crusade with you, isn't it?"

"Yes," Cone says. "I think we better meet. I've got some things for you."

"And you want something from me?"

"That's right. Why don't we stop playing games? I've only got a week to clear this."

"A hotshot like you should be able to do it in a day or two. How's about I drop by your palace around eight o'clock?"

"Sounds good to me."

"This is my week for scotch," Davenport says. "Pick up a jug, will you? I'll pay for it."

"I can afford it," Cone says. "You want soda with it?"

"Are you out of your frigging mind?" the detective says.

He buys a bottle of Chivas Regal, drives home, feeds Cleo, and eats some cold leftover lasagne. He sits at his desk and stares at that scrap of paper Ed Griffon left in his file: DUM?

"That's what I am," Cone tells Cleo. "Dumb."

Davenport arrives, wearing a clear plastic raincoat and a plastic cover on his fedora. Both are sparkling with raindrops.

"It's raining?" Timothy asks.

"No," the city detective says, "I ran under an open hydrant. Of course it's raining. Where the hell have you been for the last two hours?"

"Sitting here."

"You never look out the window?"

"What for?"

"Good answer," Davenport says. "My God. Chivas Regal! Are you trying to bribe an officer of the law? If you are, you're succeeding."

They sit at the crippled desk, feet up, and sip from jelly jars filled with the scotch whiskey.

"I got to get home," the city dick says, unwrapping a fresh stick of Juicy Fruit, "or the wife will kill me. So let's make it fast. Why did Clovis cancel the deal?"

"Because they're running scared," Cone says.

Then he tells Davenport about his confrontation with Anthony Bonadventure. About Apicella's report on the out-of-state banks. About Joe Washington's failure to examine applications for new bank accounts in the Union Square area.

"That's where you come in," he says. "Griffon was down there on something connected with the Clovis-Evanchat deal; I'm convinced of it. But I'm getting nowhere. I want you to check the area and see if anyone from Clovis applied for a new account the day Griffon was killed."

"What's so important about the banks?" he wants to know. "You don't think they're being cased for holdups, do you?"

"Nah, nothing like that. These people aren't shoot-'em-up types; they wear white collars. But whatever the con is, it's got something to do with their banks."

"Okay," the NYPD man says equably, "I'll give it the old college try. We're getting nowhere on the Griffon kill. Our witness can't remember another goddamned thing."

"But he still thinks it was a woman who pushed Ed?"

"He *thinks* it was, but the guy's a flake. No way are we even going to get an indictment on his testimony. We need more."

Cone ponders a moment. "You got a buddy at the local IRS office?" he asks finally.

"Maybe," Davenport says cautiously. "What's on your mind?"

"I'm not sure. But I thought it might be interesting if you could get a look at the returns of all the Clovis people involved."

"That would take a month of Sundays," the detective says. "But I can ask my pal if any of them are under audit and for what. It's Bonadventure we're interested in most."

"If push comes to shove," Cone says, "I think you can lean on Grace Clovis. That lady is ready to shatter into a million pieces. I think she'll admit Anthony is supplying her with nose candy. Then you can hit on him, and God knows he's no Rock of Gibraltar. Maybe he'll work a deal and sing like a birdie."

"Do you also believe in the tooth fairy?" Davenport drains his Chivas in two deep gulps and smacks his lips. "That stuff's really sippin' whiskey, but I haven't got the time. I'll check out those Union Square banks for you. What'll you do for me?"

"I'm getting into the Clovis apartment on a charity house-tour. Maybe I can come up with something."

"What are you smoking these days?" Davenport asks. "I'd like to try some of it."

"I'm going to break this thing," Cone says. "You'll see."

The detective stands and makes the sign of the cross in the air. "Bless you, my son," he says.

Two days later (both spent tailing Constance Figlia), Cone drives the Honda up to East Seventy-seventh Street, to the headquarters of the charity sponsoring the house tour. He is wearing his raggedy tweed jacket, a plaid shirt open at the neck and showing a T-shirt beneath, and his stained flannel slacks. It is, he believes, a costume suitable for visiting the homes of the rich and the famous.

The charity is located in a townhouse inhabited by what appear to be similar organizations: Society for this and Association for that. The one Cone seeks is apparently devoted to the welfare of an American Indian tribe he's never heard of, but hé assumes needs all the help it can get.

The tour is assembling on the sidewalk, next to a small chartered bus. A young woman and young man, both pale, long-haired, and earnest, continually count their flock, checking off each new arrival against a clipboard list.

"Timothy Cone," he reports to the young woman. "From Haldering and Company."

"Splendid," she says brightly, ticking off his name. "You're the last. Now we can get this show on the road. Horace," she calls, "everyone present and accounted for."

"Splendid," he says, and then in a louder voice: "May I please have your attention, ladies. And gentleman," he adds, with a bob of his head in Cone's direction. "Today we're going to visit six absolutely splendid homes. We will spend approximately thirty minutes in each house. In most cases the owners will be present to conduct the visit and answer your questions. Please, I entreat you, stay together and do not wander. Remember, you are invited guests, and I know you will conduct yourselves as you would expect guests to act in your home."

They all pile into the bus: twenty-two women—mostly middle-aged matrons with blue hair and white gloves—

and Timothy Cone. He maneuvers to get a seat next to Horace.

"When do we get to the Clovis apartment?" he asks.

Horace consults his clipboard. "Third on the schedule," he reports. "Why? Is it of particular interest to you?"

"I hear it's a classy joint."

"It's splendid!" Horace enthuses. "A triplex with divinely proportioned rooms. And wait'll you see their collections of African masks and pre-Columbian sculpture."

"I can hardly wait," Cone says.

The first home is a nine-room apartment on East Seventy-ninth Street, decorated in what the owner calls "New York Victorian."

"The real stuff," he says proudly. He's a stubby man, in his sixties, chewing on an unlighted cigar.

The living room walls are covered with flocked paper in a hellish design of mythical beasts. There are swagged velvet drapes and more gilt-framed oil paintings of dead fish than Cone has seen outside of Manny's Restaurant on the San Francisco wharf. There are also antimacassars, and a polished brass gaboon on a rubber mat. The only piece of furniture Cone admires is an armchair made of deer antlers. It looks like a sitting-down version of the iron maiden.

The second home on the tour is a Park Avenue duplex decorated in a style the gushy resident terms "French Provincial, with just a wee touch of your English manor house." This one is a little more attractive, with a lot of flowered fabrics on furniture, walls of Oriental paper, and carpeting with a pile so deep it could swallow a hundred contact lenses.

Finally the bus pulls up in front of the Clovis building on Third and Eighty-fifth. It takes two elevators to get the tour group up to the triplex. Waiting to greet them are Stanley and Lucinda, both wearing silvery jumpsuits, and if they don't exactly match, they're close enough to make Cone think of a song-and-dance team.

The main floor of the apartment is really something. The foyer is as large as Cone's loft, and the living room stretches away like a basketball court. A handsome copper staircase rises to the upper floors, although Stanley assures his awestruck visitors that there's a small private elevator to the terrace, swimming pool, and sauna.

Brother and sister chatter on, often completing each other's sentences. They name the Brazilian who designed the custom-made leather furniture, the Italian who did the marble fireplace, the Frenchman who painted the walls, and the Austrian who etched the glass for the doors.

"And who designed *le tout ensemble?*" one of the blue-haired matrons asks. "The overall creative concept?"

"We did," Stanley and Lucinda say in unison, with such an expression of satisfaction that Cone can hardly stand it. He turns and stares at a fiendishly baroque nineteenth-century grand piano, hand-carved with painted cupids, curlicues, leaping harts, crouching hares, and a wealth of other excrescences devised by a demented woodcarver.

What interests the Wall Street dick is that on the closed lid of this monstrosity are files of standing photographs framed in silver, leather, shell, aluminum, or dark wood. Cone moves sideways behind the tour group to get a closer look. It appears to be a collection of family photos: grandparents, children, relatives, friends. And one row of Stanley and Lucinda, from the time they were toddlers to their present state of physical and spiritual perfection.

"And now," Stanley says, "before we show you the upstairs—"

"—we'd like you to see our collection of pre-Columbian art," Lucinda finishes.

"Including some really rare and amusing artifacts," Stanley says. "You won't see anything like it anywhere else."

"We hope you won't be shocked," Lucinda adds, and brother and sister giggle.

The group moves to the end of the living room, where the

art collection is housed in lighted glass cases recessed into the wall. With everyone's back turned, Cone steps swiftly to the piano and scans the photographs more closely.

In the front is a four-by-five color shot of Stanley, Grace, and Lucinda Clovis, Anthony Bonadventure, and Constance Figlia. The photo is framed in blue leather. It was obviously taken on a beach somewhere. The five, wearing bathing suits, are standing in a row, arms about each other's waists, laughing at the camera.

Cone looks up to make certain he's unobserved, then swipes the framed photograph. He slides it inside his jacket, holding it clamped under his left arm. He rejoins the tour group, troops upstairs with the others to inspect the master bedroom, dominated by a "genuine Chinese opium couch."

When the visit is finished, he goes down to the street with everyone else but doesn't board the bus. Instead, he walks rapidly westward, the purloined photograph still concealed under his jacket. He doesn't take another look at it until he's back in the parked Honda on East Seventy-seventh Street.

There they all are—a grinning group, holding each other and squinting against the bright sunlight. Grace Clovis is wearing the world's tiniest bikini. Lucinda is wearing a skimpy maillot with the legs cut up to her waist. Constance Figlia is swaddled in something with a ruffled skirt. The two men are wearing conventional swimming trunks. All look healthy, happy, and maybe just a little drunk or stoned.

The photograph infuriates Cone because it refutes the scenario he had imagined, which goes like this:

Grace Clovis somehow gets evidence of her husband's incestuous relationship with his sister. In a coked-up state, Grace delivers the evidence to Anthony Bonadventure. That bandito, realizing he's onto a good thing, confronts Stanley and Lucinda and in return for his silence lures the brother and sister into some kind of a bank scam, with Constance Figlia doing the donkeywork on that computer at New World Enterprises.

That plot has a lot going for it—until Cone stares at the color photograph of five friendly people and sees how content they are with each other. And didn't he see them all drive away in a stretch limousine, laughing and chattering?

Who the hell socializes with his blackmailer? No, they're all in it together. All five are on a high, laughing up a storm as if they have the world by the nuts.

"Greed," the Wall Street dick says aloud. "It's got to be greed. Them and their African masks and private elevator and stupid piano. Screw 'em!" he adds wrathfully.

Joe Washington is a good man, thorough and conscientious. But he's not as driven as Cone. Who is? So when Joe reports he can find no pattern in Constance Figlia's bank visits, Timothy has to check it out himself.

He can be methodical when he has to be. He keeps a detailed log of Figlia's bank visits, and eventually all those hours and days spent skulking around the lobby of Clovis headquarters on East Fifty-seventh Street begin to pay off. There *is* a pattern, a rough one, but what it might signify, Cone can't yet grasp.

The woman, frequently accompanied by Anthony Bonadventure, goes to the tellers' windows at Merchants International and Manhattan Central at least once a day. On Thursdays and Fridays she makes bank visits twice or maybe three times. And on the days before a bank holiday, she's especially busy, running in and out of the two banks like some kind of a nut.

Cone is still trying to puzzle this out when, on a Wednesday afternoon, he picks up his salary check at Haldering & Co. and takes it around the corner to a branch of Workmen's Savings, where he keeps an interest-bearing checking account. He deposits his check and then draws $100 in cash. The teller punches out his number on a computer terminal to make sure he's got enough in his account, then flips out five twenties.

Cone stares at the bills and begins to get a glimmer.

"Listen," he says to the wan teller, "if I had wanted to draw against the check I just deposited, could I do it?"

The teller takes another look at the salary check Cone has just deposited. "It's local," he says, "but not our bank. Unless you can get one of our officers to okay it, better figure about five days before you can draw on it."

"Does it always take five days to clear a local check?"

"It depends."

"On what?"

"Is it a weekend? A holiday? Then it might take longer. But generally it's three to five days before a local check clears. Faster for city, state, and federal checks."

"What about checks drawn on out-of-state banks?"

"Figure ten days to two weeks before you can draw on them."

Before Cone drives home, he stops at a discount store and picks up a pocket calculator for $10.95. It's got a lot of keys he doesn't understand, but it adds, subtracts, and multiplies, and that's all he needs.

Back in the loft, he gives Cleo a dish of fresh water and some old barbecued rib bones and pulls a chair up to his desk. He gets to work with a chewed pencil stub, a pad of scratch paper stolen from his office, and his new calculator.

He works for almost an hour, interrupting his task only long enough to pop a can of cold Bud. The phone rings and rings. But he doesn't answer it. He sticks with his figuring, punching the little calculator keys carefully with his bony fingers.

When he finishes, he looks at the results with awe. He can't believe it. So he goes through his computations once again. It comes out the same way. He sits back and smiles grimly. It's a sweet scam. Simple but sweet. He can appreciate the temptation—but that's no excuse.

The next day he's back on the trail of Constance Figlia. But now that he suspects what's going down, her many bank visits don't seem so strange.

He's double-parked in the Honda across Fifty-seventh

Street on Thursday afternoon after the banks have closed. He watches Bonadventure pick up Constance Figlia in the silver LeBaron. Cone makes an illegal U-turn, ignoring the horns of furious motorists, and takes off after them. He thinks he knows where they're heading, but he wants to make sure.

It's a loose tail so they won't spot the Honda. But when he gets to New World Enterprises, the silver car is parked inside the fence, next to the office. Cone drives past slowly, sees no sign of activity, and then starts back to Manhattan.

"It's computer time," he says aloud, certain he's right.

He finds two urgent messages on his desk, both asking him to call Detective Davenport immediately. He lights a cigarette and smokes awhile, staring at the ceiling. Then he picks up the phone and dials.

"Davenport."

"Yeah, this is Cone. You wanted to talk to me?"

"What are you—some kind of fucking genius or something?"

"What's that supposed to mean?" Cone asks.

"I start checking out banks in the Union Square area, telling myself I'm stupid to listen to your idiot ideas. And the second bank I hit they say, Yeah, on the day Griffon got chilled, they had an application for a new account from New World Enterprises. How do you like that?"

"I like it."

"I even saw the application," Davenport says. "Wanna guess who signed it?"

"Constance Figlia, the corporation secretary," Cone says.

"Bingo! Go to the head of the class. And also Anthony Bonadventure, the corporation treasurer. I'm going back to the bank with a mug shot of Bonadventure to see if the officer who handled the application can definitely identify him. But I don't have a photo of Constance Figlia."

"I do," Cone says.

"Oh? Where'd you get that?"

"I stole it—on that charity house-tour I told you about."

The city detective laughs. "You're a pisser, you are. Can you get it over to me so I can nail this thing down?"

"Wait a minute," Cone says. "Let me think . . ." They're both silent a moment. Then: "Can you come over here tomorrow morning? Say about ten?"

"You got something for me?" Davenport asks.

"Another of my idiot ideas. Also, you better be here when I talk to our chief CPA, Sidney Apicella. I want to get his take on what I have to tell you."

"Will it help put Bonadventure on ice?"

"For years to come," the Wall Street dick says with more assurance than he feels.

"You think he pushed Griffon?"

"No," Cone says. "I think Figlia did that. But maybe you can get Bonadventure as an accessory."

"Okay, Cone, I'll be there. You'll have the Figlia photo for me?"

"Of course. Haldering and Company is always anxious to cooperate with New York's Finest."

"Son," Davenport says, "you've got more crap than a Christmas goose."

Cone stops by Apicella's office to make sure he'll be in on Friday morning and available for a short conference. Sid grumbles but agrees to meet with Cone and Davenport at ten o'clock.

Then Timothy pauses at Samantha Whatley's office and peers in. She's watering her scrawny philodendron. She looks at him without expression.

"Who are you?" she says.

"Your humble and obedient servant, ma'am," he says.

"You're a stranger to me," she says in a low voice. "I called you last night. No answer. I guess you were out."

"I was in," he says. "I just wasn't answering the phone."

"Prick," she says. "I needed to talk."

"I needed to clear the Clovis-Evanchat thing. You gave me a lousy week—remember?"

She brightens. "You're going to do it?"

He nods.

"And get Ed Griffon's killer?"

"Sure. With a little bit o' luck. How about Saturday night? I'll tell you all about it then."

"Okay," she says. "I forgive you, your place or mine?"

"Mine," he says. "What do you feel like eating?"

She grins at him.

"You're a depraved lady," he tells her.

"Guess who taught me," she says.

They're sitting in Apicella's office. Cone is dragging on a Camel. Davenport is starting on a new stick of Juicy Fruit. Sid is stroking his swollen beezer tenderly. They look at each other.

"Well?" Sid asks. "What's this all about?"

"Tell us about kiting checks," Cone says.

The CPA stares at him. "Kiting checks? Don't tell me you've never kited a check?"

Cone stirs restlessly. "That's neither here nor there. I just want to start from the beginning. How do you kite a check?"

Apicella sighs. "Okay, I'll give you a basic course. You got, say, five hundred bucks in your checking account. But you got a mortgage payment of, say, a thousand that's due immediately. So you write a check for the thousand because you know that before your mortgage payment check clears, you're going to be able to deposit enough in your account to cover it."

"That's illegal?" Davenport says. "I've been doing it all my life."

"Who hasn't?" Apicella says wearily. "That doesn't make it any less illegal. It's against the law to write a check for funds you don't possess at the time the check is written. What you're doing is taking advantage of the float—the time it takes for a check to clear from one bank to another. Two to five days for local banks.''

''Meanwhile you're using the bank's money,'' Cone says. ''Right? I mean, you're writing a check against money that doesn't actually exist in your account.''

''Correct,'' Sid says, nodding. ''But if you cover your check in time, no one's the wiser. That's the simplest form of check kiting. There are others.''

''Yeah?'' Davenport says. ''Like what?''

''Like overdrafting,'' the CPA says. ''Suppose you have a lot of bucks in a checking account that pays no interest— or very little. So you draw a check on much more than you've got in the account because you've got an opportunity to make a hot, short-term investment—commercial paper, a money market fund, or maybe even a race at Belmont—that pays more than the bank. In effect what you're doing is borrowing the bank's money to make more money for yourself. If you're lucky, you earn enough to cover your overdraft plus a profit. If you're unlucky, you go to jail.''

''Look,'' Timothy Cone says, ''I got a plot I want to throw at you and see what you think. Now suppose I have a million dollars.''

''That'll be the day,'' the NYPD man says.

''Well, just *suppose*. I got a million, and I open accounts at two different banks. In one I deposit the minimum required to keep the account active. In the other I deposit what's left of my million. Most of it. Okay so far?''

''So far,'' Sid says. ''You haven't broken any laws.''

''I don't mean to,'' Cone says. ''These are interest-bearing, day-of-deposit-to-day-of-withdrawal checking accounts. Okay? Now, on a Thursday, I write a check for about a million against my big account, and deposit it in my little account. Both banks pay, say, six percent. So my million is making about a hundred and sixty-five dollars a day in interest. But before my check clears, I'm making that much from *both* banks. You follow? I've still got the million in my big account because the check hasn't cleared, and the little account starts paying interest the moment I make the deposit. If it takes the check five days to clear, I've made about sixteen hundred bucks in interest from *both* banks. That million dollars is working twice.''

Apicella and Davenport stare at each other. But Cone doesn't wait for their comments.

''Now what I want to know is this: Is what I'm doing against the law? I mean, when I write a check for a million against the big account, the money is there. I'm not drawing against funds that don't exist. So is what I'm doing illegal?''

''It's got to be,'' Apicella says. ''I don't know the applicable law, but what you're doing, in effect, is doubling your money. You've got a million in two different banks—the same million!—and you're drawing interest on both balances. That's got to be against the law.''

''It is,'' Davenport says, ''and you've got to consider intent. Why are you flying that million bucks back and forth? Your interest is to defraud the banks, isn't it?''

Cone suddenly smiles. ''Okay, that's the way I see it. Now listen to this: Instead of switching a million dollars back and forth between two banks, I'm switching a hundred million. The interest on that, at six percent, is six million annually, or about sixteen thousand five hundred a day. If I can con both banks out of an extra five days of interest, I'm making eighty-two thousand five hundred a week. That comes to about four-and-a-quarter million a year. But what if I do it more than once a week? What if I use more than two banks where the float can be as long as ten days? That's ten days' interest on a hundred million bucks! How much am I going to take the banks for in a year?''

''Whee!'' Davenport cries, throwing up his hands. ''It's Looney Tunes time, folks!''

Sid rubs his nose. ''Is that what Clovis and Clovis are doing?''

''That's what they're doing.''

''Thank God the Evanchat deal was canceled,'' Sid says.

"But wouldn't the bank's computers pick up on all those big checks flying back and forth?"

"Not necessarily. Essentially, banks' computers are data-processing machines. They keep a record of deposits and withdrawals, but they're not programmed to flash a red light when a fraud like this occurs. If no bank employee takes a look at the computer printout and screams, no one's going to realize what's happening."

"Son of a bitch," Davenport says, shaking his head. "Clovis must be making zillions."

"They are," Cone says, "because they had the heavy loot to start with. That's why they set up New World Enterprises as a dummy corporation with such a big capitalization. Then, when that worked out so well, they switched their other subsidiaries' banks to Newark, Chicago, and San Diego to take advantage of the longer float. It sure beats building luxury high-rises. I'll bet the whole scam was Bonadventure's idea. It's got his prints all over it."

"I feel sick," Apicella says.

"Why?" Cone asks. "Because you don't have a piece of the action? Be happy, Sid. Haldering is out of the picture, and your ass is safe—until the next time."

Back in Cone's office, he and Davenport face each other across the desk.

"I don't want to tell you how to run your business," the Wall Street dick says, "but—"

"But you're going to," the city detective interrupts.

"Well, yeah. If I was you, the first thing I'd do is tell Merchants International and Manhattan Central to run a computer check on the deposits and withdrawals made over the past year by Clovis and Clovis and New World Enterprises. If I'm wrong, then the whole thing is dead in the water."

"And if you're right?"

"Then do the same with the out-of-state banks Clovis's subsidiaries use. It won't take them all that long to spot what's going on and you can dump the whole investigation in the DA's lap.''

"Then what do I do, teacher?" Davenport says with heavy irony, unwrapping a fresh stick of chewing gum.

"Look," Cone says, still leaning forward over his desk. "As far as I'm concerned, this bank fraud is a sideshow. I want Griffon's killer."

"As if I didn't know."

"I still say Grace is the key. The woman's a balloonhead. A little pressure and she'll explode. If you get sufficient evidence on this check-kiting scheme, you should have probable cause to get into the Clovis apartment without a warrant. Maybe the lady's got some coke on the premises. Even if she doesn't, you can lean on her about her association with Bonadventure. She'll break—I swear she will—and admit he's her candyman. Then you move in on Mr. Pinkie Ring himself. That guy has got nerves of Silly Putty. Mark my words, he'll cop a plea if you tell him his cock is on the block for the murder of Ed Griffon. I guarantee he'll name Constance Figlia as the actual killer—after he makes a deal with the DA."

Davenport shakes his head. "I don't even know what I'm going to have for lunch today," he says, "and you've got all this wrapped up in a neat package with a ribbon on it."

"It'll work," Cone says. "They're all going to take a fall, one way or another. There's only one thing I want."

"Uh-huh, had to be. What?"

"I want to be there when you pick up Anthony Bonadventure. I figure if you move fast, you should be able to cuff him by tomorrow. I'll stick close to my phone. Will you let me know when you're moving in?"

"Yeah," Davenport says, rising heavily to his feet. "I owe you that."

"Wait a minute," Cone says, fishing the leather-framed photo from his top desk drawer. "Don't forget to get into the New World warehouse in Brooklyn and grab that computer. That'll give the DA all he needs for a bank-fraud indictment. And show this photo of Constance Figlia to your flaky witness and tell him she's under arrest. Maybe he'll be willing to identify her.''

"Maybe," the NYPD man says, inspecting the photograph. "Worth a try. Which one is she?''

"Second from the left.''

"And who's the blond broad in the bikini?''

"That's Grace Clovis.''

"Oh, yeah," the city cop breathes. "I think I'll interrogate her personally.''

"You're a dirty old man," Cone says.

"I was a dirty young man," Davenport says. "I haven't changed.''

He doesn't leave the loft on Saturday morning, not even to run out for a paper. He's afraid he'll miss Davenport's call and blow a chance to be in on the kill. So he drinks black coffee, smokes cigarettes, and vapors aloud, addressing Cleo but really talking to himself.

"I may be wrong on some of the details, kiddo," he says, "but nothing important. Ed Griffon, a smart guy, caught on faster than I did and got himself knocked off. Because he wasn't smart enough to watch his back. You don't trust anyone in this world, Cleo—not even yourself. You trust me to feed you, give you fresh water, change your litter. So you're content. But what if some night I don't come home, and never do again? Who'll feed you then? Ahh, you'll make out somehow, you little shit. You're a survivor.''

So the morning crawls away. Around eleven o'clock he pours himself a brandy to stun the butterflies in his stomach. It isn't impatience so much as anger, and he knows his furies will devour him if he can't narcotize them with caffeine, nicotine, and alcohol—a well-balanced diet for what ails him.

The phone rings a little before noon, and he walks toward

it slowly, too proud to send up a prayer that it'll be the call he's waiting for.

"Yeah?" he says.

"Everything's coming up roses," Davenport sings. "The two local banks worked through the night. They figure that in the past year, Clovis has clipped them for about fifty million. The out-of-state banks are still figuring their losses. We grabbed the computer at New World, and some hotshot expert in the DA's office says it's got a complete record of everything. I mean they were *flying* those checks, and had to use a computer to keep track of deposits, withdrawals, and interest earned."

"What about the people?" Cone demands.

"We picked up Constance Figlia this morning. Then, about an hour ago, we moved into the Clovis apartment and grabbed Stanley, Grace, and Lucinda."

"Find anything?"

"Oh, yeah. A packet of happy dust in Grace's handbag."

"Did she break?"

"Even before we could question her. She went hysterical on us, and she's in the hospital. Under treatment and under guard. I think she'll spill."

"Sure she will. What about Bonadventure?"

"After I left you yesterday we put a tail on him. Our guy says that right now he's in his brownstone. We're going to take him at twelve-thirty. Want to watch the circus?"

"Wouldn't miss it for the world," Cone says. "I'll be there."

"As an observer," Davenport warns. "Just stand back and watch. This is our job."

"Of course," Cone says.

It's a drizzly day, the sky steel, the light brass, the air tasting of a copper penny. Cone is wearing his black flapping raincoat over his corduroy suit.

He's there before Davenport arrives, leaning against a lamppost one door down from Bonadventure's brownstone. He spots the police tail: one guy in an old, dented Plymouth parked across the street. Cone waits as patiently as he can, chain-smoking. He leans down once to touch the shin holster through his pant leg. It's there.

Then two cars pull up, moving slowly, and double-park in front of the brownstone. The squad car has two blues in the front seat. The other is a smart, clean Buick with three men in mufti. Davenport gets out of the Riviera first and looks around. He spots Cone and waggles his fingers. Then he directs the others.

The squad car goes around the block. The three cops trudge up the stoop and disappear into the vestibule. Cone straightens up and moves closer.

He waits almost ten minutes, tense and agitated. Then the front door opens and a procession comes out: the three NYPD detectives and Anthony Bonadventure, hands manacled behind him. He's coatless, but wearing a beautifully tailored suit of silvery sharkskin. One of the detectives is gripping him firmly by the upper arm.

Cone has a surge of hot blood, feels his face flushing. A wild, violent thought: He could bend swiftly, slip the Magnum from the ankle holster, and plug Bonadventure. He's close enough so that he wouldn't endanger the detectives. Just take one step forward, point, and *pow!*

But Davenport is staring at Cone and sees something in his face. He steps quickly to put himself between his prisoner and the Wall Street dick. He moves to Cone and gives him a fierce, stern look. He stands there a moment, not speaking, his eyes locked with Cone's.

Then, apparently satisfied with what he sees, he turns away, and Anthony is hustled into the Buick. But as he goes, he looks back at Cone, his handsome features distorted with puzzlement and fear.

Timothy, madness passing, contents himself with giving Bonadventure the finger, twisting his hand in the air.

"Ta-ta," he calls.

He still stands in the drizzle after the police car has pulled away. Then, when his trembling has eased and he has control, he goes back to his Honda. He knows how close he came, and wonders if he's ever going to grow up.

He has shopping to do, up and down lower Broadway, and in all the funky little stores in his neighborhood. He buys a couple of barbecued chickens, some salad stuff, a package of potato skins, which he dearly loves, and a smoked chub, which Cleo dearly loves—including head, skin, bones, tail, and all.

He also buys a bottle of Korbel Natural champagne.

Samantha Whatley shows up a little after five o'clock. She brings dessert: four rum balls covered with chocolate sprinkles, sinfully rich but looking like elephant droppings.

"Well?" she demands. "What happened? Tell me this instant!"

"A drink first," he says. "My first of the day."

"Ha-ha," she says.

He mixes vodkas and water. They sit at the desk, slouched on the wooden kitchen chairs, while he tells her all about it. She listens intently, not interrupting. They're on their second drink before he finishes with an account of Anthony Bonadventure's arrest.

"I almost blew him away," Cone confesses. "Maybe I would have if Davenport hadn't stepped in."

"But why Bonadventure?" Samantha asks curiously. "You say it was Constance Figlia who pushed Griffon onto the tracks."

"Sure it was, but don't you see—Bonadventure engineered the whole thing. I'm convinced of it. I mean, here were all these people—Constance, Stanley, Grace, and Lucinda—no more larcenous than the rest of us—and then Bonadventure appears on the scene with his get-rich-quicker scam and ruined all their lives."

"You think he hooked Grace on coke?"

"I'd bet on it. And Stanley and Lucinda probably made no objection. Anthony took Grace out of the picture, and they could go on holding hands forever."

"Gross," Sam says.

"Yeah. All it took was a devil like Bonadventure to lead the way. That's why I wanted to blast him."

"I'm glad you didn't."

"I am, too—I guess. But I'll probably spend the rest of my life regretting it."

"An unarmed prisoner with his hands cuffed behind him? You'd have blown him away?"

"Hell, yes," Cone says. "You'd shoot a rattlesnake just lazing on a rock, wouldn't you?"

She looks at him a moment, then shakes her head. "Tim, you scare me. You keep forgetting you're back in civilization."

"Is that what it is—civilization? But enough of this; let's celebrate the happy ending. Isaac Evanchat escaped a fate worse than death, and Haldering and Company did its civic duty. Maybe H. H. will get a scroll or plaque or something from the city, saying what an upright citizen he is."

"He'd love that," she says, smiling.

"I'll talk to Davenport. He'll put in a good word for us. Listen, I have barbecued chicken and champagne. How does that grab you?"

"Just right," she says, "but let's eat later."

It's really raining now; they hear the drumming on the roof, but the loft is dry, warm, shadowed.

"This place is like a cave," Samantha says, undressing. "There's something primitive about it."

"Yeah," Cone says. "The plumbing."

They're naked together on the mattress and she is reaching for him when he suddenly rolls away and climbs to his feet.

"Now what?" she wails. "Where are you going?"

"Forgot something."

He goes to the kitchen cabinet and comes back with a gift-wrapped package tied with a bow. He lies down beside her again and pokes the gift at her.

"For you," he says gruffly.

She looks down at the package, then looks up at him, not believing.

"For me?" she says. "What is it?"

"Open it, for God's sake."

She strips the wrapping away with shaking hands, lifts the lid, finds a necklace of chunky beads, alternating ebony and crystal. She takes it out, eyes widening, and strokes it tenderly, then puts it around her neck. They both see the shine and glitter against her dark skin.

"It's beautiful," she says in a choked voice, and begins weeping.

"Aw, shit," the Wall Street dick says, taking her into his arms.

There is joy and shouting that night.

BOOK TWO

The Whirligig Action

1

LATE IN OCTOBER of that year a dramatic story from Glendale, California, titillated and bemused the entire nation. As reported in newspapers, magazines, and on network television, the facts were these:

Laura Bentley (nineteen) and Gerald McPhee (twenty-two), residents of Glendale, had met at a church barbecue and were attracted to each other. They dated for a period of ten months and then became engaged.

In addition to their youth and good looks (both blue-eyed and flaxen-haired), they had other commonalities. Both were transplanted easterners. Laura had been born and spent the first fourteen years of her life in Baltimore, Maryland. Gerald had been born and lived in Washington, D.C., for fifteen years.

In addition, both young people were fatherless, both living with their mothers. Laura's father had deserted his wife and daughter when she was nine years old. Gerald's father had died when the boy was thirteen.

During their courtship Laura and Gerald had several times discussed the possibility that both might have been adopted. It seemed all the more reasonable to them because neither resembled their mothers, and they could find no physical likeness in the photographs that had been preserved of their fathers.

Both questioned their mothers. Mrs. Bentley refused to

discuss the subject with her daughter. Mrs. McPhee continually assured Gerald that he was, in fact, her natural child.

So the young people were married. Both being employed, they decided to wait a period of time until they could afford a small home before having "at least two children and maybe more."

Approximately a year after the marriage, Mrs. Bentley became seriously ill. She was diagnosed as suffering from an ovarian tumor, and surgery was scheduled. On the day before the operation, frightened and wanting to prepare for any eventuality, she confessed to her daughter that she, Laura, had been conceived by artificial insemination with sperm from an unknown donor.

Laura reported this to her husband, and they stared at each other, both suddenly aware of a dread possibility. Gerald McPhee then confronted his mother again and demanded to know the truth about his birth. Mrs. McPhee, in tears, finally admitted that Gerald, too, had been conceived by artificial insemination.

Thoroughly distraught, the young couple consulted an attorney. He immediately wrote the Washington, D.C., fertility clinic where both mothers had been impregnated. While awaiting a reply from the clinic, the lawyer sternly urged Mr. and Mrs. McPhee not to have sexual intercourse, even with contraceptive devices.

The worst fears of the young people were realized. A check of the fertility clinic's records revealed that Laura and Gerald had been conceived with live sperm from the same anonymous donor. They were half-brother and -sister. Their marriage was annulled.

This unusual incident was a brief sensation in the news media, but gradually faded from interest as more earthshaking stories took over the headlines.

But it was to have an unexpected and dramatic effect on several financial institutions on Wall Street.

*   *   *

"How could such a thing have happened?" Lester Pingle
asks. He strokes his bare upper lip with a knuckle. That flap
of flesh had once borne a scraggly black mustache—until
the night his wife, emboldened by two brandy stingers, told
him it made him look like a moth-eaten Groucho Marx.
Since then the lip has been naked. "Don't you people keep
records?"

Dr. Victor January tries to smile. "We at Nu-Hope certainly keep records. Computerized, I might add. We also
warn patients of the possibility of incestuous relationships
between offspring of the same donor. The whole subject is
covered in our presentation."

"Pages thirty to thirty-four," Dr. Phoebe Trumball says.

"The chance always exists," January goes on, "but it
can be minimized by the exchange of sperm, fresh or
frozen, between fertility clinics in different cities, or in
different countries."

Ernest Pingle stirs in his heavy club chair. He sweeps a
palm over a brush of white hair, cut as short as a drill
instructor's. "Tell me, Wictor," the old man starts, then
asks, "You don't mind if I call you Wictor?"

"Not at all, sir," Dr. Victor January says.

"You ship this—this stuff to other countries?"

"Frozen human sperm? Yes, we airlift it in special containers. Foreign fertility clinics sometimes have requests for
an American donor."

"And you buy sperm from foreigners?" Lester Pingle
says, rather indignantly.

"Very infrequently," Dr. January says. "New York is a
cosmopolitan city. We have an extensive file of available
sperm donors of almost every nationality. If a Liberian,
Korean, or Icelandic client requests impregnation by a male
of her country, we can usually provide it. We had an odd
one about a month ago. A woman of the Navaho Indian
tribe requested she be inseminated by the sperm of a

Navaho male. We were finally able to locate frozen Navaho sperm in a Phoenix, Arizona, sperm bank.''

"Look," Lester Pingle says hesitantly, "suppose a woman wants a tall guy with blond hair and blue eyes. You can provide that?"

"We try to answer all our clients' requests," Dr. Trumball says. "No guarantees, of course; genetics is not *that* exact a science. But we've found that a woman who requests a blond, blue-eyed donor is perfectly satisfied if she gives birth to a dark-haired, brown-eyed baby. Motherhood conquers all."

Old Mr. Pingle shakes his head dolefully. "I can't keep up," he complains. "The world changes so fast. When I was young, boys worried about getting a girl knocked up. You wanted sex without pregnancy. The girl did, too. Now women want to be pregnant without sex."

"More and more of them every day," Phoebe Trumball says, nodding. "Including many single women who, for a variety of reasons, don't wish to be married but do want a child of their own. Our Artificial Insemination Department has never been busier."

"Understand," Dr. January says hastily, "frequently the donor is the husband, where for one reason or another the couple cannot conceive by normal sexual intercourse."

"Tell me this," Lester Pingle says. "Suppose that young couple in Glendale had never discovered they had the same donor as a father, and they had a baby. Would it be normal?"

Dr. January shrugs. "No one can say. The Egyptian Ptolemies frequently entered into incestuous marriages. But I would hardly recommend it. Too much danger of genetic damage."

"Their having a child together would be only one danger," Dr. Trumball says thoughtfully. "What about this possibility: The young married couple never discover they are half-brother and half-sister. But, for whatever reasons, the man discovers he has infertile sperm, and they decide the wife will have artificial insemination. Given the improvements in the technology of freezing human sperm, she might have been impregnated by her father. That's a very remote possibility, I admit, but it does exist.''

The four stare at the walls, no one wishing to comment. Finally old Mr. Pingle looks at his son and says, ''You have more questions, Lester?''

They are on the eighth floor of a Water Street office building that has all the grace and delicacy of a woolly mammoth excavated from a Siberian bog. But the conference room of Pingle Enterprises, Inc., is comfortable enough, with oak wainscotting, leather chairs, and a fireplace that appears to be veined white marble and is actually a very artful vinyl compound.

''If it's the morality of our business that bothers you,'' Dr. January says, ''let me say this—that up to five years ago, we also provided an abortion service. But the hassle proved more than we could handle—what with the constant picketing and demonstrations. Today we are solely concerned with pro-life activities, helping people have healthy babies. There can be no legal or moral objections to that. We've included all the recent judicial decisions on our activities in the presentation.''

''We've already read it,'' Lester Pingle says, ''and we are interested. Aren't we, Father?''

''Interested,'' the old man says. ''Not conwinced.''

''As I understand it,'' Lester goes on, ''you want to expand the Nu-Hope Fertility Clinic into a nationwide chain, either privately owned or by franchise.''

''A worldwide chain,'' Dr. January says earnestly. ''Eventually.''

''And these fertility clinics would be located in shopping malls and other high-traffic areas?'' Lester asks.

''For maximum exposure,'' Dr. Phoebe Trumball says.

''More important,'' Dr. January says, ''we see a growing need for an organization that dominates the human fertility business. It would enable us to have a centralized computer system that could help prevent potential tragedies like that Glendale incident. Also, the various clinics could exchange fresh and frozen sperm, eggs, and embryos much more efficiently than a hundred clinics operating under individual ownership. We have given you our balance sheet. You can see how our business has boomed in the past three years.''

"Our pregnancy rate is the best in the country," Dr. Trumball says. "Perhaps the best in the world. And, as head of our Research and Development Department, I can assure you that our successes with artificial insemination and in-vitro fertilization will continue to increase as we refine our techniques and improve quality control.''

"Tell me, Wictor," Ernest Pingle says, "how did you come to pick our company for this project?''

Dr. January has an answer ready, so ready it might have been rehearsed. ''Shelby and Hawthorne have been our financial advisers for several years. When we decided we wanted to expand, we asked them how we might locate a partner willing to make a substantial cash investment. Shelby and Hawthorne suggested we approach a venture capital company, and recommended Pingle Enterprises because of your success in raising funds for the E-Z Ortho dental chain and the Walksoft podiatric clinics.''

"We have also done pizzas and tacos," the old man says wryly.

His son rises abruptly. "Thank you for coming by," he says to the two doctors. "It's a very interesting concept. But of course we'll want our attorneys to give an opinion and our accountants to go over the numbers.''

"And when may we expect to hear from you?'' Dr. January asks.

"Within a month," Lester Pingle promises.

His father stands up slowly and everyone shakes hands. Then Lester walks the visitors to the elevator. After they have departed, he returns to the conference room, where his father is again slumped in the club chair at the head of the table.

"I like it," Lester says.

"I don't," his father says. "Take my adwice, it's not for us."

"Why not? The numbers look good."

"It's not for us," the old man repeats stubbornly.

His son sighs. "Pop, like you said, the world is changing. We've got to keep up. What don't you like about it?"

"I don't know," Ernest Pingle says slowly. "Something isn't kosher. That Doctor Wictor—a very smart man. He talks well. The woman also is smart. They have all the answers. Even before you have the questions, they have the answers." The old man makes a soft fist and thumps his round belly. "Something here," he says. "Something in my gut tells me we should pass this one by."

"You and your gut!" his son scoffs. "Pop, if we had listened to your gut we never would have done that software deal in Massachusetts. And look how much money we made."

"Not so much," Ernest Pingle says. "I didn't understand software. I don't understand this. Frozen sperm and eggs and embryos. Feh! Frozen pizza and tacos I can understand."

"Think about it," his son urges. "Will you just do that? I really believe it's a hot proposition. Listen, I'm going to run out for some lunch. Can I bring you anything?"

"No," the old man says. "I'll have Mrs. Scherer make me a nice glass of tea and maybe I'll have one of those English biscuits. You'll be back when?"

"In an hour. At the most. And then we'll talk more about the Nu-Hope deal."

His father nods. "Something is wrong here," he says, tapping the bound presentation.

"We'll talk about it," his son says again and hurries out.

Lester Pingle, a tallish man with round shoulders and a pot that will one day rival his father's, walks quickly to the South Street Seaport. As usual, the sidewalks are crowded, and he makes better time by scuttling along the narrow streets, dodging traffic rather than trying to shove through the mob of sightseeing pedestrians.

It's a kaleidoscope, a carnival, a merry-go-round, a festival and entertainment, it's a carousel, a funfair. The costumes! The players! Everything is awhirl, and he is dizzied by the movement, colors, a shattering cacophony. Everything gigs him, and he yearns for quiet, solidity, truth—and cannot find them.

But he does find his man, browsing in a trendy shop offering maritime artifacts, including a selection of plastic scrimshaw that looks like the real thing—if you've never seen the real thing.

The man is wearing a double-breasted topcoat of herringbone tweed. It accents a barrel chest and broad shoulders: a thick, stumpy body topped with a bullethead. And atop *that,* an incongruous green felt fedora with a little clump of bright feathers in the band.

The two men stand close to the scrimshaw display and converse in low voices. The tweedy one handles a fake whalebone letter opener while Pingle fondles a darning egg.

"How did it go?"

"All right," Lester says. "Very alert, knowledgeable people. They handled themselves well."

"So you're taking them on?"

"Well—ah—not yet. It wouldn't do to make an immediate decision. It has to be vetted by our lawyers and accountants, or someone is sure to ask questions. We don't want to attract attention to this deal, do we?"

The other man turns his head slowly to stare at Pingle. His eyes are a startling blue: electric eyes. "No," he says, "we don't want to do that. But the investigation will be just routine, won't it?"

"Oh, sure. No problem. However . . ."

"However what?"

"The old man doesn't like it. But I'll bring him around," Pingle adds hastily.

"I'm sure you will," the man says with a mirthless

smile. "That's what we're paying you for, isn't it? Mr. D. is very interested in this project. Personally interested. It wouldn't do to have it fall through."

No menace. Just a flat statement.

"I understand that," Lester says, replacing the plastic darning egg. "It won't fall through. By the way, how did you know Nu-Hope would come to us? They said we were recommended by their financial advisers, Shelby and Hawthorne."

Again that mirthless smile. "I thought you knew. We own Shelby and Hawthorne."

Pingle is too keyed up to pause for lunch. He scurries back to the office and finds his father still in the conference room, sipping his glass of tea and nibbling on a biscuit from a big English tin.

Lester doesn't even take off his hat or coat. "About this Nu-Hope deal," he says abruptly.

His father looks up at him. "You read about the Clovis scandal?" he asks.

The son stares at him in astonishment. "Of course I read about it. They were stupid. How long did they think they'd get away with it? But what has the Clovis swindle got to do with us?"

"Haldering and Company uncovered it," the old man says. "They were hired to inwestigate, and one of the Haldering detectives found out what was going on. I want to hire Haldering and Company to inwestigate Nu-Hope for us."

Suddenly hot and sweating, Lester takes off his hat and coat. "Come on, Pop," he says, "there's no need for that. We've got a lot of high-priced lawyers and accountants who can do all the investigating we need."

Ernest Pingle bares his dentures. It's intended as a smile, but looks more like a snarl. "You're outwoted," he says. "You're still a junior partner—remember? We either hire Haldering to inwestigate Nu-Hope or the whole deal is dead as far as we're concerned."

Lester has no choice. "Okay then," he says, trying to make it casual, "we'll hire Haldering. I guarantee they'll find Nu-Hope is on the up-and-up."

"You're all perspiry," his father says. "Calm down and have a biscuit. They're wery good."

On this particular afternoon, Hiram Haldering is in an expansive mood. His sausage fingers are laced across his double-breasted vest as he lounges in a high-backed leather swivel chair, beaming at two expressionless employees: Samantha Whatley and Timothy Cone.

"Pingle Enterprises, Incorporated," Haldering says happily. "They're a venture capital outfit. I met with them this morning. Checked them out first, of course. They've got a good track record. Served as general partners in a number of private and public limited partnerships. Made a mint when they took a pizza chain public. Most of their other deals have paid off. No problems with the SEC or IRS. Their reputation on the Street is as good as any risk capital company.

"Anyway," H. H. continues, "I talked to the principals: Ernest Pingle, who looks to be one year younger than God but has all his marbles, and his son, Lester, a sweaty fat guy who looks like he might enjoy a career as a flasher. Well, to make a long story short—"

"Too late for that," Cone mutters, and Samantha glares at him furiously.

"To make a long story short," Haldering repeats equably, "Pingle Enterprises has been approached by an uptown outfit called Nu-Hope Fertility Clinic."

"I know it," Sam says promptly. "They used to be into abortions, but now they only do artificial insemination and test-tube babies."

"Kee-rect," H. H. says. "Sex without joy."

His jape convulses him with laughter, and the other two smile weakly.

The boss recovers slowly. "Nu-Hope," he says, "wants

to go nationwide with a chain of fertility clinics, and wants the Pingles to set up the financing. Lester, the son, is hot for the deal. The old man, Ernest, doesn't like it. He says it just doesn't smell right. He wants this Nu-Hope Fertility Clinic checked out six ways from the middle. It's a great opportunity for us. A nice fee, and a chance to get our foot in the door to the venture capital business.''

''Why did they pick us, Mr. Haldering?'' Whatley asks.

''Well . . .'' he says, ''I gather they read the news stories on the Clovis case and were impressed by our work. As they should have been; it was a neat job.''

He beams at them, and they look at him with some trepidation, knowing what's coming.

''I've alerted our attorneys and accountants,'' Haldering goes on, ''and they're checking to make sure Nu-Hope Fertility Clinic is soundly run and on the up-and-up. But we also have to run a check on the principals. That's where you two come in.''

Sam and Timothy glance at each other, shifting uncomfortably in their rigid office chairs.

''Whatley,'' H. H. says, ''I want you to work with the lawyers and accountants. Cone, the actual investigation's your baby. Hey! You'll be investigating a fertility clinic, and I say it's your baby. That's funny!''

Cone doesn't think so. ''Why the hell me?'' he demands. ''I don't know a goddamned thing about artificial insemination.''

Hiram Haldering slowly lights a cigar and blows a plume of smoke over their heads. ''Learn,'' he says. ''Buy some books and read up on it. Ernest Pingle says he's alerted the doctors at Nu-Hope, and they promise to cooperate fully with our representatives. Besides, old man Pingle insisted that the detective who broke the Clovis swindle work on this one. So you're elected. Keep me informed. We want to do a bang-up job.''

Samantha and Timothy push back their chairs, wander down the corridor.

"Lots of luck," Sam says. "Do a bang-up job and keep me informed."

"Up yours," the Wall Street dick says. "What in God's name do I know about sperm banks?"

"Learn," she repeats. "Buy some books and read up on it. Who knows, maybe you'll become a donor."

"Not me," he says. "I haven't got any to spare."

He is mollified somewhat when Sam promises to relieve him of his current caseload and parcel out his files to the other Haldering investigators. Back in his cramped office, he begins to get his notes in order. Since the Clovis scam his assignments have been dull stuff, involving mostly routine phone calls and research at Dun & Bradstreet. Nothing with any pizzazz.

He is opening his second pack of Camels of the day when his phone rings, and he reaches for it absently. "Yeah?" he says.

"Mr. Timothy Cone?"

A man's voice, kind of creaky.

"That's right," Cone says. "Who you?"

"My name is Ernest Pingle. Mr. Haldering has just informed me that you have been assigned to the inwestigation of the Nu-Hope Fertility Clinic."

"I guess," Cone says, sighing. "And you're the client?"

"I am. I was wondering, Mr. Cone, if you and I could meet personally. I would appreciate it wery much."

"Sure," Cone says. "Where and when?"

"Could you make it this evening at, say, nine o'clock? At my apartment?"

"Sounds okay. Are you in the book?"

"Yes. The only Ernest Pingle listed. On Fifth Avenue. I can expect you at nine?"

"Sure, I'll be there. I don't have to dress up, do I?"

"Dress up?" the old man says, astonished. "Why should you dress up?"

"I don't visit on Fifth Avenue very often."

Pingle laughs, a nice, bubbly sound. "Don't worry about it," he says. "This will be a wery informal wisit."

"I'll be there," Cone promises.

On his way out, he stops at Samantha Whatley's office. She's pulling yellowed leaves from her mournful little philodendron. Cone stands in the doorway and watches her.

"Why don't you get rid of that thing," he says. "It's dead."

"It's not dead," she says indignantly. "Just a little peaked. All it needs is tender, loving care."

"Who doesn't?" he says. "Listen, I just got a call from Ernest Pingle. The old man. He wants to see me tonight at his place."

Sam looks at him. "What for?"

"Didn't say."

"Well, will you try to spruce up a little before you meet him?"

"Why should I? It's just an informal wisit."

"A *what*?"

"That's the way he talks. It's a wery informal wisit."

"Good night, asshole," she says in a low voice.

"Good night, shithead," he says.

On his walk uptown, Cone stops at a discount bookstore and buys three volumes on artificial insemination, test-tube birth, and human embryo transfer. Then, closer to his loft on lower Broadway, he picks up a pepperoni pizza and a cold six-pack of Bud.

The moment he's inside the door, Cleo smells the hot pizza and comes growling up to rub against his shins.

"Take it easy, monster," he tells the cat. "You'll get yours."

He cuts the pizza into six wedges and gives one to Cleo. Then he pops a beer, starts on the pizza, and begins reading the first of his three books.

It's not a thick volume, and he finds he can do a lot of skipping and skimming and still pick up the gist. Unexpectedly, he finds the subject fascinating. A paragraph that blows his mind suggests that with current techniques, it would be possible for a child to have five parents: The egg of a donor and the sperm of a donor are joined in vitro. Two parents. The resulting embryo is then implanted in a surrogate mother. The third parent. After birth, the baby is adopted by a childless couple. The fourth and fifth parents.

"And nobody got fucked," Cone marvels aloud to Cleo, who has leaped up onto the table and is licking up pizza crumbs. "What *is* the world coming to, you crazy cat? Who are the legal parents of the child? The lawyers are going to have a field day with that one."

He doesn't exactly spruce up for his meeting with Ernest Pingle, but he does change his shirt, discarding a faded flannel plaid number for a clean white broadcloth. He checks the short-barreled .357 Smith & Wesson Magnum in his ankle holster, then starts out, waving a hand at Cleo.

"No self-abuse," he cautions.

He takes a cab uptown, figuring H. H. is so happy with the new client that he won't scream too loudly at Cone's expense account. He arrives at Ernest Pingle's apartment house, on Fifth Avenue just north of Sixty-fourth Street, a few minutes after nine. It's a cold, sharp night, a zillion stars whirling in a cloudless sky over Central Park.

The lobby has all the charm of a crematorium, and when Cone finally gets up to Apartment 24-A, he discovers it's a gloomy cavern big enough to breed stalactites. The only thing that saves it are the floor-to-ceiling windows facing west; the view is spectacular.

Ernest Pingle, apparently the only person present, turns out to be a chubby, shortish gaffer with a big head of bristly white hair. His face may have as many lines as a Rand McNally road map, but his eyes are bright, sharp, and, Cone figures, rarely have the wool pulled over them.

"I thank you for coming on such short notice," he says, shaking hands. He takes the detective's anorak and hangs it away in a closet that looks to be as large as Cone's loft. "The truth is, it's our maid's night off, and also it's Mrs. Pingle's evening with her mah-jongg club. So I thought it would be a good opportunity to inwite you up to have a little talk."

It seems like a long, unnecessary explanation to Cone, and he wonders if this bustling little man might be a trifle nervous.

"Tell me," Pingle says, "do you take a drink?"

"Now and then," Cone says, sitting on an enormous brocade couch. "This is one of the 'now' times. It's cold out there."

"So it is, so it is. To tell you the absolute truth, I like a drop of schnapps myself. The problem is this: My wife, God bless her, has wery firm opinions about strong drink and won't allow any in the house. So, to be perfectly honest, I hide a bottle on the premises. Now, you are a detective—tell me, where do you think I conceal it?"

He stands, grinning like a plump Buddha, ready to make his startling revelation.

Cone stares at him thoughtfully. "If the cork is tight, Mr. Pingle, the best place to keep it would be in the toilet tank in your bathroom. I doubt if your wife would ever lift the lid. And you'd be helping the city's water shortage by cutting down on the volume of the tank."

"*Gott im Himmel!*" Ernest Pingle says, gasping. "You are exactly right. You are a wery smart man, Timothy. I may call you Timothy?"

"Of course. But I'm not so smart. The toilet tank is the first place every cop looks when he's tossing a place."

Pingle goes off, shaking his head in wonderment. He comes back a few moments later, using a hand towel to wipe a bottle of kirsch. He disappears again and returns with two small glasses. He fills them to the rim with the cherry brandy.

"This should warm you up," he says.

Cone looks at his glass. "This should combust me," he says. He raises the drink. "*Prosit!*"

"*Prosit!*" his host responds, and they both take swallows. Not sips, but gulps.

"Oh, boy," Cone says, shuddering. "Through the teeth

and around the gums; look out stomach, here she comes. Wow! That's something, that is.''

"You said *Prosit*. You know German?''

"No,'' Cone says, "I only know *Prosit*.''

Pingle smiles. "It's enough,'' he says. Then he sits silently, moving the glass of brandy slowly between his blotched hands. Again, Cone gets the impression of nervousness—or at least hesitancy.

"You wanted to talk to me about the Nu-Hope investigation, Mr. Pingle?''

"Well, in a way . . .'' Pingle says in a low voice. "My son . . .'' Then he looks up from his brandy glass to stare directly at the detective. "Lester is a good boy, and I love him wery much. He is our only child. We lost a daughter to meningitis when she was wery young. Lester is all we have, and we want his life to be happy. You can understand that, can't you?''

"Sure.''

Pingle takes a deep breath. "You've got a closed mouth, Timothy? You can keep it shut?''

"I don't blab,'' Cone says.

"Good. My son is married. I have two adorable grandchildren, God bless them. But Lester's wife, my daughter-in-law, Sarah, she is a problem. She suffers from shopitis. You know what shopitis is?''

"She likes to spend money?''

The old man claps a palm to his cheek. "Oy, does she like to spend money! And I'm not talking about a dress now and then, a new lamp, maybe a jar of caviar. I'm talking about a Rolls, a ski lodge in Vermont, a condo on the Costa del Sol, a summer place in East Hampton, investments in Broadway shows that close the first night. That's the kind of money I'm talking about. It is a sad situation.''

"Why doesn't your son clamp down on her?''

Pingle shrugs. "He loves her, or thinks he does—which is the same thing. Also, Lester is not the handsomest man in the world. But Sarah! What a beauty that woman is! A

lovely face and a gorgeous figure. Lester is proud to be
married to her. He will give her anything to keep her happy.
He makes a good dollar—I see to that—but he is barely
keeping his head above water. This is all confidential, you
understand; I am trusting you.''

Cone nods.

''So now Lester wants us to take on this Nu-Hope Fertility Clinic. He is insistent about it. I know my son, and this
deal is wery important to him. Why this particular deal?
Why is he perspiry over it? I don't know.''

''And you want me to find out?'' Cone asks.

''If you can,'' Ernest Pingle says humbly. ''But only as
part of your inwestigation into Nu-Hope. You'll find out the
truth, won't you?''

''That's what I get paid for.''

''Of course. I'm asking you this as a father: If you should
find that my son is into something he shouldn't be in, will
you tell me first? I have a lot of money, Timothy; more than
I can ever spend in my lifetime. Lester will get most of it
anyway, but maybe if he got some of it now, it might save
him from some foolishness that would disgrace him, and
me, and his mother, and the company I worked so hard to
build. I don't want that.''

Cone makes no reply, but finishes his brandy and rises.
The old man gets the parka from the closet and stands on
tiptoes to help the detective shrug into it.

''Sometimes I wonder if I know my son,'' Ernest Pingle
says gloomily. ''Sometimes I think he's a stranger.''

''Thanks for the brandy,'' Cone says. ''I really appreciated it.''

''And you'll let me know if you find out anything bad
about Lester? I'll take care of you.''

''That won't be necessary,'' Cone says. ''You're the
client. Good night, Mr. Pingle. Better put your bottle back
in the toilet tank.''

He taxies back home, slumped in the corner of a ratty
gypsy cab with no heater. But the radiators in the loft are

hissing and thumping away like crazy, so that's a plus. The minus is that Cone is faced with the ancient axiom: "Beer, whiskey: rather risky. Whiskey, beer: have no fear." So he has a beer.

He gives Cleo a dish of fresh water and finds a slab of old lasagna in the fridge. Cleo takes it happily under the bathtub.

Cone tries to read more about human birth by syringe, birth by needle and microscope, birth in laboratory dishes. And the genesis of life kept frozen in cryogenic tanks. Who do all those rigid sperm, eggs, and embryos belong to? What parents? What families?

But his thoughts keep returning to Ernest Pingle, a nice old geezer troubled by his natural son, fearful that his heir may be acting stupidly because he's pussy-whipped by a beautiful and profligate wife.

Timothy Cone has no desire for children. No need or hope for immortality by siring a son who might beget a son, and that grandson beget, and that great grandson beget, and on and on, making the name Cone last for all time. Screw that.

"Cleo," the Wall Street dick says aloud, "when you're dead, you're fucking dead."

And he wonders if all the potential sons and daughters preserved in glass might not be better off remaining frozen forever.

The Nu-Hope Fertility Clinic occupies adjoining town-houses on East Seventy-first Street, a few doors east of Madison Avenue. The two buildings, designed by the same architect in 1928, are handsome structures of gray stone with red brick trim around bow windows on the second and third floors and mullioned windows on the top three floors.

The entrances are elegant, and the heavy front doors can be opened to the public only from within, after visitors are inspected and questioned through a grilled judas. Patients are admitted only to the west wing, where examination rooms, treatment facilities, X-ray machines, a pharmacy, and recovery rooms are located. The east wing contains executive offices, computerized record storage, and the sterile research laboratories.

Walls have been broken through between the two buildings on the third floor, but the steel door of this passageway is kept locked, and only executives and a few research staff members are provided with keys. Both structures are equipped with elevators, large enough to accommodate only one gurney at a time. Each wing has a wide staircase rising to the sixth floor.

Friday mornings are set aside for staff meetings for all Nu-Hope personnel who are not busy treating patients. These gatherings are generally held in the fourth-floor Doctors' Lounge in the west wing. It is a large, open chamber, painted a light green, looking somewhat like a factory canteen with steel tables, each set with four metal chairs. The walls are lined with machines (not coin-operated, but free) that vend everything from hot soup to plastic-wrapped wedges of apple pie.

On this particular Friday morning, the assembled staff listens to short speeches by the administrator who, as usual, urges frugality in the use of hospital supplies; by the head of data processing, who reels off the most recent statistics on new patients, sperm inseminations, and embryo transplants; and by Dr. Phoebe Trumball, who reports progress in determining the optimum time of ovulation by hormone analysis.

These mercifully brief reports concluded, Dr. Victor January stands to address his staff.

"If you can stay awake for just a few more minutes," he says, grinning at his audience, "I'd like to bring you up-to-date on the project I revealed to you a few months ago: the proposed expansion of Nu-Hope into a nationwide chain of fertility clinics. And eventually perhaps all over the world. I don't need to tell you what a marvelous opportunity this would be for all of us: an enormous increase in our caseload, our responsibilities and our income.

"I am pleased to say that the first step has been taken to make our dreams come true. We have approached Pingle Enterprises, a reputable venture capital firm, in an effort to obtain financing for our projected expansion. Their first reaction, I must tell you, was very favorable indeed. But naturally, before making a commitment, they want to know more about us.

"So I want to alert you that during the next few weeks you may see and meet several strangers wandering about the premises to size us up. These visitors will be attorneys, accountants, and private investigators from Haldering and Company, employed by Pingle Enterprises. Haldering is an organization specializing in corporate information and intelligence.

"Doctor Trumball and I will be able to handle most of their inquiries, I'm sure. But I want to make this perfectly clear: If you are questioned by any of the Haldering representatives, I want you to speak freely and answer their questions truthfully. If you have any criticism of our operation, you're completely at liberty to voice it. As far as I'm concerned, we have nothing to hide, and being absolutely honest is the best way to ensure that all our hopes become a reality. Thank you for your attention and cooperation. Now go back to work, you slaves!"

There is laughter and a spattering of applause. The lounge gradually empties out. Drs. January and Trumball, nodding and smiling at the staff, walk down to the third floor. January unlocks the steel door and they enter the east wing, going directly to his office. It is an austere, uncluttered room, with a private lavatory and small kitchen attached. He has a personal computer on his desk that can tap into the clinic's big mainframe.

They sprawl on a leather couch, look at each other.

"I think it went well," he says. "Don't you?"

"It went all right," Dr. Trumball acknowledges. "But you're taking a chance telling them they can shoot off their mouths to the Haldering people."

"What should I have told them—to clam up? That could put the quietus on the whole deal. We've got to project an open and honest image if this thing is to go through. Besides, none of these people know anything. I'm glad your crew wasn't there."

"They know enough to keep their mouths shut."

He stares at her. "Now," he says, somewhat bitterly.

"Yes," she admits. "Now."

"I hope so. How are we doing on the time, Phoebe?"

She glances at the chunky digital watch strapped tightly to her slender wrist. "It's getting close. Where are we going to meet him?"

"In Central Park. Same place. I hate this cloak-and-dagger stuff."

She shrugs. "It's got to be done," she says stonily. "He explained why we couldn't get the grant. We were such innocents when we filed. We didn't even consider the political implications. We're lucky they're doing it this way. Proves they're definitely interested."

"I guess so," January says fretfully. "Well, let's get going. It's a nice day; we'll walk over. Meet you downstairs."

The city sparkles. Light dances in spins and spirals like a giant bejeweled whirligig. The sun is a diamond, sky turquoise, pearls of tiny clouds, and all of it scintillant. The air itself seems alive and dazzling. This brilliant world promises hope and conquest.

Victor January glances at the woman striding along at his side. She too brims with purpose and resolve.

Phoebe Trumball is a tall woman, lean and hard: a greyhound look, as swift and keen. She is as slender as he, and as pale. They could be brother and sister, these two, sharing a dancer's grace. Her face is long, with wedge of chin, scimitar nose, and widely spaced dark eyes that look out at life with courage and contempt.

"One of these days I'm going to marry you," he says,

and she smiles and lets her swinging hand touch his knuckles.

"Tonight?" she asks.

"No," he says. "Regretfully, no. Martha has family in from out of town. We're feeding them before the theater. Some silly musical that's been running for centuries. I've got to play the faithful hubby."

"All right," she says equably. "I'm not going to pout and stamp my foot."

"You never have," he says. "You don't even make me feel guilty."

"You?" she hoots. "Guilty? That'll be the day!"

And they both laugh.

They find their man on the same park bench where they met before, on a narrow path northwest of the zoo. There are pedestrians, joggers, babies being pushed in prams, lovers, a professional dog-walker with six hounds on tangled leashes, and one old woman trying to sell licorice strips. But the man they seek sits quietly and alone on a slatted bench, motionless and serene.

He has introduced himself as J. Roger Gibby, and that is the name on the identification he offered, along with his photograph. They checked with his directorate, of course, and were told he was a bona fide employee. But January and Trumball know that could be a cover. J. Roger Gibby could be working for one of a dozen other agencies.

He is well and strongly built, not so dapper as to be vulgar, but he shrieks with understated elegance. It is his calm, gentle manner, the doctors agree, that convinces them of his probity. That and his deep gazelle eyes that seem to have seen everything and are still ready to understand and forgive.

He does not stand when they approach, nor offer to shake hands. They sit together on his right, a little removed, and when any of the three speaks, it is with a thousand-yard stare directly ahead.

"Well . . ." Mr. Gibby says, "how did it go?"

January gives a brief precis of their presentation to Pingle Enterprises. Trumball adds that Haldering & Co. has been retained to investigate the clinic.

"Haldering?" Gibby says. His voice is velvet. "I know them. Hiram Haldering is an ex-FBI man. If there are any problems, I'm sure he'll be amenable to reason. During your discussion with the Pingles, was anything said about how the financing would be structured?"

"No," January says, "we didn't get into that."

"We would prefer a public limited partnership," Gibby says. "We can guarantee it would be totally subscribed. By our friends, of course. A private offering might prove more difficult, as would a bank line of credit. But first things first: The most important step right now is to get you approved by Pingle. I assure you the funding is there; it's just a question of getting it funneled through legitimate sources so we're completely out of the picture. Meanwhile your research is continuing?"

"As much as we can," Trumball says. "The expenses are horrendous. Do you know what a healthy rhesus monkey costs, or a mature, virile chimp?"

"I can imagine," Gibby says with a small smile, "although I haven't bought any lately."

"We may require some recombinant DNA workups," Trumball says. "I hope you're aware of that."

"We are indeed, but genetic engineering is not your responsibility. As I told you, this project is being pursued on a number of fronts. Eventually it will all come together."

"You're very optimistic, professor," January says.

"I believe that in the world of science, if it can be done, it will be done."

"And I believe," January adds, "that a life devoted to science is a life devoted to art. Are you predicting a masterpiece?"

"That's exactly what I'm predicting," Gibby says with his sweet smile. "Other people are working toward the same goal, you know. I'm sure you realize the consequences if their masterpiece is created before ours.''

They are silent then, staring out at skeleton trees sharp against a pellucid sky. All is clear, clean. It seems a washed world in late October, the final glimpse of bright before the darkness of winter.

"One other thing," J. Roger Gibby says. "Did the Pingles tell you who Haldering is sending to investigate?"

"They mentioned a man named Timothy Cone," January says. "Apparently he is not an attorney or an accountant. Just an investigator. A detective, I suppose you could call him. I promised complete cooperation."

"Timothy Cone," Gibby repeats. "A detective. Yes, by all means cooperate with him. Meanwhile I'll do a little detecting on my own. I must leave now. Please wait a few minutes before you depart. I'll be in touch through the usual channel. Nice to see you again. Be well."

He rises and moves slowly away. The two doctors turn their heads to watch him go.

"Do you trust him?" January says.

"Do we have a choice?" Phoebe Trumball asks.

"No," he says, sighing, "I guess not. But he's so damned smooth, it worries me. He acts as if every problem can be solved."

"Don't you believe that?" she demands. "If not, we never should have started this thing in the first place."

"I believe," January says hastily. "Because I believe in you."

She glances at him with an amused smile. "But you've got to go to the theater tonight with your wife."

"Yes," he says, "I do."

"Tomorrow?"

"Oh, God, yes!" he cries. "Definitely tomorrow!"

Cone arrives at his office at nine-thirty—early for him—and over coffee and a bagel begins reviewing the legal PIE on Nu-Hope. Nothing in the report alerts him. Nu-Hope is legally chartered and licensed. No tax problems. No liens or lawsuits. No record of hearings before medical boards. The PIE goes into some detail on Nu-Hope's past history as an abortion clinic. It was a legal enterprise, apparently efficiently run, with no history of malpractice suits.

The changeover from abortion to fertility clinic occurred four years ago after continued harassment of patients by antiabortion groups severely interrupted business. Personal threats against January and his staff had been reported to law enforcement agencies.

Nu-Hope is totally owned by Dr. January, although he has established a very generous pension, retirement, and profit-sharing plan for his employees. In brief, the clinic appears to be a legitimate, successful enterprise, much admired in the medical community for its profits, high pregnancy rate, and the quality of its research department, headed by Dr. Phoebe Trumball.

Cone tosses the report aside and pulls his phone forward. He calls Neal Davenport, the NYPD detective he met on the Clovis swindle. It takes three calls to locate the city dick, but he finally comes on the phone.

"Timothy Cone?" he says. "The financial sherlock and Wall Street whiz? How're you doing, buster?"

"Surviving. And you?"

"Likewise. How did you like those newspaper stories on the Clovis scam? Haldering got a nice plug—right?"

"Right," Cone says. "The old man was flying."

"And that's why you're calling—to thank me. Correct?"

"Not exactly."

Davenport laughs. "I didn't think so. What do you want?"

"I got two names for you. I thought you might run them through Records and see if either of them has a sheet."

"Now why should I do that?"

"Just for the fun of it."

"Kid, you've got chutzpah. Who are these people?"

"A couple of doctors. They run a fertility clinic on the Upper East Side."

"Fertility clinic? What the hell's that?"

"They get women pregnant."

"I used to do that," Davenport says, "but not recently. What's Haldering's interest in a fertility clinic?"

"We're checking them out for a venture capital outfit. The clinic wants to go national."

"All right," the NYPD man says, sighing. "I guess I owe you one. Give me the names and I'll see if we've got anything on them."

Cone spells out the names of Drs. Victor January and Phoebe Trumball.

"Okay," Davenport says, "I'll check and get back to you."

"Today?"

"Don't push your luck, sonny boy. This is going to cost you a couple of belts in that Garden of Delights you call home."

"Anytime," Cone says, and they hang up.

He broods a few moments, then wanders down the corridor to the office of Sidney Apicella, chief of Haldering's CPAs. As usual Sid is furiously rubbing his bugle when Cone enters.

"Leave it alone, Sid," Timothy advises. "You're just going to irritate it more."

"It irritates me," Apicella grumbles, "so why shouldn't I irritate it. If you're looking for the accounting PIE on the Nu-Hope Clinic, it's not completed yet. You'll get a copy when it is. Now leave me alone; I've got work to do."

"This isn't about Nu-Hope," Cone says. "Can you get me a financial rundown on Lester Pingle?"

Apicella looks at him with astonishment. "Since when do we investigate clients? Pingle Enterprises is in the black; we checked them out before we took them on."

"I know," Cone says patiently. "It's not the company I'm interested in; it's Lester, the junior partner. I want to know his cash assets, liabilities, and investments. You can find out.''

"My God, Tim," Sid says, groaning, "that'll be a day's work—and a pain in the ass.''

"Sure it is," Cone agrees cheerfully. "So is everything else around this joint. Let me know when you've got some numbers. And stop massaging your schnozz. You know, W. C. Fields had the same thing, and he used Allen's Foot Ease on it.''

"No kidding?" Apicella says, interested. "You really think it'll help?''

"It couldn't hurt.''

Cone goes back to his office, calls a local deli and orders a cheeseburger, fries, a dill pickle, and a cold can of Black Label Light.

On a sloppy day like this, everyone is eating in, so it's almost an hour before his lunch is delivered. Meanwhile he hacks away at the weekly progress report Samantha What-ley demands of all her detectives. That woman is a holy terror, Cone decides, and pads his expense account out-rageously.

After finishing his lunch he types up the progress report on the old Remington standard that's been allotted to him. The keys haven't been cleaned in years, and all his two-finger typing comes out with the o's, p's, a's and e's filled in. Cone's finished manuscript looks like the Rosetta stone.

He takes it down to Samantha's office, hoping they'll have a chance to exchange intimate insults, but she's not in. So he flips his report onto her desk and wonders if he should go home. He's not doing any good sitting at his desk, staring at the walls. At least, back in his loft, he can read more of the books on artificial birth and discuss original sin with Cleo.

It's almost two-thirty in the afternoon, and he's preparing to make his break when the receptionist calls and tells him Detective Davenport is there and wants to see him.

"Yeah," Cone says, "send him in.''

Neal K. Davenport, a big, overweight guy, shoves into Cone's office, wearing a soaked raincoat, a plastic cover on his fedora, and carrying a dripping umbrella that he props in a corner, letting it piddle on the floor.

"How come you're not out detecting?" he says. "A glorious day like this. You got anything medicinal? I think I'm coming down with something."

"Terminal thirst?" Timothy says. "I haven't got a drop, but maybe I can find something. Wait a minute."

"I'm not going anywhere," the cop says. "I just got here."

Cone goes down the corridor to Sol Faber's office. Sol isn't in, but Cone knows he keeps a pint of gin in the bottom drawer of his desk, which Cone finds, half-empty. He takes it and leaves a note scrawled on Sol's desk calendar: "I lifted your jug. The Masked Marvel."

He stops at the water cooler to pull out two paper cups, then goes back to his office. Davenport has taken off his raincoat and condomed hat, and is sitting placidly in one of the uncomfortable office chairs, unwrapping a fresh stick of Juicy Fruit. He looks at the paper cups and the half-filled pint of gin.

"Bless you, my son," he says. "May your tribe increase. I never drink gin except on the third Tuesday of every month, but in this case I'll make an exception."

Cone closes the door and fills their cups. They're little triangular dunce caps—you can't set them down—so both men hold their drinks, sipping as they talk.

"Nice of you to stop by," the Wall Street dick says. "I suppose you were out for a stroll on this pleasant afternoon and just found yourself in the neighborhood."

"Uh-huh," Davenport says, drinking and chomping on his wad of chewing gum. "Something like that. You know those two names you gave me this morning? The doctors? Well, they're clean. We've got nothing on them."

"And you waded through muck and mire just to tell me that? Come on!"

"Ordinarily," the city dick says, "I wouldn't have been in any hurry to check out those names. Just something to do when I got around to it. I mean I got a full plate. You can understand that, can't you?"

"Sure. So why all the speed?"

"Funny story. Not funny ha-ha, but definitely oddball. I work out of an office with another guy, a dick too. Our desks butt up against each other. He's a nice guy, Nick Galanis, a Greek. A very sharp eye. He always smells of garlic, but that's neither here nor there. Anyway, this morning he's sitting there and he hears me on the phone repeat those two names you gave me: Doctor Victor January and Doctor Phoebe Trumball. When I hang up, he wants to know what that was all about. I tell him a guy I know wants those two people checked out—and what's it to him."

Davenport pauses to reach across the desk for the gin bottle.

"Finish it," Cone says. "The booze and your story."

"All right," the cop says, "don't mind if I do."

He empties the bottle and shakes it carefully to get the last few drops.

"Well, here's what happened: A few months ago, Nick caught a squeal from the Fulton Fish Market. You know those guys down there go to work like at two in the morning. There's a Volkswagen parked right in front of a loading dock. So the first guy to show up for work looks in and sees a Caucasian male in the driver's seat with half his head blown away. They call us, and Nick Galanis goes down to take a look.

"It turns out the clunk's name is Harold Besant. That's the name on his driver's license, and that's who the Volkswagen is registered to. There's a Charter thirty-eight Special on the seat to his right, like it's fallen from his hand. One round fired. The slug that killed Besant went into his right temple and took a lot of his brains with it when it came out. Powder burns around the entrance wound. The only prints on the gun were Besant's. So what does that tell you?"

"Suicide," Cone says.

"Sure it was suicide," Davenport says, almost angrily. "Open and shut. But why did he pick the Fulton Fish Market? Who the hell knows? But Nick Galanis gets a hair up his ass. You know how you feel when a case is so neat and clean; you begin to wonder if you might be missing something. So Nick starts snooping, mostly on his own time. He finds out the dead guy was a research assistant at the Nu-Hope Fertility Clinic."

"Oh-ho," Cone says.

"Yeah oh-ho. That's why Nick perked up his ears when he heard me repeat those names. He had questioned Doctor January and Doctor Trumball. They claimed the guy had been depressed lately, and his fellow workers agreed he'd been in a down mood."

"Did you trace the gun?"

"Of course we traced the gun. It wasn't registered. I mean Besant had no permit. The piece was part of a shipment swiped from a Jersey warehouse. It was probably sold on the street."

"Did Besant leave a suicide note?"

"No, but that doesn't necessarily mean anything. He could have done it on the spur of the moment. Entrance wound in the right temple with powder burns. Gun found on the seat by his right hand. No prints on the gun but his. So where does that leave Detective Nick Galanis? In no-wheresville—right? He figures he's making a big something out of nothing. The file is closed as an apparent suicide. The ME says it was, so the Department's home free and clear."

"You should have been an actor," Cone says. "You're leading up to your great dramatic moment—I can feel it coming."

"Yeah," Davenport says, grinning, "something like that. This Harold Besant's closest relative is an uncle who's in the merchant marine, and he was on the other side of the world when Harold shuffled off this mortal coil. About a month ago, the uncle gets back to New York and looks up Nick Galanis, wanting to know how his nephew died. Nick tells him, and the uncle says no way; it was imfuckingpossible. You know why?''

"I'll bite. Why?''

"Because, according to the uncle, Harold Besant was left-handed.''

"Son of a bitch,'' Timothy Cone says.

Whatley and Cone are lounging in Sam's ruffled apartment. They've had a fast dinner of grilled franks, baked beans, and cold sauerkraut, washed down with bottles of Dark Heineken. While she stacks the dishes in her little kitchen— trim as a ship's galley—Cone tells her about the books he's been reading on artificial insemination, in vitro fertilization, and embryo transfer.

"Keep talking,'' Sam says, "but pick up a dish towel. I'll wash and you wipe.''

He complies and goes on describing the laboratory technique for conception without intercourse.

"No sweat,'' he says, "and no grunting. No 'Was it as good for you as it was for me?' A lot of single women are doing it. Interested?''

"No, thanks,'' she says, swabbing out the sink. "The patter of tiny feet doesn't interest me. Besides, I've had all my plumbing excavated; I told you that.''

"You could always adopt.''

"Who?'' she asks. "You?''

He finishes the last plate, and she takes the damp towel from him and hangs it away carefully to dry.

"And now,'' she says, "the surprise.''

"Oh, God,'' he says. "You're sending me home?''

"Not yet. You know what negus is?''

"Negus? Never heard of it.''

"Red wine, hot water, sugar, lemon juice, and cinnamon. I came across the recipe in an old cookbook and stirred up a batch. Want to try it?''

"Sure," he says bravely. "Sounds like it'll go great with beans and sauerkraut."

She heats the negus in a saucepan until it begins to bubble. Then she pours it into thick mugs and adds a sprinkling of nutmeg.

"Go ahead," she commands. "Try it."

He sips cautiously. "Hey! Not bad."

"Not bad, you asshole? It's delicious."

"It's okay. A great winter drink. It warms the heartles of my cock."

"You're disgusting," she says, smiling. "I'm going to trade you in for a new model."

"Nah," he says. "You get used to an old clunker, and you never want to scrap it."

They take their mugs of hot negus into the living room and sprawl on one of the rag rugs.

"You know," Sam says, "you're the most unromantic man I've ever met. But while you were talking about those test-tube babies made in the lab, I got the feeling that you don't really approve."

"Sharp lady," he says, blowing on his drink to cool it. "To tell you the truth, I'm not sure how I feel about it. I understand that it's a boon for couples who can't have kids naturally. But something about the whole idea turns me off. It's so goddamned mechanical. Like making sausages or stamping out widgets. How do you feel about it?"

Whatley shrugs. "I guess if women want kids so bad they'll go through all that, then more power to them. It's legal, isn't it?"

"I guess so. Nu-Hope isn't breaking any laws that I know of." He pauses a moment, wondering if he should tell her about that questionable suicide of a research assistant. He decides to keep his mouth shut—about that and Ernest Pingle's fears for his son.

"You're holding out on me again, aren't you?" Sam

says, looking at him closely. "You get a thousand-yard stare in your eyes, and I know something is going on in that tiny, tiny brain of yours."

"Nah," Cone says. "I'm just brooding about babies coming off a kind of assembly line. What a weird world it is."

The empty mugs are set aside.

"Bed?" she asks.

"I like it right here."

"Suits me," she says. "You don't know what a pleasure it is not to have the damned cat biting my toes."

He watches her undress, admiring the sharp-edged body, hard flanks, the twist of muscle and tendon. When she raises her arms to let down her long auburn hair, he sees the play of soft light on dark skin, warm shadows. Her body is as tight and bony as his, but the curves of hip, waist, and back are more elegant, smoothly glossed.

"At least," she says throatily, "take off your stupid work shoes."

He undresses quickly.

Their lovemaking, as usual, has a desperation about it, but never more than that night. Their coupling is a punishing duet, played furioso. They seem determined to rend walls of flesh and penetrate to a bliss that might consume them both. Perhaps their tumultuous striving springs from their talk of a brave new world with life manufactured in a sterile lab, all the ecstasy and pain of creation banished forever, along with joy and suffering, grief and laughter.

Their violence could have been a protest. Or it could have been an act of affirmation, asserting their humanness.

Whatever, it is one hell of a bang.

2

TIMOTHY CONE FIGURES he could call the Nu-Hope Clinic
and tell them he's coming up to make a white-glove inspection. But the smart way to do it, he reckons, is to waltz in
unexpectedly before they have a chance to sweep dirt under
the rug or pop a skeleton into a closet.

He gets up to East Seventy-first Street about three o'clock
on a dull, grimy day, a smell of snow in the air, and stands
across the street a few minutes eyeballing the two townhouses. They look solid, dignified, well-maintained. There
are big pots of ivy outside, still green, and all the windows
are sparkling.

He dodges through traffic and crosses to the east wing,
rings the bell beside the heavy front door. The judas is
opened almost immediately; Cone can see only the eyes and
white cap of what appears to be an extremely short nurse.
He holds up his identification card for inspection.

"Timothy Cone," he says. "From Haldering and Company. I'd like to see Doctor Victor January."

"Just a moment, please, sir," she chirps, and the judas is
closed.

He waits patiently, stamping his feet a bit to chase the
chill. It is almost three minutes before the door is swung
open by a tall woman in a light-green lab coat. She holds
out her hand, smiling.

"I'm Doctor Phoebe Trumball," she says. "Do come
in."

155

Her handclasp is hard and dry.

"Doctor January is busy with a patient," she explains, "but he'll be able to join us shortly. Meanwhile, may I give you the fifty-cent tour?"

"Sure," Cone says. "I guess you were expecting me sooner or later."

"Better sooner," she says almost gaily. "Now let me put away your coat and we'll get started. I suppose you'll want to see everything. I think it best if we begin next door in the patients' wing. That's really where most of our work is done."

She takes him up to the third floor, chattering on about the architect of the townhouses and how originally they were private residences of two brothers in marine insurance. Both of them died on the _Morro Castle_.

"Which," Dr. Trumball says, "is rather ironic—don't you think?"

"Yeah," Cone says.

She reminds him a lot of Samantha. The two women have an attractive angularity and bold features. But Sam is dark, and you can read everything she feels in her eyes. Phoebe Trumball is pale and all closed in. Cone bets she's not usually so chatty. Maybe not devious, he acknowledges, but calculating.

They walk through the third-floor passageway to the west wing. Cone notes the doctor unlocking the door.

"Security," Trumball explains. "Our research labs in the east wing are sterile and off-limits to patients."

"What's in the labs?"

"You'll see them. That's where the embryos are formed. And our sperm, egg, and embryo banks. Temperature control is very important."

"Listen," Cone says, unable to resist. "I've been doing some reading about artificial insemination, and I have a question, a silly one, but it's been nagging at me. When a guy sells his sperm—well, what do you collect it in?"

Dr. Trumball laughs. "Believe it or not," she says, "we use empty baby food jars. Sterilized, of course."

They go on a whirlwind tour of the west wing, with Trumball introducing staff and answering questions before Cone asks them. She makes certain he sees it all, except the rooms where patients are being treated. He is shown offices, labs, lavatories, X-ray rooms, examination rooms, the pharmacy, recovery rooms, and the Doctors' Lounge, where they pause at one of the steel tables and have a black coffee from one of the vending machines.

"Well," Trumball says, "what do you think so far?"

"Impressive," he says honestly. "Everything clean and neat. Looks like you run a tight ship."

"We try." She looks down at her coffee cup. "Something I haven't mentioned. . . . You must realize, Mr. Cone, that most of the women and couples who come to us are under a great deal of emotional stress. They are frantic to have children. Occasionally they cause some unpleasant scenes when we are not able to help them on the first try. I just thought I'd mention it."

Cone nods. "Do you have children, doctor?"

"No," she says. "Finished your coffee? Now let me show you around the east wing. I'm sure Doctor January will be with us soon."

Back they go through that third-floor passageway. As Trumball is unlocking the door, Timothy raps on it.

"Steel," he says. "Expecting a terrorist attack?"

"Oh, no," she says, laughing, "nothing like that. Just super security."

He has the feeling that she's laughed more in the last hour than she has in the past month. This is not, he decides, a normally laughing woman. So she's nervous about passing the Haldering inspection. Which is normal. But still . . .

In the east wing, Cone peers into executive offices, the main computer room, a few open labs. One locked chamber has a thick plate glass window fronting on the corridor. He sees busy employees bending over microscopes or using stainless steel machines he can't identify. All the workers are swaddled in wrinkled green trousers and jackets, with caps that cover their hair. Some are wearing surgical masks.

"Your research lab?" he asks.

"One of them," Dr. Trumball says shortly. "We have another where you have to enter through a special air lock. I'd invite you in, but decontamination takes at least twenty minutes, including a shower. The air inside is specially filtered."

"I'll skip," Cone says.

"Don't blame you," she says. "I rarely go in there myself. It's easier to use the intercom to check on what's going on."

He finds it difficult to move away from that plate glass window. He watches the activity inside. Workers in their wrinkled green uniforms. Glittering machines. Huge tanks that steam when the lids are lifted. Computer monitors flickering. Tapes whirling around and around. A factory.

"Making babies," the Wall Street dick says.

"Trying to," Dr. Trumball says. "That's what we're here for."

"Hello, there!" Dr. Victor January carols, coming up with hand outstretched to Cone. "Sorry I'm late. A small crisis. Very small, thank God! I'm January, and you must be Timothy Cone from Haldering. Happy to meet you. Phoebe been taking care of you, has she? The grand tour?"

Cone nods, shaking the soft, slender hand. This guy, he immediately decides, is Mr. Charm himself. It comes out his pores, with a deliberate theatricality that mocks itself. "Look, I'm putting on an act. You know it and I know it. But it's fun, isn't it, and no one's getting hurt."

January herds them into his private office and closes the door. He gets them seated in directors' chairs and then flops into his own swivel chair behind the big, cluttered desk. The chair is covered with zebra skin. Very dramatic.

"All right," he says, grinning fiercely, "let's have your questions. I'm sure you've got a hundred."

"No," Cone says, "not really. I did have some, but Doctor Trumball answered them. There is just one thing I'd like to know: Where do you get your customers?"

January gives him a roguish smile. "Customers? Well, yes, you're right. We prefer to call them patients or clients—but who's fooling whom? They *are* customers. Let me get you the latest numbers."

He leans forward, punches keys on the computer terminal on his desk, peers at the screen.

"As of last week," he reports, "approximately eighty-seven percent of our patients were referrals from other doctors, clinics, and hospitals. About ten percent came in on recommendations of other patients. The rest are what we call walk-in trade. Women or couples who have read about us or have seen me on TV talk shows. Okay?"

"Sure," Cone says. "You guarantee results?"

"Of course not," Trumball says rather crossly. "How could we possibly do that? Before we accept a patient, she—or she and her husband—go through an hour-long orientation lecture. We make certain they fully understand what's involved. And then they sign a five-page legal release that spells out in exact detail what we hope to do and what they can expect. But no guarantees."

"We've been lucky," Dr. January says, rapping the wooden top of his desk. "No lawsuits—so far. We really never promise more than we can deliver. This is not an exact science, Mr. Cone. And lots of things can go wrong. Gradually we're improving our pregnancy rate, but it's still a chancy proposition. We make no secret of that, and especially not to our patients. We make certain they know the odds."

Cone reflects what a nice, amiable gathering this is, all of them sitting about a warm office on a biting November afternoon, smiling at each other. He decides to shake them up.

"A guy named Harold Besant," he says casually. "He used to work for you. Research assistant. A couple of months ago he blew his brains out down at the Fulton Fish Market."

If he expects to rock them he's out of luck. Their faces

become suitably grave, their expression of sorrow suitably solemn.

"A terrible tragedy," Dr. January says.

"Dreadful," Dr. Trumball says. "The poor boy. We knew he was upset. Spells of silence. Once a horrible fit of weeping—and he couldn't, or wouldn't, give a reason for it."

"All the symptoms of depression," January says mournfully. "We tried to get him to our resident shrink, but he refused. I blame myself; I should have insisted."

"It wasn't your fault, Victor," Phoebe Trumball says.

"Did he have any close friends?" Cone asks. "Anyone on your staff?"

"No," Trumball says, "and I think that was part of his problem. We're really a family here, but he was never really a part of it. Was he, Victor?"

"No," January says. "The man was an outsider, a loner. And very talented. Too bad."

Their sadness seems genuine enough, but Cone, that cranky, misanthropic man, can't totally buy it. Maybe because January is everything Cone is not: handsome, impeccably dressed, with a magnetic appeal.

But to Cone, his gestures are too flamboyant, his smiles too wide, the waves in his blond hair too elaborate. Look for sincerity, Cone decides, and you find greasepaint.

"Are you married, Doctor January?" he asks suddenly.

"I am indeed," the man says promptly. "With two marvelous bambinos. I have their photos in my wallet—but I'll spare you that!"

Everyone laughs politely and the Wall Street dick stands up.

"Thanks for your help, folks," he says. "At the moment I can't think of anything else I need. But I may give you a call or stop by again. Okay?"

"Of course," January says, with a billowy wave of his hand. "We're anxious to get this thing approved, and we're happy to cooperate in any way we can. Our staff has been

instructed to answer all your questions fully to the best of
their ability. We have nothing to hide.''

"Glad to hear it," Cone says, shakes hands with January
and follows Phoebe Trumball down to the street floor,
where he reclaims his parka. He shakes hands with her and
walks out into a gloomy evening, the sky paved with slate
and a mean wind gusting. He pulls his hood over his spiky
hair, shoves his hands into fleece-lined pockets, and tramps
over to Park Avenue.

Then he stops, reflects a moment, and retraces his steps.
He takes up station across the street from the Nu-Hope
Fertility Clinic. It's a few minutes after five o'clock, and he
decides to give it an hour. If nothing happens by six, he'll
split and go home. He pounds up and down the block to
keep the circulation going.

It's almost six o'clock before January and Trumball come
out. They're hatless, and Cone spots them immediately:
tall, willowy blonds walking with a jaunty grace. Timothy
trudges behind them. After a while he begins to wonder if
they're heading for the South Bronx. But on Eighty-third
Street they turn eastward. And just before they come to
Third Avenue, they scurry up the steps of a nicely restored
brownstone.

Cone waits a few minutes and then climbs the stairs and
inspects the names listed on the brass bell plate. Dr. P.
Trumball occupies Apartment 4-B.

He wanders away. The two doctors could be having a
business meeting. It could be a cocktail party with Dr.
January's wife present. It could be—

Ah, shit. Cone knows what it is.

"Big deal," he says aloud, and a bag lady mooching past
him turns sharply and snarls, "Go fuck yourself."

"Don't think I haven't tried," he yells after her.

The next morning Cone gets to work about a half hour
late—which is as close to promptitude as he can come—
and finds a note on his desk to call Lester Pingle. He lights

his third cigarette of the day while he ponders what the guy might want. He decides it will be a stern demand to hurry up the Nu-Hope investigation.

But when Lester answers the phone, he is all sweetness and light.

"Thank you for calling back," he says. "I understand you're Haldering's investigator on the Nu-Hope Fertility Clinic deal."

"That's right."

"I was hoping we could get together for a few minutes. There are certain factors involved I think you should be aware of."

"Like what?"

"Well, that's what I wanted to talk to you about," Lester says, "but not on the phone."

"Okay. You want me to come to your office?"

"No, no," Pingle says hastily. "This is, uh, confidential. You know where Trinity Church is?"

"Sure."

"Can you meet me outside the main entrance in, say, twenty minutes?"

"I'll be there," Cone says. "How will I know you?"

"I'm wearing a black overcoat with a fur collar. And a black bowler."

"And I'll be wearing an olive-drab parka," Cone says. "No bowler."

Pingle laughs somewhat nervously and hangs up.

Timothy takes his time and ambles down Broadway to Wall Street, pausing to look idly in shop windows. When he gets to Trinity, he sees a tall gink in black overcoat and derby pacing back and forth in front of the church. Cone lights a Camel before he goes up to him.

"Lester Pingle?" he says loudly.

The guy jumps like he's been goosed with an icicle, then whirls around. "Yes," he says, "yes, that's right. You're from Haldering?"

"Uh-huh. Timothy Cone. Want to see my ID?"

"No, no," Pingle says, "that won't be necessary. I just thought I'd tell you what's on my mind so you'll know what's involved."

Cone nods.

"We can just walk up and down here for a few minutes. I'd have asked you to the office, but the walls have ears."

"People keep saying that, but I've never seen a wall with ears. Although potatoes have eyes."

Pingle looks at him doubtfully, trying to decide if Cone is making a joke or is simply demented. The detective's bland expression gives him no clue.

Cone notices that although it's a nippy day, Lester's pale face is sheened with sweat.

They tramp up and down before Trinity Church as Lester launches into a spluttering monologue. Hiring Haldering was his father's idea. Lester, in his own mind, is certain that the Nu-Hope deal is clean and a potential moneymaker.

"It rates high when you consider the risk-benefit factor," he says.

The stumbling block is Ernest Pingle. Lester's father is getting on in years, and he's not keeping up so well, but without his approval, the deal is dead.

"So?" Cone says. "What do you want me to do about it?"

Well, Pingle says wiping a palm across his forehead, his father trusts Haldering because of their role in uncovering the Clovis swindle. And Lester just wanted Cone to know how hidebound his father has become, and how he seems to be prejudiced against Nu-Hope. It would be a personal favor to Lester if Cone would okay Nu-Hope as soon as possible. In that event, there would be more assignments for Haldering; Lester would see to that.

"We call them as we see them," Timothy Cone tells him.

"Of course," Pingle says, "but everyone who's looked into Nu-Hope agrees it's a sweet piece of business, so there's really no reason to stall."

"I'm not stalling," Cone says stonily. "I've just started my investigation."

Then, looking straight ahead, Lester Pingle says in a low voice: "You scratch my back, I'll scratch yours. I want this Nu-Hope deal. You okay it and there's a nice piece of change in it for you."

"Yeah?" Cone says. "How much?"

"How does five thousand sound to you?"

"Doesn't sound like much," Cone says. "This could mean millions for Pingle Enterprises."

"Ten," Pingle says desperately, still not looking at the detective. "Ten thousand. Okay?"

"No, thanks."

"Why are you so stubborn?" Lester cries.

"I work at it," Cone says and walks away.

He doesn't look back, which is a mistake. If he had, he'd have noted that Lester doesn't leave. He continues his parade back and forth in front of Trinity. In a few moments a man comes out of the church. He's wearing a herringbone tweed topcoat and a green felt fedora with a clump of bright feathers in the band.

Pingle is surprised. "You were inside the church, Martin?"

"Why not? I'm entitled. Besides, I wanted to get a look at Cone. Scruffy character, isn't he?"

Three months previously, when they first met, the barrel-chested man had introduced himself simply as Martin. Lester Pingle didn't know if it was Martin Something or Something Martin. Later, doing some investigating of his own, he learned it was Martin Gardow. He was chief of special projects for one of the country's largest conglomerates, ruled by a tyrant whom Wall Street insiders called Mr. D.

"How did it go?" Martin asks.

"It didn't," Lester Pingle says miserably. "He turned down the offer of more jobs. He turned down the ten thousand."

"You think he wants more?"

"No. I just don't think he can be bought."

"Don't tell that to Mr. D.," Gardow says with his mirthless smile. "He believes that every man has his price. But the price doesn't necessarily have to be in dollars. Our contact at Nu-Hope tells us that Cone is very smart, very inquisitive, and very persistent. We'll just have to find out what his price is."

"No violence," Pingle says, wiping the sweat from his forehead again. "I hate violence."

Martin turns to look at him. "I know you do, Lester," he says softly.

Then the two men separate, walking off in opposite directions. By that time, Cone is back at Haldering's. He goes directly to Sam's office.

"I want to tell you something," he says when she looks up. "I'll put it on paper, but I want you to know—just in case he decides to play rough."

"What the hell are you talking about?"

He tells her about Lester's proffered bribes.

"Son of a bitch," Sam says thoughtfully. "Ten thousand? Weren't you tempted?"

"Nah," he says. "My heart is pure."

"And your disposition is rancid. I better tell H. H. about this."

"No," he says quickly, "don't do that."

"Why not?"

He looks at her. "Because after striking out with me, Lester will probably try to get to Hiram himself. I want to find out just how anxious he is to seal the Nu-Hope deal."

"Jesus Christ," Sam says. "What's going on here?"

"Beats the shit out of me," he says. "I can't get a handle on the thing."

He's still brooding an hour later when his phone rings.

"Timothy Cone?"

"Yeah. Who's this?"

"Detective Nick Galanis, NYPD. I work with Neal Davenport. He says he mentioned me."

"Sure he did. What can I do for you?"

"Neal says you're investigating the Nu-Hope Clinic. Right?"

"Yeah. For a proposed expansion deal. They want to become a chain. Like fast-food joints or something."

"And he told you about Harold Besant? The alleged suicide?"

"He told me."

"Look, Cone, I had to drop that thing after the ME's report. Also, there was too much new stuff coming along. You can understand that, can't you?"

"Sure."

"But the damned thing still bugs me. I got the feeling someone's jerking us around, and I don't like it. Anyway, while you're looking into Nu-Hope, I wish you'd ask a few questions about Besant."

"I already have. The two top doctors up there tell me he was depressed."

"Yeah," Nick Galanis says, "that's what they told me, too. Did you talk to Jessie Scotto?"

"Jessie Scotto? No. Who she?"

"Works at Nu-Hope. A nurse in the west wing. She was Harold Besant's girlfriend. As a matter of fact, they were living together on the Upper West Side. I questioned her right after Besant's death, but she was shook and I got nothing from her. Maybe I'm blowing smoke, but I thought she was scared shitless and just wasn't talking. But that was like two months ago, and maybe she's calmed down by now. I'd appreciate it if you'd talk to her and see what you can get—if anything. Neal says you're a bulldog, so give it a try. That so-called suicide is still on my brain. I think about it every day."

"Well, yeah," Cone says, "I can do that. Jessie Scotto? What kind of a woman is she?"

"A little mouse," Detective Galanis says. "Don't lean

on her or she'll fold. Just play the sympathetic daddy and maybe she'll talk.''

"All right,'' Cone says. "Thanks for the tip.''

"You'll let me know?''

"Of course.''

It's an hour after he hangs up that Cone remembers the doctors had told him that Harold Besant had no close friends on the staff.

The black Cadillac de Ville is parked in a No Parking zone just north of Broome Street. Standing alongside is one of the biggest guys Cone has ever seen: a young hulk who looks like he's wearing football pads under his gray whipcord jacket. As Cone goes by on his way to work, the monster steps in front of him.

"Mr. Timothy Cone?'' he asks pleasantly.

Cone looks up at him. About six feet six, he figures, at least 280, with a neck as wide as the detective's thigh. He looks as if he's got the muscle to toss Timothy over to Lafayette Street if the mood takes him.

"Yeah, I'm Cone. Who are you?''

His question is ignored. The giant gestures toward the back of the Cadillac. "A gentleman here would like to speak to you for a few minutes.''

"No, thanks,'' Cone says. "Mommy told me never to accept rides from strangers.''

"We're not going for a ride,'' the young behemoth says. "Just a little talk right here. Come on, Mr. Cone, be nice.''

"And if I'm not nice?''

The guy shrugs. "Then I get back in and drive away.'' He sounds disappointed.

But Cone believes him. He bends down to peer in the window. The man sitting back there looks innocent enough. He's elegantly dressed, with a miniature orchid pinned to the lapel of his taupe gabardine topcoat. He sees Timothy staring through the glass, gives him a sweet smile, and makes little beckoning motions with his fingers.

"Okay," Cone says.

The bodyguard, or chauffeur, or whatever the hell he is, opens the rear door and Cone slides in. He sits far back and crosses his knees so he can get to his ankle holster in a hurry if he has to.

The man turning sideways to face him has deep, soft eyes, a gentle manner. He's pushing sixty, Cone reckons, and looks like he has a massage and a manicure every day. He's wearing a cologne that makes the inside of the Cadillac smell like a cedar chest.

"Please forgive this unconventional method of meeting you, Mr. Cone," he says in a quiet voice. "I suppose I could have written you a letter or called your office for an appointment, but it didn't seem wise."

"Why not?" Cone asks.

No answer to that. "First let me introduce myself." The man slides a pigskin case from his inside jacket pocket, extracts a plastic ID card, and hands it over.

The Wall Street dick takes a quick look at it. "This doesn't mean much," he says. "I could buy a fake on the street for maybe fifty bucks."

"I don't think so," the guy says, flashing his sweet smile again. "That particular card has a microchip embedded in it."

"Well, well. Will wonders never cease?"

"No," the other man says. "They won't."

"And what's this battle monument commission? I never heard of it."

"Not many people have. It's just another federal bureaucracy."

"You promote battle monuments?"

"Among other things."

"J. Roger Gibby," Cone reads from the card. Then he looks up to stare into those dark, shadowed eyes. "That name rings a bell." He pauses a moment, then snaps his fingers. "Got it. I've been reading books on artificial insemination. They keep mentioning Professor J. Roger Gibby. That's you—correct?"

"I *was* a professor, but not any longer. Just another government employee."

"But you did a lot of work on test-tube babies. So the reason we're having this confab is the Nu-Hope Clinic investigation. Am I right?"

"Exactly right."

"Let me make another wild guess," Cone says. "You want me to okay the Nu-Hope deal. How'm I doing?"

"Batting a thousand."

"What the hell is Uncle Sam's interest in Nu-Hope?"

"They're doing some excellent original research. The federal government is vitally interested in furthering technology in their area."

"Bullshit," Cone says roughly. "What's the research you're interested in—how to get more sperm donors to jack off into empty baby food jars?"

Gibby gives him a wry look. "You have a colorful way of speaking, Mr. Cone. I'm afraid I can't be more specific about our interest in Nu-Hope."

"Okay," Cone says. "If that's the way it is, that's the way it is. Nice talking to you."

He reaches for the door handle, but Gibby puts a light hand on his arm.

"Just a moment, Mr. Cone. Please. I've gone to a great deal of trouble to look up your record. Marine Corps. Vietnam. Your medals. You served your country well."

"Oh-oh," Cone says. "Here it comes. Hearts and flowers. Be a patriot. Do what Big Daddy in the White House wants you to do. Is that right?"

"Not quite. There are others as anxious about Nu-Hope's research as we are."

"Jesus Christ, now it's help defend America against Godless Communism. You're really pulling out all the stops."

"No," Gibby says seriously, "I'm not suggesting that at all. I'm sure the Soviets are doing research along similar lines. But that doesn't concern us at the moment. There are others interested in the same subject."

"Others? What others?"

"That, I'm afraid, is also privileged information."

Cone nods. "Glad to have met you," he says. "As for the US of A, I've paid my dues. As for Nu-Hope, I'm going to keep digging. If they're clean, that's what I'll report. And if they're dirty, likewise."

He climbs out of the de Ville. The bruiser, still standing on the sidewalk, glances at him but lets him go. Cone tramps angrily southward on Broadway.

He's only an hour late for work, and gets a wrathful look from Samantha when he passes her in the corridor. But he's in no mood to endure a reaming out for his tardiness, and without even a good morning to her, heads for his office.

"Grouch!" she calls after him.

He sits at his battered desk, fishes out a cigarette, and rumbles stuff around in his brain, trying to find some logical pattern: Lester Pingle offers a bribe for an okay on the Nu-Hope deal. Cone tells him to get lost. The next morning, the U.S. Gov't., in the person of J. Roger Gibby, makes the same pitch.

Does that mean that Pingle's bribe money was going to come from the taxpayers? Or is Lester buddy-buddy with the "others" Gibby mentioned? Finally, why is everyone so goddamned interested in Nu-Hope? And why did January and Trumball lie about Harold Besant?

The whole thing reminds Cone of that nonsense riddle he loved as a child: "If it takes fourteen geese to get down off an elephant, how many Palmolive wrappers does it take to paper a boxcar?" He groans, pulls the phone toward him, and calls Jessie Scotto at the Nu-Hope Fertility Clinic.

He identifies himself, says he's coming up to the clinic to speak to several of the employees, and would like to talk to her for a few minutes.

"I'm very busy," she says in a voice so low he can hardly hear her.

He won't let her get away with that. "Doctor January told me he instructed the staff to be as cooperative as possible. Is that right?"

"Yes," she says faintly, "he told us that."

"Well, then? It won't take long."

"All right," she says. "If it's only for a few minutes."

"In the Doctors' Lounge," he suggests, "in about an hour. We'll have a coffee or something. I'm wearing an old parka, but you'll have to identify yourself."

"All right," she says again, sounding like she hears the tumbrils rolling.

At the clinic Cone flashes his ID and has no trouble getting into the west wing. He takes the elevator to the fourth floor and is happy to find the Doctors' Lounge empty. He treats himself to a free cup of black coffee and a wedge of apple pie. It comes with a plastic fork. Pie and fork taste alike.

He's on his second cup of coffee when a little nurse scurries into the lounge, looking like she's pursued by wolves. Cone rises, forces himself to smile, holds out a hand.

"Miss Scotto?" he says. "I'm Timothy Cone from Haldering. Thank you for meeting with me."

She looks like she's expecting him to slap her. But she gives him a brief, limp handclasp, then collapses into a metal chair at his table. Detective Galanis was wrong, Cone thinks: Two months haven't restored Jessie Scotto's nerves. She looks ready to shatter into a million pieces.

"Can I bring you a coffee?" he asks.

She shakes her head, so he sits down again, opposite her, and hunches over the table. He speaks quietly, trying to play the sympathetic daddy. But it's difficult; she won't look at him.

"Just a few questions," Cone says soothingly. "I know how busy you must be."

Like Galanis said: She's a little mouse. Diminutive, with frizzy hair and pale, watery eyes. She's not wearing makeup, and swims in a nurse's uniform too large for her. It's hard to believe she was living with Harold Besant. She looks like someone's maiden aunt.

"How long have you worked at Nu-Hope, Miss Scotto?"

"Six years."

"Like it?"

A nod.

"What are your duties?"

"I prep patients."

As they talk, people begin to wander into the lounge and use the vending machines. Cone notices a number of them glance curiously at Jessie and himself. He leans farther across the table, deciding he better cut this short before the place is jammed by the lunchtime crowd.

"You knew Harold Besant," he says, more of a statement than a question.

She looks up at him fearfully.

"Look, Jessie," he says, trying to keep his temper under control, "whatever you say is just between you and me. I swear to God I'll never repeat a word. You and Harold were living together."

She nods.

"Did you know he had a gun?"

"He didn't," she bursts out. "I know he didn't."

"The night he died, did he tell you where he was going?"

"No. He just said he'd be gone for an hour or so. He said he had to meet someone."

"Did he say who?"

"No."

"Do you think he was depressed, like everyone says?"

"He was—Harold was worried."

"About what?"

"His work."

"What was his work, Jessie? What did Harold do in that research laboratory?"

She looks directly into his eyes, unblinking, and Cone knows she's going to lie.

"He never discussed his work with me," she says. "I know nothing about it."

Cone sits back and regards her gravely. "There's no way I can help you if you won't let me."

She begins weeping, covering her eyes with a palm. "Just leave me alone," she says in a muffled voice. "Just go away. Please."

"All right," he says, sighing. "Haldering's phone number is in the book. If you change your mind, you can reach me there."

People look at him as he stalks out of the Doctors' Lounge, leaving Jessie Scotto alone at the table, her eyes covered, thin shoulders bowed and trembling.

He takes a cab back to John Street, furious with his failure, but not seeing how else he could have handled it. At least he learned that Harold Besant hadn't owned a gun. Or, if he had, Jessie Scotto wasn't aware of it. But if she was living with the guy, you'd think she'd know.

Back in his office, he puts in a call to Detective Nick Galanis. But Galanis has the day off, so Cone leaves a message he called and will call again tomorrow.

He leans back in his swivel chair and stares at the ceiling. He keeps seeing Jessie's pinched features and tear-filled eyes. She's such a defeated little woman, bowed by the heavy load she's carrying and too frightened to get out from under. A loser.

"Just like me," Cone says aloud.

"Who's just like you?" Sidney Apicella asks. "Typhoid Mary?"

The CPA stands in the doorway, gently rubbing his swollen beezer.

"You don't look happy, Sid," Cone says, "but then you never look happy."

"How can I be happy when you keep tossing me curve balls? Remember asking me to check Lester Pingle's financial situation?"

"Of course I remember. Well?"

"Pingle Enterprises is in good shape. A nice balance sheet. But Lester is close to being a bankrupt. The guy hasn't got two kopecks to rub together. How do you like that?"

"I like it," the Wall Street dick says.

* * *

The loft phone explodes, and he rouses from a heavy sleep. He pushes himself off the mattress and staggers over to the wall phone in his minuscule kitchen.

"H'lo?" he says sleepily.

"Jesus Christ," Davenport says, "you still snoozing? It's eight o'clock already."

"Big deal," Cone says, yawning. "What's this, a wake-up call? To get me to work on time?"

"No," the city detective says, "it's more than that. Jessie Scotto got scragged last night."

Silence.

"Cone? You there?"

"I'm here," Timothy says, slumping and wanting to upchuck. "She's really dead?"

"As a doornail. Looks like a B and E. Too bad you never got a chance to talk to her."

"I did," Cone says. "I talked to her yesterday morning."

"You son of a bitch!" Davenport yells at him. "Why didn't you tell us about it?"

"I tried. I left a message for Galanis. Ask him."

There's a moment's silence, then the cop comes back on. "Yeah," he says, "sorry. Nick's got your message on his desk. Anyway, the lady's dead. We just got it over the wire. Nick and I are going up there to take a look. Want to tag along and inspect the corpus delicious?"

"I don't want to," Cone says, "but I better."

"Okay. We'll pick you up outside your palace in about fifteen minutes. Don't make us wait."

"I'll be there," Cone promises.

They're in a dusty blue Plymouth, both city detectives in the front seat. Timothy scrambles into the back and is introduced to Nick Galanis, who's driving. He's a short, swarthy guy with a thick black mustache.

"This stinks," he says wrathfully. "A fake suicide and now Besant's girlfriend gets chilled. You're telling me it's a coincidence? *Bullshit!*"

"Calm down, Nick," Davenport advises. "Your ulcer will be acting up again. Cone, we picked up some black coffee. Here's yours."

He hands over a big cardboard container.

"Thanks," Timothy says gratefully. "It's plasma. When was she killed?"

"Don't know," Davenport says, gulping his coffee. "We got none of the details. Just that a Caucasian female identified as Jessie Scotto was found dead in her apartment on West Seventy-fourth. Homicide suspected. That's all they put out."

"You talked to her yesterday?" Galanis demands angrily. He's gnawing on his long mustache, reaching up with his bottom teeth.

"That's right."

"Get anything?"

"She said that Besant didn't own a gun."

"Goddammit!" Nick says furiously, banging the steering wheel with his palm. "I didn't even ask her that. I'm a fucking idiot!"

"She was still shook," Cone says. "She knew something but wasn't talking. I pushed it as far as I could, but she started crying and there were a lot of people around, so I split."

"What makes you think she knew something?" Davenport asks.

"She lied to me. She said she knew nothing about Besant's work at Nu-Hope. A woman lives with a guy and doesn't know what his job is? Maybe—but I can't buy it."

"Anything else?" Galanis wants to know.

"Yeah, she said that on the night Harold died, he told her that he was going out for an hour or so to meet someone. She claimed she didn't know who it was."

"Uh-huh," Nick says. "She told me that, too. I think the part about him going out to meet someone was the truth. But I think she knew who it was."

The brownstone on West Seventy-fourth Street, just east of Amsterdam, is roped off with sawhorses and wide Crime

Scene tapes, holding back the usual crowd of rubbernecks. There are three squad cars and a meat wagon double-parked. The morgue attendants are playing gin rummy on the fender of their van. Davenport and Galanis clip their IDs to their jacket pockets.

"C'mon," Neal says to Cone. "We'll get you in. I want to make sure we're all talking about the same woman."

The blue at the door glances at the detectives' tags, then looks at Cone.

"Who's he?" he asks.

"A witness," Davenport says, and the three of them push through the door. They tramp up a stairway covered with threadbare carpeting. The place reeks of roach spray. On the third floor, another uniformed officer stands guard before a closed door.

"A witness," Davenport repeats, jerking a thumb at Cone. "Keep an eye on him; he's a dangerous character."

"Thanks a lot," Timothy says.

The two city detectives disappear inside. Cone waits in the hallway. He and the uniformed cop eye each other warily. After about three minutes, Davenport comes out.

"What did you have to eat this morning?" he asks.

"Just the black coffee you gave me."

"Try to keep it down," the city dick says. "I had my shoes shined, and I wouldn't want to get them splattered. C'mon in."

Later, Cone has a confused recollection of a squeezed one-bedroom apartment that's been thoroughly trashed: rugs torn up, pictures yanked off the walls and smashed, lamps overturned, all the shelves in the kitchen emptied onto the floor, chair and sofa cushions slashed, clothing spilled from bureau drawers.

All he remembers clearly is the body on the bed.

Davenport pulls down the bloodied sheet with his fingertips. "This the woman you talked to yesterday?"

"Yeah," Cone says, swallowing.

"What the fuck's this all about, Neal?" a plainclothesman says indignantly. "This is my squeal."

"Don't get your balls in an uproar, Harry," Davenport says. "We're not moving in on you. This one is all yours. But she was questioned yesterday on another file, and I just wanted to make sure of the ID. What made all those puncture wounds?"

"You want me to guess?" the doctor from the ME's office says, snapping shut his black case. "I'd guess a sharpened ice pick. Most of the holes look to be no more than an inch deep. Painful but not fatal."

"I saw something like that before," Nick Galanis says. "Jabs from the little blade of a jackknife. To get a guy to talk. But why did they cut off her nipples?"

"Maybe she wouldn't talk," Cone says stonily. "Then they really went to work on her."

"She was tied up and gagged when she was found," Harry says. "The legs of a pantyhose was shoved down her throat."

"I can't say definitely until the PM," the doc says, "but I think that's what killed her. Probably choked to death on her own vomit. Not a nice way to go."

"At least they spared her face," Cone says, staring at those pale, pinched features. The little mouse, trapped and destroyed.

"How do you see it, Harry?" Davenport asks.

"A junkie," the plainclothesman says promptly. "Trying to score. Maybe he heard she had money up here. When she wouldn't talk, he tortured her. Then, after she died, he tore the place apart."

"It's all yours," Davenport says, nodding. "Lots of luck."

Back on the sidewalk, the three men take deep breaths. Even the grimy city air tastes good.

"A nice way to start the day," Cone says.

"I'm hungry," Davenport says. "What say we go over to Amsterdam and get us some breakfast?"

Ten minutes later they're sitting at a table in a white-tiled dairy restaurant on West Seventy-second Street. They're all having the same thing: tomato juice with a wedge of lemon, scrambled eggs with lox and onions, french fries, toasted bagels, and more black coffee. They eat busily.

"Do you buy what Harry said about a junkie?" Cone asks.

"Harry's a good cop," Davenport says, smiling, "but when God was passing out brains, he was pretty far back in the line. I think the woman was tied and gagged, and then the place was torn apart. When the killer couldn't find what he was looking for, he went to work on her with ice pick and knife. She croaked before she talked."

"What was he looking for?" Galanis says, wiping ketchup from his mustache with a paper napkin. "She couldn't have had much cash or jewelry. Look at that apartment. You know you're not going to strike it rich in there."

"Poor Harry," Davenport says, unwrapping a stick of Juicy Fruit and sliding it into his mouth. "I got a feeling this is going to be an F and F case. File and forget."

"I know who killed her," Cone says in a low voice.

The two NYPD men look at him, blinking.

"Who?" Galanis says.

"I did," Timothy Cone says, pushing back from the table and taking out his pack of Camels. "Because I've got no more brains than Harry. I questioned the poor woman in the Doctors' Lounge. Someone saw us talking and told someone else. And that was the end of Jessie Scotto."

"What the hell are you talking about?" Davenport wants to know.

"Just blowing smoke," Cone says, lighting a cigarette.

They drive him back to John Street. But before he goes into the office, he walks around the corner to a discount bookstore on Broadway. After searching the shelves, he buys two more books on new techniques in laboratory conception. He has a vague idea of what Jessie Scotto's killer was looking for.

But it doesn't make him feel less guilty.

They're in Hiram Haldering's office.

"Now tell me," Hiram is saying, stubby fingers laced across his pot. "How are we coming along on the Nu-Hope deal? Everything hunky-dory?"

"We're coming along fine," Samantha says. "No red flags have turned up yet. Have they, Tim?"

"No," Cone says, "not yet."

H. H. stirs restlessly. "The Preliminary Intelligence Estimate from the accounting section just came in. The CPAs give the deal a go-ahead. Ditto from the legal section. So all that's missing is an okay from you people."

"I'm working it," Cone says.

The benign smile disappears. "How much more time do you need on this, Cone?"

"Hard to tell."

"Well, Pingle Enterprises is getting anxious. I got a call from Lester this morning. They want our evaluation so they can get rolling."

"Rolling on what?" Cone asks.

"On the expansion plans for the Nu-Hope Clinic," Haldering says, staring at him like he's an idiot.

"I mean how are they going to handle it?" Cone explains patiently. "Did Lester say? A limited partnership, public or private? A franchise setup or a public offering of stock?"

Haldering leans forward, frowning. "They didn't say, and I didn't ask. What the hell business is it of ours? Listen, I want you to know I'm under considerable pressure to complete this investigation."

"I'm sure Tim is giving it every priority," Samantha says. "Isn't that right?"

"Sure," Cone says. "Every priority."

Haldering looks at him suspiciously, then turns to Whatley. "I'll give you one week, Sam, and that's it."

They walk back to Samantha's office. She motions him inside but leaves the door open.

"I love the way you show respect for your employer," she says.

"What the hell was that all about?" he asks her. "He's never been so antsy."

"Well, he said Lester Pingle called him."

"Yeah, but I got the feeling someone else is leaning on him."

She stares at him a long moment. Then: "I told H. H. that no red flags had turned up on this deal, and you agreed with me. Was that the truth?"

"No," Cone says. "Red flags are flapping all over the place."

Samantha groans. "I know it's hopeless to ask what's going on—you're such a closemouthed bastard."

"All I've got are bits and pieces," he tells her. "Nothing you can take to the bank. When I've got something I can put on paper, I'll do it."

"Can you give me a glimmer, for God's sake? Do you think the Nu-Hope deal stinks?"

"To high heaven," he says.

He goes back to his office and finds, on his desk, a PIE from the accounting section.

According to Sid Apicella's gnomes, Nu-Hope is in great shape. They've got a couple of low-interest bank loans they're paying off on the button. Their cash flow is being smartly managed, and gross income shows a satisfying year-to-year increase since they converted from an abortion clinic.

But their operating expenses have also increased. Part of that is due to an enlarged staff. But a lot of it, Cone notes, is because of ballooning expenditures on research and development. The present and projected allocations for R & D seem inordinately high.

That night Cone heats up two cans of chili con carne, sparked with an extra sprinkling of chili powder. He eats that with a package of soda crackers and a cold can of Heineken. Cleo has the same thing, except for the beer. The cat sniffs at that, then wrinkles its nose and turns away.

"You're no son of mine," he tells the castrated tom.

He spends the evening reading and trying to understand the first of his two new books on artificial conception. He smokes half a pack of Camels and drinks three vodkas and water. Near two o'clock, he's dizzy with nicotine, alcohol, and all those long words in the book. What, in God's name, is ectogenesis?

He gives Cleo fresh water and promises the cat new litter in the morning. He's just beginning to undress when the phone rings.

"Yeah?" he says.

"Timothy Cone?"

"That's right. Who's this?"

"I'm the super in the building where Samantha Whitley lives."

"Whatley," Cone says. "Samantha Whatley. Is anything wrong?"

"Well, we had some excitement here. Someone tried to break into her apartment. The cops are here now."

"Jesus Christ," Cone says. "Is she all right?"

"Well, she got banged up a little. She asked me to call and see if you'd come right over."

"Sure," Cone says, thinking of Jessie Scotto. "Tell her I'll be right there."

He hangs up, rebuttons his shirt, pulls on corduroy jacket and parka. He straps on his ankle holster with the shortbarreled .357 Magnum.

"Hold down the fort, kiddo," he tells Cleo, then goes clattering down the six floors of iron staircase, trying to figure his best bet at finding a taxi at that time of night.

But he doesn't have to worry about a cab. He trots about twenty feet toward Spring Street when two men come out of the shadows and close in on him.

"Suckered," Cone says aloud, knowing Sam is okay. He backs slowly away, arms half-lifted, palms turned outward.

They're not tall guys, but they've got heft. They're not wearing overcoats or topcoats or raincoats or hats. Just dark suits. They look like twin undertakers. They're both smiling, like they came to escort him to a surprise party.

"You Cone?" one of them asks.

"I gave at the office," Timothy says, hands still raised.

"You hear that, Sol?" one of them says. "He gave at the office."

"Funny," Sol says. "The guy's a comedian. Ask him if he's got any other jokes."

"Look," Cone says, "I don't know what—"

The punch comes out of nowhere, and he's not fast enough to slip it. It catches him at the corner of his mouth and splits his lip open. He tastes the blood, and Sol steps in with a short, hard jab to his gut. These guys are real bullyboys.

They swarm all over him, jackhammering with hard fists. The pile-lined parka helps, but not enough. He tries to tuck in his head and cover up, but they straighten him with stiff pokes, then bend him over with hooks to his kidneys. Professionals.

Before he knows it, he's down on the sidewalk. He vaguely remembers a lecture on unarmed combat at Quantico. "Your eyes and your nuts," the instructor had cautioned. "Always protect your eyes and your nuts." So Cone curls into a fetal position on the cold pavement, arms across his face, while the two thugs give him the boot.

They don't intend to kill him, he knows that; they just want to hurt. And they do. He takes a kick to his temple that almost chills him. And finally they both jump in the air and come down hard on his ribs.

Meanwhile they haven't said a word. Just breathing heavily. Doing a job of work. When the punishment ends, he stays curled up, eyes closed. Then, suddenly, the chili comes up.

"Jesus Christ," one of them says disgustedly, as if it's all Cone's fault.

"You got the message?" Sol says to Cone. "From now on do what you're told. Be smart. Play along."

He hears them moving away. He's almost out, but hangs on to consciousness, telling himself those are the two cruds who cut off Jessie Scotto's nipples. That gives him strength to open his eyes and lift his head from the concrete.

He sees them moving away in a misty haze to a parked car. He makes it to be a four-door, black Pontiac Bonneville, but can't be sure. He knows they'll have to drive by him down Broadway. He slides a hand to his ankle holster.

When they pull out with a squeal of tires, he's ready for them, forearms propped on the sidewalk, gun held in both hands. It's wavering, he knows, but at that distance he can't miss.

He shoots steadily, following the car, pumping off rounds like he's on the range. The damned car seems to absorb his shots with no effect until, thirty feet down Broadway, the Pontiac suddenly veers, climbs the sidewalk, and smashes through the plate glass window of a trendy new restaurant that serves quiche and spinach salad.

The car plunges into the darkened interior with a screech of torn metal and a crunch of splintering wood. Cone is hoping for an explosion and fire, but no such luck. Now he sees a few people on the street, running toward the crash.

Cone drags himself slowly to his feet. Stands wavering. Everything seems to be working. He goes back to his loft. It takes him almost twenty minutes to climb those six flights of iron steps, resting on every landing. Finally, he gets inside, turns on the lights, locks and bolts the door. Cleo takes one look at him and retreats under the bathtub.

"C'mon," Cone says, "I don't look that bad."

But when he strips and inspects himself in the medicine cabinet mirror, he calls to the cat, "You're right."

He knows he was conned, but he's got to make sure. So before he doctors himself, he phones Samantha. She picks up on the sixth ring.

"Wha'?" she says sleepily.

"Cone. You okay?"

"Of course I'm okay. What time is it? Oh, my God.

What are you, drunk or something, waking me up at this hour?''

"Just checking," he says. "Go back to sleep."

"You sound funny," she says. "You're not talking right."

"I think I got the flu," he says. "Maybe I won't be in tomorrow. Good night. Sweet dreams."

He takes a healthy belt of vodka and uses a little soaked in a paper towel to swab off his torn lip and assorted cuts. The adrenaline is wearing off and he's really beginning to ache.

Finally he hears the sounds of sirens and buffalo whistles, and knows that the police have come to investigate the car that crashed into the restaurant. He hopes it'll be a job for Homicide.

He finishes washing up and puts his parka in a plastic garbage bag, ready for the dry cleaners. He tries stretching, cautiously. No permanent damage that he can find. Just a bad beating. He's had that before.

He bends down slowly and collapses onto the mattress. After a while Cleo comes padding over to him, sniffs at his wounds, and whimpers.

"Yeah," Cone says drowsily. "I know."

Getting up in the morning is something else again. Every joint stiff, every bone ready to snap. He turns on the shower and stands under hot water until he begins to look like a six-foot prune. Then steps out and inspects himself in the mirror. Beautiful. Yellow, red, black, purple, blue.

"Just call me the Rainbow Kid," he tells Cleo.

He pads naked around the loft, reflecting that it might not be the Taj Mahal, but there's always plenty of heat and hot water.

The cat gets fresh water and a chunk of kosher salami. Cone has black coffee and a Camel. Because he has no intention of going into the office, he sees no point in shaving. Especially since his face is lumpy with welts, and that split lip wouldn't take kindly to a razor. So he pulls on a grungy costume of Jockey shorts, faded jeans, and a Stanley Kowalski T-shirt.

It's about nine-thirty, and he's settling down with another black coffee and another cigarette when Davenport calls.

"Taking a day off, sherlock?" the city dick says breezily. "I tried you at your office, but they said you're not coming in."

"Yeah, that's right. I think I've got the flu or something."

"Well, there's a lot of that going around these days. And you sure sound funny. Like you got a mouth full of marbles. Hey, what do you think about the excitement in your neighborhood last night? On your block, as a matter of fact."

"What excitement?"

"A car plowed into a restaurant. You didn't know about it?"

"Not a thing. What happened?"

"Just what I said: A new Pontiac Bonneville drives through the plate glass window of a restaurant. You didn't hear anything?"

"What time did this happen?"

"About two-thirty in the morning."

"I was asleep. Dead to the world."

"Sure," Davenport says. "Anyway, when they dug out the car, there was a stiff in the front seat. He was ID'd as Bernie Snodgrass. How do you like that for a moniker? Bernie had a rap sheet as long as your arm, so good riddance. Guess what killed him."

"The crash?"

"Nope," the NYPD man says cheerily. "A slug in the back of the head. Fired from maybe twenty or thirty feet away. There were some other bullet holes in the car and we recovered a slug from a three-five-seven Magnum. You pack a piece like that, don't you, Cone?"

"Yeah," Timothy says. "An S and W."

"I thought so," Davenport says. "Interesting. We've got

statements from witnesses who say they saw a second guy running away from the scene. I thought you'd like to know.''

"No skin off my ass,'' Cone says, "but thanks for telling me. Did you ID the car?''

"Now that *is* interesting. It's a company car, registered to Rauthaus Industries. They're on Wall Street. Ever hear of them?''

"Yeah, they make robots and industrial computers for assembly lines. A division of International Gronier, a conglomerate that owns half the world.''

"Well, Rauthaus Industries claims the Pontiac was stolen from their company garage on Cedar Street. They say they weren't even aware it was missing until we called them.''

"Uh-huh,'' Cone says, grinning at the phone. "There's a lot of that going around these days. Listen, will you do me a favor?''

"Will it cost me?''

"Nah. Just a phone call. You know the guy Harry who's handling the Jessie Scotto kill?''

"Yeah.''

"Could you find out if they picked up any prints in Scotto's apartment.''

"I doubt if they did, but I'll ask him.''

"Well, if they did, will you ask him to check them against Bernie Snodgrass'? You said he had a record.''

Silence. Then:

"You son of a bitch, Cone!'' Davenport yells at him. "You're holding out on me again, aren't you?''

"Why should I do that?'' Cone says mildly. "We're both working the same side of the street, aren't we?''

He hangs up softly.

He inspects the ancient, waist-high refrigerator, hoping it'll contain enough rations so he won't have to make a trip outside. But it's hopeless. There's some dried-out Havarti with dill, a chunk of moldy kielbasa, an opened tin of brisling sardines, and two cans of Heineken. That's about it. And there's that smelly parka in the garbage bag that has to be taken to the cleaners.

Groaning, he does what he has to do: Strips, cleans, assembles, and reloads his S&W Magnum, and straps it to his shin. Pulls on gray wool socks from L. L. Bean, and his scuffed yellow work shoes. Dons his cruddy raincoat and a sailors' knitted watch cap. Then, carrying the bagged parka, he sallies forth. Thank God the big freight elevator is working at that hour, and he doesn't have to pound down six floors.

Less than an hour later he's back in the loft with two twine-handled shopping bags. He's got a bottle of Italian brandy, a liter of vodka, a carton of Camels, a can of human-type tuna for Cleo, and some packages of frozen food: short ribs, spaghetti and meatballs, beef stew, and lasagna.

He gets everything stowed away, gives Cleo half the tuna, and changes the litter in the cat's pan. He starts to hunker down with a small vodka and resume reading one of his new books on artificial conception when there's a knock on the loft door: Samantha's signal—two short raps, pause, one more. Sighing, Cone goes to open up.

Sam starts to say, "Hello, asshole," but only gets as far as opening her mouth when she sees Timothy's face. "Oh, my God," she says. "That's what you call the flu?"

Inside, door locked, she examines him more closely. She reaches out to touch the bluish lump on his temple, but he winces away.

"Drunken brawl?" she asks.

He shrugs. "Just one of your ordinary, run-of-the-mill muggings. No big deal."

"I thought you sounded chopped last night. Why the hell didn't you tell me? I'd have come over. I don't suppose you have any Band-Aids or any other first aid supplies in this swamp."

"Will you stop trying to play Florence Nightingale?" he says crossly. "I'm okay. Just a little achy, that's all."

"Did you report it to the cops?"

"Of course not. You know what they'd say: 'Tough shit.'"

She stares at him, frowning. "You're not telling me the truth," she says finally.

"Shut up," he says roughly, "and have a vodka."

"At this hour?"

"Why not? It's noon somewhere in the world."

They sit at his table-desk, sipping their vodkas and water from jelly glasses. She opens her suede trench coat. She's wearing a black gabardine pants suit.

"You look okay," he tells her.

She ignores that fulsome compliment and inspects him narrowly. "Where did they hurt you?" she asks. "Besides your empty head. Ribs?"

He nods.

"Not the *cojones,* I hope!"

"No," he says, "the family jewels are safe and sound."

"What did they get?"

He shrugs again. "A couple of bucks. Maybe twenty. It really wasn't worth their time."

"When did this happen?"

"Hey," he says, "what's this—the third degree? I got mugged, lost a few dollars, and that's it. Just drop it—all right?"

"Christ, you're a pain in the ass."

"Did I ever deny it?"

They sit staring at each other with wary hostility.

"Thanks for coming to check up on me," he says grudgingly.

"You want off the Nu-Hope case?" she asks him.

"No," he says. "By tomorrow I'll be up to speed. I'll come into the office."

She nods, finishes her vodka, rises, and belts her trench coat. She stoops to scratch Cleo, who's been rubbing against her ankles. "You never let me do anything for you," she says in a low voice.

"Well, I'm about to ask you something now. You know that dinky little pistol you own. The nickel-plated job."

"Yes."

"Where is it?"

"Top drawer of my bedside table."

"Loaded?"

"Of course."

"Do me a favor, will you? Start carrying it in your pocket or handbag. Will you do that?"

"What for?"

"Just do it," he shouts.

"I can take care of myself," she says hotly. Then she softens. "Okay, if it'll make you feel better, I'll pack it."

"Yeah," he says, coming close to slide an arm across her shoulders, "it'll make me feel better. Give us a kiss, will you? If you can find an undamaged patch."

She kisses him softly on the cheek, then holds his arms.

"Take care. I'll call you tonight to see how you're doing."

"If a woman answers," he says, "hang up."

"Up yours," she says, grinning. And then she's gone.

He goes back to his reading, and finally figures out what ectogenesis is. It makes sense to him. They already have incubators that can keep premature kids alive. It seems reasonable to believe that eventually a laboratory womb could be developed in which an embryo might live and flourish until it reaches birth weight.

He puts the book aside and goes to his kitchen wall phone.

"Mr. Ernest Pingle," he says. "Timothy Cone of Haldering and Company calling."

"Just a moment, please."

The old man comes on almost immediately. "Hah!" he says. "And how is my favorite inwestigator?"

"Okay," Cone says. "And how are you, sir?"

"I wasn't listed on the obituary page this morning," Pingle says, "so I got up. You have something to tell me?"

"Not exactly, Mr. Pingle. But I've got a couple of questions. Maybe the answers would help my investigation."

"Of course. The questions?"

"Has your company ever done any business with Rauthaus Industries?"

Silence.

"Mr. Pingle? You're there?"

"Where else would I be? Why do you ask about Rauthaus?"

"Their name came up in connection with the Nu-Hope Clinic."

Pingle sighs. "Let me tell you, young man, those people at Rauthaus are nogoodniks. They are owned by International Gronier, who are double nogoodniks. And Mr. Leopold Dewers, who owns everything, is the biggest nogoodnik of them all. To answer your question, yes, we did business with Rauthaus Industries. Once. They are not nice people, Mr. Cone. We were lucky to get away with the fillings in our teeth. I am sorry to hear they are inwolved in the Nu-Hope deal."

"I'm not sure they are, Mr. Pingle. It's just one of several leads I'm working on. Their name came up."

"If they are inwolved, then I know the Nu-Hope business is definitely not for us. Tell me this, Mr. Cone: Is my son Lester mixed up with Rauthaus?"

"I don't know for sure."

"I think maybe I better have a little talk with that meshuggener."

"Please don't do that," Cone says hastily. "I have absolutely no hard evidence your son has contacts with Rauthaus. Give me a little more time before you do anything."

Quiet for a moment. "I'm thinking," Ernest Pingle says, "I'm thinking. All right, I'll give you more time. I'll say nothing to Lester. But if he *is* mixed up with those shtarkers, it would be with a man named Martin Gardow. You have that?"

"Martin Gardow? Yes, I'll remember."

"He is a nasty piece of goods. He does all the dirty work for Mr. D. That's Leopold Dewers. Martin Gardow is presentable, well-dressed, soft-spoken, but the man is a bum. That is my personal opinion, but you can tell anyone you like that I said it."

"I don't intend to tell anyone," Cone says, admiring the gaffer's feistiness, "but I'll keep the name in mind. Thank you for your help, Mr. Pingle."

"Don't be such a stranger. Maybe someday we'll go to lunch together and tear a herring."

"I'd like that," Cone says.

He never did think J. Roger Gibby engineered last night's assault. Nor does he believe Lester Pingle has the balls to order up a beating. But Martin Gardow has the resources and apparently the ruthlessness to apply a little physical persuasion to convince Cone to okay the Nu-Hope deal.

And that conclusion doesn't do a goddamn thing to help solve the big problem: What is going on at Nu-Hope to make the U.S. Government and International Gronier so frantic to pump money into a fertility clinic?

One of those wild, giddy November days in Manhattan . . . wind gusting, dying, gusting again . . . sun blaring, then swallowed by scummy clouds . . . spatters of rain . . . newspapers blown high . . . rumble of thunder from somewhere . . . and suddenly a blue sky . . . dust devils go bouncing . . . as men hang on to hats, women hang on to skirts, and all go bowling along, buffeted and spun.

Timothy Cone, leaning against the swirly day, fights his way down to John Street. He goes directly to the office of Sidney Apicella, who leaves off stroking his swollen nose to stare at Cone's face.

"Holy Christ," he says, "what happened to you?"

"Got caught in a revolving door. Listen, Sid, I know you've got a lot of contacts. Will you see if you can pick up any poop on a guy named Martin Gardow? He works for Rauthaus Industries.''

"Why should I do that?'' Apicella asks.

"Because you gave an okay on the Nu-Hope Clinic deal, and if it turns sour, you're going to look like an A-Number-One schlemiel.''

The CPA, who has anxiety attacks every hour on the hour, says, "You think it's going to turn sour?''

"I'm beginning to see the dark at the end of the tunnel. Check on Martin Gardow for me, Sid, and I'll say in my report how cooperative you were.''

"That's extortion,'' Apicella cries desperately.

"Of course,'' Cone says. "What else?''

He goes to his office. Maybe it's because he still feels the dull throbs of the beating or maybe it's the mixed-up day, but he's in a cantankerous mood and knows it. He feels he's being jerked around, doesn't like it, and resolves to do some jerking of his own.

He calls Nu-Hope and asks to speak to Dr. January. The doctor is so full of charm that Cone can hardly stand it. He tells January he wants to come up for another meeting "to clear up a few points.''

"Come right ahead,'' January says heartily. "We can always make time for you.''

Cone hangs up, wondering why he instinctively mistrusts cheerful people.

When he gets to East Seventy-first, he stands across the street a few minutes, just scoping the clinic. He's convinced that the answers to all his questions lie behind the handsome façade of those two townhouses. But the polished windows return his stare blankly, and he's left frustrated and growly.

Phoebe Trumball is in January's office, and Cone once again thinks of how physically similar the two doctors are. He brushes aside their queries about his battered face and says, "I read about Jessie Scotto in the paper.''

Immediately their faces congeal into suitable expressions of sorrow.

"A tragedy," January says. "What a city this is. A jungle."

"Just dreadful," Trumball says. "She was such a sweet girl. Quiet and shy."

"Yeah," Cone says. "Now two of your staff have died violently. I hope your other employees aren't spooked."

"Oh, no," January says. "Everyone is depressed, naturally, but things like that do happen in the city."

"Just coincidence," Trumball says. "The two deaths."

"Sure," Cone says. "But that's not what I came to talk about. I think I should visit your research labs. The ones behind the locked door. Just so I can complete my report."

"As I explained to you," Trumball says tartly, "it's a sterile lab. You would be required to strip, shower, change into a special lab uniform. It's a tedious process."

"I don't mind," Cone says.

"And then," Trumball goes on, "I'm afraid all you'd see is our research staff hunched over microscopes or taking blood samples from our experimental animals. Not very exciting."

"That's all right," Timothy persists.

"There's a legal problem involved too," January adds, frowning. "There's always a possibility of infection from our animals. We have liability insurance, of course, but it only covers our staff. I'm afraid it's just too much of a risk, Mr. Cone. For you and for us."

Cone understands that he's not going to get into that lab. "Okay," he says, "but why don't you tell me what you're working on in there?"

"Phoebe," he says to the other doctor, "that's your bailiwick. Can you give Mr. Cone a quick rundown?"

"Of course," she says crisply. "Basically, we're trying to refine optimum periods of ovulation. Especially as they relate to body temperature and hormone release. The goal is to maximize our pregnancy rate. It's a very tricky business. In the field of in vitro fertilization, we're trying to improve techniques using frozen sperm and eggs to bring the success percentage up to that of live.''

"When you fertilize in vitro," Cone says, "you produce more than one embryo?"

"Frequently. Especially if fertility drugs have been used. Then we select the embryo we believe is the strongest, for implantation in the host mother."

"And what happens to the other embryos? Down the sink?"

Dr. January stirs restlessly. "Not always," he says. "Some may be frozen. I hope you're not going to accuse us of abortion."

"Abortion? I never thought of it that way—although I suppose some people might."

"Yes," January says darkly, "some people do."

"What about ectogenesis?" Cone asks. "Doing any work on that? Or cloning?"

"Oh, my," Dr. Trumball says, almost mockingly, "you have been doing your homework, haven't you?"

"I've been reading some," Cone admits.

"Well, to answer your question, no, we are doing no work on ectogenesis or cloning. Although other people are."

"No money in it," Dr. January says, turning on the charm. "Besides, it's way in the future. All we're concerned with is helping women have healthy babies."

"So that's the extent of your research in the locked lab? Ovulation timing and in vitro fertilization with frozen sperm and eggs?"

"That's it," Dr. Phoebe Trumball says.

Cone remembers the children's rhyme: "Liar, liar, pants on fire." But he doesn't recite it.

He stands and thanks them for their time. Trumball conducts him down to the street. Then she returns to January's office and slumps into one of his directors' chairs.

"He suspects something," she says somberly.

"You think so?" January says, nervously gnawing at a thumbnail. "I thought he was just fishing."

"I don't think so. He seems to know just enough to be dangerous. I think we better call Gibby. Maybe he can take care of Cone."

"You really feel that's necessary?"

"I do. And when you speak to him, tell him about Cone's face. The man has been beaten up."

"So? What has that got to do with us?"

"Just tell Gibby about it," she says patiently. "It may mean something to him."

"If you say so. You know where I'd like to be right now?"

"Yes," she says, smiling. "We could take a long lunch hour, but call Professor Gibby first," she insists. "There's too much riding on this to let Cone upset things."

"You're right," he says. "It's my whole future."

"*Our* future," she says, looking at him queerly.

"Of course," he says hastily. "*Our* future."

Back in his office, Timothy puts his feet on his desk and tries to sort out his suspicions. Nearly an hour passes before he's interrupted by the phone. When he picks it up and says, "Yeah?" all he gets is a lot of static. He holds it away from his ear and finally the line clears.

"Yeah?" he says again.

"This is J. Roger Gibby. I'm sorry we have a bad connection, but I'm calling from my car."

"Your *car?*" Timothy says, amused. "Don't you have an office?"

"I do," Gibby says. "In Washington. I'd like to talk to you, Mr. Cone."

"In your car? Where are you—on the Long Island Expressway?"

"As a matter of fact, I'm parked right outside your office. I was hoping I might prevail upon you to drop down and chat for a few minutes."

"A lot simpler than your coming up here, huh? Okay."

He takes his time pulling on his raincoat and knitted cap. He also checks his ankle holster. When he gets down to the street, the black Cadillac de Ville is not hard to spot. The young bodyguard is lounging against the front fender, examining his fingernails.

"Nice to see you again," Cone says. "How're the folks?"

The giant doesn't respond, but politely opens the back door. The car is filled with the scent of cologne. The government man is as spiffily dressed as ever, wearing a fawn wideawake and a little sprig of greenery pinned to the lapel of his topcoat.

"Parsley?" Timothy asks.

"Pine," Gibby says, smiling. "Thank you for joining me." Then he examines Cone's face. "They did a job on you, didn't they?"

"They? Who's they?"

The other man sighs. "Could we stop playing games for a moment? I just wanted to assure you that I had nothing to do with the attack."

"Why should I believe that?"

"It's simply not my style."

"Is it your style to lean on my boss, Hiram Haldering, to get quick approval of the Nu-Hope Clinic deal?"

"Yes," Gibby says calmly. "Haldering is an ex-FBI man with very strong patriotic convictions. I attempted to present his government's position. But I did not have you assaulted."

"Never thought you did," Cone says. "You're not going to tell me what this is all about, are you?"

"No. I can't."

"So why did you want to talk to me?"

Gibby gently strokes his chin, as if he had once had a Vandyke.

"Mr. Cone," he says, "I think you're a very perspicacious man."

"Perspicacious? What does that mean?"

"Keen. Shrewd. I need your advice. You've met Doctor January and Doctor Trumball how many times—twice?"

"That's right."

"I was hoping you might give me your impressions."

"Why the hell should I?" Cone asks. Then, when Gibby looks startled, he adds: "Professor, I'm in the information business. If the outfit I work for can't use it, I trade it for something I want to know. What have you got to trade?"

Gibby draws a deep breath. "All right, Mr. Cone, how's this: The Nu-Hope Fertility Clinic is engaged in original biotechnological research that could—and I emphasize *could*—have a vital effect on the security of our country. I can tell you no more than that, except to say that what we're concerned with may sound like science fiction, but it is actually in the realm of the possible. Others, individuals, are interested in that research for personal gain. Other countries are interested because they wish to remain on the cutting edge of modern science. And that, I'm afraid, is all I have to trade. Is it enough?"

Cone ponders a moment. "Okay," he says finally. "If you want my take on January and Trumball, here it is: I think he's a charm boy. A strong puff of wind would blow him away. Not only is he ambitious, he's greedy. He wants all the goodies: money, power, and maybe a Nobel Prize. Doctor Trumball is the brains of that outfit. She knows exactly where she's going. Research is her shtick, and she couldn't care less about the perks."

Gibby is silent for a moment. "Thank you, Mr. Cone. What you've said reinforces my own feelings. My fears, I should say. I think I may have a problem there."

"Welcome to the club," Timothy says. "Can I go now?"

The government man gives him one of his sweet, slow smiles. "Of course. Do watch your back, Mr. Cone. The others are not nice people."

"So I've learned." Cone starts to climb out of the car, then turns back. "By the way, Professor, here's a freebie for you: January and Trumball are rubbing the bacon."

"Yes," Gibby says, expressionless, "I am aware of that."

They stare at each other silently, hearing all the noises of
the streets: the carousel city whirling to a tinkly tune.

Cone returns to his office and slumps in his swivel chair,
still wearing his raincoat and knitted cap. He's brooding on
the little that Gibby told him when Sid Apicella stops by.

"You coming or going?" he says.

"I don't know," Cone says, "and that's the truth."

"You asked me to find out about Martin Gardow."

"And?"

"Gardow's title is chief of special projects for Rauthaus
Industries, but he's really the hatchet man for International
Gronier, which owns Rauthaus. Gardow is a shark and
takes orders only from Mr. D. That's Leopold Devers, who
runs the whole shebang. Gardow has a nasty reputation. He
broke a strike at one of Gronier's factories. Three workmen
were killed and one was crippled for life. Gardow is also
reputed to be head of industrial espionage for Mr. D."

"Sounds like a real charmer."

"Oh, he is. Apparently he handles Gronier's political
payoffs and bribes, and is supposed to have a hefty slush
fund. All Mr. D. is interested in are results. Tim, this guy is
strictly bad news. What's his connection with the Nu-Hope
Clinic deal?"

"Maybe he wants to make a contribution to their sperm
bank," Cone says, and that's all he'll tell Apicella.

3

CONE GETS BACK to the loft that night with a small barbecued chicken and two chilled bottles of Löwenbräu dark.
He and Cleo share the chicken and he's about to get back to
his reading on artificial conception when there's a sharp
knock on his door. It's not Samantha's signal, and Cone
approaches the door warily, standing to one side.

"Yeah?" he calls.

"Davenport. Let us in, for Christ's sake. We're not
going to bust you."

Cone unlocks, unbolts, unchains the door. Neal and Nick
Galanis are standing there.

"How did you get in downstairs?" Cone wants to know.

"Your outside door has been jimmied."

"Again?" Cone says, sighing. "Second time this month.
Come on in."

"How do you like this joint?" Davenport asks Nick
Galanis. "Luxurious—no? That monster under the bathtub
is supposed to be a cat." He turns to Cone. "Aren't you
going to offer us a drink?"

"What will you have? I got beer, vodka, red wine, a little
brandy."

"Vodka for me. You, Nick?"

"I'll have wine," Galanis says. "I gotta get home. My
daughter's birthday party. If I miss that or turn up bombed,
I'm in deep shit."

They sit around the desk, the NYPD men still wearing their windbreakers and looking grim.

"Okay," Cone says, "what's the beef? You look like you're ready to roust me."

Davenport stares at him thoughtfully, unwrapping a stick of Juicy Fruit. "You're holding out on us again. Harry pulled some prints in Jessie Scotto's apartment. They belonged to Bernie Snodgrass, the punk who got killed a few doors down the block from where we're sitting. Now how did you know the prints would match?"

"I didn't *know,*" Cone says. "It was just a guess."

"Listen," Galanis says. "Is there any connection to Harold Besant's death? Was Snodgrass in on that, too?"

"Look," Cone says, "you're asking me questions I can't answer. If you want me to guess, I'll try. There probably is a connection. If Besant was scragged, Snodgrass was in on it. Him and his buddy."

"His buddy?" Davenport says. "The guy witnesses saw running away from the crashed Pontiac?"

Cone nods.

"What happened?" the city dick says. "You get bush-whacked?"

"Yeah," Cone says reluctantly. "I was suckered into coming down to the street. They jumped me and did a job."

"You get a make on the other guy?" Galanis demands.

"Snodgrass called him Sol. About five-ten, maybe one-eighty. Heavy through the chest and shoulders. Wearing a dark suit. A real thug. I've got the marks to prove it."

"Could you pick him out of a lineup?" Davenport asks.

"Sure," Cone says with more conviction than he feels. "Why don't you start with Snodgrass's pals. Maybe he and that Sol did time together. You'll find him."

The two cops stare at him, expressionless, then lean forward and top their jars.

"And that's all you're going to give us?" Davenport says. "A guy named Sol?"

Cone is silent a moment, sipping his brandy and doing

some fast thinking. He knows he's going to need help from these guys, and if he keeps stiffing them, they won't even return his calls.

"The way I figure it is this," he says finally. "Bernie Snodgrass and Sol were two hired hands. The kind of guys who'll take credit cards for a kill or a beating. But there's got to be a moneyman behind them—right? I have absolutely no hard evidence, but I'll give you a name: Martin Gardow. He's with an outfit called Rauthaus Industries. From what I hear, the guy's a villain, but a real handle-with-care case. I mean he's got a lot of money and political clout behind him."

Davenport pulls out a notebook and ballpoint pen. "Martin what?"

"Gardow. G-a-r-d-o-w."

"And what's his company?"

"Rauthaus Industries. They're on Wall Street."

"What's his connection with Besant and Scotto?" Galanis asks.

"Beats the hell out of me," Cone says, "and that's the truth. But Gardow has a heavy interest in this Nu-Hope Fertility Clinic I'm investigating. Exactly what, I don't know. But Besant and Scotto both worked there, and my guess is that Gardow arranged both their deaths."

"Why?" Galanis says.

"Maybe Besant was going to spill the beans," Cone says, rubbing his forehead. "Maybe he had some reports or papers or something. Maybe it was just because of what he knew. After they kill him they're afraid he may have told his girlfriend, so Jessie Scotto gets whacked, too. I know I'm blowing smoke, but it does make a crazy kind of sense. Something's going on in a locked research lab at Nu-Hope, and a lot of people are interested. Interested enough to kill to keep it a secret."

"And you have no idea what it is?" Davenport asks.

"No, not yet. But I'll find out."

"Sure you will," Davenport says, finishing his drink and

standing up. "And when you do, we'll be the first to know—right?"

"Absolutely," Cone says.

"When shrimp fly," Davenport says good-humoredly. "Okay, sherlock, we'll see what we can dig up on Sol and Martin Gardow. Thanks for the booze."

"Yeah," Galanis says. "Thanks." He stands and, unexpectedly, reaches to shake Cone's hand. "I knew that Besant suicide was a fake. It's been eating at me. Now we've got something to work on. Not much, but *something*. Keep in touch."

When they're gone, Timothy goes back to his books and reads about motile sperm fighting their brave way upstream to find a welcoming egg. Thinking of that, he's tempted to call Samantha Whatley, but resists. He has no desire for progeny. Still . . .

They're having an office party. Apicella's secretary is getting married, and the festivities have overflowed into the corridor. Sid has sprung for a few bottles of hard booze, mixers, colas, and platters of glutinous noshes hustled up from the local deli. The bride-to-be opens her presents with giggles and blushes.

Cone, who bought her a gross of Sheiks, stands in the hallway, nursing a plastic cup of warm vodka and listening to the sounds of joy. Samantha Whatley comes up to him, glowering.

"That was a nice, romantic gift you gave her," she says.

"What the hell," he says, "it's practical. If she doesn't want to use them, she can always fill them with water and drop them out the window. Bomb the pedestrians."

"You're nuts, you know that? Totally nuts."

"So what else is new?"

"I'll tell you what's new," she says. "Or old. The Nu-Hope Clinic case. Time's running out. H. H. gave us a week—remember?"

"Tell me about it," he says bitterly. "I'm moving on it. I really am. Things are beginning to come together."

She looks at him. "You're shitting me," she says.

"Yeah," he admits, "I am."

"Tim, why can't you tell me what you're up to? After all, I am your boss; I ought to know what the hell is going on."

"Sam, I'm spinning. It wouldn't do any good to explain what's going on. It's a fucking merry-go-round."

"If you'd tell me, maybe I could help. I do have a brain, you know."

"I know you do, but—"

Then other people crowd up to them and for almost ten minutes they're part of a laughing, chattering group. Finally the others drift away and Whatley and Cone are standing alone again.

"Another thing . . ." she says in a low voice. "You know how long it's been since we've been together?"

"Too long," he says, groaning. "Every time I sneeze, dust comes out my ears."

"Just how long do you expect me to wait?" she demands.

He gets pissed off. He can't stand to be leaned on.

"You're free, white, and twenty-one," he tells her.

She stares at him. "You really are an asshole. Who the hell but me would put up with your nasty moods?"

"Cleo," he says.

She can't help smiling, but moves away from him. He pours himself more warm vodka from Sid's bottle and carries it back to his office. That exchange with Samantha has shaken him more than she knows. She's right: What other woman would put up with his lousy disposition and cruddy habits?

But he can't waste any more time brooding about his personal happiness, or lack thereof. He's got a job to do.

He remembers a lecture on small-unit infantry tactics delivered by an old, grizzled colonel who had so much fruit salad on his chest that he listed to port. The problem posed was how to take a bald hill held by an enemy ensconced on the heights. No ravines, no natural cover, no artillery or air cover. What do you do?

"Go home," someone suggested.

"No," the colonel said, "you go up the hill and take it."

"We'd get our ass shot off," someone else said.

"Probably," the colonel said, smiling bleakly. "But what the fuck do you think they're paying you for?"

So, knowing what he is paid for, Timothy wonders how he can take that goddamn hill and keep his ass intact. He remembers what Gibby said about January and Trumball: "I think I may have a problem there."

With both doctors? Or with one? Maybe there's trouble in paradise.

He puts in a call to Victor January, but the doctor is in surgery and will get back to him as soon as possible. Cone waits patiently, sipping his drink and chain-smoking, wondering idly which will wear out first: heart, lungs, or liver.

"Hello there, Mr. Cone!" Dr. Victor January says, finally calling back. "What can we do for you today?"

"I was hoping we could have a talk."

"Of course. You want to come up here?"

"No," Cone says. "A private talk. Just you and me. I would prefer Doctor Trumball not be there."

Silence. Then, slowly: "I see. Well, I suppose that could be arranged. Any suggestions?"

"You know the Hotel Bedlington? Not too far from your place. Can you meet me there? Around three o'clock?"

"What's this about, Mr. Cone?"

"Just a meeting for our mutual benefit."

"All right," January says. "The Bedlington bar at three. I'll be there."

"If I were you," Cone says, "I wouldn't mention this to your partner or anyone else."

Again a long pause. "Very well," January says, "I won't."

After he hangs up, Cone sits back, satisfied. So far, so good. He's confident that January is going to take the bait.

He returns to Sid's office, but the party is over; no more free food or vodka. So he pulls on his newly cleaned parka and goes downstairs to have a cheeseburger and fries at a fast-food joint where he stands at a chest-high counter.

Then he cabs up to the Hotel Bedlington, and is pleased to find the cocktail lounge almost deserted. Just the bartender and one guy mumbling into his martini. Cone orders a draft Heineken and takes it to a corner table where he has a good view of the glass door leading to the lobby.

January shows up a few minutes after three. He looks around, spots Cone, and comes striding toward him with one of his sugarcane smiles. "Fink," Cone says—but not aloud.

"Hi!" January says brightly. "This was a splendid idea. I'm ready for a break."

"You'll have to order from the bar," Cone tells him. "There's no waiter working."

The doctor comes back with a tall drink. "Amaretto and soda," he declares. "Delicious and refreshing."

"Uh-huh," the Wall Street dick says, realizing that with very little effort he could learn to loathe this man.

"Cheers," January says, then sips his drink and flaps his lips appreciatively. "Good, good, good! You sounded very mysterious on the phone, Mr. Cone."

"Did I?" Timothy says. "Not much mystery about it. I believe in putting my cards on the table. That's okay with you?"

"Of course. Everything up-front."

"Sure. Well, here's the way I figure it: If Haldering gives the green light, Pingle Enterprises will work the deal. They'll structure it as a public or private limited partnership, or maybe as a franchise setup, or a public stock offering. However they do it, there's going to be a lot of bucks involved, and you'll come out of it a rich man."

"Not me," January says, smiling, "the clinic."

"But you *are* the Nu-Hope Fertility Clinic, aren't you? I mean you own the whole kit and caboodle. Right now,

here's how things stand: Our legal and accounting depart-
ments have given go-aheads. The final report has to come
from me. I can turn thumbs up or down.''

''Well, I certainly hope you'll give us your approval,''
the doctor says warmly. ''We've done everything we can to
cooperate with your investigation.''

''Maybe not everything,'' Cone says, staring at the other
man. ''Like that locked research laboratory you won't let
me see. I wouldn't like to insist that we bring in an independent team of scientists to see exactly what you're doing in
there.''

January drains his drink, rises abruptly, goes to the bar,
and returns with a refill.

''Thirsty,'' he says. ''A difficult morning in surgery.
Now then, why should an independent scientific investigation be necessary?''

''It may not be,'' the Wall Street dick says. ''Not if I file
a favorable report.''

They look at each other, eyeballs locked.

''How much?'' January says hoarsely.

Now it's Cone's turn to make a trip to the bar for a refill.
He takes his time, chats a moment with the bartender, letting the doctor sweat. Then he goes back to the table.

''How much?'' January repeats.

''I figure if the deal goes through, you're going to end up
a multimillionaire. It only seems right and decent that I
should get a little piece of the pie. To guarantee my goodwill, you understand.''

''How much?'' the doctor says for the third time.

''Oh,'' Cone says, waving a hand, ''I figure fifty thousand is a reasonable fee.''

January tries to hide his shock but doesn't succeed. The
hand that hoists his Amaretto and soda is trembling and
some of the drink spills down his chin. He wipes it away
with a cocktail napkin.

''That's ridiculous,'' he says, not looking at Cone.

''Is it? Doesn't seem so to me. I reckon I'm in the catbird

seat. If I say go, it's go. So fifty grand doesn't seem like such a big chunk of cash.''

When he planned this scenario, Cone figured this was the turning point. If January told him to go screw himself or stalked out in a snit, then Cone's house of cards would collapse with a crash that would splinter his femurs. In addition, if the doctor went to Haldering, screaming extortion, Cone would find himself out on the street. And then who would change Cleo's litter box?

But January doesn't react with anger, outrage, or even surprise. Instead, he lifts his glass a bit and replaces it on the table, several times, making a chain of interlocking damp rings.

"Fifty thousand," he says reflectively. "A lot of money."

"Not really. Not when you think of what's at stake."

January raises his eyes to look at Cone directly. "I didn't think you were that kind of a man."

"What kind is that? You're looking out for Number One, aren't you? So am I. What's so terrible about it?"

"I can't give you an answer right now."

"Of course you can't. Didn't expect you to. Just think about it awhile. Remember what I said about calling in outside MDs to investigate your research lab. And figure what you've got to gain and what you've got to lose. You can read a balance sheet as easily as you read a temperature chart. The one problem we've got is that my boss wants my report in a couple of days."

Victor January drains his drink, stands. He reaches for his wallet, but Cone holds up a palm.

"No, no," he says. "I'll take care of the tab."

January gives him a thin smile. "Thank you. I'll let you know tomorrow. About your, ah, proposition. Will that be satisfactory?"

"Sure," Cone says. "I'm as anxious to see Nu-Hope work this deal as you are."

"That I doubt," January says.

Cone watches him leave. Then he sits there, sipping the remainder of his beer. He knows the risk he's running. He's charging up that hill like a maniac, screaming and firing at anything that moves. There's just a small chance he might gain the summit, dazed, shaken, look around at the carnage and say, "Who needs the fucking hill?"

A sodden morning, with the broken skylight dripping onto the linoleum floor of the loft. Cone puts a battered saucepan under the leak, and Cleo pads over to lap at the collected rain.

"Crazy cat," Cone says grumpily.

At the office he sits at his desk, wondering if the actors in his script are going to play the roles he's assigned them. Just to kill time, he fiddles his swindle sheet, doubling all his expenses. He knows Samantha Whatley will halve them. It's a game.

His phone rings a little after ten A.M. Being a superstitious man, he crosses his fingers before he picks it up.

"Yeah?" he says.

A woman's voice, chirpy: "Mr. Timothy Cone?"

"That's right."

"Just a moment, sir. Mr. Martin Gardow calling."

Cone smiles coldly at the phone. Bingo!

"Cone?"

"Yep."

"Martin Gardow here. I think we better have a talk."

"Sure," Cone says. "Where and when?"

"Eleven o'clock at the South Street Seaport. You can make it?"

"I'll make it. How will I recognize you?"

"I'll recognize *you*," Gardow says. "There's a shop that sells nautical stuff. It's got a big tin whale over the entrance."

"I'll find it."

"Eleven o'clock," Gardow says. "Be there."

Slam!

Timothy Cone is happy. "My fondest dreams are coming true," he sings aloud to the peeling walls, and checks the short-barreled Magnum in his ankle holster.

He decides to be on time, to prove his sincerity. The drizzle has dwindled to a freezing mist. By the time he arrives at the Seaport, his parka and leather cap are pearled, and his feet feel like clumps. A fog hangs over the river, and the few tourists who have braved the lousy day look shrunken and sour.

He finds the shop that sells marine artifacts. He's hardly taken two steps inside when a thick, stumpy guy shoves in front of him. He's wearing a tweed topcoat, beaded with rain, and a green felt fedora with a sprig of feathers in the band. His face is meaty, but there's nothing soft about his eyes.

"Cone?" he says.

"That's right. You Martin Gardow?"

"Yes. The rain bother you?"

"Not so much."

"Good. Let's take a walk."

The Wall Street dick doesn't like that. Inside, he's relatively safe. Out on an almost deserted street, anything could happen. Like a long gun trained on him from a parked car. But he figures he'll get nowhere being timid with this hardnose.

They stroll along the waterfront, the river swathed with fog, tugs hooting. It's real graveyard weather, with a damp cold that eats into bones and promises death.

"Just what the fuck do you think you're doing?" Martin Gardow asks quietly.

"Trying to scorch your ass a little," Cone says. "I thought that was obvious."

"Fifty thousand?" Gardow says. "Are you really that greedy?"

"Oh-ho," Cone says, knowing now that he guessed right. "January told you, did he? Nah, I'm not greedy. But there's so much bread involved here, I thought I'd pick me up some crumbs.''

"I don't think you're stupid. But you're costing me more time than you're worth. Do you realize how *small* you are? Do you know what you're up against? You're a fly, Mr. Cone. You keep making trouble, you're going to get swatted.''

"Maybe," Cone admits. "You tried it once, didn't you? And now Bernie Snodgrass is pushing up daisies, and the buttons are looking for his pal Sol. Maybe they'll find him and crack him. Worried about that, Mr. Gardow?"

"I don't know what you're talking about."

"Sure you do," Cone says.

Then, infuriated by Gardow's calm confidence, the Wall Street dick suddenly plucks the little bunch of feathers from the man's hat band and tosses it over the railing into the East River.

"I hate those things," he says.

Gardow glances a moment at his bright feathers floating away on the scummy tide, then turns to stare at Cone.

"You're not long for this world," he says.

"I know. None of us are."

They're facing each other now, and Gardow's blue eyes are sparking. Timothy thinks the guy is going to get physical. He can see it in the flushed skin, bunched shoulders, the fast pump of the big chest. But gradually Gardow gets control of himself. When he speaks, his voice is as toneless as ever.

"I think it's time to lower the boom. You turned down Lester Pingle's offer of ten grand. Then suddenly you brace January for fifty. Did you learn something? I'm betting you didn't. I think you worked January to get to me. A nice move—but not too smart. All right, now you know: I've got Lester Pingle and Victor January by the balls. So? What are you going to do about it?"

"Blow the whistle on the Nu-Hope deal," Cone says, dreading what's coming next. "What else?"

"I'll tell you what else," Gardow says. "I don't know what the relationship is between you and your boss Samantha Whatley, and I couldn't care less. All I know is that when those two bandits suckered you down to the street at two in the morning, they did it by telling you Whatley was in trouble. That's got to tell me something—right? She's *your* short hair, isn't she, Mr. Cone? And that's my leverage."

"You prick," Cone says.

"You know what happened to Jessie Scotto. Want to see Samantha Whatley with her tits cut off? Think about it. I'll give you two days. Forty-eight hours. If I haven't heard that you've okayed the Nu-Hope deal by then, we go after your friend."

"You're dead," Timothy Cone says. "As of now, you're dead."

"I don't think so," Gardow says with his mirthless smile. "As my boss says, every man has his price. I think I've discovered yours, and it isn't money. As a matter of fact, you're not going to get fifty thousand out of this deal, or even ten. You're getting Samantha Whatley. Two days, Mr. Cone. Nice to have met you."

He tips his hat with an ironic little gesture, turns, walks slowly away through the thickening mist. I could drop to one knee, Cone thinks, pull my iron, and put six between those thick shoulders.

He stands trembling, fighting down the hot anger. He doesn't doubt for a second that Gardow is capable of doing exactly what he threatens. But wasting the guy would solve nothing. His boss, the legendary Mr. D., would just come up with another Martin Gardow. And the whirligig will keep spinning.

Cone's hands are shaking so badly that it takes three matches to get his Camel lighted. And then, after two drags, the damned thing is snuffed out by moisture dripping from the beak of his black leather cap. He tosses the wet cigarette away and plods westward. He knows what he's got to do.

In the lobby of Pingle's office building Cone takes off his parka and leather cap and shakes them vigorously, spattering the marble tile with rain. The maintenance man, who's pushing a big mop back and forth to keep the floor dry, looks at him and says, "Thanks a lot."

"Listen, if it wasn't for shlubs like me, you wouldn't have a job. I mean, we muck up your floor so you can clean it. Then you've got a job—right?"

"That's one way of looking at it," the guy says.

"It's the only way," Cone assures him, and takes the elevator up to the eighth floor. "Timothy Cone," he says to the receptionist. "To see Mr. Ernest Pingle . . ."

"Just a moment, sir."

She mutters into a phone. Cone waits patiently. In a few minutes an elderly lady comes out, leaning on a cane. She's got a man's pocket watch pinned to the bosom of her black dress. She gives Cone a suspicious, angry stare.

"He's having his lunch," she says.

"I'll wait."

"No," she says grudgingly, "come on in."

She conducts him, hobbling on her stick, down a long corridor. Throws open a door.

"You want a glass tea?" she asks. "Coffee?"

"No," he says. "But thank you."

Ernest Pingle is propped behind an old oak desk with a glass of tea before him and an opened tin of English biscuits. There's an extra armchair in the tiny room and an old-fashioned oak filing cabinet. A bentwood coat tree. A brass wastebasket. And that's about it.

"This place is almost as small as my office," Cone says, looking around. "I thought you Wall Street types lived high off the hog."

Ernest Pingle shrugs. "I've got a telephone. What more do I need? How are you, Mr. Cone?"

"Damp, but I'm surviving," Timothy says, hanging his wet parka and cap on the coat tree. "You okay?"

"Rheumatism," the old man says. "In this weather, it

acts up. Which is why I'm not standing to greet you. But I would like to shake your hand.''

Cone reaches across the desk, then slumps into the armchair alongside the desk.

"Tea?" Pingle asks. "Maybe coffee?"

"No, thanks. Your secretary asked me."

"Mrs. Scherer. She's been with me almost fifty years. Would you believe?"

"Yeah, I'd believe."

"At least have a biscuit," the old man says, shoving the tin toward him. "They're wery good."

Cone inspects the contents, then selects a swirled round with a dot of chocolate in the center.

"A wise choice," Pingle says, nodding. "You've got something to tell me, Mr. Cone?"

"Something to tell you," Cone says, "and something to ask you. You've treated me square and I've got to level with you. Drop the Nu-Hope Clinic deal."

"It's not for Pingle Enterprises?"

"Or anyone else. But a lot of very strange people are interested in it. My advice is to bail out. But I've got to admit I can't give you any logical reasons. Except that I think it stinks."

"I agree," Ernest Pingle says equably. "I felt in my gut from the start that it was not for us. So I'll call Nu-Hope and cancel the deal, and I'll call Haldering and tell him to end the inwestigation."

"No," Cone says quickly. "Please don't do that. Give me another one or two days before you pull the plug. I think I'll have it wrapped up by then."

Pingle looks at him curiously. "One or two days? So why are you telling me now I should cancel?"

"Because I think my boss is under pressure and might give you a go-ahead without waiting for my report. Don't listen to him, Mr. Pingle. It's a sour deal."

The other man nods. "I'd offer you a bonus," he says, "but I know you wouldn't accept it."

"You're right; I wouldn't."

"See!" the old man says gleefully. "I know people. The first time I met you I said to myself, 'There's a man I can trust.' You know why I said that?"

"Because you offered me a kiss then, and I turned you down."

"No, that wasn't it. Maybe you turned me down because you were owned by someone else. But you thanked me for that little bit of schnapps I gave you. I said to myself that a man so polite can't be a thief."

"Don't be so sure," Cone says. "The most successful con men are the most courteous."

The old man shakes his big head. "Not you," he says. "I *know*. All right, I kill the Nu-Hope deal, but not for a couple of days. You'll let me know when I can move?"

"I'll let you know."

"Meanwhile, what about my son Lester? He's inwolved in this?"

"Up to his pipik."

"With that shtarker Martin Gardow?"

"Yes," Cone says. "Gardow has him on a string."

"Lester is in danger? Physical danger?"

Cone ponders a moment. "He may be," he says finally, "but the chances are small. I think it's worth the risk. I'm hoping to slice Gardow off at the knees before he can spring, and then your son will be home free. Mr. Pingle, I hate to give advice to anyone as smart as you, but why don't you read the riot act to your son? Cut him down to size. Then bail him out of his money troubles and put him on an allowance. Tell him and the wife to straighten up and fly right. If they haven't got themselves squared away in, say, a year, then kick them out of the nest."

"Wery good adwice," Ernest Pingle says sadly. "His mother would kill me, but sometimes it's necessary to be cruel to be kind."

Cone nods, rises, struggles into his damp parka. "That's it," he says. "I saw my duty and I done it. Thanks for the cookie."

"Biscuit," the old man says, flashing his dentures. "The English call them biscuits."

"Whatever," Cone says. "It was good."

Timothy reaches across the desk to shake that unexpectedly sturdy paw.

"Are you married, Mr. Cone?" Pingle asks.

"No."

"Would you like to meet a wery nice girl?"

"No," Cone says, "thanks. I already know a nice girl."

"God bless her!" Ernest Pingle cries.

He decides not to go back to the office. He doesn't want to bump into Hiram Haldering just yet and he's afraid that if he sees Sam, he'll lose his brio and, remembering Martin Gardow's threats, insist that she take off immediately for Hong Kong, or at least go visit her parents in Idaho. Then she'll want to know why he wants her out of town and, if Cone explains, she'll be outraged and claim she is completely capable of taking care of herself.

Cone doesn't need that kind of hassle. He decides his best bet is to stay the course, do what he's doing, and eliminate the danger before telling Samantha she might be in danger. If he fails, there will be time enough for damage control.

It's impossible to get a cab, and all the buses are jammed with damp mobs that he knows will be smelling of mothballs. So he walks all the way back to his loft, cursing the wet, the gloom, and especially Martin Gardow. But not forgetting to stop at neighborhood stores to pick up a smoked chub for Cleo, a package of frozen spaghetti and meatballs for himself, and a bottle of Korbel brandy to chase the chill.

In the warm loft, he tosses the chub to Cleo and fixes his own dinner. When he's finished, he decides on a short nap. Cleo comes padding over to fit into the bend of his knees, and the two of them fall asleep.

It's almost ten P.M. when he wakes up and settles down with one of his new books on artificial conception, still seeking a clue to what's going on in that sealed research laboratory at the Nu-Hope Clinic. He sticks with it, trying to understand the techniques involved.

He's demolished a half pack of Camels and is on his second brandy when he reads a long footnote in print so small he has to play the book like a trombone, moving the page back and forth until the type comes into focus. Then he reads it again.

He looks up blinking. He thinks he's got it. It explains why the U.S. Government is interested. And why Leopold Devers, the redoubtable Mr. D. of International Gronier, would order Martin Gardow to get a lock on the research.

Timothy stares at Cleo, who is sitting primly on his desk, paws together, regarding him with cold, glittery eyes.

"Holy Christ!" Cone says to the cat.

He thinks it through carefully. If he calls Phoebe Trumball at night and demands to see her, she's going to be wary about asking him up to her place. Or even venturing out after dark to meet him at a bar. And he doesn't want to brace her in public; this has got to be a one-on-one in private.

Also, if he calls in the evening, there's always the chance January will be with her. Cone has no desire to take on the two of them together; they'll draw too much strength from each other.

So he waits until morning and calls the clinic around seven-thirty, asking when they expect Dr. Phoebe Trumball to arrive. He's told she usually checks in at nine o'clock. He thanks them, says he'll call back. But instead, he calls her home.

"Hello?" she says.

"Doctor Trumball? Good morning. This is Timothy Cone."

A short pause. "My," she says, "you *are* an early riser."

"Yeah," he says, "sometimes. Listen, something very important has come up. I was hoping you'd be willing to talk to me this morning. Not at the clinic; it can't be there."

"What is this about, Mr. Cone? If it's the Pingle deal, then I think Doctor January should be present."

"No, it's about that research you're doing. I really think we should have a private talk."

"Goodness," she says with a nervous laugh, "you sound very mysterious."

"Just give me a half hour," he persists. "And then, if I'm not making sense, tell me to get lost and I'll go. Okay?"

"Well, all right," she says finally. "How soon can you be here?"

"Twenty minutes," he says happily.

There are a lot of empty cabs going uptown after dumping their fares on Wall Street, so Cone has no trouble getting a hack. He spends the trip rehearsing what he's going to say. He decides to come on hard, throw it all at her before she can get her defense organized.

She's wearing a black wool jumpsuit. Zippered and form-fitting. He's never seen her without either a lab coat or street coat before, and he's surprised at the willowy strength of her body.

She takes his parka, but offers no coffee or anything else.

"Now then, Mr. Cone," she says, all business. "What's this all about?"

He's sitting in an uncomfortable, linen-covered armchair, and he hunches forward, elbows on knees, hands clasped.

"The deal with Pingle Enterprises is dead," he says, looking directly at her. "I killed it. I told Ernest Pingle yesterday, and he agreed to pull out."

It takes a moment for that to sink in, and it really rocks her. Then she gets indignant.

"But *why*? What gives you the right to wreck our plans? Haven't we cooperated with you every step of the way? Why on earth would you turn us down?"

"Well, let me talk awhile, doctor. Most of it is guess-work, but it fits the facts I know.

"First of all, I think I've found out what you're doing in that locked research laboratory of yours. It's okay by me. If you're not doing it, someone else is or will be. But it's a long, expensive project. I figure you might have applied for a federal grant. Instead, Gibby shows up, representing a government agency that funds scientific research. Mostly on the sly. How am I doing so far?''

"I'm listening," she says stonily.

"Gibby explains that Uncle Sam is interested in your project, but there's *no* way a grant can be made. The media might get hold of it and there'd be political hell to pay. But Gibby suggests you could get the money you need for research by going to a venture capital outfit like Pingle Enterprises. It could be structured as a limited partnership or franchise, but the government would guarantee that Nu-Hope's expansion would be oversubscribed through a lot of dummy investors who would be shoveling in the taxpayers' money. That makes sense, doesn't it?''

She doesn't answer.

"I've got no objections to that scam," Cone says, figuring he's on a roll. "If that's all there was to the deal, I'd have okayed it. If the U.S. Government wants to play cute, it's no skin off my nose. But then two people got murdered, and the whole thing went sour."

She stares at him, and he believes she is genuinely bewildered.

"Two murders? What are you talking about?"

"Harold Besant and Jessie Scotto. They got dusted because your playmate, Doctor January, is a very ambitious, very greedy man—and you know it. The deal suggested by Gibby wasn't good enough. If the government funded your research, it wouldn't put any bucks in January's pocket, so he engineered another deal. A sellout I don't think you know a thing about."

"You're lying!" she says angrily. "He wouldn't do anything like that."

"Sure he would," Cone says. "For enough money and fame. He makes contact with a guy named Martin Gardow, who's the hit man for an outfit called Rauthaus Industries, which, in turn, is owned by International Gronier. The top man at Gronier is Leopold Devers, known as Mr. D., who, from what I hear, makes Attila the Hun look like a Boy Scout."

"You can't prove any of this!" she says furiously.

"The only thing I can't prove is how January and Martin Gardow got together. Maybe your partner approached Gardow. Maybe you've got a snitch in your lab who tipped off International Gronier to what's going on, and Gardow was handed the assignment. However they got together, Mr. D. and Gardow now own January, lock, stock, and test tube. That connection I *can* prove. A couple of days ago I met with January in private, and suggested he pay me fifty thousand to okay the deal with Pingle Enterprises. January said he'd think it over. The very next day I get a call from Martin Gardow, who's yelling at me for holding him up for fifty big ones. Is that proof enough for you?"

She doesn't want to believe, but Cone can see she's beginning to. He decides he never could have convinced her so quickly if she didn't already have some secret doubts about January.

Cone is silent, giving her time to absorb the shock. They're sitting there, staring at each other, when a phone in the next room rings.

"Let it go," Phoebe says dully. "It's probably the clinic wondering where I am. Would you like some coffee? I think I better have something."

"Sure," Cone says, "that would be nice. Black, please."

While she's in the kitchen, he looks around her trim living room and spots a couple of ashtrays, so he figures it's okay to smoke. He lights up a Camel, inhaling gratefully. He's satisfied with the way it's going—so far. The crunch will come when he leans on her.

She returns with a tray loaded with a Chemex of coffee, cups, saucers, packets of Sweet 'n Low.

"There's more, isn't there?" she asks, pouring.

Cone nods. "The murders. Harold Besant's death was a
setup. Someone sat beside him in the car, put a gun to his
head, and blew his brains out. Made it look like Besant
committed suicide. The killer placed the gun as if it had
fallen out of Besant's right hand, but the police learned later
Besant was left-handed."

She shudders, takes a gulp of her coffee.

"Jessie Scotto's death was an obvious homicide," he
goes on. "Very brutal, very nasty. The murderer was looking for something he thought she had, or was trying to get
her to talk. The cops found fingerprints belonging to a punk
who worked for Martin Gardow, your playmate's pal."

"Will you stop calling him my playmate," she says
furiously. "It's disgusting and I resent it."

"Okay," Cone says equably, "I won't call him that
again. But there's hard evidence tying Gardow and his
thugs to Jessie Scotto's murder."

"Why are you telling me all this? What do you *want?*"

"I want to hang Martin Gardow up to dry. I want to get
that villain off the streets. But I need a motive. Why did
Gardow kill Besant and Scotto? I think you can guess, and I
was hoping you'd tell me. Harold Besant worked in your
research lab. You saw him every day. I figure he knew
exactly what was going on, and it bothered him. He was
ready to go public. Did Besant have access to your lab
records?"

"Of course."

"Is anything missing?"

"Not to my knowledge."

"Do you have a copier in the lab?"

"Yes."

"So it's possible he could have made a complete record
of what's going on in there?"

"Yes, it's possible. But we trust our staff. We don't
search them every night when they leave."

"Maybe you should. Was Harold Besant acting strangely
in the weeks before he died?"

"Well, he was depressed. Everyone noticed it."

"Did he ever object to the work you're doing?"

"He never said anything about it to me."

"Did he talk to Doctor January shortly before he died? Did they have any private meetings?"

She finishes her coffee, and when she sets the cup down, it rattles against the saucer.

"He might have," she says cautiously. "But I wouldn't have any idea what they talked about."

"Uh-huh," Cone says, knowing she's lying. "Did Besant ever threaten to quit?"

"He seemed, ah, dissatisfied," she says vaguely.

"Doctor Trumball," Cone says, "it's possible, just possible, you may be required to testify about these matters under oath. I think you're holding out on me. I think you're remembering a lot of things. Why don't you think of yourself, your professional career, and tell—"

Just then the outside door buzzer sounds, four short, angry bursts. Phoebe is startled.

"That's Victor's ring," she says confusedly. "I'll have to let him in."

"Sure," Cone says, rising. "You do that."

January comes in fast. "Darling," he says worriedly, "is everything all—" Then he sees Cone. "Oh," January says, trying to twist his face into a smile. "I didn't know you had a guest."

"Doctor Trumball and I have been having a little discussion," Cone says.

The three stand in a tense triangle.

"A discussion?" January says. "About Nu-Hope?"

"Mostly about you," Cone says. "Your connection with Martin Gardow. How deeply you're involved in the murders of Harold Besant and Jessie Scotto. That's what we've been discussing. Stuff like that."

Suddenly, unexpectedly, Victor January falls into a martial-arts crouch. Hands clenched into fists. Arms extended.

Shoulders hunched. His pale face is frozen. He shuffles toward Cone. "Hah!" he shouts.

The Wall Street dick stoops swiftly, draws his Magnum from the ankle holster, straightens, and aims casually.

"Hah yourself," he says to January. "You pull that karate shit with me and I'll pop your kneecaps. You'll spend the rest of your life wheeling around on skateboards. You want that? Or maybe I'll go for the cajones, and you'll be singing soprano in the shower. Come on, try me. At this range I can't miss."

The doctor glares at him, then melts. His arms fall to his sides. Fists open. He stands slumped. His face sags, mouth partly open. All his charm is gone. He looks spectral, leached out.

"Now behave yourself," Cone says. "I know what you're doing in that locked lab. So you can wave goodbye to the Pingle deal. To Gardow and his dirty bucks. To the Nobel Prize and TV talk shows and all that crap. Do your job, Doctor January. Help women have babies and be satisfied with that. A tycoon you ain't, and never will be."

"Oh, darling, darling!" Phoebe Trumball cries. She moves to the demolished man, embraces him. He puts his head down on her shoulder.

Cone hears sobs, but who is weeping, or if both are, he cannot tell. He slips his iron back into the holster, finds his parka and cap, and heads for the door. He knows he's gone as far as he can go with those two simples. But it was worth the try.

He turns at the door to look back. They're still hugging. Phoebe Trumball is murmuring, stroking Victor January's hair.

She's in love with the guy and won't squeal.

That's okay. Cone can understand that.

He spends the afternoon in his office, snarling at everyone who comes by, including Sam. Around one o'clock he calls down for a cheeseburger, fries, and two cans of cold Bud.

Meanwhile, he's trying to devise a way to slip the blocks to Martin Gardow, that monster.

Cone knows he'll never get anywhere trying to pry testimony from Drs. January and Trumball. At the moment, those two schlumphs are probably making nice-nice and talking about how they can get out of the mess they are in with their asses unscarred.

Nor can Cone expect any assistance from J. Roger Gibby. The government man will never cooperate on any plan that might attract media attention to Uncle Sam's interest in a scientific research project that would bemuse half the nation and scarify the other half.

No, the only possibility is to use Martin Gardow's cockiness to demolish him. Timothy Cone has a few ideas on how that might be done. But he's got time working against him, Sam to protect, and his own fury to contain. One of his imagined solutions is to find Gardow, blast the fucker, and wait patiently for the blues to arrive and take him away.

He leaves the office a little after five o'clock, still seething, and is only a few feet from Broadway when a short beep from a car horn makes him look up. It's the city's dusty blue Plymouth, illegally parked, with Detectives Davenport and Galanis in the front seat. Davenport waves him over. Cone climbs into the back.

"What's up?" he says.

"My cock," Davenport says. "Watching all the young ginch stroll by." He turns sideways in the front passenger seat so he can talk to Cone. "We picked up that pal of Bernie Snodgrass. Only his name is Sal, not Sol. Salvador Guiterrez, a real sweetheart with a sheet as long as your schlong. Nice stuff, like attempted rape, assault with a deadly weapon, battery, and so forth and so on. And would you believe he's never spent a day in the slammer?"

"I believe it," Cone says. "Where is he now?"

"He walked," Nick Galanis says gloomily. "What could we hold him for?"

"Assault," Cone says. "I can ID him."

"Big deal," Galanis says. "His word against yours. And he'll come up with four witnesses who'll swear that at the time of the alleged incident, Salvador Guiterrez was in Bayonne, New Jersey, eating scungilli. It's no use, Cone. The sonofabitch knows we've got nothing on him."

"Did you run a trace on Martin Gardow?"

"Oh, yeah," Davenport says, unwrapping a fresh stick of Juicy Fruit. "He's everything you said, and more. If he was whacked, they'd narrow the list of suspects to about a thousand."

"And I'd be one of them," Cone says. "I had a meet with the guy."

Both city detectives snap their heads around to stare at him.

"About what?" Davenport demands.

"About the Nu-Hope Fertility Clinic. I told him I wanted fifty grand to okay the deal. He said I'd either okay it without the loot or he'd cut off my girlfriend's tits. Isn't that lovely?"

"Beautiful," Galanis says bitterly. "That's what happened to Jessie Scotto. You think Gardow was behind that?"

"Had to be. He bankrolled it, and Snodgrass and Guiterrez did the job. That's why Sal is hanging tough. He knows he's got money for the legal eagles."

"So?" Davenport says. "Where do we go from here?"

"I got an idea," Cone says. "A long shot, but it might just work."

"Yeah?" Galanis says hopefully. "Let's hear it."

Cone explains what he has in mind, and the two cops listen intently. When he finishes, they look at each other.

"We could set it up," Davenport says slowly. "I know a great tech. It could be done. But if it turns sour, you know what's going to happen to you, don't you?"

"Oh, yeah," Cone says, "I know. You want to fly it?"

"Why not?" Galanis says savagely. "It's got a chance."

"Okay," Davenport says.

So they talk ways and means, set up a schedule, look for loopholes and close them. When Cone gets out of the car, they all shake hands.

He walks home and feeds himself and Cleo. He gives the cat fresh water and changes the litter. He does some laundry in the kitchen sink, smokes half a pack of Camels, and drinks more Popov than he should. Meanwhile he's muttering to himself, rehearsing the part he's going to play the next day.

"Academy Award, kiddo," he tells Cleo. "I'm going to get an Oscar for this one."

He sleeps badly that night: dreams haunted with images of a war he thought he had forgotten. Once he is awakened by his own groans, to find Cleo bending over him, almost nose to nose, mewling sadly.

"Beat it," Cone says, pushing the cat away.

He tries to get back to sleep again, but it doesn't work. He finally gives up and waits for dawn, lying supine on that scruffy mattress on the floor, staring up at his broken skylight and wondering what it's all about. It's that kind of night.

He's an hour late getting to work in the morning, which is bad even for him. But he has to fight fears gnawing at him like the leeches in Nam. A terrible lassitude saps his resolve, and he beats it only by thinking of Sam and what might happen to her if he fails.

His first call is to Ernest Pingle.

"Mr. Pingle," he says, "you can pull the plug now. The Nu-Hope deal is dead."

"Wery good," the old man says. "I'll call Haldering and tell him to stop the inwestigation and send me a bill."

"It would help me," Cone says, "if you just told him you decided to withdraw from the deal without giving him any reason."

"Of course," Pingle says. "What else? Are you all right, my young friend? You sound wery tight."

"Just winding this thing up. With luck, it'll be finished today."

"Is there anything I can do to help?"

"No, thank you," Cone says gratefully. "Did you talk to your son?"

"I talked," Ernest Pingle says. "To him *and* his wife. I think maybe they'll behave."

"I think maybe they will," Timothy says, smiling at the phone. "Nice meeting you, Mr. Pingle. I hope our paths cross again."

"Why shouldn't they? I want to hear the whole story about Nu-Hope. When it's ower."

"You will," Cone promises. "I'll tell you, but you won't believe it."

"At my age I'll believe anything."

Cone's second call is to Martin Gardow. But the secretary tells him Mr. Gardow is in conference and suggests he call back in a half hour. Cone waits forty-five minutes before trying again. This time Gardow comes on the line.

"Cone?" he says. "I was expecting to hear from you."

"Yeah, I guess," Cone says, trying to make his voice as servile as he can. "I've been doing some thinking about what we discussed."

"Glad to hear it. And?"

"I don't see why we can't get together. I mean we're both reasonable men—right?"

"I hope so," Gardow says, "for your sake. So you've decided to okay the Nu-Hope deal?"

"Well, I'd like to talk to you about it first."

"What's to talk about? You know what your choices are."

"Well, sure," Cone says, "but it doesn't seem right that I come out of this empty-handed."

Martin Gardow sighs. "Another cheapski," he says. "All right, Cone, I may toss you a cookie if I'm in the mood. I'll see you at the Seaport, same place, this afternoon."

"Meeting out in the open like that gives me the willies," Cone says. "I like my back to a wall."

Unexpectedly, Gardow laughs. Not a nice laugh. "Yes," he says, "I can understand why you might feel that way. What do you suggest?"

"There's a place on Madison. The Hotel Bedlington. They got a cocktail lounge that's usually deserted in the afternoon. I thought we might meet there about three. Have a friendly drink. Our business won't take long."

There's silence, and Cone's afraid he's lost.

Then Martin Gardow says, "The Bedlington? Yes, I know it. Just let me check my appointment book."

The fink!

"All right," Gardow says after a pause, "I'll meet you at the Bedlington bar at three o'clock this afternoon. Be on time. I don't like to be kept waiting."

Cone's next call is to Davenport.

"It's on," Cone tells him. "Three this afternoon at the Bedlington."

"Okay," the cop says. "We're ready to roll. The hotel people are cooperating. We'll get there an hour ahead of time and set things up."

"Follow the script," Cone warns him. "It's my cock on the block."

"We'll do our job. Nick can't wait to get his hands on this guy."

"Like I told you," Cone says, "even if the charge doesn't stick, just busting the guy might convince Sal Guiterrez to turn canary."

"It's worth a try," Davenport acknowledges. "Stay cool."

"Yeah," Cone says. "See you later."

He gets up to the Hotel Bedlington a little before two-thirty and heads directly for the gents'. There's a sign on the door: CLOSED FOR REPAIRS. PLEASE USE THE MEN'S ROOM ON MEZZANINE. Satisfied, Cone goes into the cocktail lounge. There's one bartender, handicapping a racing sheet, one bored waiter, examining his nails, and one young couple at the bar, heads together and giggling.

The Wall Street dick takes a small table in a shadowed corner and sits with his back to the wall, where he can watch the entrance. The waiter brings him a paper napkin and a little dish of salted peanuts. Cone orders a bottle of Heineken, and when it comes, he goes to work on it as fast as he can.

The beer finished, he catches the waiter's eye and signals for an encore. When the waiter brings the second bottle, he starts to remove the empty, but Cone stops him.

"Leave it," he says. "I want to keep track."

"Whatever you say, sir," the waiter says, sighing. But Cone knows what he's doing. Those two beer bottles on his table are theatrical props.

Gardow comes striding in a few minutes after three. He looks around, spots Cone, and comes over. He's wearing his double-breasted topcoat but no hat. Cone wonders if he discarded the green fedora after the feathers drowned in the East River.

Gardow takes off his coat, folds it neatly, and places it atop Cone's parka on a nearby chair. When the waiter comes over, Gardow orders a scotch mist with a twist of lemon peel. The drink is served with a short straw, and Cone is amused to note that Gardow actually uses it.

Gardow glances at the two beer bottles. "You like the suds?" he asks. "That figures. I'll bet you go bowling, too."

"Yeah, well, sometimes," Cone says sheepishly. "Good exercise—you know?"

Gardow could have taken a chair across the table from Cone, but instead he has seated himself on the vinyl-covered banquette next to Cone. Their knees are almost touching.

Gardow takes another sip through the straw, then reaches into his jacket pocket and pulls out a small black box, no larger than a pack of cigarettes. It is inset with a switch, a round grille, two lights, and a needled dial.

"Know what this is?" Gardow says, holding it out.

Cone shakes his head.

"It's a miniaturized electronic debugger. My company makes them. In Taiwan. For instance, suppose you came in here wired with a recorder, maybe even a transmitter, to pick up our conversation. This little—"

"Wired?" Cone says, astonished. "Why would I want to do that?"

"Just suppose you did," Gardow says, staring at him. "This little beauty would tell me in a minute."

He turns the switch on with his thumb, then begins to move the little black box across Cone's shoulders and chest, around his waist, down his legs. A green light on the box is glowing. Gardow watches the dial, paying no attention to the stares of the waiter and bartender.

Finished, he flicks off the switch and slips the device back into his jacket pocket. "You're clean," he says. "But if you had been wired, I'd have known it. You've got heavy metal on your lower right leg. What is it?"

"I carry a piece in an ankle holster. I've got a permit for it."

"Sure you do," Gardow says, going back to his scotch. "You weren't thinking of plugging me, were you?"

"Come on," Cone says. "I put it on every morning like underwear. I've never fired it off the range."

"Uh-huh," Gardow says. "Tell that to Bernie Snodgrass. After you dig him up."

"Look, Mr. Gardow," Cone says, finishing his second beer, "this kind of talk is getting us nowhere. I want to discuss the Nu-Hope deal."

"So you said on the phone. And I asked you what there is to discuss."

"Wow," Cone says, "those beers . . . My back teeth are floating. Let me take a quick trip to the john and then I'll tell you what's on my mind."

"Go ahead," Martin Gardow says casually. "I'm comfortable here."

Got him!

At the entrance to the men's room in the lobby, Cone knocks three times, rapidly. Davenport opens up.

"Okay?" he asks.

"So far," Cone says, starting to take off his corduroy jacket and flannel shirt. "This is one suspicious bastard. He's got a debugger, like I figured. More than three minutes and I'm in *biiig* trouble."

"We'll make it," Nick Galanis says. "This is Marve Heimholtz, a genius. He's going to wire you. Marve, this is Cone."

"Hi," the bespectacled tech says, stripping adhesive tape off a wide roll. "I'm giving you a mike on your chest, a transmitter on your ribs, a recorder in your jacket pocket."

"Left pocket," Cone says. "He's sitting close to my right side and might feel it."

"Okay, the recorder goes in your left jacket pocket. We've also got a pickup under the bar in the cocktail lounge and another in here. We should get results from one or another. They're all miniaturized units. Japanese. Try not to cough, sneeze, or scrape things. Keep your voice loud and clear. It wouldn't hurt to lean toward him as closely as possible without spooking him."

As he's talking, the tech is wiring Timothy Cone's bare torso, carefully applying strips of tape to keep the mike, wires, and transmitter in place.

"Two minutes," Davenport says, looking at his watch. "Move it along, Marve."

"Almost done," Heimholtz says. "Put on your shirt and jacket again."

Cone buttons up, and the tech slips the recorder into his left jacket pocket. The three cops examine him.

"Looks good to me," Galanis says.

"Could you button your shirt up to the neck?" Marve says. "Just to make sure he doesn't spot the tape."

"I could," Cone says, "but the top button was open when I left him. If I close it now, he might notice. He's a real wiseguy."

"Okay," Davenport says, "leave it open." He glances at his watch again. "A bit over three minutes. Out you go. We'll listen in here. If you get anything, we'll put the arm on him when he leaves."

Cone nods, tugs down his jacket. "I'd really like to take a leak," he says, "but we haven't got the time."

"Cross your legs," Galanis says.

"What a relief that was," Cone says, sliding back onto the banquette. He notices Gardow has ordered a fresh scotch mist. Cone raises his hand, catches the waiter's attention, motions toward his empty beer bottles.

"By the way," he says to the other man, "this is my treat."

"Of course," Gardow says. "Cone, I'm going to finish this drink and take off. So if you have anything to say to me, you better spit it out now."

"Yeah, well, I wanted to talk about Nu-Hope. When I got assigned to that thing, I really didn't know how important it was."

"It's important," Martin Gardow says. "Mr. D. gives it the highest priority."

"Well, I didn't realize how much muscle was behind it. Lester Pingle tries to buy me off with ten grand, and I figure there's more there than I thought."

"Pingle handled it stupidly," Gardow says. "The man's a fool."

"Yeah, he is, you're absolutely right. Then I learn about Harold Besant and Jessie Scotto and I began to catch on to how big this thing is."

Gardow shrugs. "It had to be done. Besant was threatening to go public. Jesus, that's all we needed. So he had to be taken out."

"And you figured he had told his girlfriend?"

Gardow looks at him. "Wouldn't you?"

"I don't know. You're much smarter than I am, Mr. Gardow. I mean, you're way ahead of all of us. It's just that I saw the girl's body. Snodgrass and Guiterrez must be a couple of creeps."

"They are, but you work with what you can get. How did you find out those two slugs whacked Besant and Scotto?"

"I didn't find out; the cops did. Besant was left-handed, but the gun was dropped like it had fallen from his right hand. And they found Bernie Snodgrass's prints in Scotto's apartment."

"Shit!" Gardow says disgustedly. "How stupid can you get? Well, Snodgrass is feeding the worms, and I'll have Guiterrez taken care of. Mr. D. doesn't like loose ends."

"This Mr. D.," Cone says, "he sounds like hell on wheels."

"He's a rotten, no-good sonofabitch, but he pays a good buck for results. Well, enough of this bullshit. Have you okayed the Nu-Hope deal?"

"Not yet," the Wall Street dick says. "I guess January told you I know what's going on in that secret research lab of theirs."

"He told me. So?"

"Well, I can see how important it is."

"I told you what would happen to your girlfriend if you don't produce."

"I know, Mr. Gardow. And I know you're not just making noise. But it seems to me a little bonus would be a nice gesture on your part."

"What do you call a little bonus?"

"Well, of course I don't expect fifty grand. I just mentioned that number to January to smoke him out. But you had Lester Pingle offer me ten grand. Could you still spring for that?"

Gardow finishes the remainder of his drink and rises. "That was before I learned about Samantha Whatley. I could stiff you completely, and you'd produce just to keep her breathing. But I'm a forgiving man. The moment I hear you've okayed the deal I'll get a thousand to you—just for goodwill."

"Gee, Mr. Gardow," Cone says, whining, "can't you do better than that?"

"Take it or leave it," Gardow says, pulling on his coat.

"I'll take it," Cone says hastily.

"I thought you would," the other man says. "I deal with sleazes like you all the time. You start out ten feet tall and end up on your knees. Don't call me again."

He starts toward the glass door leading to the lobby. Cone hurries after him. He wants to give Davenport and Galanis a chance to get in position.

"When will I get the cash, Mr. Gardow? I can really use it."

"You'll get it when I feel like it."

Both men go out into the lobby. The cops are waiting, IDs in their hands.

Davenport steps up. "Martin Gardow?"

"Yes. Who're you?"

"Detective Davenport, New York Police Department. This man is Detective Galanis. Here is our identification."

"What the fuck is this?" Gardow says wrathfully.

"You're under arrest," Davenport says. "Open your coat, please. We have to search you."

"Arrest," Gardow says, stunned. "For what?"

"Conspiracy to commit murder, for starters," Galanis says. "We'll probably come up with more when Salvador Guiterrez starts singing. Hey, Neal, how's about sending a cassette of this schmuck's remarks to Mr. D.? He'll get a big kick out of it—especially that part where his faithful employee calls him a rotten, no-good sonofabitch."

"I don't know what the hell you're talking about," Gardow says, his face suddenly tight and pale.

"Martin, baby . . ." the Wall Street dick calls softly.

Gardow whirls on him. Cone has unbuttoned his jacket and shirt. He displays the electronic gear taped to his bare torso.

"Surprise!" he says.

Gardow stares, shocked, then raises his eyes to glare. "I am going to have you popped," he says slowly, biting off each word.

"You think I care?" Timothy Cone says, much amused.

The whirligig is slowing down. Some of the people have been thrown off, some are still riding. But the merry-go-round is coasting now, music dying. Cone feels the tension seep out of him. It was a fast, frantic ride on the carousel, but it's good to stand on solid ground and see things in focus rather than a dizzying blur.

He figures there is no point in going back to the office. So he takes his delayed leak and lets Marve Heimholtz strip the electronic gear from his body before taking a cab down to his neighborhood. Before going up to the loft, he stops off to buy some salami and eggs, and a can of tuna for Cleo. Let the moth-eaten cat celebrate, too.

He's unlocking the loft door when his phone starts ringing.

"I'm coming!" he yells at it, and wonders, not for the first time, why people shout at a ringing phone.

"Yeah?" he says.

"What the hell are you doing home?" Sam yells. "You work here—remember?"

"I also work outside the office, and I've been busting my butt on the Nu-Hope Clinic deal."

"Forget it," she says. "Pingle Enterprises called and signed off. The case is dead."

"No kidding?" Cone says.

"You devious bastard, I'll bet you finagled it."

"Listen," Cone says, "I just picked up some salami and eggs. How's about coming by for dinner?"

"You got any salad stuff?" she asks in a low voice.

"I got a tomato. It's a little spotted."

"Beautiful," she says. "All right, I'll pick up some mixed greens at the deli. See you about six?"

He gives Cleo half of the tuna and puts fresh water in the cat's coffee can. By the time Samantha arrives, he's working on his second vodka and third Camel, and he's in a mellow mood. Not ecstatic, but satisfied every time he recalls the look on Martin Gardow's face when that yahoo realized he had been royally screwed.

"I want to know what you've been up to," Sam says angrily the moment she's inside the door.

"Calm down," he tells her. "Take off your coat, relax, have a drink."

"Don't try to sweet-talk me, buster," she says. "I always know when you've been conniving; you get that shit-eating grin."

"Christ, you're in a lovely mood," he says. "I'll tell you, I'll tell you. Just sit down and be nice."

Grumbling, she puts her package of salad stuff in the refrigerator and pours herself a jar of white wine. She sits at the table and scratches Cleo's ears.

"All right," she says, "let's have it. All of it."

He doesn't tell her *all* of it. Not about the threats to her safety. If he had mentioned that, she'd have cut him to ribbons, demanding to know what right he had to think she couldn't protect herself. She is that kind of a woman and, being that kind of a man, he can understand it.

So he tells her about J. Roger Gibby, Martin Gardow, Mr. D., Drs. January and Trumball, and the murders of Harold Besant and Jessie Scotto. Samantha listens intently, not interrupting. When he's finished and says, "That's it," she pours herself another glass of wine.

"No," she says, "that's not it. Not all of it. You still haven't told me what the McGuffin is. Why were the government and Mr. D. so interested in what Nu-Hope was doing in that research lab?"

"You won't believe it," Cone tells her.

"Try me," she says.

And, right on cue, there's a gentle rapping at the loft door.

"Now who the hell can that be?" Cone says. He slips the Magnum from his ankle holster and moves to the door, standing well to one side. "Who is it?" he shouts.

"Roger Gibby. May I come in for a moment?"

The Wall Street dick opens the door cautiously, peeks out, then pauses to slide his iron back into the holster.

"How did you get in downstairs?" he wants to know.

"I fear your outside door has been jimmied," Gibby says.

"Oh, God," Cone says. "Again? Well, come on in."

Gibby enters slowly. He's as impeccably clad as ever, wearing a trim chesterfield with a velvet collar, a black bowler, and carrying a pair of fawn gloves. There's a sprig of edelweiss pinned to his lapel.

"Where's your muscleman?" Cone asks.

"Downstairs, guarding our hubcaps." Gibby sees Samantha and removes his hat. "I beg your pardon, ma'am," he says with a small bow. "If I had known Mr. Cone had guests, I would have come at another time."

"Sam," Cone says, "this is Professor J. Roger Gibby."

"Former professor," he says with his sweet smile.

"This lady is Samantha Whatley, my boss at Haldering."

Gibby shakes her hand. "A pleasure," he says. "I envy you for having such a clever and diligent investigator on your staff."

"Oh, Cone's a pisser," Sam says, and if Gibby is shocked by her language, he doesn't reveal it.

He looks slowly about the loft. "Different," is his verdict. "And what, pray, is that animal under the bathtub?"

"Cleo," Cone says. "A sort of a cat. Take off your coat and pull up a chair. Have a drink."

"I'm only staying a minute," Gibby says, "but I would appreciate a small drink. It's been a long day."

"I've got some brandy."

"Excellent. Just a pony, if you will."

Gibby seats himself at the desk and is not at all disconcerted when Cone brings him the brandy in a jelly jar.

"Your health, ma'am," he says. "And to your continued success."

"Thank you," she says faintly.

Gibby takes a sip. "Quite nice," he says. "I presume that Mr. Cone has told you about his investigation of the Nu-Hope Fertility Clinic."

"He's told me everything except the reason everyone was so interested in them. I mean why were the U.S. Government and International Gronier involved?"

"The U.S. Government is no longer involved," Gibby says, looking at Sam steadily. "As of this afternoon we have terminated all connections with Nu-Hope. And, after the arrest of his underling, I suspect Leopold Devers of International Gronier has done the same."

"How did you find out about Gardow's arrest?" Cone asks curiously.

"Oh . . ." Gibby says vaguely, "I have contacts."

"So that's the end of it?" Cone says. "The government is dropping the whole thing?"

"Well . . ." Gibby says, "I wouldn't exactly say that, Mr. Cone. We're certainly dropping Nu-Hope. But not the project. I'm a great believer in redundancy in scientific research. It would have been foolish to have depended on one source. Actually, we have a number of teams developing the same thing. The work will continue."

"Yeah," Cone says. "That figures."

"Just to satisfy an old man, will you tell me how you got on to it?"

"I read a book," Cone says. "It was the only thing it could have been."

"Read a book," Gibby repeats, nodding. "The best way."

"Goddammit!" Samantha Whatley explodes. "Will the two of you tell me what the hell you're talking about!"

"I can understand your curiosity, ma'am," Gibby says, smiling gently, "and I see no reason why you shouldn't know. If you decide to go public—which I doubt very much you will wish to do—I can assure you there is no evidence confirming the government's interest."

"What *is* it?" Samantha cries desperately.

"It's called hybridization," Gibby says, staring thoughtfully into his jar of brandy. "An extremely complex project to explore the possibility of combining human sperm and eggs with the sperm and eggs of certain other primates, such as rhesus monkeys, chimpanzees, and others. It also involves the possibility of embryo transfer from one closely related species to another."

Sam turns her head slowly to stare at Timothy. "You were right," she says. "I don't believe it. Mate a woman with a monkey?"

"Oh, no!" J. Roger Gibby protests. "No, no, no. Actual sexual intercourse has never been suggested. We're concerned merely with laboratory techniques."

"Merely," Whatley says. "I love that merely. And you think someday you can produce a half-human/half-chimp?"

"Are you asking for my personal opinion?" Gibby says. "Yes, I think it's possible. In fact, there are reports that it's already been done by a Chinese doctor. Unfortunately, his laboratory and experiment were reportedly destroyed by terrified peasants."

"That I can understand," Samantha says.

"Look," Cone says. "Supposing the government or someone else spends a zillion dollars on this thing, finances a lot of research teams, and eventually succeeds, producing an ape-man. What I want to know is, what the hell's the *point?* Why spend so much money? Go to so much trouble?"

"Think about it, Mr. Cone. You're a smart man; just think about it. Envision any of these possibilities: an army composed of soldiers, vicious as baboons, with no imagination and hence no fear of death. Or intelligent semi-humans bred to fit into the tight, computerized cockpits of tomorrow's fighter planes. Or gifted animals able to withstand the boredom and terrors of long space flights."

"All right," Cone says grimly, "that's the government's interest. What was Mr. D.'s?"

"International Gronier is a worldwide conglomerate with

factories all over the globe, a great many in third-world countries. Leopold Devers was prescient enough to realize how hybridization might revolutionize the labor force. Imagine half-animals bred to exact specifications. The missing link between robots and humans. Why, you might develop workers with abnormally long arms, prehensile toes, superior eyesight, or any other physical quality desired for efficient and low-cost production. Brilliant animals with no desire for unions or a say in management.''

"Just toss them a banana," Cone says.

"Yes," Gibby says quite seriously. "That's the bottom line. Profit. Greed. That's what motivated Mr. D."

"I don't like this conversation," Sam says.

Gibby finishes his brandy, rebuttons his chesterfield, reclaims his bowler and gloves. He looks at Samantha with his kindly smile. "Religion, morality, ethics?" he says. "Is that what you're thinking about? I must tell you that science and technology have a momentum all their own. It makes no allowance for religion, morality, ethics. It's a different world. I am fond of remarking that if it can be done, it will be done. You cannot put a cap on man's creativity. It is hopeless to try by threat or edict."

"What you mean," Timothy Cone says, "is that science is your religion."

Gibby thinks about that for a moment. "Yes," he says finally, "I suppose that is what I mean: Science is my faith."

He thanks them for their hospitality, shakes hands, and flaps his gloves at Cleo, who is standing in the center of the floor, regarding him with hard, shining eyes. Then Gibby departs, and Cone locks, bolts, and chains the door behind him.

"Salami and eggs?" he asks Sam.

"Yes," she says, "that's what I need."

They speak very little that night, both burdened with secret thoughts, oppressed by nameless fears. They eat, drink, smile at Cleo's crazy antics. But it is a subdued evening, the whirligig finally stopped, music dead, lights dimmed.

It has seemed so before, and now once again that bedraggled loft becomes a cave, a refuge. Cleo is certainly not their child, but that dilapidated cat—in a manner they cannot comprehend—completes a family huddling in shelter, safe from the dark forces gathering outside.

Aloneness silences them, and it seems more a time for reflection than joy. They ponder existence and question their roles in the universe: leaves, grains of sand, dying stars. All their hopes, dreams, ambitions brought low. Evanescent things. Doomed to perish.

"What a drag," Whatley says.

"Yeah," Cone says.

They come out of it, as they inevitably must if they are to survive. They look at each other with glassy grins, tickle Cleo's ribs, stack the dishes, have another drink, embrace in a quick, clumsy dance step to no tune, fling off their clothes, have a vertical hug, flop onto the floor mattress, have a horizontal hug, nibble, yelp with laughter, stroke, the warmth and fever of living coming back now.

He stares entranced at her small, elegant breasts.

"Thank God," he says, "they're still there."

"Tim, what the hell are you talking about?"

"Just talking," he says, bending to kiss.

BOOK THREE

A Covey
of Cousins

1

WALL STREET, AS everyone knows, is a short, narrow, bustling thoroughfare that runs from a river to a graveyard. But it is more than a passage from deep water to deeper earth.

It is not a street at all, but a community whose backroom workers might toil in Queens, Hackensack, or Peoria. Indeed, Wall Street encompasses the world via a bewildering array of speedy electronic communication equipment: telephones, cables, satellites, facsimile reproduction, television and, faster than all of these, rumors.

Wall Street is fueled by greed and oiled by cupidity. It is a state of mind, a culture, a never-never land with all the hopeful romance of the Roseland Ballroom and the grungy despair of a Bowery flophouse. Men have soared on Wall Street—and not all of them through the nearest window because they guessed wrong.

It is a mystery, even to experienced insiders. It is a rigorous mathematical puzzle and simultaneously the most emotional and irrational of human institutions. Dealers come and go, customers come and go, but Wall Street endures, a series of nesting boxes so enormous, so artfully contrived and frustrating, that no one has ever uncovered the final secret.

Players on Wall Street, addicted to the madness, have coined a number of pithy aphorisms to serve as guides to financial adventures:

"If it sounds too good to be true, it *is* too good to be true."

"Never panic—but if you do, make sure you're the first to panic."

"Happiness can't buy money."

There are many fine buildings channeling the Street. Some house prestigious trading firms whose probity cannot be questioned. And then there are concrete barns with stalls for cash cows and others for spavined beasts not worth the feed to keep them alive, although they continue to exist until fatally stricken by Chapter Seven.

It is in one of the thriving establishments just east of Nassau Street, on a nippy Monday morning in mid-December, that the passion, the fervor of Wall Street may be glimpsed in all its crass, exciting glory. For there, on the premises of Laboris Investments, Inc., a throng of the covetous are attempting to follow the dictum of Sophie Tucker: "I've been rich and I've been poor, and believe me, rich is better."

The outer office is plain enough: plywood walls, plastic plants, and furniture that looks as if it has been rented from an outfit that supplies political campaign headquarters. The air is gummy with smoke, and the two begrimed windows look out on a shadowed airshaft that plunges to a concrete courtyard, bare and cold.

But the people coming through the door in a constant stream care nothing for the surroundings. The light of avarice is in their eyes. Many carry ads torn from newspapers, magazines, and direct-mail solicitations.

There to greet them are three personable employees of Laboris Investments, Inc. The two young men and one young woman wear large badges inscribed: ACCOUNT EXECUTIVE. And below: HI! and their names.

Each new arrival is handed a flier that, in four pages, describes the Laboris investment philosophy and technique. The thin brochure is mercifully free of the usual legal gobbledygook that fills thicker and more impressive Wall Street prospectuses. It also has the grace to state that "This is a high-risk investment, neither approved nor disapproved by the SEC, and investors should be prepared to lose the total sums invested."

But even this chilling disclaimer cannot cool the passion of the mob. They arrive with checkbooks at the ready, with money orders, even with wrinkled bills stuffed into Bloomies' shopping bags. The account executives are frantically active, answering questions, passing out applications, writing out receipts for cash received.

There is fever in the air, and all are infected. Some of those arriving are already Laboris clients come to make an additional contribution, and they happily tell strangers of a 30-percent return on their money. "Monthly checks—regular as clockwork!" And so the contagion spreads, many angry because the account executives cannot accept their money quickly enough.

For every exultant customer who departs, two nervous hopefuls appear. There is apparently no end to the enthusiasts. The crowd importuning Laboris to take their life savings grows and grows. And all share a common affliction: the something-for-nothing syndrome for which modern medical science can offer no cure.

"Here's a crazy one," Samantha Whatley says. "Right up your old kazoo."

"How come I get all the nut cases?" Timothy Cone says grumpily. "Are you trying to tell me something?"

"Well, if you want to know, the customer asked for you, so just shut up and listen." She opens a folder and starts reading. "A private client. Mrs. Martha T. Hepplewaite. A widow. Lives in her own brownstone on East Thirty-eighth. With her only child, a daughter named Lucinda. Mrs. Hepplewaite wants us to investigate an outfit called Laboris Investments. The guy running it is Ingmar Laboris."

"Ingmar Laboris? What's that—a Swedish mouthwash?"

"Funny," Sam says without changing expression. "The legal and accounting sections already have their marching orders. You go see this Mrs. Hepplewaite and find out what the hell she wants. H. H. says she was very vague on the phone."

"How come she latched onto us?"

"Says we were recommended by Ernest Pingle, who mentioned your name. Hiram checked with Pingle, and he says the lady's got all the money in the world. Her husband was a Kansas City meat packer who dropped dead on the eighth green at St. Andrew's."

"What happened—did he miss a six-inch putt?"

Samantha shoves the file across her desk. "It's all yours. Go see the lady, and for God's sake this time keep me up to speed on what's going on."

"Don't I always?"

"Get lost," she tells him.

He takes the folder back to his office, parks his scuffed yellow work shoes on the desk, and scans the file. It doesn't tell him much more. But it does include address and phone number. So he calls.

"Hello?" A woman's voice. Cautious.

"Mrs. Martha T. Hepplewaite?"

"No, this is Lucinda Hepplewaite. May I ask who's calling, please?"

Cone tells her.

"Just a moment, please," she says, and the Wall Street dick reflects she's got a lot of "please" in her.

That's daughter Lucinda. When mother Martha comes on, she sounds like a drill instructor. No "please" at all.

"You're Timothy Cone of Haldering and Company?" she demands.

"That's correct, ma'am. I was hoping you'd have time to see me today."

"You have my address?"

"Yes."

"Five o'clock this afternoon. Precisely."

Slam!

Cone sits looking at the dead phone.

"And I love you, too," he says aloud.

He gets up to East Thirty-eighth Street ahead of time, to give himself a chance to scope the building. It snowed early that morning, a couple of inches, and it's cold enough to keep the white stuff crunching underfoot, like a beach of crusty sand. He stomps back and forth, hands in the fleece-lined pockets of his anorak.

The brownstone looks well-maintained, windows shiny and the sidewalk swept. Five stories high with bow windows and a mansard roof. Maybe seventy-five years old, he figures, and at today's prices worth a mil. At least. In the gloomy December twilight, there are lights burning in rooms on the first two floors.

The young woman who answers the door is tall, bony, and has a few too many teeth for her mouth. She's wearing an old-fashioned sweater set, a flannel skirt, and brogues almost as heavy as Cone's work shoes. A tentative smile lights her horsey face.

"Mr. Cone?"

"That's right. Miss Lucinda Hepplewaite?"

"Yes. This way, please."

He follows her down a narrow corridor and into a parlor that appears to have been untouched since World War I. Everything heavy, dark, carved, and embellished, with dried flowers under bell jars, crocheted antimacassars, needlepoint footstools, faded photographs framed in wood, an old wind-up Victrola, and whatnots and curios without end.

It's all so dated and evocative that Cone has a strong desire to cry: "Great heavens! The Boche have invaded Belgium!"

"Please take off your coat and, uh, cap," she says, "and make yourself comfortable. Mama will be with you in a moment."

She clumps away, and Cone takes off his parka and, uh, cap. But he can't see anyplace to put them. There's already *something* on every flat surface in the room, and the chairs and couches are so precisely arranged that he's afraid to desecrate them. So he stands there, holding both.

Lucinda doesn't return, but Mama comes stumping in, leaning on a cane as thick as a mizzenmast.

"I'm Mrs. Martha Hepplewaite," she declares, halfway between a bark and a snarl. "You're Timothy Cone from Haldering?"

"Yes, ma'am. Would you care to see my identification?"

"Not necessary. Ernest Pingle described you."

She makes no effort to shake hands, but plumps down in an armchair and looks up at him. He wonders if she intends to keep him standing during this interview.

"Sit down, man," she says testily.

He looks about warily and finally perches on the edge of a couch that looks deep and soft enough to swallow him.

"You're not much to look at," she says, "but I hear you know your job."

Cone remains silent, wondering whether he'll turn to stone if he stares at her long enough.

She's a massive woman, with enough wattles and dewlaps to make a bloodhound jealous. Timothy guesses a lot of good beef and bourbon went into that raddled face. Like her daughter, she's wearing two sweaters. But her broad hips are wrapped in a tweed skirt as heavy as a horse blanket. And she's also sporting a string of pearls that looks like the real thing.

"Would you like a glass of water?" she asks suddenly.

"No, thank you," he says. "But it's very kind of you to ask."

She looks at him suspiciously, but his expression is grave and attentive.

"Very well," she says gruffly. "I suppose you want to know what this is all about."

He nods.

"What do you do with your money?" she demands.

He decides it's time to clamp down. "None of your business," he says. "What do you do with yours?"

"None of your business," she replies. "But you do know something about investing, don't you?"

"A little."

"I know a lot," she says flatly. "My husband left me well-off, and I had to learn how to manage it. It wasn't easy, but I succeeded. One of the things I discovered along the way is how many crooks there are in the world."

"Yeah," Cone agrees, "you could say that."

"I *do* say it. Now my only child is engaged to be married."

"Congratulations."

"The man is a dolt," the old lady says. "But at her age and with her looks, she's lucky to get anyone."

Cone is getting pissed-off at this harridan. "I think your daughter is attractive," he states.

She ignores that. "Her fiancé is a pediatrician. Doctors are notorious for being the world's worst money managers. Because they can lance a boil, they think they can deal with options, indexes, futures, and commodities. They're the favorite targets of every con man in the country. Lucy's husband-to-be is putting a lot of money into a company called Laboris Investments. Have you heard of it?"

"Not until this morning when I was assigned the case."

"Well, it's run by a man named Ingmar Laboris."

Cone doesn't make many jokes, but when he finds one he likes, he sticks with it.

"Sounds like a Swedish mouthwash," he says.

"Don't waste your wit on me, young man," Mrs. Hepplewaite says sharply. "I warn you, I have absolutely no sense of humor. This Ingmar Laboris is promising a return of thirty percent. What would you do if someone offered you a return like that?"

"Run the other way," Cone says. "How does he claim to do it?"

"Currency trading," she says. "Switching dollars to

pounds or francs or yen or pesos. Rates between various national moneys are constantly changing. I admit there are profits to be made in such trading, but it demands split-second decision-making by very experienced and knowl-edgeable traders. I've checked my sources on Wall Street, and no one's heard of this Ingmar Laboris. He seems to have come out of nowhere, and has no track record. Yet here he is promising a thirty-percent return. I don't like it.''

"It doesn't sound kosher," Cone acknowledges. "To run a currency-trading operation you need a worldwide net-work: open telephone lines, computers, agents in every country—the whole bit. Has Laboris got all that?''

"How on earth would I know?" she says angrily. "What do you think I hired Haldering for? To find out. I don't want Lucy marrying a bankrupt doctor. I have no intention of bailing them out.''

Cone ponders a moment. "Have you any idea how much your daughter's fiancé has invested with Laboris?''

"I don't know exactly. I'd guess it's almost a hundred thousand.''

The Wall Street dick whistles softly. "A tidy sum. Can he get it out?''

"That's what infuriates me," Mrs. Hepplewaite says. "Apparently he can withdraw his money anytime he wishes, and he *has* been earning thirty percent on his invest-ment. Of course he's delighted—the idiot!''

"Have you tried talking to him about it? Or to your daughter?''

"I've talked—to both of them. Should have saved my breath. They're convinced this get-rich-quick scheme, whatever it is, will make them wealthy. The children!''

"All right," Cone says, "you've given me enough to go on. I'll look into it.''

"That's all you're going to tell me—that you'll look into it?''

"That's all I'm going to tell you," he says stonily, stand-ing up and putting on his parka. "When I have something to report, you'll hear from Haldering. Not before.''

"You're snotty," she says. "You know that?"

"Sure, I know it," he says. "And you're a mean old biddy. You know that?"

Unexpectedly she laughs. At least her spongy face creases into a grimace that might pass as a grin. She waves her cane at him menacingly.

"Stop wasting time," she says, "and go to work. That's what I'm paying you for."

He's plodding down the long corridor toward the front door when Lucinda Hepplewaite steps out of the shadows and puts a soft hand on his arm. Startled, he turns to face her.

"Please be kind," she whispers, and then she's gone.

He stands there a moment, flummoxed. Then he exits into a chilled mizzle that's put glittering halos around the streetlights. It takes him almost twenty minutes to find an empty cab, and then he gets a hackie who barely speaks English and has to be told when to turn left or right.

Cone arrives back at his loft in a foul mood, not improved when he discovers Cleo has upchucked in the middle of the linoleum floor.

"You sonofabitch!" he yells at the cat. "You been eating cockroaches again?"

He cleans up the mess, rinses his hands, pours a heavy Popov over ice. Lights a cigarette. Puts his feet up on his desk-table. Cleo comes purring over, wanting to make up.

"Miserable cat," Cone says, but he reaches down to scratch the torn ears, which the scarred and denutted tom dearly loves.

He sits there for maybe a half hour, wondering what she meant by "Please be kind." To whom? Herself, her fiancé, her mother? To everyone and everything: animal, vegetable, and mineral?

Grunting, he rouses from his reverie and opens a big can of beef stew. He heats it up in a battered saucepan. When the fat has melted and the stew is beginning to bubble, he pours out about a third of it into Cleo's feeding dish (a chipped ashtray), and eats the remainder himself, spooning it directly from the pan into his mouth. He pauses just long enough to dust some chili powder into it, then finishes. It's okay. Not a lot of meat, but okay.

He goes back to Popov and Camels for dessert. But not before he digs out the Manhattan telephone directory from the cabinet under the sink. He looks up Laboris. To his surprise, he finds three listings: Laboris Investments, Inc., on Wall Street; Laboris Importers, Inc., on Nineteenth Street at an address that would put it just west of Fifth Avenue; and Laboris Gallery of Levantine Art on upper Madison Avenue.

Cone circles the three names with a black Magic Marker, then tears the page out of the directory. *Three* Laborises? It's such an unusual name, he figures Ingmar is either running all three outfits or there's a family connection.

He calls Samantha.

"Hello?" she says.

"Yeah," he says. "Cone."

"Call back; I'm eating dinner."

"This will only take a minute. You know everything; what does Levantine mean?"

"Jesus, you're a pain in the ass," she says disgustedly. "Can't you look it up? The Levant is a term used to describe all the countries around the east Mediterranean. Like Turkey, Syria, and Iran."

"Okay," he says. "Thanks."

"How did you make out with—"

"See you tomorrow," he says and hangs up.

He sits there, wondering if Laboris Investments is financing that 30-percent return from the profits of Laboris Importers and the Laboris Gallery of Levantine Art.

"Not fucking likely," he says aloud to Cleo, who is under the bathtub, sleeping off the beef stew. The cat opens one eye to stare at him, then shuts it again.

Feeling his own eyes beginning to close, Cone finishes his last drink and last cigarette of the day. He checks the door to make certain it's locked, bolted, chained. Then he

undresses, first unstrapping his ankle holster and placing the
.357 short-barreled Magnum close to the mattress on the
floor.

He's lying there in his skivvies, waiting for sleep, when
Cleo comes padding over to curl up in the bend of his knees.

"Please be kind," he says to the cat.

He doesn't bother checking in at the office the next morning, but goes directly to Laboris Investments, Inc., on Wall
Street. It's only a little after nine-thirty, but the joint is
already jumping. There's a crowd swamping the three account executives and, from what Cone can see, they're all
eager to plunk down cash for a ticket on the gravy train.

It's a crazy mob, hard to categorize: dowagers in ankle-
length minks; starchly clad executive types carrying alligator attaché cases; cops and Sanitation guys in uniform;
housewives, one with her hair in curlers; a gentleman wearing a clerical collar; a couple of punk rockers; a woman who
looks like a bag lady; and two bums who look like they
spent the night on the IRT subway grille.

What they all have in common, Cone decides, is a gallop-
ing case of the gimmies.

He picks up one of the skimpy prospectuses and reads it
carefully. But it's weasel-worded: No promises are made,
no profits mentioned. "It is hoped . . ." and "It is expected that . . ." and "Possible returns might . . ." And
then the disclaimers: You could lose your entire investment,
and there is no guarantee that past success will continue in
the future. All legal, the Wall Street dick reflects mournfully, and all designed to get the chief gonnif off the hook.

The most interesting thing in the brochure is a photograph
of Ingmar Laboris himself, grinning happily at the camera.
He's a swarthy, plump-faced man with a heavy head of
slick black hair and a brush of mustache thick enough to
clean out a bird cage. Small ears flat to his skull. Full lips
with a pouty look. The eyes are squinched with innocence
and glint.

"May I help you, sir?" an account executive carols, suddenly appearing at his elbow.

He looks at her badge. "Maybe you can, Gwen. Any chance of my seeing Mr. Laboris?"

"Oh, I'm sorry, sir, but Mr. Laboris is out of the country at present. Expanding our operation overseas, you know."

"Uh-huh."

"Is there anything I can help you with? Do you have any questions?"

"Can I get a thirty-percent return?"

"Oh, sir, we can't guarantee any rate of return. The prospectus spells that out very clearly."

"Sure it does," Cone says genially. "But I can get my money back whenever I want it?"

"Of course, sir. We maintain a special redemption fund."

"Glad to hear it," Cone says. "You accept cash or tellers' checks?"

"Or money orders," Gwen says proudly. "And all major credit cards up to the limit of your credit rating."

"Thank you very much," Cone says. "You've been very helpful."

"Would you care to invest now, sir?"

"Not at the moment. I'd like to think about it."

Her smile flicks off, and she turns away. She's working on commission, he figures, and why should she waste time with a turd-kicker like him when there are so many other applicants with deep pockets?

He leaves Laboris Investments, not much wiser than when he arrived. The whole operation smells, but he figured that from the start. Going down in the elevator, he looks again at Ingmar's photograph and thinks: Would you buy a used Oriental rug from this man?

He stops at the office on his way uptown, just to let people know he's still alive. There are no messages and no memos on his desk, which is okay with him. Still wearing his parka and black leather cap, he wanders into Sidney Apicella's office.

"Oh-oh," Sid says, rubbing his red nose. "Bad news—I just know it."

"Nah," Cone says. "Just a question or two about the Laboris Investments case . . ."

"My God, Tim," Apicella says, "we haven't even started on that one."

"Well, could you check out our foreign contacts and see if any of them have ever heard of Ingmar Laboris? He's supposed to be a hotshot international currency dealer."

Sidney stares at him. "But you think he's a phony?"

"Yeah," the Wall Street dick says, "that's what I think."

He could take an uptown bus, but he cabs instead. He knows the client will be billed for his expenses. He figures Mrs. Martha T. Hepplewaite for a tightwad and imagines with pleasure how she's going to yelp when she gets the itemized invoice.

It's his military training; he's got to make a personal reconnaissance of the territory. So he walks up and down West Nineteenth Street, getting a feel of the neighborhood. Office buildings, lofts, small manufacturers, fabric houses, a couple of dingy bars, and a lot of importers and exporters of this and that.

Laboris Importers, Inc., is a block-wide emporium with huge plate glass show windows—and a roll-down steel shutter for nighttime protection. Dominating the window display is a six-foot brass Buddha, arms raised, belly shined. The statue stands on a dark wood base carved to resemble a rock outcrop.

Timothy Cone pushes open the door, which jangles a bell suspended overhead. He hasn't seen a gizmo like that in years. But the alarm seems to alert no one. There are maybe a half-dozen customers wandering the aisles. And in the back, behind a counter, five salesclerks are nattering and laughing. Apparently Laboris Importers doesn't believe in the hard sell.

Cone looks around, making a zigzag path through the big sales floor. He's never seen so much junk in his life. Someone has combed the world for tasteless trinkets and mass-produced art—and here it all is, displayed under fluorescent lamps in a Manhattan showroom.

Primitive African statuettes—probably made by computerized lathes in Nigeria. Imitation Navaho silver jewelry, set with stones that look like unchewed bubblegum. Moth-eaten red fezzes with limp black tassels. Glass paperweights filled with tiny Swiss chalets and a snowstorm of rice. Cigarette lighters shaped like Colt pistols. Planters' hats from Panama and puppets from India. Mexican wedding dresses and carved wooden rabbits from Guatemala. A set of Scottish bagpipes and a rack of chino pants from Taiwan. Enormous leather hippopatami from somewhere and just as large porcelain elephants from somewhere else. And tons and tons of similar stuff.

It is, Timothy Cone decides, awed, the greatest collection of schlock he's ever seen in his life.

"May I be of service, sir?" someone asks, and Cone turns slowly, hearing the hisses rather than the words.

It's a short, chubby gink, swarthy, a toothbrush mustache and teeth so white they seem to have been sandblasted. He's wearing a cologne that smells of defunct roses. And he looks like he's been dipped in Mazola.

"Just wandering around," Cone says. Then: "I hope you don't mind my asking, but does this store have any connection with Laboris Investments on Wall Street?"

The glittery teeth become more prominent. Cone figures it's a smile.

"But of course," the man says happily. "He is our cousin." He waves a hand at the other salesclerks still chattering away in the rear of the store. "We are all cousins. The Laboris family is very large. Did you invest with Ingmar?"

Cone nods. "Do you think I did the right thing?"

The guy puts a soft hand on his arm. "The wisest decision you have ever made in your life. Ingmar is a financial genius. All the cousins have invested with Ingmar."

"Glad to hear it," Timothy says. "And may I ask what your name is?"

"Sven Laboris. Amusing, no? The combination I mean. Ingmar and Sven with Laboris. I think maybe a Swede lady took one look at the Mediterranean and decided to stay."

"Yeah," Cone says, "that could happen." And then, because Sven has been so pleasant and forthcoming, he looks around for something cheap he can buy. There's a table filled with dark wooden Buddhas. They look like small versions of the big brass job in the store window.

"Those Buddhas . . ." he says. "What kind of wood is that?"

"Oh!" Sven says. "Very nice. Solid teak from Burma. All hand-carved, of course. Each one different."

He picks up one of the statuettes and hands it to Cone. "One solid piece of wood. Very hard. Very difficult to carve. Look at the detail."

The figure is about twelve inches high, and unexpectedly heavy. Arms are raised, plump belly protrudes, and the face has an expression of beneficent joy. It is posed in a carved rock, fists clenched, the whole posture one of jaunty pleasure.

"What are you asking for it?" Cone says.

"Oh, this must be $29.95. Import duties, you know."

Cone starts to replace the Buddha on the table. "That's a little more than I wanted to spend."

"However," Sven Laboris says hastily, "because you have invested with our cousin, I can make you a special price. Twenty?"

"Okay," Cone says.

"Also," Sven says, giggling, "I must tell you about a special bonus. It is something that will delight you. If you rub the belly of a Buddha—here, let me show you how; stroke gently, like so—well then, you will have good luck for many years and all your wishes will come true."

"No kidding?" the Wall Street dick says.

He emerges from Laboris Importers, Inc., carrying the

wooden Buddha swaddled in tissue paper and thrust into a brown paper bag. He figures he'll give it to Sam. If she doesn't want it, she can always give it to some relative for a Christmas present. In any case, Cone is going to put the twenty bucks plus sales tax on his swindle sheet. Let Martha Hepplewaite scream when she sees that Haldering & Co. is billing her for "One Buddha, teak, hand-carved."

He cabs on uptown, exhilarated with all the client's cash he's spending. He knows upper Madison Avenue, he doesn't have to reconnoiter the ground. A splashy neighborhood. Big bucks and big greeds. Very little schlock here. Just bring fresh money.

The Laboris Gallery of Levantine Art fits right in. It's an elegant three-story building, the entire façade covered with faded blue tiles in a vaguely Persian pattern; foliage and beasts, bearded warriors and scimitars—all contained within a severely geometrical border. Timothy Cone, who knows Manhattan real estate values, can guess what that little gem of a building cost.

There's very little of the Levantine in the interior. It's all high-tech, with white walls, track lighting, and Lucite cubes, containing works of art, set on solid ebony pedestals. Soft music is coming from somewhere: a meringue of plucked strings and flutes that is simultaneously lulling and lascivious.

"May I be of service, sir?" she says, and again he hears the hisses and not the words.

He turns to look, and curses himself inwardly for being a filthy beast, because his initial reaction is: What a *dish!* He suddenly remembers a gyrene buddy of his spotting a similar woman on the street and remarking admiringly, "All you need with *that* is a spoon and a straw."

She is young, short, chubby: a butterball. Olive complexion, killing eyes, and a smile to melt titanium. Long black hair to her buns, and such a bursting, fleshy, burning look about her that the Wall Street dick is distraught enough to remove his leather cap—more from homage than politeness.

"Miss Laboris?" he asks, scarcely believing that croak is his voice.

"Yes," she says, "I am Ingrid Laboris."

"You own this gallery?"

"Oh, no," she says, laughing gaily. "That is Erica Laboris, my cousin. You would like to see her? She has just stepped out for a moment, but she should be back shortly."

"Okay," Cone says, "I'll wait. Meanwhile I'll just look around."

"Please do," Ingrid urges. "We have so many beautiful things."

He watches her move away, knowing he could get twenty years for what he's thinking. "Down, boy," he tells himself, and resolutely makes a tour of the gallery, inspecting all those splendid antiquities locked within Lucite cubes.

There are urns, vases, plates, silver jewelry and golden bowls, lapis lazuli necklaces, clay rhytons in the shape of rams' heads, volumes of poetry, miniatures, illuminations, scraps of textiles and calligraphies, book bindings and manuscripts. There is even a crouching sphinx in faience, and two terra-cotta monkeys copulating ferociously.

No prices are posted, but he knows he can't afford a single item even if he wanted it—which he doesn't. He abjured coveting *things* years ago, when he returned from Nam. But that doesn't prevent him from recognizing museum-quality art when he sees it.

"May I be of service, sir?" she says, and once again he hears the hisses.

She has approached so quietly that he hasn't even been aware that she was in the gallery. Her fragrance should have been the tipoff: the same rose-scented cologne Sven was wearing on Nineteenth Street. Cone figures the Laboris family is importing the stuff.

"Were you looking for something special, sir?" she asks, and he realizes all the cousins have trouble with their sibilants. A lot of spit there. Maybe, he thinks, it's a genetic defect—like his own impulse to say "thoity-thoid." His old man always called it a "horspital."

"Not really," he tells her. "You're Miss Erica Laboris, the owner?"

She nods with a two-bit smile.

"I just stopped in by accident," he explains. "I was down on Wall Street at Laboris Investments, and then came uptown and was walking by and saw your name. Is there any relation?"

"Oh, yes," she says, the faint smile flickering again. "That is Ingmar, our cousin. I hope you invested."

"I did. Do you think I did the right thing?"

"Absolutely," she says firmly. "Ingmar knows all about currency trading. I've invested money with him myself."

"Glad to hear it," Cone says. "Tell me something: Where do you get all these great old things you have here?"

She starts telling him about her frequent trips to the eastern Mediterranean, how she buys from traders and private collectors, how she'll have nothing to do with grave robbers and museum thieves, how every piece in the gallery is authenticated and has an impeccable provenance.

As she's speaking, he's staring. Erica is taller than Ingrid, older, and not as bloomy. But she is a striking woman, impressive, with the oiled Laboris skin, chalk teeth, and smoldering look that could be either unspent passion or dyspepsia.

From her polished spiel and slightly aloof style, Timothy figures her for a very brainy lady. And better a friend than an enemy. He notes her fingernails: long, narrow, and lacquered a deep indigo. Want those reaching for your carotid? No, thanks.

"That's very interesting," he says when her lecture ends. "To tell you the truth, I'm out of my depth here. I'm not a collector. I know from nothing about antique art. Maybe I better stick with Laboris Importers on Nineteenth Street."

"Oh," she says with her cool, brief smile, "you've been there, have you? Sven is another cousin. He carries some nice things. Very modern. But we have many casual visitors like yourself, Mr.—"

"Cone. Timothy Cone."

"Casual visitors like yourself, Mr. Cone. But sometimes they return, captured by the beauty, the mystery, the allure. It is an introduction to a vanished world of great creativity. Perhaps you, too, will return."

"Maybe I will."

"If you would care to leave your address, I would be happy to send you an advance notice when we have a special exhibit."

"That's nice of you," Cone says. He digs the battered wallet from his hip pocket and searches. Eventually he finds a dog-eared business card stuck to a small photo of Cleo that Samantha Whatley took with her Polaroid. The cat looks depraved. Cone peels away the card and hands it to Erica Laboris.

"So glad to meet you, Mr. Cone," she says. "Do stop by again. We're always getting in new things. New *old* things. Who knows—you might find something that you *must* have. To make your life complete."

"Yeah," he says, "that could happen."

He leaves the gallery and trudges slowly south on Madison Avenue. A miserable December day. A sky that looks like beaten lead, and an icy wind that just won't quit. He stops at a corner phone booth and calls Sam.

"Wanna eat Chink tonight?" he asks. "I'll spring for it. Your place. Around seven o'clock."

"Why, Mr. Cone!" she carols. "Ah sweah you sweep a gal right off her feet."

"Stuff it," he tells her and hangs up.

They're sitting on the floor, on one of Samantha's oval rag rugs, surrounded by cardboard containers of pork lo mein, shrimp with lobster sauce, sweet and sour chicken, fried rice, barbecued ribs, egg rolls, wonton soup, and six bottles of cold Tsingtao beer.

"You bought enough to feed a regiment," Sam says, gnawing on a rib.

"Well, whatever we don't finish, I'll take home. Cleo can live off the leftovers for a week."

"So?" she says, slurping wonton. "How you coming with the Hepplewaite case?"

"Okay," he says, stuffing his face with an egg roll.

"That's all you're going to say—okay?"

"That's all."

"Jesus," she says disgustedly, "you're at it again. I'm your boss—remember? Is it too much to ask that you keep me informed?"

"I'm in a mulling mood," he yells at her. "You know what mulling is? It means I don't know my ass from my elbow."

"All right, all right," she shouts back. "I should have known better than to expect any cooperation from a crotchety bum like you."

"Screw you," he says.

"Fuck you," she says.

They glower at each other, then go back to the pork, chicken, and the shrimp, spooning it over the rice and gobbling the mess with soy sauce squeezed from little packets.

"You going home for Christmas?" he asks, not looking at her.

"Yes, I'm going home for Christmas. What are you going to do?"

"Who the hell knows? Make a tree for Cleo. Deck the halls with matzo balls. Get drunk. You'll be back for New Year's?"

"Sure," she says, "I'll be back."

"Good," he says. "Then I can drink champagne out of your combat boots."

She tries not to smile, still sore at him. They finish most of the food, and what's left is spooned into a plastic bag for Cleo. All the empty containers are dumped in the garbage can, and they settle down with the remaining beer.

"Why are you such a prick?" she asks him.

"Because I enjoy it. Why are you such a bitch? Hey, I've got something for you."

He rises from the floor and goes over to the cretonne armchair where he's tossed his parka. He pulls a brown paper bag from underneath and hands it to Samantha.

"What's this?" she demands. "A bomb?"

"It's for you. Open it."

"My God," she says, "don't tell me you bought me a present. For Christmas?"

"Hell, no. I'm going to put it on my expense account. It's part of the Hepplewaite case. Go ahead, look at it."

She unwraps the tissue paper, holds the carved, grinning Buddha in her hands.

"From Laboris Importers," Cone explains. "Cousins to Laboris Investments. If you don't want it, give it to your folks when you go home."

Sam inspects the statuette, turning it around and around, then looks at the little sticker on the bottom.

"Made in Burma," she reports. "You know, I like it. It's cute."

"Cute, for God's sake? Well, it's hand-carved teak. One solid piece of wood."

"I definitely like it," she says, nodding. "I'm not giving it to anyone; I'm keeping it. How much did this little gem cost?"

"Twenty bucks, plus tax. The greaseball who sold it to me claims that if you rub the belly all your wishes will come true."

"Hey," she says, "that's cool." She starts rubbing the plump belly of the Buddha.

"What are you wishing for?" Cone wants to know.

"That's between me and Izzy here."

"Izzy?"

"That's what I'm going to call him—Izzy."

"You're gone," he tells her. "You should be committed. Izzy! That happens to be a religious statue."

"What the hell do you know about religion?"

"I'm religious," he protests. "I worship."

"Yeah? Like what?"

"Let me show you."

They're out of their clothes like a shot and snuggling under the quilt on her bed.

"You son of a bitch," she says, "why can't you be nice to me."

"Come off it," he says. "Niceness you don't need. It would just turn you off."

"You're right," she says, sighing.

They've given up trying to understand the pleasure they derive from their obsessive hostility. They're able to remain lovers as long as they remain adversaries. They hide their fears with bravado and think bullying will mask their vulnerability.

Perhaps the enigma is what keeps them socked together. Mystery adds spice when the glands take over, and in their lovemaking there is always the sinful excitement of coupling with a stranger.

But that night, under the quilt, randy as all get-out, neither is concerned with self-analysis. Trading wonton breaths and soy sauce kisses, they come together as if the third week in December were the rutting season in Manhattan, and each must prove a holiday passion.

With grunts and groans, sighs, and yelps, they make great sport of demolishing each other, their bodies fevered and agile. If they could slam foreheads and lock horns, they would. For when the hormones gush, they become insensate to tenderness, love, or compassion, and know only the glory of their sweaty struggle.

What a game they play! With coarse oaths and sweet whimperings, they deflower each other for the nth time. The contest ends a draw; no winner, no loser; just two exhausted and loony combatants staring at each other with wild and wondering eyes.

Until Samantha reaches out languidly to touch the belly of the Buddha she has placed on the bedside table.

"You know," she says softly, "it really works."

Cone gets to the office a half hour late, as usual, and sits at his desk without removing his parka or cap. He lights his third cigarette of the day, coughs, and calls Neal Davenport.

"My God, sherlock," the NYPD detective says, "I haven't heard from you in two weeks. I was afraid you were mad at me."

"Nah," Cone says, laughing, "nothing like that. Whatever happened to Martin Gardow?"

"Made bail and took a powder. We're not even looking for him. We've got Guiterrez on a homicide rap. He'll probably bargain it down, but he'll still spend a few years in the slammer where he can play pick-up-the-soap in the shower with guys bigger and tougher than he is. Is that why you called—to get caught up on my caseload?"

"Not exactly. There's something else."

"No kidding?" Davenport says. "I never would have guessed. What do you want now?"

"There's an art gallery on upper Madison, the Laboris Gallery of Levantine Art. I thought there might be someone in the Department who could give me a rundown on the place."

"What are they doing—fencing?"

"I don't know," Cone says, frowning at the phone. "I went up to talk to the lady who runs the joint, and before I know it, she's telling me how she will never have anything to do with grave robbers and museum thieves. When someone tells me how honest they are, the first thing I do is count my rings and check the fillings in my teeth."

"Yeah," the cop says, "I know what you mean. What's your interest in this art gallery?"

"The owner is a cousin of a guy who runs an outfit I'm investigating: Laboris Investments on Wall Street. They're paying out more than anyone could reasonably expect. I think there's a scam going on there, but I have no idea what it could be."

Davenport sighs. "You really come up with some dillies. I know a sergeant who works out of the Special Robberies Division. He's supposed to be a hotshot on art thefts. His name is Terry MacEver. I'll give him a call and tell him what you want. If he's interested, he'll call you back. If he doesn't, forget it.''

"Fair enough," Cone says. "I'll be in the office all morning."

Then he takes off his anorak and cap, and wanders down to Apicella's office. Sidney looks up indignantly, and Cone holds up a palm.

"Don't get your balls in an uproar, Sid," he says. "I know it's too soon to hear from your foreign contacts about Laboris. I just wondered if you had anything at all on the case."

"A little," the CPA says grudgingly. "Laboris Investments has a nice bank balance. They've also got a special fund set aside for redemptions. As far as I can tell from the first look, they're solid."

"Yeah," Cone says, "and I'm Queen of the May."

"That's possible, too," Sid says.

Cone goes back to his office and lights a Camel, dreaming up loopy criminal connections between Laboris Investments, Laboris Importers, and the Laboris Gallery of Levantine Art. But none of his fantasies work; it's all smoke.

He spends almost an hour working on his swindle sheet and weekly progress report to Samantha. They're smoke, too. When his phone rings, he grabs it in a hurry, hoping.

"This is Sergeant Terry MacEver, Special Robberies Division, NYPD. I got a call from Neal Davenport. He told me what you do and gives you high marks. That's the only reason I'm calling, d'ya see."

"Yeah, well, Neal and I have helped each other out on a couple of things."

"So he says. You're interested in the Laboris Gallery?"

"Sort of."

"Got anything on them?"

"Nothing," Cone says fretfully. "But when I was up there, I was the only customer in the place. If they own that building, it must have cost a mint. And if they're renting, I don't see how they're making it."

"They're renting," MacEver tells him. "From a cousin named Leif Laboris."

"Another cousin," Cone says, sighing. "That figures. Listen, can I buy you dinner or a drink? I've got an expense account I can fiddle."

"Not dinner," the sergeant says. "I've got to get home to walk my dachshund, d'ya see, and then get uptown for an art auction. But I'll take you up on the drink."

"Good enough. Where and when?"

"You know Pete's Tavern?"

"Sure I do. East Eighteenth Street."

"Right. I'll meet you at the bar there at four o'clock. Okay?"

"Fine."

"How will I make you?"

"A little under six, about one-seventy, spiky hair, dirty parka, black leather cap. I'll be drinking vodka, and I'll have a pack of Camels on the bar in front of me."

"That should do it," MacEver says. "If I'm a little late, don't get antsy; I'll be along."

"I'll wait," Cone promises, and hangs up, feeling a lot better. If a hotshot cop who specializes in art thefts knows about the Laboris Gallery, there must be some action there.

He gets to Pete's about twenty minutes early. He sits at the bar, still wearing his parka but with his cap off, rolled, and jammed in his pocket. He puts his pack of Camels on the bar and treats himself to a Finlandia on the rocks.

He's just started his second, and it's almost four-fifteen, when someone taps his arm.

"Timothy Cone?"

"That's right."

"Terry MacEver. Sorry I'm late."

"No sweat," Cone says, and they shake hands.

The sergeant isn't dressed like a cop, even one in mufti. He's wearing an Irish field hat, an unbuttoned Burberry trenchcoat, a suede sport jacket, tattersall waistcoat, doeskin shirt with a paisley ascot at the throat. Trousers are pinkish cavalry twill. Shoes are oxblood loafers with tassels.

MacEver sees the Wall Street dick eyeballing him, and laughs. "You like the threads? No, I'm not a *fagela*. This is my working uniform, d'ya see. I spend most of my working hours at art galleries and auctions and in antique shops. If I went in dressed like your average harness bull with a gravy-stained brown suit off plain pipe racks, I'd get nowhere. Listen, I'm going to have a gin martini straight up with a twist. Then let's take a booth where we can have a little privacy."

They sit across from each other, parka and trenchcoat off and folded on the bench seats alongside them. MacEver takes a gulp of his martini and squints his eyes with pleasure.

"First today," he says. "Plasma."

He's small for a NYPD cop, but Cone notes that the shoulders under the suede jacket are hefty enough, and the guy moves well. He's got a neatly trimmed chestnut mustache and a lot of wavy chestnut hair that looks like it's been styled and blow-dried. Everything about him is so neat and well-groomed that he makes Cone feel like a slob.

"Neal Davenport says you're a screwball," MacEver says briskly, "but a valuable screwball. So when you mentioned the Laboris Gallery I figured I'd take a chance. You scratch my back and I'll scratch yours."

"What else?" Cone says.

"Look, I'm going to talk fast because I don't have too much time. Let me give you a rundown on what I do. Now, how many art galleries and antique shops do you figure there are in New York?"

"A couple of hundred?" Cone guesses.

"How does sixteen hundred grab you? And that's only in Manhattan. And there's only me and a couple of part-timers I can call in to cover them all. Don't get me wrong; most of those sixteen hundred places are on the up-and-up. But there's a lot of fencing going on, some contract burglaries, and a lot of gonnifs in the business who wouldn't blink an eye if a Bowery bum showed up with a couple of antique miniatures painted on ivory and claimed he found them in a garbage can. You follow?''

''I follow,'' Cone says.

''Well, these places are licensed, but we can't cover them all. Occasionally the Consumer Fraud Department gets a complaint that a 'genuine Louis XIV chair' was actually made in Grand Rapids. Generally, the complaint ends up on my desk and I have to check it out. Dull stuff. But most of my job—the fun part—involves big-money thefts of art and antiques. We get alerts from Interpol and from a special outfit that sends out regular bulletins on art work swiped from museums and private collectors.''

''How much of that stuff is there?'' Cone wants to know.

''Art thefts worldwide? Last year about five thousand were reported.''

Cone whistles softly. ''Let me get us a refill,'' he says. He goes to the bar, comes back with another round, slides into the booth again.

''Thanks,'' the sergeant says. ''If I ask for a third, turn me down.''

''The hell I will,'' Cone says. ''This is *my* third. Listen, you said there were five thousand reported art thefts last year. You mean some are unreported?''

''Sure,'' MacEver says cheerfully. ''I'd guess at least double that number. For every one reported, the cops never hear about two others. Because the private collector who got ripped off bought his painting or silver chalice or whatever from a crook who stole it in the first place. So he can't go screaming to the cops, d'ya see. We'd want to know who he bought it from, how much he paid, does he have the proper documentation. The best part is this: The crook who lifted the work of art from the private collector is probably the same villain who sold it to him. There are supposed to be guys in the business who make a good living stealing and selling the same work of art over and over again.''

''That's beautiful,'' Cone says.

''Isn't it? Can I have one of your cigarettes?''

"Sure. Help yourself."

"I'm trying to quit smoking by not buying cigarettes. Now I find myself bumming them from other people. I'm going to die a mooch with lung cancer."

MacEver lights his Camel with a gold Dunhill, inhales deeply. The smoke doesn't seem to come out mouth or nose. It just disappears. He takes another sip of his martini. "Alcohol and nicotine," he muses. "Why don't I just slit my wrists and be done with it."

"Too fast," Cone says. "We've all got to suffer first."

"Yeah," the sergeant says. "Well, let's get back to art thefts. There's something else you should know about them: They run in cycles. One year it will be French Impressionist paintings. The next year it will be pre-Columbian statuettes. Even thievery has its trends—usually following what's bringing high prices at the big auction houses. That's where the Laboris Gallery comes in."

"That I *don't* follow," Cone says.

"Well, for the past year or so, the really 'in' fashion in stolen art has been stuff from the Near East. You know what things are like over there: bombings and raids and everybody shooting at everyone else. In the process, a lot of museums and private collections have been looted. So there's plenty of Islamic and pre-Islamic art work up for grabs, and it's dollars-to-doughnuts that most of it will end up in New York."

"*Now* I follow," Cone says. "But how are they getting the stuff into the country?"

"Good question. The Customs guys do what they can, but they're as understaffed and overworked as we are. Suppose a shipment of ten thousand wax bananas comes in from Columbia. You think *every* banana can be checked? No way. So Customs spot-checks and finds only wax bananas. But five hundred could be filled with pure cocaine. Who's to tell? Now, to get back to art thefts from the Near East, you think a pirate is going to airmail his loot directly from Beirut to New York? Fat chance! That valuable work of art is going to be transshipped and travel halfway around the world before it gets into this country, maybe from Mexico or Canada. We had a case about six months ago: a sword with a silver hilt set with diamonds and rubies. A real beauty. It was swiped in Lebanon, went to Turkey, to India, to Korea, to Taiwan, to Venezuela, to Cuba, to Miami, and eventually ended up in Manhattan as part of a shipment of office furniture. And the guy who engineered all this lives in Switzerland. How do you like that?''

"Did you nab him?'' Cone asks.

"Couldn't touch him. But we recovered the sword. We're holding it until the rightful owner can be determined—which will probably never happen. Anyway, right now the art scene in New York is being flooded with booty from Iran, Lebanon, Iraq, and Turkey.''

"Where do you start on something like that?''

"Since I'm such a cynical bastard, with the apparently legitimate art galleries and dealers who handle Islamic stuff. Some of them sell to the public, some only to private collectors. I've got a list of about fifteen possibles. The Laboris Gallery is one of them.''

"Oh-ho,'' Cone says.

"Yeah, oh-ho. But I've checked them out and they seem to be clean. You don't think so?''

Cone takes a swig of his vodka. "Don't know. All I can say is that they're occupying a prime piece of Manhattan real estate and aren't exactly thronged with customers. And the owner, a deep lady named Erica Laboris, made a point of telling me how honest she is. I'm itchy about that place.''

Terry MacEver sighs and finishes his martini. "See what you can come up with,'' he says. "Anything, and I do mean *any*thing, will be gratefully appreciated.'' He fishes in his inside jacket pocket, pulls out a pigskin wallet, extracts a card, and hands it across the table to Cone. "There's my number. If I'm not in, you can leave a message and I'll get back to you. Right now this whole business of smuggled

Near East art is driving me right up the wall. Listen, I've got to run. Thanks for the refreshment.''

They shake hands, and then Sergeant MacEver is gone. Cone carries the empty glasses and his parka over to the bar and orders another Finlandia. His third or fourth? He can't remember—and who the hell cares?

He sips his fresh drink slowly, smoking another Camel and reviewing all the stuff MacEver told him. Good background, he decides, but what has it got to do with Laboris Investments on Wall Street? Is Ingmar paying that 30 percent from the proceeds of smuggled Levantine art? Ridiculous. Who ever heard of a thief needing financing and going public? It would be like the Mafia selling shares.

Because MacEver was so ready to meet with him, Cone figures the sergeant is holding out. He knows something, or suspects something, about the Laboris Gallery he's not mentioning. That's okay; Cone said nothing to him about Laboris Importers on Nineteenth Street.

He looks into his empty glass of vodka and reflects that everyone wants the glory of the collar. It's understandable; it comes with the territory. But cops—locals, state, Feds, or whatever—have to think about their records and their careers. All Cone has to think about is his own satisfaction.

"Another, sir?" the bartender asks.

"Splendid idea," the Wall Street dick says, wondering if he'll get home alive.

It's a honey of a hangover. Nausea, dry heaves, headache, tremors, a parched throat, a cold sweat, gummy eyes, cramping of the bowels, self-disgust—the whole bit. Cleo looks at him sorrowfully.

"Don't *you* start," he tells the cat.

He drinks a quart of cold water, two cups of black coffee, pops four aspirin, takes a hot shower, starts a cigarette, and puts it out. He inhales twelve deep breaths, striding up and down the loft, tries to drink a cold beer and puts it back in the fridge. He belches, frequently, and Cleo retreats under the bathtub.

He's getting it together, pulling on his white wool socks with trembling hands, when his phone rings.

"The boss," he says to Cleo.

"Where the hell *are* you?" Samantha Whatley demands angrily.

"On my way," he says. "I overslept."

"Horseshit," she says. "I can smell your breath over the phone. Come to my office as soon as you get in. I've got something to show you."

"I've seen it," he says.

"Very funny. Just *be* here."

He walks to work as usual, figuring the fresh air will perk him up. But it isn't fresh; it's thick and smells of snow and sewer gas. He plods along, all scrunched up in his parka, heavy work shoes slapping the pavement, and wonders why he smokes too much, drinks too much, and generally plays the fool. He can solve other people's mysteries, but he can't solve his own.

"Screw it," he says aloud, and passersby glance at him nervously.

He lumps into Samantha's office, still wearing his cruddy cap and parka. She stares at him.

"Jesus!" she says. "You didn't shave, did you? Afraid you'd slit your throat? You look like the wrath of God."

"I *am* the wrath of God."

"Did you remember to feed Cleo?"

"Yes, I remembered to feed Cleo. Is that what you wanted to see me about?"

"Sit down," she says, "before you fall over."

He slumps gratefully into the armchair alongside her desk.

She looks at him a long, sad moment. "You're killing yourself," she says.

"Tell me about it," he says bitterly. "Come on, lectures I don't need. What's up?"

"You know that Buddha you gave me? I broke it."

He straightens in his chair. "You *broke* it? How? With a sledgehammer? That was one solid piece of teak."

"The hell it was," Sam says. "I didn't exactly break it, but take a look at this."

She reaches into the well of her desk, pulls out a Macy's shopping bag, and plucks out the Buddha.

"Looks okay to me," he says.

"Yeah?"

With a hard twist of her wrists, she separates the Buddha into two parts, base and figure. She displays the sections.

"Son of a bitch," Cone says wonderingly. "The momser who sold it to me swore it was one solid piece of wood."

"That's not all," Samantha says. "It unscrews the wrong way—clockwise. And then there's this . . ."

She holds up the butt of the separated Buddha. There's a hole drilled into the figure, about an inch in diameter and three inches deep.

"What the hell," Cone says. "Now why did they do that? To lessen the weight for shipment? Nah, that doesn't make sense. Listen, how did you find out it comes apart?"

"This morning I reached to shut off my Snooz-alarm and knocked him onto the floor. When I picked him up, I noticed the base was loose. I couldn't figure out how the two parts were connected until I tried twisting it the wrong way."

"It's interesting," Cone says. "Let me take it."

"I want it back," Samantha says sternly. "It's Izzy, and I love him."

"Cut the shit," Cone says roughly. "Give me the goddamned thing. I'll let you know what I find out."

"In a pig's ass," Whatley says, but she lets him take the Buddha dumped into the Macy's shopping bag.

He goes back to his office, takes off his cap and parka, and lets them fall to the floor, because some office bandit stole his coat tree. Then he sits down to examine the Buddha. He screws the two parts together tightly, turning them counterclockwise. When they're snug, he leans forward to examine the joint. You'd never notice if you weren't looking for it. Nice workmanship. The little label MADE IN BURMA is still stuck to the base.

He puts the Buddha under his desk and shambles down the corridor to the legal department. He's passing Apicella's office when the CPA calls, "Hey, Tim, got a minute?"

Cone pauses.

"Listen," Apicella says. "I got cables from three of my overseas contacts. None of them ever heard of this Ingmar Laboris. If he's trading in foreign currencies, he's got to be doing it through fronts. I don't like it."

"I don't either," Cone says. "Take my advice, Sid, and hold off on your PIE until I can get more skinny on this guy."

"Keep me informed," Apicella says anxiously.

"Oh, sure," Cone says, and continues on to Louis Kiernan's office.

"Hey," Cone says, "we got like an atlas or an encyclopedia around this joint?"

The young paralegal peers at him over his reading glasses. "No big encyclopedia," he says. "I've been trying to get a set of the Britannica, but Mr. Haldering won't okay the cost. But he did spring for a one-volume job. It's that thick book in the white cover on the top shelf."

Cone takes down the heavy volume and flips through it. He reads the paragraph on Burma. Chief products: teak, rubies, sapphires, and jade. He closes the book, replaces it on the shelf, starts out of the office.

"Find what you were looking for?" Kiernan asks.

"Who the hell knows?" Cone says.

Back in his own office, he separates the Buddha again and peers at the hole drilled into the base of the figure. It's a nice, smooth job. He can't see the residue of anything. He sniffs at it, but all he can smell is oiled wood. He puts the figurine aside, digs out his wallet, and calls Terry MacEver.

The sergeant is on another phone, so Cone leaves a message and waits patiently. Meanwhile he turns the Buddha over and over in his hands, shaking it once or twice. Nothing rattles. But closer inspection does reveal a lot number burned lightly into the bottom of the base—30818-K. Whatever that means.

True to his word, MacEver calls back.

"You got something for me?"

"More questions," the Wall Street dick says. "Yesterday, when you were talking about smuggled Levantine art, I didn't ask what the stuff was. Paintings? Sculpture?"

"A lot of things," MacEver says. "Miniatures. Manuscripts. Figurines. Illuminations. Weapons. Could be almost anything."

"Listen," Cone says, "could any of that fit in a container about an inch across and three inches long?"

"Very little of it. Maybe coins, a gold chain, a rolled-up page from a book. But we're talking about drinking cups and statuettes and old weapons."

"Yeah," Cone says. "Thanks for your time. I'll keep in touch."

"You do that," MacEver says.

After he hangs up, Cone realizes he is ravenous, having drunk his dinner the night before. He pulls on parka and cap, takes the Buddha along in the shopping bag, and leaves the office. He heads for a sloppy Irish pub on Broadway where he stuffs himself with Dublin broil, hashed browns, overcooked string beans, a lousy salad, four slices of soda bread, and two bottles of Harp.

Feeling a lot better, his violent eructations reduced to gentle burps, he takes a cab up to West Nineteenth Street to pay another visit to Laboris Importers.

The huge brass Buddha is still in the show window, a king-sized version of the teak job Cone is carrying in his shopping bag. While staring in the window, he spots something he hadn't noticed before: a small sign propped on a bamboo easel. LABORIS IMPORTERS, INC. THE DIFFERENT AND THE BEAUTIFUL FROM ALL OVER THE WORLD. STORES IN NEW YORK, BOSTON, BALTIMORE, WASHINGTON, ATLANTA, MIAMI, NEW ORLEANS, DETROIT, CHICAGO, ST. LOUIS, DENVER, LOS ANGELES, SAN FRANCISCO.

Cone is impressed. He hadn't realized this House of Schlock was a nationwide chain. He has a sudden vision of an army of grinning teak Buddhas, arms raised in triumph, taking over the country.

The store has plenty of customers prowling the aisles. Cone goes directly to the table where his Buddha had been displayed. It's laden with a phalanx of little stuffed rabbits from Taiwan. When you wind them up, they twirl and bang tiny cymbals affixed to their paws.

He marches to the sales counter at the back. There's a flock of clerks twittering away to each other. They all look like Laborises: swarthy skin, flashing eyes, teeth like sugar cubes. He can even smell that rose-scented cologne.

He holds up a hand, and a little lady comes scampering over.

"May I be of service, sir?" she asks with the familiar hiss.

"I'll bet you're a Laboris," he says.

"Oh, yes," she says, giggling. "I am Karen Laboris. We have met?"

"No, but I know some of your cousins." He fishes into his shopping bag, hauls out the Buddha. "Listen, I bought this a few days ago."

"And it's damaged? Your money will be cheerfully refunded, sir. No trouble at all."

"No, no," he says hastily. "Nothing like that. It's just that I like it so much—and my wife does, too—that we'd like to buy another one. But I can't seem to find any on display."

"Ahh," she says, "that was a very popular item. Handcarved. One solid piece of teak. So enchanting, don't you think? I am afraid we are out of stock."

"Oh, no," he says. "I promised I'd get one for my mother-in-law, who is in a nursing home, wasting away. Don't you have a single one left?"

She frowns. "Let me look in the stockroom, sir. It's possible there may be one on a back shelf."

"Thank you," he says. "I'd appreciate that."

While she's gone, he takes a look around. There's a lot of

new stuff that wasn't displayed on his first visit: suits of armor from Spain, Korean chests with brass hardware, enormous marionettes from India, leather hassocks from Turkey, quilts from Iowa, Portuguese wine flasks, and cuckoo clocks from Switzerland.

Cone is examining a Brazilian armoire when Karen Laboris comes trotting up to him, carrying a teak Buddha.

"I found one!" she announces happily. "The last in the store. You are in luck."

"Hey, that's great," he says, taking a quick look at the Buddha she's holding. It appears to be a double of the one in his shopping bag.

"That will be thirty-five dollars," she says. "Plus tax."

He doesn't quibble about the price. While she's making out the sales slip, he says, "I suppose your stores all over the country carry this."

"Oh, yes, sir," she says. "Everyone loves it. We've sold hundreds. If you rub the belly, it will—"

"I know," he says. "And I've been told it really works."

"It does," she says, giggling again. "Sir, Laboris Importers is going into the mail-order business. We plan to bring out a catalog of our most enchanting items twice a year. If you would care to leave your name and address, we will be happy to add you to our mailing list."

"That would be enchanting," he says, and gives her his name and home address. "That's a lovely perfume you're wearing," he adds.

"You like it?" she says archly. "It's made exclusively for us. It is called *Nuit de Fou*. I think that means Night of Craziness. Or something like that."

"Yeah," Cone says. "It figures."

He cabs back to the office, toting the two Buddhas in the Macy's shopping bag. He resists the temptation to inspect his new purchase until he's safely seated behind his desk. It appears almost identical to the first. A few variations here and there—but no more than you might expect from hand-carved works.

He picks up the latest acquisition, grips it firmly, and tries to unscrew the base. Nothing. He applies more force. Still nothing. He looks more closely, his nose squashed against the Buddha's belly. No hairline joint. The new statuette really is one solid piece of teak.

"Son of a bitch."

Cone sits back in his creaking swivel chair and glares at the two figures. Four arms upraised, two shiny bellies, two plump faces with beneficent grins. Cone grabs the latest purchase, turns it over, inspects the base. There's the label MADE IN BURMA. But the lot number reads 30818-M. So? The two Buddhas were imported in different lots, maybe different shipments.

He puts them close together on his desk, lifted arms almost touching, and he sits there, brooding. The more he stares at those plump, smiling faces, the more they remind him of something.

It doesn't take him long to make the connection. That stupid prospectus he picked up at Laboris Investments with the photo of Ingmar on the cover. Shave off the bushy mustache and he would look exactly like the grinning Buddhas.

2

"WELL, MAN," Mrs. Hepplewaite says. "What do you have to report?"

"Nothing," Timothy Cone says.

"Nothing?" she repeats angrily, thumping her heavy cane on the floor. "Then what am I paying you for?"

"You want me off the case? Call my boss and ask for a replacement. If you want to fire Haldering and Company, then fire them. It's your decision."

She glares at him. "You're as snotty as ever," she says.

"It's my nature," he tells her. "Look, if it'll make you feel any better, I think Ingmar Laboris is running a scam. But I've got absolutely no hard evidence. As of now, the guy is delivering, and apparently no one has lost any money."

"Did you check his background?"

"Yeah. No one's ever heard of him, in this country or overseas. He came out of nowhere."

"I told you so," she says triumphantly.

"So what? He could be trading currencies through agents or front companies. It's done all the time. And he's got a solid bank account with a special fund for redemptions."

"The man is a thief," she insists.

Cone stands and fastens the toggles on his parka. "Is that why you brought me up here? You could have told me on the phone. Now you're going to be billed for my transportation. By cab. Think of that."

She stares at him fixedly. "I don't like you much," she says.

"Welcome to the club," he says, stalking out.

"I expect immediate results!" she yells after him.

He can think of several choice rejoinders, but he doesn't voice them. He's halfway down the block, heading toward Madison Avenue, when he hears the sound of running feet. He turns and sees Lucinda Hepplewaite flying toward him, a big green loden cape floating out behind her.

"Hi," he says.

"Mr. Cone," she says breathlessly, "have you found out anything?"

"Nothing definite."

"Mama thinks Francis is a dolt," she says with an anxious, toothy smile. "But he's not."

"Francis? Your fiancé?"

She nods. "He's trying very hard to prove to Mama that he can take care of me. She doesn't think he's right for me. She doesn't think *any* man is right for me. Because she doesn't want to let me go. She wants a companion in her old age."

"I get the picture," Cone says.

"Please, Mr. Cone, if you hear anything bad about Laboris Investments, will you tell me first, before you tell Mama?"

He doesn't answer. "Is your fiancé still getting checks from Laboris?"

"Oh, yes."

"Thirty percent or more?"

"Well, the last check he received was a little under twenty percent. But that's still good, isn't it?"

"Uh-huh."

"And you'll tell me if you find anything wrong?"

"I'll see what I can do," Cone says, and watches her go running back to the brownstone, the cape billowing behind her.

He continues on to Madison Avenue and takes an uptown

bus. He doesn't know why he's decided to stake out the
Laboris Gallery of Levantine Art for a few hours. Maybe,
he admits, because he hasn't anything better to do.

He walks by the place and looks through the window.
Lights are on, the gallery is open, but it looks empty. No
customers, no Ingrid or Erica Laboris. Cone crosses
Madison and starts tramping up and down the other side of
the street, his eyes on the gallery entrance.

It's a cruel, naked December day with a wind that flays
and a lowery, sunless sky that presses down. Cone lights a
cigarette, stuffs his hands into the pockets of his anorak,
and plods back and forth, figuring he'll give it till noon.
Then maybe he'll grab a Coney Island red-hot, with all the
trimmings, from a street vendor, have a wild cherry cola,
and then head back to the office.

He's been patrolling for almost a half hour when he sees
two mink-clad matrons enter the gallery. They're inside for
maybe fifteen minutes and then come out and go on their
way. They weren't carrying any packages when they entered, and none when they exit. Zero plus zero equals zero.

During the next hour the gallery has two more visitors: a
big, heavy man in a tweed coat, and a spindly woman
wearing a knapsack over her down jacket. Neither stays
long, and Cone figures maybe they just went into the gallery
to look around and warm up.

It's about 11:45 when he spots another visitor. A shortish
man wearing a beret and a three-quarter-length coat of black
fur pops inside so quickly that Cone can't get a good look.
But he has an itchy feeling that he's seen the gink before. So
he takes up station almost directly across Madison and
keeps watching the gallery, though sometimes it's difficult
because the Christmas traffic is murder.

He stands there, stamping his feet and smoking his third
Camel. Eventually, almost a half hour later, the gallery
door opens. The beret starts to exit, then ducks back inside
for a moment. Finally he comes out, closes the door, moves
to the curb. He starts waving a hand for a taxi. Cone takes a

long look and makes him. It's Sven from Laboris Importers on Nineteenth Street.

"Hello, there," the Wall Street dick says softly.

It takes Sven almost five minutes to get a cab. Cone watches him go, then trudges eastward to Lexington or Third, looking for his Coney Island red-hot. He tries not to make too much of Sven's visit to the Gallery. They're all cousins, aren't they? The family that plays together, stays together. Whatever the hell that means.

Except that when Sven entered the gallery, Cone could swear he wasn't carrying anything. But when he came out, he was lugging a bulging briefcase.

It's almost two o'clock before Cone gets back to the Haldering office. There's a memo from the receptionist centered on his bare desk: Please call Terry MacEver. So, his stomach still grumbling from that hot dog with sauerkraut, onions, piccalilli, and mustard, the Wall Street dick calls the sergeant.

"Listen," MacEver says, "I've been thinking about your interest in the Laboris Gallery, d'ya see, and I did something I should have done before: I ran the owner, Erica Laboris, through Records."

"And she's got a sheet?" Cone says hopefully.

"Nope, she's clean. But Neal Davenport told me you were interested in Laboris Investments on Wall Street. What's the name of the boss?"

"Ingmar Laboris."

"Shit," MacEver says. "Close but no cigar. Nothing on Ingmar. But the computer did cough up the name of Sven Laboris. Does that mean anything to you?"

Cone is silent a moment. "Yeah," he says finally, "Sven works at a place called Laboris Importers on West Nineteenth. I think maybe he's the boss."

"Is that so?" the sergeant says, his voice suddenly cold. "You didn't mention Laboris Importers before. Not holding out on me, are you?"

"I wouldn't do that," Cone says righteously. "You're

interested in smuggled art. Laboris Importers is a junk shop. Besides, they're listed in the telephone book; it's no secret. Nah, I wasn't holding out on you. I just didn't think it was important.''

"Look," MacEver says, "if you and I are going to work together, just tell me what you know and let me be the judge of whether it's important or not. Okay?"

"Of course. Absolutely. So Sven Laboris has a sheet?"

"Not much of one. About six months ago the blues busted an after-hours joint on East Eighty-third Street. A penthouse yet! They shook down all the customers, which was probably a stupid thing to do because their warrant only covered the owners. Anyway, when they frisked Sven Laboris, they found a glassine bag of shit in his jacket pocket.''

"No kidding. Was he held?"

"Maybe for a couple of hours. But he had no needle tracks, no previous criminal record, and there was no evidence that he was dealing in what the government laughingly calls a 'controlled substance.' So he walked. Happens all the time. But here's the kicker: When the lab analyzed the heroin he was carrying, they said it was the purest they had ever seen. That stuff could have been cut six ways from the middle and still zonked fifty junkies. Shoot it uncut and it's instant DOA. Sven Laboris claimed someone must have slipped the skag into his jacket pocket after the blues broke in.''

"Oh, sure," Cone says. "And that's it?"

"That's it," the sergeant says. "I don't know if it means anything, but I'm giving it to you. Now what have you got for me?"

Long pause.

"Come on, come on," MacEver says impatiently. "There are no freebies in this business—you know that. What have you got?"

Cone decides he better play along; so he tells MacEver how he staked out the Laboris Gallery that morning and saw

Sven Laboris enter empty-handed and emerge about a half hour later carrying a briefcase.

"What has that got to do with your guy on Wall Street?" asks MacEver.

"Beats the hell out of me," Cone admits. "I can't see Ingmar financing drug or art smuggling with investors' funds and then paying off thirty percent. Banditos don't go looking for public money. They've got other ways to raise cash. Mostly from their profits on the last deal."

"I know what you mean," the sergeant says. "Well, you keep plugging, and I'll keep plugging, and maybe between us we can make a score. I won't hold out on you, but you don't hold out on me. Understood?"

"Oh, sure," Cone says, hanging up. And if you believe that, there's a swell bridge to Brooklyn you may be interested in buying.

He lights a cigarette and ambles down to Joe Washington's cubicle. It's identical to his own, except that Joe has a coat tree and a coffee maker he locks up in his desk every night.

"Hey, it's the Cone-head," Washington says, looking up. "How's it going, old buddy?"

"Getting by. And you?"

"Surviving. What're you doing for the holiday?"

"Celebrating Christ's birth."

"Yeah?" Joe says, looking at him closely. "Wanna come out to my house for Christmas dinner? Roast turkey, mashed potatoes with gravy, cranberry sauce—real honky soul food."

"Nah," Cone says. "You'll want to be alone with your family. But thanks anyway. Listen, I need some poop. Didn't you work a drug case about two years ago?"

"Closer to three," Washington says, leaning back in his swivel chair and laughing. "What a giggle that was! The client was a brokerage house on the Street. They suspected one of their account executives was dealing, so they called us in. Dealing? That idiot was trying to become the IBM of dope. He had even started a mail-order business. If we hadn't scuttled him, he'd have been selling futures in heroin and cocaine. The guy was blitzed out of his gourd.''

"You worked with the City on this?"

"Oh, sure. An undercover narc named Petey Alvarez. A wonderful guy. I still see him for drinks occasionally. What's your interest, Tim? You got a drug case?"

"I don't know what the fuck I've got," Cone says fretfully. "But there may be a heroin angle. The stuff usually comes over in kilo bags—correct?"

"Yeah. Two-point-two pounds."

"Where does it come in?"

"Boston, New York, Baltimore, Miami, the Texas coast, Los Angeles, San Francisco, Seattle. Here, there and everywhere."

"And how does it come in?"

"Hidden away in everything from office furniture to VCRs. There's a million ways to get the shit into the country. Every time the Feds close off one pipeline, ten new ones open up."

Cone is silent, thinking that over.

"Mostly from where?" he asks finally.

"Oh, hell," Joe Washington says. "A hundred places. If the climate is right, you can grow opium almost anywhere. The guy I helped nab was getting his supply from Turkey and Iran after it was processed in Marseilles and Sicily."

Cone perks up. "Turkey and Iran? The Middle East?"

"Yeah, but that was three years ago. Turkey and Iran claim they've put the opium growers out of business. Fat chance! Look, if you're a piss-poor farmer, you know you can make more money squeezing a poppy than growing rutabagas. So I'd guess there's stuff still coming from the Middle East. And of course there's always Cambodia, Vietnam, or Laos."

"And Burma?" Cone asks.

"Burma? Sure, Burma."

"Listen, Joe, could you call this Petey Alvarez and pick his brains a little?"

"I guess I could," Washington says slowly. "What do you want to know?"

"Well, you keep talking about how things were three years ago. Ask him about how things are now. Is there a lot of heroin on the street in New York? Or is it all cocaine? And does he have any idea where it's coming from and how it's getting in?"

Joe looks at him. "He could probably tell me all that, Tim, but what's in it for him?"

"Maybe a nice bust, maybe nothing. Will he go along with you on that basis?"

"I'll try," Washington says, sighing.

Cone goes back to his office and finds two file folders Samantha Whatley has dropped on his desk. Two new cases.

"Goddammit!" he shouts.

He sits down in his swivel chair and flips through the files. They look dull: Check out a proposed merger of two outfits that sell water pumps, and investigate a franchiser who's selling a chance to get rich by raising worms in your basement. The Wall Street dick already knows the answer to that one.

He tosses the folders aside, lights a Camel, leans back to review the day's happenings. He's got a possible drug-smuggling caper. He's got a possible art-theft scam. But what—if anything—is the connection with Laboris Investments on Wall Street?

Maybe, he thinks morosely, Ingmar is the Mr. Nice Guy of the family and strictly legit.

"And I also believe in the Tooth Fairy," Cone says aloud.

He gets up early the next morning, shaves, and even takes a shower. Cleo looks at him in amazement.

"What are you staring at?" he asks the cat. "It's Christmastime, isn't it?"

Sitting in his skivvies, he has two cups of black coffee, each with a cigarette. Then he sips a small shot of Italian brandy because he feels in a festive mood. He lets Cleo lick the rim of his empty glass.

"Stick with me, kiddo," Cone says, "and you'll be wearing diamonds."

He puts on what he calls his "good suit": a frowsy tweed jacket with suede patches on the elbows, flannel slacks (not too stained), a plaid shirt open at the neck to reveal a clean but somewhat grayish T-shirt. He straps the Magnum to his ankle and is ready for a fight or a frolic.

When he gets outside, he finds it has snowed during the night; there's almost an inch of powder on the sidewalks. But it's melting rapidly, and the air is razory, the sky washed. As usual, he hikes down Broadway to the Haldering office on John Street. Before he goes up, he stops at the deli for a container of black coffee and a buttered bialy.

At his desk, working on his breakfast, he calls Laboris Investments, Inc. If he can get through to Ingmar, he's decided to zap the guy with honesty. Not too much, of course, but enough to get him interested and willing to talk.

"Has Mr. Laboris returned from overseas?" he asks the perky receptionist who answers the phone.

"May I ask who's calling, sir?"

"My name is Timothy Cone, and I'm with Haldering and Company on John Street. I'd like to speak to Mr. Laboris if he's available."

"Just a moment, please," she chirps—from which Cone figures Ingmar is on the premises.

He munches on his bialy a couple of minutes before she comes back on the line.

"Thank you for waiting," she says. "Could you tell me what this is in reference to?"

He's got his scenario plotted. "Haldering and Company represents a private client who would like to make a substantial deposit with Laboris Investments. We have been asked to investigate. I was hoping for the opportunity to have a personal interview with Mr. Laboris."

"Just a moment, please, sir," she repeats, and she's gone again. He has finished his breakfast and lighted his third cigarette of the day before she comes back on again. "Mr. Laboris is tied up at present," she says. "But if you'd care to leave your number, he'll get back to you as soon as possible."

"That'll be fine," Cone says, and gives her the Haldering number.

"Thank you, sir," she says.

He sighs, hangs up, and doesn't do anything but smoke and count the walls for the next twenty minutes. He hopes Ingmar has taken the bait and is checking out Haldering & Co. When his phone rings, he picks it up, determined to be humble.

"Timothy Cone," he says instead of his usual "Yeah?"

"This is Ingmar Laboris speaking."

"Thank you for calling back, Mr. Laboris. I realize what a busy man you are, but I was hoping you might be able to give me a few moments to discuss an investment one of our clients wishes to make."

"So I understand," Ingmar says. The voice is plummy, with the churchy resonance of a monsignor or a proctologist. No hisses for Ingmar. "I must tell you I do not ordinarily meet with individual investors or their representatives. My time is almost totally devoted to managing our currency portfolio."

"I appreciate that, Mr. Laboris, but perhaps you'd be willing to make an exception in this case. The investment our client is planning is of such a size that we feel a personal interview is necessary."

"What amount are we speaking about?"

"A quarter of a million," Cone says, hoping that won't be too small to turn Ingmar off or too large to make him suspicious.

"I see," the other man says thoughtfully. "Well, let me take a look at my appointment calendar."

Got him! Cone exults, recognizing the ploy.

"If you can be here at ten-thirty this morning," Laboris says, "I will be able to fit you in. But I must tell you it can only be for a limited time. I am flying to Zurich at noon."

"I appreciate your help," Cone says. "I'll be in your office at ten-thirty on the dot."

It's only after he hangs up the phone that he says, "Fink!"

He gets to Laboris Investments ten minutes early, intending to scout the territory. The outer office is crowded with plungers, but nothing like the mob scene he had witnessed on his previous visit. Speculators are still signing up and plunking down their bucks, but Cone wonders if the bloom is off the rose.

He wanders about, picks up one of those skimpy brochures and reads it again, once more noting the caveat: "Past performance is no guarantee of future results." And then there's the photo of Ingmar: plump, glossy, with that gleeful look of the Buddha statuettes.

And when Cone is ushered into the inner office, the man himself, standing behind an enormous mahogany desk, looks even more like a mustachioed Buddha, for he has a smooth, round belly that bulges his vest. His skin has the Laboris margarine sheen, and his handclasp is slippery.

"Mr. Cone," he says in that orotund voice. "Delighted to make your acquaintance."

"Likewise," the Wall Street dick says. "I certainly do appreciate your making time for me in your busy schedule."

Laboris waves that away, and with the same gesture indicates the leather armchair facing his desk. But he doesn't, Cone notes, offer to relieve him of his anorak. Since the office is overheated, that's probably Ingmar's tactic to make his visitor's stay as short as possible.

"Would you be offended if I smoked a cigar?" Laboris asks. "I fear I am addicted."

"Go right ahead," Cone says. "As long as I can light up a spike. I'm hooked, too."

"Of course," Ingmar says, moving a heavy ashtray halfway between them. It's a solid chunk of smoky quartz, faceted like a diamond but with a shallow depression to hold ashes. "A Nepali prince gave me that. It's amusing—no?"

"Yeah," Cone says. "Amusing."

He watches solemnly as Laboris goes through the slow ceremony of lighting his cigar.

"Now then, Mr. Cone," he says, "how may I be of service?"

"I don't know if you're familiar with Haldering and Company, sir, but we do financial investigations for corporate and individual clients. You can check us out if you like."

"I already have," Laboris says with a soft smile. "You're not one of the biggest firms in that business, but you have a good reputation."

"Well, we try. Anyway, we have a client who wants to put a quarter-million in your operation and is paying us to take a look-see. No reflection on you, of course; it's just prudent investing."

"I understand. And naturally you cannot reveal the name of this client."

"Naturally."

Ingmar regards the lengthening ash on his cigar with pleasure. "I must tell you," he says, "each time I smoke I play a game to see how long an ash I can produce before it falls off. To prove the steadiness of my hand."

"It looks steady enough to me," Cone says, realizing that there is no way this guy is going to be surprised, shaken, or angered.

"Foreign-exchange trading is a minute-by-minute thing, isn't it?" Cone asks. "How do you keep up?"

"Through open telephone lines to my chief agents overseas. We avoid computers and telecommunications equipment, but I must tell you, I am in constant touch with market changes, no matter how frequent or how small. The exchange rate between, say, British pounds and Israeli shekels may suddenly vary by a tenth of one percent. Doesn't sound like much, does it? But when you're dealing in hundreds of millions, as I am, there's money to be made on that tenth.''

''Or lost.''

''That,'' Ingmar Laboris says, ''I try very hard not to do.''

''You mentioned your overseas agents. We've checked with currency traders in several European cities, Mr. Laboris, and none of them has ever heard of you.''

The ash falls from Ingmar's cigar onto the polished desktop. He makes no effort to scoop it up or brush it away, but looks at it sorrowfully. ''What a shame,'' he says. ''I had hoped to grow it longer. About my not being known to foreign-exchange traders overseas, I must tell you that I am delighted to hear it. You see, Mr. Cone, I deal daily in vast sums. If I did it in my own name, my trades would be sufficient to quirk the market. Even a rumor of my interest might destroy a potentially profitable deal. So I am happy to remain anonymous. I employ almost a hundred agents all over the world who trade for me and who are wise enough, I trust, not to mention the name of Laboris Investments. I must tell you that money trading is a very ancient and arcane art.''

''Yeah,'' the Wall Street dick says. ''Jesus drove them from the temple, didn't he?''

Laboris tries to smile. ''I believe the biblical reference is to money *changers*. Somewhat different from modern currency traders.''

Cone could have argued that but decides he's pushed it far enough. ''Mr. Laboris, I haven't seen anything that looks like an annual report. You issue them, don't you?''

Ingmar sets his cigar carefully aside in the quartz ashtray. ''I certainly intend to. I must tell you that Laboris Investments has been in existence for less than a year so, as of this date, no annual report has been issued. However, I have organized a special staff for that purpose, and we anticipate having a complete report available by the middle of March.''

He glances at his gold Rolex, and Cone know's he's not going to prod this guy into making any mistakes or unexpected disclosures. Sitting back, manicured fingers laced across his vested belly, Laboris looks bland, oiled, and satisfied. The slick black hair is without a wayward strand, and the full lips are rosy enough to be rouged. He's wearing a suit of smooth gray flannel. He also sports a gold pinkie ring with a rock just slightly smaller than the Kohinoor.

''A couple of final questions,'' Cone says. ''What is the minimum investment you accept?''

''Five thousand. But additional funds may be deposited in existing accounts in thousand-dollar increments.''

''And what is your current rate of return?''

Ingmar pauses a moment, then sighs heavily. ''Unfortunately, at present it is only a little over ten percent—due mainly to the unexpected rise in value of the Japanese yen.''

''Uh-huh,'' Cone says. ''The yen'll do you in every time.''

''However, I have every confidence that we will improve on net profits in the next few weeks. I am especially interested in the relationship between German marks and Swiss francs. It's a very volatile situation, and I think there's a small fortune to be made.''

''Yeah,'' Cone says, ''if you start with a large fortune.''

Both men laugh heartily, each as falsely as the other, and Cone rises to leave. Ingmar comes up close to give him that slick handshake again. Cone gets a whiff of the familiar Laboris scent: desiccated roses.

''I certainly hope I have addressed all your questions adequately, Mr. Cone.''

''You've impressed me,'' the Wall Street dick says.

''And you'll recommend Laboris Investments to your client?''

"I'll certainly make a recommendation. You'll probably be hearing from us shortly. Thank you for your time, Mr. Laboris."

He can't wait to get into the hard, clean December sunlight. The stench of con is overpowering, and it takes the long walk back to John Street to rid himself of that odor of glib thievery. What *is* the sonofabitch up to?

Back in his office, the answer still eludes him. He doodles a rough equilateral triangle on a scratchpad. At the apexes he writes the names of three cousins: Sven Laboris, Erica Laboris, Ingmar Laboris. Sven gets the notation: "Possible dope smuggling." Erica gets "Possible art theft" after her name. And Ingmar gets a big, fat question mark. It's a triangle, Cone is convinced, but he can't see the connection between cheap gimcracks, expensive Levantine antiques, and Laboris Investments, Inc., of Wall Street.

"Screw it," he says aloud, and calls down to the deli for a hot corned beef on rye, with cole slaw, a half-dill pickle, and two cold cans of Michelob Light.

That afternoon, Joe Washington comes slouching into Cone's office and finds Timothy drowsing, chin down on his chest. Joe grins and calls softly, "Hey, Tim, got a minute?"

Cone opens his eyes. "I got a lot of minutes—all empty. Pull up a chair."

"You feeling okay?"

"If I felt any better I'd be unconscious. What's doing, Joe?"

Washington pulls a small notebook from his jacket pocket and starts flipping pages. "I talked to Petey Alvarez, that narc pal of mine."

Cone straightens in his swivel chair. "That's great. Come up with anything?"

"More than you want to know," Joe says, reading his notes. "The opium poppies are squeezed in Bhutan, Bangladesh, Laos, Thailand, Vietnam, Cambodia, Burma,

Turkey, Iran, Pakistan, Afghanistan, and points north, east, south, and west. The raw stuff used to be sent to Marseilles and Sicily for processing, but most of those labs have been busted. The latest thing is to set up plants close to the source of supply. Cut out the middleman. So the shit is coming in from all over the Middle and Far East.''

"That's nice," Cone says.

"Yeah. Some of it is quality, some of it probably has sand, sugar, or talcum powder mixed in. To answer your specific questions, the price on the street right now has gone up. You get less in your nickel and dime bags. But there's plenty available. If you've got the gelt, you get your melt.''

"And that's it?"

"Just about," Joe says, closing his notebook. "One more thing: Petey says in the last six months or so, some really high-quality smack has been coming in. Which means a small amount goes a long way after it's been cut. And that's all I got. Any help, Tim?"

"Who the hell knows?" Cone says. "But thanks anyway."

After Washington leaves, Cone opens the bottom drawer of his desk and stares down at the two Buddha statuettes. It takes him a moment to identify his first purchase, the one with the removable base. He separates the two sections and peers into the neat hole drilled up into the figure.

That hollow could never contain a kilo. It might, he estimates, hold six ounces of a white powder packed tightly. Six ounces. Not much. He pulls a scratchpad toward him and does some quick figuring.

Say Laboris Importers brought in a thousand hollowed Buddhas for distribution all over the country. Six ounces of heroin per Buddha. Six thousand ounces. About 375 pounds. Or about 139 kilos. If the stuff is pure, maybe they could get $30,000 per kilo. More than four million for the lot. Nice. And then, because the cousins are all business, they sell the emptied Buddhas in their schlock shops.

And the solid Buddha, the one that doesn't separate?

Maybe that's one of the dummies put up front in the shipment in case Customs wants to take a look.

And, Cone realizes, they would use more than the Buddha statuettes. The stuff could be hidden in leather hassocks from Turkey, porcelain elephants from Korea, huge marionettes from India. Those things are big enough to contain a whole kilo of shit.

And also, Cone thinks, big enough to conceal Levantine art, like urns, bowls, rhytons, manuscripts, weapons—anything. What a sweet setup. You deal in crazy cuckoo clocks and end up with a zillion bucks from smuggled dope and stolen art work. Beautiful.

But all smoke, he acknowledges. He hasn't got a smidgen of hard evidence to prove what he guesses is going down.

He puts the two teak Buddhas away and slams the desk drawer. He's no sooner done that than Samantha Whatley comes storming into his office.

"Where's Izzy?" she demands. "I want him back—now!"

"What's the rush?" Cone says mildly. "You'll get him back eventually."

Sam leans down and lowers her voice so no one will overhear. "Listen, bubblehead," she says, "you don't give me so many gifts that I'm going to give up Izzy without a fight. You give me something and then you take it back. What kind of bullshit is that? And if that isn't enough, you cheap bastard, you're not even paying for it; it's on your swindle sheet, for God's sake. Come on, let's have it."

Sighing, Cone opens the lower desk drawer, fumbles inside, pulls out the solid Buddha, and shoves it at her.

"Here," he says, "take the goddamned thing."

Samantha takes a close look at the statuette and then, without even trying to untwist the base, glares at Cone wrathfully. "What are you trying to pull? This isn't Izzy."

He groans. "How do you know?"

"Because my Izzy has a cute little dimple in his chin. This one doesn't."

"A cute little dimple? Jesus Christ!" He hauls the other Buddha from the desk drawer and hands it to her. "Go ahead, unscrew the base. The first one is a solid piece of wood."

Sam inspects the two statuettes carefully, then looks at Cone, perplexed. "What the hell's going on, Tim?"

"Damned if I know."

"Oh, you know," she says angrily. "You're just not telling me."

"Nothing to tell."

"What a hardass you are. Well, I don't care, I'm taking Izzy with me."

"Okay, but keep it safe; I may have to borrow it again one of these days."

"Lots of luck," Samantha says, sweeping out of his office, the Buddha cradled in her arms.

Cone opens a fresh pack of Camels, lights his umpteenth cigarette of the day. He sits smoking slowly, staring at the solid teak statuette on his desk. Its arms are stretched high in a banzai gesture, plump face creased in a happy grin. Finally, he pulls the phone close and calls Sergeant Mac-Ever.

"What's happening?" MacEver wants to know.

"Nothing's happening; that's why I'm calling. I've got a wild idea I want to try on you."

"About the Laboris Art Gallery?"

"Yeah. Would you be willing to try a sting?"

"How do we do that?"

"Well, you told me you get reports from Interpol and other places on stolen works of art. Right?"

"That's correct."

"Suppose you pick out one of the items and we send someone to the Laboris Gallery to ask if Erica can find them a similar item. If she refuses to bite, she's clean. If she says she'll see what she can do and then actually delivers, we've got her. What do you think?"

Silence.

"Sergeant?" Cone says. "You there?"

"I'm here," MacEver says finally. "It's not a *bad* idea, but it needs a lot of work. Most art galleries get photos and descriptions of stolen objects, so you can't just waltz in, describe a piece of loot, and say you want to buy it. That would alert any art dealer, especially if they don't know you from Adam."

"Yeah, I can see that. So you think a sting is out?"

"I didn't say that. But it would have to be rigged very carefully."

"Have you ever met Erica Laboris?" Cone asks. "Would she recognize you?"

"No, I've never met her, and I doubt if she'd make me."

"Okay, how about this: I go up to the gallery and tell Erica I've got a wealthy brother-in-law who's a nut on collecting antique daggers or pisspots or whatever. You select the item from your list of stolen stuff. I say the guy is coming to New York from Topeka on a business trip and he'd like to stop by and see if she's got anything to add to his collection. You follow? We suck her in slowly."

"And I play the brother-in-law?"

"Sure," Cone says heartily. "I mean, you know the business, don't you? This is one shrewd lady, and she'd know in a minute if you're a genuine expert or just a plant."

"It just might work," the sergeant says slowly, "but I may have some trouble convincing my boss. At any rate I'll give it the old college try. I'll get back to you as soon as possible."

Cone hangs up, satisfied that he's started one wheel turning. Figuring he's given Hiram Haldering enough sweat for one day, he pulls on his parka and cap, shoves the solid Buddha in Samantha's shopping bag, and, carrying that, heads for home.

As he leaves the building, he spots a tall, scrawny guy wearing a ratty trench coat and a black slouch hat, like a foreign correspondent from the 1930s. He's leaning against a mailbox, mumbling to himself and shifting his weight slowly from foot to foot.

Just one of your Manhattan weirdos, Cone figures, and turns north on Broadway. Two blocks later, he stops for the sign to change from DON'T WALK to WALK, and sees the nut case in the trench coat standing at his elbow, still mumbling.

Having learned to live defensively in New York, Cone slows to let the mumbler get ahead of him. But no dice; the trench coat begins to saunter, too, staying about fifteen feet behind the Wall Street dick. Cone stops to look in a shop window with a tasteful display of plastic Christmas trees and Styrofoam ornaments. The weirdo stops and stares around vaguely.

If he's shadowing, Cone figures he's got to be the most inept tail since General Hood lost track of General Sherman at the Battle of Atlanta. The mumbler sticks at Cone's heels for three more blocks. Then the investigator decides to dump him. Cone darts out into oncoming traffic on Chambers Street, sprinting, pausing, pirouetting like a ballet dancer. He makes it to the other side, bones intact, ignoring the screams of infuriated drivers. He looks back. The trench coat is still hesitating on the curb, waiting for the light to change.

He walks home at a faster pace, proud of his performance. He stops at a local deli, picks up barbecued pork ribs, a container of potato salad, and a cold six-pack of Heineken. When he comes out of the store, the mumbler is across the street, inspecting the heavens.

''Shit!'' Timothy says aloud, startling a young couple who are walking by, holding hands.

Up in the loft, door locked, bolted, and chained, he sets out his evening meal. Cleo sits patiently on the floor at his side, waiting for discarded bones.

Cone works his way through two pounds of ribs, a half pound of potato salad, and two cans of beer. Then he goes to the front window and pulls the torn shade aside. The tall, scrawny guy is standing in the doorway of a closed Japanese sushi joint across Broadway. Even at a distance, Cone can see him slowly weaving from side to side. Got to be stoned out of his gourd, Cone decides.

"Ah, the hell with it," he tells Cleo. "I shall return carrying my shield or on it."

That doesn't impress the cat at all.

He pulls on his cap and anorak. Then he transfers the .357 Magnum from ankle holster to the parka's right-hand pocket, goes downstairs, and crosses to the other side of Broadway.

"Mr. Laboris, I presume," he says, walking up to the tail.

"Beat it, bum," the guy says. He doesn't look like a Laboris: too tall, too pale, too thin. He's got a saber of a nose, his teeth are tarnished clunks, the eyes are black aggies.

"What are you on?" Cone asks. "I'll make one guess: smack—right? Really good stuff?"

"Get lost," the man says hoarsely. "I'm waiting for someone."

"You're waiting for death," Cone says. "It could be me if you keep tramping up my heels. Who hired you?"

The guy straightens up from his slouch. He takes a deep breath. "You asked for it," he says.

"Oh-ho," the Wall Street dick says. "We seem to have a little altercation brewing here. Okay, put up your dukes."

Cone raises balled fists, begins dancing about the other man, tossing short punches at the air, stubbing his nose with a thumb.

"Come on," he says. "Lay on, Macduff, and damned be him who first cries, 'Hold, enough!' "

"My name ain't Macduff."

Cone reaches out to slap the man's face lightly. "No?" Slap. "What is it?" Slap. "What is it?" Slap.

"You stop that!" a woman says. "Stop beating that man!"

Cone turns to see a middle-aged couple: mink coat and British short-warm. The man is trying to tug the woman away.

"I'm not beating him," Cone says. "I just want to punish him. He raped my cat."

"He what?!"

"You heard me," Cone says. "Bestiality. Disgusting."

"Come along, Cynthia," the man says.

"I'm going to call the police," the woman says defiantly.

"Yeah," Cone says, "you do that. Tell them I've cornered the mad cat rapist who's been terrorizing lower Manhattan."

"You prick," the mumbler says when the couple scurries away. "You're a rotten, no-good prick."

"Who hired you?" Cone asks, slapping the guy's face again, harder this time.

Cone thought he was stoned, out on his feet, but the gink moves fast. His hand comes out of his trench coat pocket, there's a snick and a click, and six inches of raw knife blade gleam dully. And he knows how to use it, not gripped like a dagger, hand raised to strike a blow, but knuckles down, ready for a smooth stab or slash.

"Come ahead," Cone says, knowing he hasn't got time to start fumbling for his iron. "Make your play. Do what you're getting paid to do."

The guy lurches, but he's clumsy, hasn't got the moves. Cone feints, then goes in under the steel. He gets a solid wrist lock, twists, then turns the whole arm. He raises his own knee and brings the other man's arm down hard. There's a satisfying *crack!* The knife clatters to the sidewalk.

"You hurt me," the man says wonderingly, looking down at his dangling arm. "I think it's busted."

"I think so, too," Cone says. "I'll bet it hurts."

Then, when the guy's eyes glaze over and he begins to fall, the Wall Street dick catches him under the arms and eases him down. He'd like to search him, but Cynthia in the mink coat might have made good on her threat to call the cops. So Cone recrosses Broadway and climbs the six floors to the loft.

He mixes a muscular vodka and water and paces up and down the loft, drinking, waiting for his adrenaline level to get back to normal, and trying to figure who sicced the mumbler on him, and for what reason. It just doesn't make sense. Why hire a spaced-out junkie to scrag someone? And Laboris Importers already knew his home address—if the hophead was paid to track him to his wallow.

He gives up trying to puzzle it out. He freshens his drink (with vodka, not water), and sits again at the rickety table. He takes the solid Buddha from the Macy's shopping bag and sets it on the floor. Cleo comes padding over to investigate.

The denutted tom stares at the statuette, sniffs it all over, then begins rubbing his flanks against the smooth teak belly.

"Keep rubbing, kiddo," Timothy Cone says, "and make a wish. Maybe you'll get your balls back."

The next morning, he's on his second cup of black coffee and second cigarette when the wall phone rings in the kitchen. It makes a loud, shrill jangle and sends Cleo scuttling under the bathtub.

"Yeah?" Cone says.

"Neal Davenport," the NYPD detective says. "Don't you ever go to work on time?"

"Nah. But I make up for getting in late; I leave early. What's up?"

"Not me, that's for sure," Davenport says. "Had your first laugh of the day?"

"I could use a mild chuckle."

"Late last night the blues in your precinct picked up a clunk in the doorway of a sushi bar right across the street from where you live. That's a laugh, isn't it?"

"A corpse?"

"Deader than Paddy's pig."

"How'd he go?"

"Knife. The preliminary report says he was stabbed three times in the gut, and then a final cut tickled his heart, and that was it. He's been ID'd as Sidney Leonidas. That name mean anything to you?''

''Yeah,'' Cone says. ''Leonidas was the king of Sparta in the fourth century B.C.''

''I don't think it was him,'' Davenport says. ''This one was a junkie. He was covered with ulcerated needle tracks. The docs figure that even if someone hadn't offed him, he'd have OD'd from shooting shit, probably sooner than later.''

''Very interesting. But why are you telling me all this?''

''Because every time something happens on your block, I get antsy about you. You do crazy things and then leave it to us to pick up the garbage.''

''Yeah, but I deliver, don't I? Maybe not right away, but eventually.''

''Well . . . maybe,'' the city dick says grudgingly. ''How's the Laboris thing coming along?''

''Slowly. Nothing to report.''

''And if there was, you wouldn't talk, you tight-mouthed bastard. Look, Cone, if you've got anything that'll help us on this homicide, spit it out.''

''I don't know a damned thing about it.''

''The guy had a busted right wing. You know anything about that?''

''Not a thing.''

''Shit!'' the city bull says disgustedly. ''You and your goddamned secrets. One of these days you're going to realize that you've got to go along to get along.''

''Did you find the knife?'' Cone asks.

''What?''

''The knife that killed this Sidney Leonidas. Did you find it?''

''That's just when I mean,'' Davenport says indignantly. ''You want to pick my brains, but you won't open up to me. All right, I'll toss you a crumb: No, we did not find the murder weapon. Now just remember you owe me one.''

''Thanks,'' Cone says. ''I'll be in touch.'' And he hangs up.

He peers out his front window and, across Broadway, sees NYPD sawhorses around the sushi bar. There's one uniformed cop on duty, talking to a few of the rubbernecks. Otherwise no activity. Cone pulls on cap and parka, checks his ankle holster, and sets out to trudge down to John Street.

Meteorologists have been predicting a white Christmas, and it sure smells like one. It's cold enough for a wet snow, and the air is thick, clotted, and beads on Cone's leather cap. He plods along steadily, reacting automatically to traffic lights and pedestrian flow, but oblivious to the cityscape. He's pondering the murder of Sidney Leonidas.

He knows from experience that nine times out of ten the solution to any problem is the most obvious one. In the case of the mumbler's death, the evident explanation is that some villain came along, maybe a junkie himself, saw a guy passed out in a dark doorway, and decided to pick him clean. But Leonidas roused and put up a fight. The knife was there, handy on the sidewalk, so the mugger grabbed it up and made the muggee's quietus with a bare bodkin.

It listens—but could Leonidas put up a fight with a busted right arm? Cone doesn't think so. A little old lady on crutches could have lifted the guy's wallet and shoes; he was in no condition to offer resistance. He was *out* when Cone left him.

So the obvious doesn't have all the answers. The next best guess is that Sidney Leonidas was done in deliberately, with malice aforethought. Someone wanted him gone.

The Wall Street dick doesn't enjoy that idea. Because the logical perpetrator might well be a guy who hired the mumbler to waste Cone and followed him to make sure the job was done properly. Then, when he witnessed the confrontation between the two and saw his assassin chopped down and laid to rest in the doorway, the boss decided he better get rid of his junked-up thug in case he had told or might tell Cone or the cops who he was working for.

That scenario holds together, but it makes Timothy look like a pointy-head. It means that while the mumbler was following him to his loft from the office, there was a second shadow behind both of them, keeping an eye on the action and ready to take over if things got hairy. And Cone had never been aware of a second tail.

He doesn't like it. There are a lot of desperadoes in New York, and the knave who hired Sidney Leonidas will probably not quit after one failure. He'll come on again. And again. That realization makes for an itch between the shoulder blades and a tendency to flinch at any loud street noise.

Now I know how the President feels, Cone thinks—but that's no comfort.

Sergeant MacEver is waiting in the reception room of Haldering & Co. He's dressed dapperly and carrying an attaché case of black alligator. Cone leads the way to his office.

"Beautiful," the sergeant says, looking around. "This place should be condemned."

"It has been," Cone tells him. "We're just waiting for the wrecker's ball. I think they're going to build a skyscraper or a parking lot or something. Take a chair."

MacEver sits down, still wearing his natty fur-collared chesterfield and a trooper's cap of black mink.

"About that sting on the Laboris Gallery," he says. "I think maybe we can finagle it."

"Good," Cone says. "Best news I've had today."

"But I don't have an absolute go-ahead. You know how the Department works; no one wants to stick his neck out, in case it ends up a complete disaster. But I did get tentative approval to put the play in action. Here's how I plot it: We follow your original scenario. You make the first approach. I'm your rich brother-in-law, in New York on a business trip. I'm a nut collector of antique swords, and I'm especially interested in getting hold of some old blades from the Near East. You with me so far?"

"I'm following."

"Okay," the sergeant says. He leans down to open his attaché case, pulls out an 8×10 b & w photo and hands it to Cone. "That's what we're looking for."

Cone inspects the grainy photograph. "Looks like a hunk of junk to me."

"Does it? Well, they're maybe seventy or eighty of them in the world that have been definitely identified and dated. This particular blade is Assyrian and was hand-forged around the sixth century B.C. They were still making iron swords then, but using bronze for the hilts. Anyway, this one was stolen from a Beirut museum about six months ago."

"What's it worth?" Cone asks.

"Hard to say. Who would want a rusty piece of old iron except a museum or a collector? It's worth whatever you can get for it. I'm just telling you all this stuff as background, d'ya see. When you make your pitch to Erica Laboris, all you know is that you've got a wealthy relative who's ape for antique swords from the Middle East."

"I dig. I make the intro and then you show up and take it from there."

"Right," MacEver says approvingly. "We'll play this very cozily and see what the lady suggests. When can you start the ball rolling?"

"Today," Cone says. "Maybe this morning. You want me to use your real name?"

"No," the sergeant says. "Too risky. I've got some business cards from an insurance outfit in Dallas that I've helped out on a few things. They'll cover for me. Here, take it and leave it with the mark."

He hands a card to Cone. It reads: J. Ransom Bailey, Agent, Fugelmann Insurance Co., Inc., Dallas, Texas.

"If Erica Laboris checks with them," MacEver says, "they'll swear I'm one of their most successful salesmen."

"J. Ransom Bailey," Cone says, pocketing the card. "Very elegant. And what are you doing in New York?"

"Attending a convention of insurance agents at the Hilton: guys who have topped fifty million in sales for the past year. It's legit; the convention is starting tomorrow, and Bailey is registered at the Hilton."

"You make a great diddler," Cone says admiringly. "Looks to me like you've covered your tracks just fine."

"Not the first time I've done this," Terry MacEver says. He snaps shut his attaché case and rises. "Give me a call after you've seen Erica Laboris and tell me how it went. Don't press too hard and don't, for God's sake, mention that stolen Assyrian sword I showed you."

"I'm not an amateur bamboozler myself," Cone says. "I'll act the rube. I'll do everything but say, 'Aw, shucks.' Don't worry; if the lady can be had, she will be had."

"Tell her I'll only be in New York till Christmas Eve, and then I'm flying back to Dallas. Just to put a little heat on her, d'ya see. When I talk to her, I'll turn the burner up a bit higher. If she's dealing stolen art, she'll want to close the deal as soon as possible."

"I'll call you as soon as I've made contact," Cone promises.

After MacEver leaves, he lights a Camel and reviews the planned sting. He can't see any glaring loopholes. If Erica Laboris is foursquare, then the whole scam is dead. But if she takes the bait, then they should be able to hang her by the heels. It all depends on the intensity of the lady's greed.

Which has, of course, apparently nothing to do with Laboris Investments, Inc., of Wall Street. This case, which started as a simple investigation of an investment firm, has now flushed a covey of cousins, and Cone is up to his pipik in possible heroin smuggling and possible art theft.

What it calls for, he decides, is juggling, sleight of hand, and a dark vision of the human race which may or may not be one of God's jokes.

He gets up to the Laboris Gallery a little before noon, and walks by once, scoping the place. As far as he can see, no customers—which pleases him.

When he goes marching in, doffing his cap, Ingrid Laboris, the cream puff, comes dollying up, giggling like a maniac.

"I knew you would return," she says. "I just *knew* it!"

"Did you?" Timothy Cone says, beaming. "That's more than I did. How'ya doing? Busy?"

"Not so much," Ingrid says, pouting prettily. "Not so many people shop for Levantine antiques for Christmas presents. You are interested in something?"

"Yeah. Your cousin Erica. Is she around?"

"Oh, yes. In the back office. I shall tell her you are here."

She sashays away. He watches her go, cursing his unbridled lust.

But then Erica comes stalking, cooling him down. She's wearing a black leather sheath that looks like a tube, tight enough to squeeze her out both ends. But there's no come-on about her; she's aloof, sure.

"Ah," she says. "Mr. Cone of Haldering and Company."

"You remembered," he says. "That's nice."

"But of course," she says with her distant smile. "How may I be of service?"

The hisses sound like a whistling teakettle.

"Listen," Cone says, "I've got a brother-in-law, J. Ransom Bailey, a rich-type insurance agent. He's in from Dallas for a convention at the Hilton. Randy is a nut on swords, and when I told him I had visited your gallery, he wanted me to ask if you had anything he could add to his collection."

"Oh?" Erica Laboris says. "What exactly is he looking for?"

Cone shrugs apologetically. "I know from nothing about swords. The one time I saw his collection in Dallas, it just looked like an assortment of junk to me. A lot of rusted iron and tarnished bronze."

"Iron and bronze? Then he's interested in antiques?"

"Oh, yeah—he's hooked. I mean he hasn't got any modern sabers or things like that; his stuff is *old*. Here's his business card."

He hands it over and Erica examines it closely.

"Fugelmann Insurance," she says, reading. "I have heard of them."

"It's supposed to be a big outfit. I guess Randy is one of their star performers. At least the Hilton convention is for hotshot insurance agents. Do you have any antique swords he might be interested in?"

Erica puts a fingertip to pursed lips and ponders a moment, frowning. "Nothing at the moment," she says. "But if you could wait a few minutes, I'll call two other dealers who handle antique weapons. We sometimes exchange requests for rare or unusual items."

"Sure," Cone says, "go ahead and make your calls. I'll just wander around and look at all your pretty things."

She's gone for almost five minutes which, Cone figures, is time enough for her to call the Hilton in New York and Fugelmann Insurance in Dallas to make certain that J. Ransom Bailey exists. When she returns, her frosty smile has thawed a bit.

"Your brother-in-law may be in luck," she says. "One of the dealers I spoke to has a very old iron blade in good condition. I'll be happy to borrow it and show it to Mr. Bailey if he'd care to stop by."

"Hey, that's great," Cone says. "He's flying back to Dallas on Christmas Eve, so he hasn't got much time. Can I tell him to call you and set up an appointment?"

"Of course. I will be delighted to meet with Mr. Bailey."

"Good enough," Cone says. "He'll be in seminars most of the day, but I'll get hold of him later this afternoon and have him give you a call. Thanks for your trouble."

"No trouble at all," she says, putting her indigo talons lightly on his arm. "That's what we're here for."

Cone walks over to Fifth Avenue to get a cab heading downtown. He reckons the meeting with Erica went okay. No evidence that she's dealing in loot, but she didn't turn him down cold either. Now it's up to Terry MacEver.

When he gets back to the office, he calls the sergeant to report.

"I told her you'd call for an appointment later this afternoon. She's going to show you an iron sword she says she's borrowing from another dealer. Is that kosher?"

"Oh, sure," the sergeant says. "Art dealers are always borrowing from each other or taking stuff on consignment. Then they split the profit. Nothing illegal about it. Did she act suspicious?"

"Hard to tell what that lady is thinking, she's so buttoned up. Let me know what happens, will you?"

"Sure I will. You got a home phone number?"

"Yeah. It's unlisted, so don't write it on any men's room walls."

He gives MacEver his telephone number and hangs up. He lights a cigarette, calls down to the deli for lunch, and starts hacking away at his expense account and weekly progress report. There are a few early Christmas parties starting in the offices, but no one invites Cone.

He plods home through the mottled dusk, using every trick in the book to make certain he isn't being tailed, and wondering if hired killers knock off work for Christmas. Why not? They've probably got family celebrations, trees to decorate, gifts to buy.

Gifts to buy? Holy Christ! Tomorrow is Christmas Eve, and he hasn't bought anything for Samantha, or for Cleo, either. The cat is easy; a big hunk of garlic salami will do the trick. But that won't satisfy Sam. Cone tells himself he can always pick up some drugstore perfume—or maybe a gag gift like five pounds of horehound candy. Whatley would get a laugh out of that.

When he gets to his building, he finds the street door has been jimmied again. It's getting to be a weekly occurrence. He climbs six floors to the loft and finds his door open a few inches. He stoops swiftly, draws his Magnum from the ankle holster.

He kicks the door wide open and goes in fast, crouching. He looks around quickly. Nothing. He turns back to check the locks and doorjamb. No nicks or scars. A nice professional job.

Cleo is cowering under the bathtub.

"You're a lousy attack cat," Cone says sourly. "Couldn't you have fought to the death to preserve the sanctity of our home?"

He wanders around a moment and soon discovers what's missing: the solid teak Buddha statuette. He stands in the middle of the loft and sniffs. No doubt about it: The warm air of the loft smells of faded roses. *Nuit de Fou.* The exclusive scent of the Laboris cousins.

Christmas Eve turns out to be a cheerless day, with a clayey sky and a wild wind that won't quit; it blows warm, then cold, dies, and revives. There are a few dusty snow flurries, but nothing to carol about.

The Wall Street dick spends the morning futzing around the office, hoping for a call from Terry MacEver. But the sergeant doesn't phone, and Cone doesn't want to bug him. Office parties are beginning to swing and, unable to endure all the jollity and high spirits, Timothy takes off and taxis uptown to buy Samantha a Christmas gift.

That task accomplished, he decides to kill time walking uptown to Central Park. It is not a pleasant hike; Fifth Avenue is scattered with last-minute shoppers scurrying to get home, and holiday decorations already look tired and worn. When he finally cabs back to his neighborhood, he stops at his local deli to pick up some beer and Cleo's garlic salami. Then to the liquor store for supplies to see him through the holiday blues. He washes up, changes his shirt, and starts out for Samantha's apartment, carrying a bottle of Asti Spumanti.

Sam is leaving for her parents' home on an early-morning flight, and she's busily packing when he arrives.

"Where the hell were you today?" she demands. "We had a great party going at the office, and everyone wanted to know where you'd disappeared to."

"I was working," he says.

"In a pig's ass. You were probably sleeping in your loft.

Listen, I want to get rid of all the leftovers in the fridge, so that's what we're going to have. Then you take off and let me finish packing and get some sleep. Okay?''

"Sure," he says equably. "Why not?"

She pulls out bits and pieces of this and that: a bowl of cold lamb stew, baked beans, a piece of flounder, some cole slaw, foil containers of creamed spinach, noodles, and green beans, a hunk of cheddar, two potato pancakes, a dish of curried rice, cherry tomatoes, a few dried-up gherkins, slices of head cheese, heels of pumpernickel. Both being blessed with efficient digestive tracts, they devour every-thing and polish off the bottle of sparkling wine.

"Hey," Cone says, "that teak Buddha in two parts— you've still got it?"

"Izzy? Of course I've got him."

"I need it for a while."

"What for?"

"Evidence."

She stares at him. "Son, you've got more crap than a Christmas goose. What evidence?"

"Just an idea."

"Tell me."

"Not yet. It's too crazy."

"That figures," she says. "All your ideas are crazy."

"Not so," he protests. "I happen to have a very logical brain."

"You haven't got a brain," she tells him. "You've got tapioca in your skull."

"Oh-ho," he says. "Now that you've worked your evil way with me and enjoyed my damp, white body, it's insult time."

"Go to hell," she says, "and let's open our presents."

She's bought Cleo a red net Christmas stocking packed with a catnip-stuffed mouse, three plastic balls, a package of munchies, a can of poached salmon, and a plastic-framed picture of Garfield. She gives Cone a cashmere muffler in a Black Watch tartan.

"Nice scarf," he says, examining it. "Thanks."

"Muffler, not scarf, idiot," she says. "And you better wear it."

"Oh, I will," he says, "I really will."

Cone gives her a $100 gift certificate from Altman's.

"That's the most romantic gift I've ever gotten," she tells him.

"Yeah, well, I didn't know your measurements, so I figured you could buy something for yourself."

She puts a palm against his cheek and looks into his eyes. "You're really a mutt—you know that? Mutt, mutt, mutt!"

"I suppose," he says, sighing.

They slow down and drink some of Sam's vodka. No sex tonight; they both know it and accept it with only a small twinge. They talk about her plans to return to New York for New Year's Eve and what they might do.

"Stay in," he says. "New Year's Eve is amateur night. We'll spend it at the loft. I'll buy balloons, a small package of confetti, and two funny hats."

"I can hardly wait," Samantha says. "I may call you during the week. Just to make sure you're not shacked up with some tootsie."

"Not me," he says. "Cleo maybe, but not a tootsie."

"Have a happy Christmas, Tim," she says. "Now drag your ass out of here. I've got to finish packing and get some sleep."

"Let me have the Buddha."

"Jesus," she says, "you never give up, do you? Will I get it back?"

"Sure you will."

"The original Izzy?"

"Absolutely."

"You better be telling the truth," Sam says, "or you'll be singing soprano for the rest of your life."

She puts his cashmere muffler, Cleo's Christmas stocking, and the two-part Buddha statuette in a brown paper sack and taps his cheek. "On your way, buster," she says.

"Yeah," Cone says. "Have a good time. Don't talk to any sailors."

She comes up close. "Take care of yourself, asshole."

"You too, shithead."

They embrace lightly, exchange a small kiss and a sad smile. Then he leaves.

He cabs back to the loft and gives Cleo the gift-packed stocking. The cat isn't interested in any of the toys but goes whacko over the empty net stocking and starts wrestling it across the linoleum.

Cone pours himself a brawny brandy.

"She's gone," he tells Cleo. "Merry Christmas, kiddo."

He sits at his desk, wraps his new muffler around his neck and sips his drink, feeling bereft.

3

CHRISTMAS TURNS OUT to be a broody day for Timothy
Cone, with not much Ho-ho-ho about it. He grumps about
the loft all morning, drinking black coffee, demolishing
cigarettes, and growling as he gives Cleo fresh water and
changes the cat's litter.

He goes out about noon to buy a paper and plods a half
dozen blocks before he finds a newsstand that's open. The
sky is low and looks like wrinkled parchment. There's still
snow in the air, and the wind is cold and sharp enough to
make his teeth ache. He returns thankfully to the warm loft
and decides to drink and sleep the day away.

There's no one, family or friends, he has any desire to
call and wish a Merry Christmas. But then his phone starts
ringing. Joe Washington wants to extend Season's Greeting. So does an uncle in Brooklyn who's full of hearty cheer
and asks to borrow a hundred bucks. Then a gyrene buddy
who served with Cone in Vietnam calls to exchange ribald
insults.

Then, later in the afternoon, Terry MacEver phones.

"Merry the hell Christmas," he says. "I should have
called yesterday, but I had a Christmas Eve party to go to
and got taken by the sauce, d'ya see."

"Yeah," Cone says, "that happens."

"Well, I went up to see Erica Laboris. Like you said,
there is one smart lady. She starts asking me questions

317

about my collection of antique swords—pumping me. I had boned up on the subject, so I think I convinced her I was a compulsive collector and knew what I was talking about. Then she brings out the blade she claims she borrowed from another dealer. It was a piece of shit and I told her so. It looked like it had been hammered from old sardine cans. That thing couldn't cut braunschweiger. She was just testing me, d'ya see. I told her I was looking for something better. She pretended to think awhile and then said a European agent she dealt with had mentioned a choice item that was available. She described it: an Assyrian relic of the sixth century B.C. It sounded exactly like that stolen sword I showed you in the photograph. She said it was museum quality. Sure it was, if it was lifted from a Beirut museum. She said the European agent wanted twenty K for it, but she thought he might be willing to come down a bit. I told her it sounded interesting, and twenty thousand didn't scare me if it was the real thing. But of course I'd have to see it first. She said she could have it flown over and would be able to show it to me in a couple of days.''

''Do you believe all that?'' Cone asks.

''Hell, no! I think she's got the sword in the country right now and scammed the story of the European agent to give herself an out if the deal turns sour. Very suspicious, our Erica. Anyway, she's going to give me a call when the blade arrives, and I promised to fly up to New York to take a look.''

''How is she going to phone you?''

''She'll call Fugelmann Insurance in Dallas, and if I'm not in—which obviously I won't be—she'll leave a message and I'll call her back. I've got all that set up with my contact there. I don't want to start celebrating, but so far it looks good. I swear she's peddling that stolen Assyrian iron.''

''I'll bet my cajones on it,'' Cone says. ''She's playing it cozy, but visions of sugarplums are dancing in her head. She thinks she's found an A-Number-One sucker. Play it out, Sergeant; I think you're going to score.''

"I'm hoping," MacEver says. "How do you figure she got the sword into the US?"

"Inside a leather hassock from Turkey," Cone says. "Or a porcelain elephant from Korea. But that's another story. Keep me up to speed, will you?"

He hangs up, convinced they're going to bust the Laboris Gallery. That leaves Laboris Importers and Laboris Investments, Inc. And how to land Sven and Ingmar snares his thoughts for the remainder of that Christmas day, which now seems suddenly merrier and more hopeful.

On the morning after Christmas, Cone gets to work late. He breakfasts at his desk (black coffee and a Mae West) while he flips *The Wall Street Journal* and the Business Day section of the *Times*. All the economic pundits predict interest rates will continue to fall, and Cone wonders how long Ingmar Laboris is going to be able to pay that high rate of return. Even junk bonds are down to 12 percent.

It's almost noon when he leaves the office and grabs a taxi up to West Nineteenth Street. Laboris Importers is crowded, which is what he figured. All those people are returning Christmas presents. The flock of cousins is busy behind the sales counter in the rear of the store, and Cone is free to wander around and take a look at the latest in imported monstrosities.

No teak Buddhas in sight, but there is a table of curious statuettes arranged in precise ranks like a company of Marines on parade. They are all about eight inches tall, and identical; no hand-carving here. They look to be a resin and sawdust compound, colored black and produced from a mold.

There is a small placard set on a bamboo easel:

THE HINDU GODDESS KALI, WIFE OF SHIVA. SHE IS KNOWN AS THE BLACK ONE, OFTEN DESTRUCTIVE. KALI IS DEPICTED IN INDIAN ART AS WEARING A NECKLACE OF SKULLS, AND SOMETIMES SNAKES. SHE IS THE GODDESS OF DEATH AND FREQUENTLY WIELDS A SWORD TO CUT THE THREAD OF LIFE. KALI MEANS "TIME" TO REMIND US OF OUR SHORT LIFE SPAN.

"Right on," Cone says softly.

Glancing around to make certain he is unobserved, he picks up one of the statuettes. Kali is standing on a low base, her hefty bosom pressing thin drapery. About her neck is a string of skulls. In one hand she holds a sword, scissors in the other. Charming lady.

Cone twists the base in a clockwise direction. Nothing. Then he tries a conventional twist to the left. Again nothing. The doodad is solid, a single casting. He replaces it on the table and tries another, with the same result. He looks around again to make certain no one is noticing his strange behavior, then continues trying other statuettes.

He hits pay dirt on the sixth; the base unscrews when turned to the left. He puts that Kali aside and goes on with his search. He finds another with a screw-on base. He takes the two to the sales clerk and waits patiently for almost fifteen minutes before he can pay for his purchases. They are swaddled in tissue paper and slid into a plastic bag. Printed on the outside of the bag is: LABORIS IMPORTERS, HOUSE OF WONDERS.

He cabs back to Haldering & Co., goes directly to his office, and shuts the door. Still wearing parka and cap, he sits at his desk, unwraps one of the Kali statuettes, and carefully unscrews the base. Drilled upward into the goddess is a hole about an inch in diameter and three inches deep. Cone peers inside, turning the figure this way and that to catch the light. He sees a slight coating of white powder.

Bingo! Maybe.

The second Kali yields the same results. Cautiously, Cone licks a finger and swabs it into the recess. It comes away with some white powder adhering. He sniffs at his finger. Nothing—except nicotine. Then he takes a small lick. The powder tastes bitter. He wonders what the hell he's doing; he has no idea what high-grade smack tastes like. It could be talcum powder for all he knows.

He sits there a long time, staring at the two disassembled Kalis on his desk. Goddess of death and destruction? Could be. He pulls the phone close and calls Neal K. Davenport. But the city bull is out, can't be reached. So Cone leaves a call-back message.

Suddenly he realizes he's famished. He phones down for a sausage hero, a kosher dill, and two cans of beer. He's finished all that and is wiping his lips and belching mightily when Davenport calls back.

"Hey, sherlock," he says. "What're you selling today—cancer?"

"Listen," Cone says, "how about having a drink with me up at my loft?"

"The Garden of a Thousand Delights?" the NYPD man says. "Why this sudden attack of hospitality? You must want something."

"You know a guy in the Department named Petey Alvarez? He works out of Narcotics."

"Petey Alvarez? No, the name doesn't ring a bell. I know some narcs, but no Alvarez."

"I was hoping you could get hold of him, and the two of you could drop by. This Alvarez doesn't know me from Buster Keaton, but maybe you could talk him into coming along."

"Now why should I do that? What's in it for me?"

"It might help solve that homicide on my street. That Sidney Leonidas who got scragged. You want to break that, don't you?"

"Not especially," Davenport says. "The guy was a doper. Who cares? His kill comes pretty far down on my anxiety list."

"Come on," the Wall Street dick says. "It would look good on your record to clear that file, wouldn't it?"

"Has this got something to do with your Laboris job?"

"Well, yeah, it might have."

Davenport sighs. "What a pisser you are. Okay, I'll try to get hold of this Petey Alvarez and see if I can con him into visiting your mansion. By the way, I'm drinking bourbon this week."

"You'll get it," Cone promises.

It's almost two hours before the city dick calls back. He's located Petey Alvarez and talked the narc into showing up at Cone's loft. The meet is set for six o'clock. And Alvarez drinks rum and 7-Up.

"Holy Christ!" Timothy Cone says.

But on his hike back to the loft that night, making certain he's not being tailed, he stops at local stores to pick up a jug of Jim Beam, one of Puerto Rican rum, and a six-pack of 7-Up. He feeds Cleo, checks his ice cube trays, and places the plastic bag with the two Kali statuettes under the table. Then adds Izzy, the two-part Buddha he borrowed from Sam.

Petey Alvarez turns out to be a short, whippy guy with a walrus mustache and hair long enough in back to support a brass barrette. He's wearing a braided Greek captain's cap and a black trench coat gray with grime. His dirty Reebok running shoes have broken and knotted laces, and a small gold ring hangs from his left earlobe.

He looks around the loft in amazement.

"Sonnenbitch," he says. "I live better than this in the barrio. Wassamatta, you busted?"

"Nah," Cone says. "I got some money."

"But you got no fucking taste," Alvarez says. "Bathtubs like that we throw out on the street."

"It's an antique," the Wall Street dick explains.

"Yeah," Neal Davenport says, "and so are you. Do we stand here passing the time with idle chitchat or do we have something to drive the chill?"

Cone gets them seated on kitchen chairs and brings them drinks. He leaves the bottles of bourbon and rum on the table so they can help themselves. He pours a jelly jar of vodka for himself.

"L'chaim," Petey Alvarez says, raising his glass.

They drink to that, and then sit looking at each other.

"So this is it?" Davenport finally says. "A nice, quiet drinking party? This is what you dragged us up here for?"

"It's a long story," Cone says.

"I got time," Alvarez says. "My woman expects me when she sees me."

Cone starts by telling them about the client, Martha Hepplewaite, who wants Laboris Investments investigated because she's suspicious of their high rate of return.

"That's Ingmar Laboris," he says. "I still don't know where he fits into this action, but I'll bet he's a nogoodnik."

Then he tells them about Laboris Importers on West Nineteenth Street and the foreign schlock they sell. Cousin Sven Laboris, he reminds them, was picked up in a raid on an after-hours joint and was found to be carrying a bag of high-grade heroin.

"Now look at this," Cone says, and pulls the two-part Buddha from beneath the table. He unscrews the base and shows them the recess drilled up into the statuette. "That's how I think they're bringing junk into the country, packed inside things like this."

Alvarez jerks a thumb at Cone. "Is this guy for real?" he asks.

Davenport laughs. "The jury is still out on that one. But he hasn't fucked me up—not yet he hasn't."

"Look," the narc says, "how much shit could you jam in that little bitty hole? It wouldn't be worth the trouble."

"Sure it would," Cone says, "if you're bringing in hundreds or thousands of these doodads. Now we're talking about kilos. And Laboris Importers has stores all over the country—a perfect distribution setup."

The two cops look at each other. Then Davenport shrugs.

"Thin stuff," he says. "All smoke."

"Well, yeah," Cone admits, "if this Buddha was all I have. But today I dropped by Laboris Importers and got these."

He drags out the two statuettes of Kali and unscrews the bases. He hands a figurine to each of the other men.

"Notice?" he says. "Same-size drilled hole. But these have some white powder in them."

They examine the Kalis, peer into the recess. Then, just as Cone did, the narc licks a forefinger and probes the hole.

"It could be flour," Cone says.

Petey Alvarez licks his finger. "Flour, my ass," he says. "High-octane horse. I be a sonnenbitch."

They all sit, staring at each other. Then they reach forward to fill their glasses.

"It's not only these statues," Cone tells them. "Laboris Importers brings in stuff from all over the world. Big clocks and porcelain elephants and hassocks and crap like that. They could be sneaking in kilo bags for all we know."

"Beautiful," Alvarez says. "I love it. But the Customs guys check shipments."

"Sure they do," Cone agrees. "But like everyone else, they're overworked and understaffed. So they spot-check. Not *all* the statuettes are going to carry junk. Just the ones with a special lot number burned into the base. The ones up on top will be legit."

The narc looks at Neal K. Davenport. "You think I should take a ride with this nut?"

"What have you got to lose? If it doesn't pan out, no harm done. If Cone's right, you got yourself a nice bust and maybe a commendation."

"Yeah," Alvarez says. "Look. Let me take one of these statues to the lab and get a test on the powder."

"Be my guest," says Cone.

"Then, while they're testing, I'll find out where this Laboris Importers has its warehouse. If they have stores all over the country, they've got to have a warehouse. Makes sense?"

"It does to me," Davenport says. "Their stock is probably trucked to the warehouse from the docks or airports after it clears Customs."

"That listens," Cone says. "Maybe they got their own trucks. I don't figure they're mailing the stuff to other cities by parcel post."

"Yeah," the narcotics man says, sniffing at the hole

drilled into the Kali figurine. "If this is as pure as I think it is, it could zonk half the junkies in the Bronx out of their gourds." He looks up at Cone. "You work with Joe Washington—right?"

Cone nods.

"I was wondering why he called to pick my brains," Alvarez says. "That's cool. One hand washes the other, and you're coming through."

"Enough of this bullshit," Neal Davenport says, pouring himself more Jim Beam and unwrapping a fresh stick of Juicy Fruit. "What do I get for bringing you two lovers together? Cone, you said something about the Leonidas homicide."

"Look," Cone says, "the guy was tailing me, and I braced him the night he was chilled. But I didn't do it. I could tell he was stoned out of his skull."

"But you broke his arm?"

"Well, yeah, but I had to; he pulled a shiv on me. When I left him, he was blotto in that doorway, and his knife was on the sidewalk."

"Uh-huh," Davenport says. "And who do you guess put him away?"

"The guy who hired him. Probably one of the Laboris cousins. Listen, this family is a fucking corporation. Like an idiot I gave Laboris Importers my home address, to get their mail-order catalog. And Ingmar at Laboris Investments has my office address. I think maybe they compared notes, got spooked at the idea that I was getting nosy and might have bought one of the hollow Buddhas. They wanted to take me out of the picture."

"What's Laboris Investments got to do with all this?" Davenport asks.

"Beats the shit out of me," Cone admits.

The NYPD detective stares at him a long time. "You're holding out on me again," he says. "You and your goddamned secrets. There's something you're not spilling. I know it when your eyes go blank."

"Hey," Cone says, "one thing at a time. If you can bust Laboris Importers for drug dealing and lean on some of the cousins, one of them is going to break and cop a plea—right? Then you'll find out who slid the blade into Sidney Leonidas. And you'll get brownie points for clearing a homicide."

Davenport sighs, turns to Alvarez. "Why do I let this fruitcake con me like this?" he says. "Every time he calls, I know it's trouble and more work."

"I don't know," the narc says. "He's beginning to get to me. And you gotta admit the price of his drinks is right."

The two cops drain their glasses and stand.

"I'll be in touch," Petey Alvarez says, shaking Cone's hand. "Thanks for the wallops."

"Where's the cat?" Davenport asks.

"Under the bathtub. Sleeping."

"That's what I should be doing," the city dick says. "See you around."

After they're gone, Cone puts the bottles under the sink and rinses out their jelly jars. He figures he's started some action, and maybe it'll pay off.

He stalks about the loft, pondering, and Cleo slithers out from under the bathtub, yawning and stretching. Then the cat starts padding after Cone, turning when he turns, sticking close to his heels, mewing steadily.

"You hungry again?" Cone says. "I've got some nice ham hocks for us. Just be patient."

He figures Petey Alvarez for a cowboy—just the kind of gritty guy needed to put the arm on Sven Laboris. Cone knew hot dogs like Petey in Nam: real outlaws who pushed and pushed until they earned medals or body bags.

Cone is happy he didn't blab about Sergeant Terry Mac-Ever and the sting planned for the Laboris Gallery of Levantine Art. Davenport and Alvarez have no need to know. And Cone likes to keep his hole card facedown until the call.

"Okay, kiddo," he says to Cleo, "let's have the ham hocks. One for you, three for me."

*   *   *

He lumps into the office the next morning, an hour late. He's carrying his breakfast in a brown paper bag: container of black coffee, buttered bagel.

"You're late," the receptionist says sternly.

"Morning sickness," Cone explains. "I'm pregnant."

"Well, you got a call. Two calls. From Mr. Ingmar Laboris. He wants you to call him as soon as you get in."

He goes back to his office, drinks coffee, eats bagel, smokes third Camel of the day. *Then* he calls Ingmar Laboris. He guesses what that oily knave wants—and he guesses right.

"Hello there, Mr. Cone!" Laboris says heartily. "And how are we this morning?"

"We're fine," Cone says. "We have a slight twinge of the liver, but we think that'll pass."

"Excellent, excellent!" Ingmar carols, obviously not listening. "The reason I called, Mr. Cone, was to ask if your client had made up his or her mind to place that investment you mentioned."

"The quarter-mil?" Cone says. "I've made a recommendation, and I expect the client will come to a decision shortly. Probably in the next day or so."

"And how do you read the client's mood? Do you feel the investment will be made?"

"I'm not allowed to comment on that," Cone says virtuously. "But I think you're in for a surprise."

"Splendid!" Ingmar Laboris, obviously a terminal optimist, says happily. "I must tell you I am deeply appreciative of your efforts on behalf of Laboris Investments. Incidentally, you might wish to consider taking a flier yourself. In all confidence, I can assure you that our future looks very bright indeed, and while I can make no promises, of course, I anticipate a very rapid increase to a thirty-percent return."

"I'll certainly consider it seriously," the Wall Street dick says.

After he hangs up, he sits staring at the phone. Ingmar's

call is worrisome. It sounds to Cone like the man is getting itchy. Maybe that mob of new investors has dwindled to nothing, or maybe Ingmar is planning a final big score before he closes up shop and walks off into the sunset.

Cone drags himself down to the office of Sidney Apicella. The CPA looks up from an enormous ledger, then sits back and begins massaging his swollen beak.

"You haven't bugged me for days," he says. "What's wrong—you sore at me?"

"One easy question, Sid," Cone says. "Remember when you checked the bank accounts of Laboris Investments for me? You said they had a special redemption fund set aside to pay off investors who wanted their money back."

"That's right; I remember."

"Do you recall how much was in the fund?"

Apicella rubs his beezer vigorously. "I think it was about a million five when I checked."

"Could you find out what it is now?"

"Oh, Christ," Sid says. "That's Ollie March at Merchants Interworld. He's done so many favors for me lately, I hate to hit him again."

"Come on," Cone urges, "it'll only take one short phone call. You can send him a bottle of booze. I'll finagle it on my expense account."

"Well . . . okay," Apicella says grudgingly. He flips through his Rolodex, finds the number, and dials.

"Mr. Ollie March, please . . . Hello, Ollie. Sid Apicella here. How are the hemorrhoids? . . . Uh-huh . . . Jesus, that's a shame . . . Ollie, I hate to bother you again—I know how busy you are—but this is important. Remember my asking you about the position of Laboris Investments? . . . That's right; Wall Street. Well, what I need right now is the current status of their redemption fund. Could you take a look? . . . Sure, I'll hang on."

He covers the phone with a palm and looks up. "The poor guy is really suffering," he says. "He has to sit on an inner tube."

"Tough," Cone says.

Apicella goes back to the phone. "Yeah, I'm here, Ollie . . . Uh-huh . . . I've got it. Thanks very much; I owe you more than one. I hope the new treatment helps . . . Right . . . I'll be talking to you."

He hangs up and swings around in his swivel chair to face Cone. "Laboris's redemption fund is down to a little below three hundred thousand."

The two men stare at each other.

"From a million and a half about ten days ago," Cone says. "Sounds like someone's pulled the plug."

"I'd say so," Apicella agrees. "Does the client have any money in Laboris Investments?"

"Not the client. The husband-to-be of the client's daughter."

"Better tell him to get it out," the CPA advises. "The sooner the better."

"Yeah," Cone says, "that's what I figure. Thanks, Sid."

"Don't forget that bottle for Ollie," Apicella calls after him.

Cone goes back to his office and calls the Hepplewaite brownstone. He's in luck; Lucinda answers the phone.

"Miss Hepplewaite, this is Timothy Cone at Haldering and Company."

"Oh, yes, Mr. Cone. Do you want to talk to my mother?"

"No, I want to talk to you. In private. Can we meet somewhere?"

Silence. Then: "Is it about you-know-what?" she asks in a whisper.

"Yes," Cone says, "it's about you-know-what. Can you get out of the house for a few minutes?"

Long pause. Then faintly: "Maybe for a few minutes."

"That's all it'll take. How about meeting me on the corner of Thirty-eighth and Madison in half an hour? If you're late, don't worry; I'll wait."

"All right," she says in her wispy voice, "I'll meet you there."

He gets up to Madison and Thirty-eighth Street about five minutes early. It's a snappy day with a sturdy westering wind and a brilliant sky. Cone stomps up and down, hands in pockets to keep his parka from flapping. He's not wearing Samantha Whatley's Christmas gift. Cleo is probably sleeping on the muffler right now.

Lucinda Hepplewaite comes flying down the block, loden cape billowing out behind her. Her long face is wrenched. She grips Cone's arm.

"I hope you have good news for me," she says breathlessly.

"I got lousy news for you. That boyfriend of yours— what's his name?"

"He's not my boyfriend; he's my fiancé. And his name is Francis."

"Yeah," Cone says. "Well, you tell Francis to get his money out of Laboris Investments as fast as he can."

"Oh, my God," she says, then grimaces. She's all teeth. "Is it that bad?"

"Bad enough."

"Are you sure?"

"No, I'm not sure," he says angrily. "But you asked me to tell you first if I found out anything, so I'm telling you: Laboris is going down the tube."

They walk up and down: ten paces, turn, ten paces, turn. Lucinda has a stride as long as his. She's huddling inside her loose cape. Once or twice she shivers. Cone figures it's the cold; he doesn't think she's nervous or fearful.

"What should we do?" she asks finally.

"No use writing a letter or phoning," he says. "That'll get you nowhere. This Francis of yours—can he come on hard? I mean can he yell, threaten, really lay on the muscle?"

"Oh, no," she says. "Francis is the dearest, sweetest man who ever lived. He's very quiet and mild. I've never heard him raise his voice in anger."

"Oh, boy," Cone says. "You're sunk."

Pace, turn, pace in silence. Then he stops. She stops. He turns to face her.

"Unless . . ." he says, "unless you can do it."

"Do what?"

"Collect Francis, and the two of you get down to Laboris Investments as fast as you can. Demand the return of Francis's hundred thousand. They'll try to stall, tell you to write them a letter, and all that. But you scream and shout and insist on a check immediately. There will probably be potential investors in the outer office, so if you create enough of a scene, they'll probably give you your money to get rid of you. Can you do that?"

"I'll do it," she says decisively, "if I have to."

"You have to," he tells her. "And the moment you get the check, take a taxi to Francis's bank and deposit it. Even then there's no guarantee; Laboris may stop payment the moment you leave. But it's the only chance you've got. If it doesn't work, you'll be listening to your mother say, 'I told you so,' for the rest of your life."

"I'll go right now," she says determinedly. "I won't even tell mother where I'm going."

"Atta girl," he says. "Remember to come on strong. Yell and stamp your foot and even squeeze out a few tears if you have to. Just don't leave Laboris without your boyfriend's money."

"My fiancé," she says.

"Whatever. Where's his office?"

"Sixth Avenue and Fifty-seventh Street."

"I'll get you a cab. Pick up Francis and go straight to Wall Street. Let me know what happens."

He puts her in a taxi, raises a hand in farewell and benediction. Then he stops another empty cab and rides down to John Street.

The first thing he does is phone Laboris Investments. Ingmar is out, which is another lucky break; Cone figures he's on a roll. He leaves a message with Ingmar's secretary:

Please tell Mr. Laboris that Timothy Cone of Haldering &
Co. called, and the investment they discussed that morning
has been approved by the client. The funds will be in Mr.
Laboris' hands within two days.

Cone hangs up, satisfied that he's done all he can to
protect the client's interest. Or rather, the client's daughter's interest. The two are not necessarily identical.

He reckons that when Ingmar hears he's getting a quarter
of a million in a couple of days, he'll be more inclined to
sign a 100-G check for Lucinda Hepplewaite's fiancé.

It takes a con man to con a con man.

Later in the afternoon, Lucinda Hepplewaite calls him, all
excited. She did just as he instructed, created a rambunctious scene at the Wall Street offices of Laboris Investments, and eventually her fiancé was issued a check for a
hundred thousand.

"Just now. We got to Francis's bank a few minutes before it closed."

"Good for you," Cone says. "Now if Laboris doesn't
stop payment, you're home free. Lots of luck."

He starts on his progress report, opening a fresh pack of
Camels—second of the day. By four o'clock he's ready to
call it quits and wander home. As a matter of fact, he's
halfway out the door of his office when his phone rings
again, and he returns to his desk.

"Yeah?" he says.

"Petey Alvarez, you crazy sonnenbitch," the narc says,
laughing. "That stuff in the statue's asshole tested out as
high-grade smack. We got a make on Laboris Importers'
warehouse. It's over on Eleventh Avenue. We haven't got
enough guys for a twenty-four stake, but we're covering the
place from midnight till eight. Listen, you wanna have
some fun?"

"Sure," Cone says. "I like fun."

"I'm taking the watch from midnight to four. How about
coming along and keeping me company?"

"Okay. Should I bring what's left of the rum and Seven-Up?"

"I was hoping you'd say that," Petey says happily. "Yeah, bring it. We can have a few and chew the fat while we're planted there. How's about I pick you up at your loft around eleven-thirty. All right by you?"

"I'll be waiting," Cone says.

He goes home, feeds Cleo, changes the cat's water, and has a belt of vodka before he lies down, fully clothed, on the floor mattress. He figures if he's going to be awake from midnight to four, he better get a start on his shut-eye.

He rouses a little after ten-thirty, fixes himself a salami sandwich with a dry slice of greenish Swiss cheese. He wolfs that down with another vodka, wondering how long his gut can take the punishment. He puts the rum and 7-Up in a shopping bag, then adds his own jug of Popov and a couple of empty jelly jars. He also adds a plastic bag of ice cubes. Timothy Cone knows how to live.

He waits outside on the sidewalk for almost ten minutes before Alvarez drives up. He's behind the wheel of a clunker so old and battered that Cone isn't sure what it is: a '74 Dodge, he thinks, or maybe a '73 Chrysler.

"Don't let the looks fool you," Alvarez says. "Plenty of horses under the hood. This baby can move when it has to."

"And nothing falls off?" Cone asks.

"What's to fall? The lights and bumpers are stuck on with picture wire and masking tape. Don't worry, sonny boy; it'll hold together."

They head north, and Alvarez fills Cone in on what he's learned, which isn't much. The heroin in the Kali statuette tested out as almost pure, probably from Thailand. The Laboris Importers' warehouse is owned by a company named Sirobal, Ltd.

"Sirobal," Cone says. "Laboris spelled backwards."

"You got it," Petey says. "The schmucks!"

He tells Cone the Customs guys have no rap sheet on Laboris, but they do a big business by ship and air. The warehouse is busy during the day, but at night there's only one watchman. The building has an alarm system, but it' self-contained, not wired to a security agency or local precinct.

"Oh, they're bringing the stuff in," Petey says. "No doubt about it. If we can't get evidence of them dealing we'll have to tell the Feds to clamp down with dog searches and all that shit. But I wouldn't like that; I want to engineer this bust myself."

"Why not," Cone says. "You're entitled."

They park in the shadows on Fifty-third Street where they have a good view of the Laboris warehouse. It's a squat ugly building with stained brickwork and blacked-out windows above the ground floor. But there are interior lights on the street level, and they can see figures moving about inside.

"Hey-hey," Petey Alvarez says, "what's this? The place is supposed to close at six o'clock when the night watchman comes on. Maybe they're having an office party."

"Yeah," Cone says. "Maybe."

They settle down, and Cone mixes a rum and 7-Up for Petey, and pours himself a jelly jar of vodka on the rocks. They drink slowly, and for almost two hours the narc regales the Wall Street dick with stories about the wild way dope is brought into the country.

In sealed condoms swallowed by couriers. In small metal containers shoved up the rectum or pushed into the vaginas of female mules. In tubes of toothpaste and jars of cosmetics. In kids' teddy bears and cripples' hollow crutches. Under toupees and inside sanitary napkins.

"How about this one," Alvarez says. "They dissolve coke or heroin in a tub of water. Then they dunk a woman's fur coat in it. Let the fur dry. She waltzes through Customs carrying the fur coat over her arm. Once she's in, they soak the fur coat again and extract the dope from the water. Isn't that beautiful? The bastards are always one step ahead of us."

But as he's talking, Cone notes, the narc rarely takes his eyes from the Laboris Importers' warehouse.

"I don't get it," Alvarez says fretfully. "The place is supposed to be closed with just a night watchman on duty. But I make out two guys moving back and forth. You see them?"

"At least two," Cone says. "Maybe three. One's a hulk. The others are small and skinny."

"Yeah," Petey says. "So what the fuck's going on at this hour?"

It's almost two A.M. when a long, silver-gray Cadillac limousine glides to a stop in front of the warehouse.

"Oh-oh," the narc says. "We got some action. Scrunch down a little. Just in case."

They watch as two men get out of the Cadillac and look around before walking up to the dimly lighted doorway of the warehouse.

"Sonnenbitch," Alvarez says softly, "I make those guys. The short one in the black leather coat is Simon Juliano, a hotshot drug dealer in East Harlem. He's a real kink. Digs little Chinese girls—and I mean *little*. The monster in the plaid mackinaw is his muscle, Ollie Jefferson. He's got feta between his ears, but he's fast."

The two men look around again, then ring the bell. In a moment the warehouse door opens and they disappear inside.

The narcotics cop drums on the steering wheel with heavy fingers. "Something's going down," he says. "It's a buy; I swear it's a buy."

They straighten, stare at the lighted ground floor of the warehouse. But there's no movement, nothing to see.

"Listen," Petey says to Cone, "you loaded?"

"Yeah. A short-barreled Magnum in a shinplaster."

"Good enough. Well, those two shtarkers weren't carrying anything when they went in, were they?"

"I didn't see anything."

"So if they come out with a suitcase or bag or whatever I'll *know* it's a buy. I'd like to bust their asses. You game?"

"Sure," Cone says. "Why not."

"Okay," Petey says, "here's how we work it. . . . If they come out with a package, we let them get in their yacht and drive away. We follow them. Because I don't want to spook Sven Laboris—not yet I don't. Then, when they're a few blocks away, we cut them off and see what they picked up at the warehouse."

"It's legal?" Cone asks.

"Hell, yes. I've got probable cause. Both those pricks have drug sheets."

"No," Cone says, "I mean my being in on the bust. I'm a civilian. I'm ready, willing, and able, but won't it put your ass on the line in the Department?"

"Fuck it," Alvarez says roughly. "I'll scam my way out of it. I've done it before."

"Then let's do it," Cone says.

He slides his .357 out of the ankle holster and holds it on his lap. Petey Alvarez pulls a cannon from a shoulder holster and places it on the seat beside him. It's the biggest handgun Cone has ever seen.

"What do you use that for?" he asks. "Elephants?"

"It'll crack an engine block," Petey says proudly. "Once I knocked off a guy standing behind a half-inch steel door. Jesus, was he surprised."

They wait in silence. It's almost fifteen minutes before the warehouse door opens again. Several men can be seen shaking hands. Then Juliano and Jefferson start back to their limousine, looking about carefully. The muscle is carrying a small suitcase.

"That's it," Alvarez says. "They made a buy. Let's get this show on the road."

The Cadillac pulls away. In a moment, the narc starts up his clunker and follows the big car. They go south for a couple of blocks, then the limousine makes an illegal U-turn and heads north. Alvarez follows, keeping a block back. The avenue is deserted; only the two cars are moving.

"They're going to get antsy in a minute," Alvarez says. 'They'll spot us on their tail and speed up. I think we better move in. You set?"

"I'll never be setter," Cone says.

The old car leaps forward. The narc wasn't lying about the power under the hood. In moments they're alongside the Cadillac, and then ahead. Petey wrenches the wheel sharply to the right.

"Whee!" he screams.

Screech of brakes. Squeal of skidding tires. Thud of crumpling metal. The limousine is forced up onto the sidewalk. It crunches to a stop, the front end digging into the tin shutters of an abandoned store.

The narc is out of the car, howitzer in his fist. Cone is close behind, Magnum gripped tightly. They rush the big car. Alvarez jerks open the door on the driver's side.

"You're dead!" he yells. "Out, out, you fuckers!"

But it's not that easy. Juliano, driving and apparently stunned, sits slumped with his head bent forward, pressed against the steering wheel. But Ollie Jefferson piles out the other side, fumbling at his hip. Cone circles behind the Cadillac and aims, crouched, with a two-hand grip on his shooter.

"Don't do it," he says, not recognizing his own voice.

But, as Alvarez said, the muscle has no brains. He pulls a revolver from a hip holster. Cone pumps off two. The first misses. The second shatters Jefferson's left kneecap, spins him around, dumps him. Cone moves in fast, kicks the revolver away. He stands over the fallen man, Magnum still gripped in both hands.

"This fink is out," Alvarez calls. "How's yours?"

"No problem," Cone says.

"Beautiful!" Petey says. "I love it!" He digs into the limousine, hauls out the suitcase, snaps it open. "Three kilos," he reports gleefully. "Everything's coming up roses. Keep an eye on these two cocksuckers, will you, while I call for backup."

The Wall Street dick stands motionless, gun still aimed,

while the narc goes back to use his radio. Then Alvarez
returns to his side and looks down at the fallen Ollie Jefferson, now writhing in pain, clutching his shattered knee.

"Suffer, you scumbag," Petey says. Then he claps Timothy Cone on the shoulder. "I love you, baby," he says.
"You did real good. But look, I think you better take off.
It'll make things a lot easier for me if you're gone when the
brass arrive."

"Sure," the Wall Street dick says. Then: "Thank you for
an enjoyable evening."

"You nutty sonnenbitch!" Alvarez cries, embracing
him. "You like action—no? Me, too. Shoot 'em up! Bang
bang!"

"Keep in touch," Cone says.

He walks over to Ninth Avenue and after waiting ten
minutes gets a cab heading downtown. He's still wired, on
high, waiting for his adrenaline to drain away. He tries to
breathe deeply and slowly. But he's still surging inside,
half-sick, half-drunk with sorrow and pride.

He left his vodka jug in Petey's car, but he's got some
California brandy in the loft. He has a beefy slug to calm the
jits while he recalls what happened that night: what Petey
said, what he said, what Alvarez did and what he did.

He lets Cleo lick a brandy-dipped finger, and the cat's
purr and lazy movements help him thaw and remember his
philosophy.

"Just don't give a damn," he advises Cleo. "That's the
secret."

He's still awake, lying in his skivvies on the mattress,
and it's almost four A.M. when his phone jangles. Oh-oh,
he thinks, Petey's in trouble.

"Yeah?" he says.

"You bastard!" Samantha Whatley wails. "Where the
hell have you been? I've been calling all night."

"I worked late at the office," he says, happy to hear her
voice.

"Bull*shit!*" she says. "You never worked late at the
office in your life. You've been out tomcatting around."

"Nah," he says, "I wouldn't do that. Where are you—back in town?"

"Coming back tomorrow," she says. "But it'll be late in the afternoon so I won't show up at the office. How are things going?"

"Okay."

"That's all—just okay? How you doing on the Laboris thing?"

"All right," he says. "Coming along."

She sighs. "What a chatterbox you are. Come over to my place tomorrow night?"

"Sure," he says. "How's about a big pizza and a jug of red ink?"

"Sounds great. I haven't had a decent pizza since I left. See you tomorrow. Good night, asshole."

"Good night, shithead," he says, and hangs up.

"Sam is coming home," he tells Cleo, and goes back to the mattress, content.

"Sergeant Terry MacEver to see Mr. Timothy Cone," the receptionist says primly.

"Yeah," Cone says, "send him in."

He hangs up the phone, stands, brushes croissant crumbs off his corduroy jacket. He drains the dregs of his black coffee, crumples the container, and tosses it at his wastebasket. Misses, and leaves the garbage on the floor.

MacEver, a dandy, enters wearing a black bowler with a curved brim. He looks at the littered office with some distaste and declines Cone's offer to take his hat and coat.

"Just stopped by for a minute," he explains. "Good news: I think Erica Laboris has taken the bait."

"Hey," Cone says, "I like that."

"She called Fugelmann Insurance in Dallas, and they got back to me. So I phoned the lady, pretending I was deep in the heart of Texas. She says she's got an iron sword that she thinks would make a splendid addition to the collection of J. Ransom Bailey. Then she proceeds to describe, almost exactly, the blade that was stolen from the Beirut museum. It's hand-

forged, Assyrian, and dates from around the sixth century B.C
I'm betting she's already got the loot in her hot little paws.

"Sounds good," Cone says. "When are you going to se
her?"

"Tomorrow," the sergeant says. "I didn't want to be to
anxious, d'ya see. So I told her I'd fly up from Dallas an
meet her in the gallery in the afternoon to inspect the me
chandise. You want to be there?"

"Hell, yes," Cone says. "If it's the genuine article
you're going to cuff her?"

"What else?" MacEver says. "I'll arrange for som
backup in case we have a hassle. I'll give you a call tomor
row morning and we'll synchronize our watches. I'm real
high on this thing, Cone; I think we're going to score."

The sergeant leaves, and Cone lights a cigarette, feelin
perky. Alvarez made a nice bust last night that will probabl
lead to the indictment of Sven Laboris. And now Terr
MacEver has a good shot at putting Erica Laboris in th
slammer. The Laboris cousins are being decimated.

But . . . but . . . Cone begins to wonder if he might b
engineering a monumental balls-up. The arrest of one La
boris cousin will surely spook the rest of the clan. Groan
ing, he gets on the horn and tries to locate Petey Alvarez
No luck; the narc is not available, and no one knows wher
he is. Beginning to sweat, Cone calls Davenport and almos
sobs with relief when the detective answers.

"Hey, sherlock," the cop says breezily, "I hear Petey
Alvarez had himself quite a time last night."

"Did he?" Cone says.

"You weren't along for the ride, were you?"

"Not me," Cone says. "I went to bed early last night
Slept like a baby."

"I know what that means," Davenport says. "You woke
up crying every two hours."

"Listen, I've been trying to locate Alvarez. Do you know
where he is?"

"Not at the moment. He's busy organizing the Shoot-ou

at the O.K. Corral. We're going to raid the Laboris warehouse tonight and really tear the place apart. I'm going to grab every Laboris cousin in sight and lean on them. Maybe I really can clear that Sidney Leonidas homicide.''

Cone takes a deep breath. ''You can't do that,'' he says.

Silence. Then: ''Why can't I do that?''

''Not you,'' Cone says. ''The raid on the warehouse—it can't go down tonight.''

''No?'' Davenport says coldly. ''Why not?''

''There's something I didn't tell you.''

''I knew it, I knew it!'' the city bull screams at him. ''Oh, you tight-mouthed idiot! I knew you were holding out on me. All right, all right, what is it?''

Cone tells him about the sting he and MacEver have planned for the Laboris Gallery. And how they're going to pull the plug on Erica Laboris the following afternoon. If the Laboris Importers' warehouse is raided that night, and a covey of cousins picked up, it'll send Erica running.

''You can see that, can't you?'' Cone says. ''She'll close up shop and get out of town. You know she will.''

''And you couldn't have told me all this before?'' Davenport demands.

''Look,'' Cone says, ''it was MacEver's deal, and I didn't want to queer it. I'm just as tight-lipped when you and I work together.''

''Yeah?'' the NYPD man says. ''Well . . . maybe. But now we got a world-class fuckup on our hands.''

''Not necessarily,'' Cone says. ''Get hold of Alvarez, explain the situation, and get him to postpone the warehouse raid until tomorrow afternoon. Then call Terry MacEver and fix it so the warehouse and the art gallery are hit at the same time. That way none of the birds will fly away.''

''Mmm,'' Davenport says thoughtfully. ''It might work.''

''Sure it'll work,'' Cone says. ''You manage the whole thing. You'll direct two important busts and probably close the Leonidas file. You'll make lieutenant out of this.''

''You really know the way to a man's heart, don't you?'' Neal Davenport says. ''You lunatic! Where were you when God passed out brains—at the end of the line? I'll give you a call if I can straighten out this mess.''

He hangs up.

Cone is satisfied that he's done all he can. From now on it's up to the Department to run the show. He's convinced they'll find enough evidence in the warehouse to justify the raid. And if Sergeant MacEver is right about the antique sword being offered by Erica Laboris, that cousin will take a fall, too.

That leaves only Ingmar Laboris.

When he goes out for lunch, he's still thinking about Ingmar and what that pascudnyak might be up to. He wanders about lower Manhattan, head bowed, shoving his way through the lunchtime throng. He buys a gyro and a cherry cola from a sidewalk vendor and continues his hike, eating and drinking as he walks.

He figures that if the coordinated busts of the Laboris warehouse and art gallery go down as planned, Ingmar might decide to make a fast exit. But Cone doesn't think so. The guy has bank accounts he'll want to clean out first. And he'll need to make cash transfers to someplace that doesn't have an extradition treaty with the US, and where government officials are not insulted by the offer of a small pourboire.

He drags himself back to Haldering, wondering how he's going to spend the afternoon while waiting for Davenport to phone and report a go or no-go. But his first call, after taking off parka and cap, is from Hiram Haldering himself.

''Cone,'' he says in his chief executive officer voice, ''I want to see you in my office right now. Immediately. Is that clear?''

''Shit!'' the Wall Street dick says—but only after he's hung up the phone.

H. H. is sunk in the high-backed swivel chair behind his desk. His muttony face is flushed with either anger or a three-martini lunch. Plump fingers are clamped across his vested belly. His balding pate gleams dully in winter light leaking through corner windows.

Alongside his desk, Mrs. Martha T. Hepplewaite sits grimly in an armchair. She's leaning forward like a figurehead, propping herself on the heavy cane. Her raddled features are as purplish as Haldering's, and all the wattles and dewlaps are quivering with fury.

They glare at Cone.

"Hi, folks," he says, and since no one asks him to sit down, he slouches limply and wonders if he'll be offered a final cigarette and blindfold before the execution.

"Cone," the boss says—a high-pitched bark—"how long have you been on the Laboris Investments case?"

"Oh . . . I don't know. Two weeks or so, I guess."

"And what, exactly, have you discovered?"

"Nothing much. Little bits of this and that."

"But you have no evidence that Laboris is a fraud?"

"Nope," Cone says. "No hard evidence."

"Then why," Mrs. Hepplewaite says, almost strangling on her wrath, "why did you see fit to advise my daughter to tell her fiancé to withdraw his investment?"

"Oh, she told you that, did she?" Cone says. "It was a judgment call. I think Ingmar Laboris is a crook. Right now I can't prove it. But I thought it best to tell your daughter about how I felt. She and her fiancé decided to bail out."

The harridan bangs her cane on the floor—two loud thumps. "Why didn't you tell me first?" she demands. "I am the client. I am paying the bills. You went behind my back."

The Wall Street dick doesn't like being hollered at.

"I'll tell you why I didn't go to you first," he says. "I called you a mean biddy, and you are—in spades. If I had told you I think Laboris Investments is probably a fraud, you might not have passed the news along to your daughter."

"Cone," Hiram Haldering says, shocked, "you're talking to a valued client."

"Big deal," Cone says. "She's a conniving old lady who wants to keep her daughter unmarried and at home, slaving as a cook, secretary, housekeeper, servant, scullion, and all-around Cinderella. She's vindictive enough so that, if I said I think Ingmar Laboris is a gonnif, she might not tell Lucinda. She might keep her mouth shut and let the investment of her daughter's fiancé go down the drain. Then maybe they couldn't get married. Then maybe she could keep Lucinda cleaning up slops and winding clocks in their mausoleum for the rest of her life. Then maybe she could keep repeating, 'I told you so,' at least once a day until she died."

Mrs. Hepplewaite collapses back into her chair. The hand holding the cane begins to tremble. "You're a dreadful man," she says in a hoarse whisper. "Dreadful."

"Sure I am," Cone says cheerfully. "And you don't do so bad in that department yourself. My advice to you, ma'am—unsolicited, and you can tell me to go to hell if it'll make you feel better—my advice to you is to make peace with your daughter, give her your blessings, and wish her the best. That lady has more gumption than you give her credit for. She's going to marry her Francis, and maybe they'll have a kid or two. You told me he was a pediatrician, didn't you? Then he should know how it's done. If you turn her out, you'll never get to see your grandchildren. Is that what you want?"

She stares at him with widening eyes, and he thinks he sees the beginning of tears, but can't be sure.

"Snotty," she says in a low voice. "The snottiest man I've ever met."

"Dreadful and snotty all in one afternoon," he says. "My my, this is my lucky day. If all goes well, your daughter's fiancé has recovered his original investment plus a nice profit. Lucinda will be married. Doesn't that bring the roses to your cheeks?"

She growls, tapping her cane angrily on the floor. The three are silent a moment. Then Hiram Haldering, unwilling to grant his employee a complete triumph, clears his throat.

"About these expense accounts you've submitted on your investigation," he says sternly. "Two teak Buddhas and two statuettes of the goddess Kali. What is that all about?"

"Yes," Mrs. Hepplewaite says, raising her head and regaining her confidence. "And all those bills for cab fares. Do you *live* in a taxi, you disgusting man?"

"All legitimate expenses," Cone says blithely. "You're also going to pay for a bottle of cognac for a banker who helped me out. I knew you were a shrew, Mrs. Hepplewaite, but I never figured you for a cheapski. Pay the tab and think of the joy you'll feel when your first grandchild pees in your lap."

And he stalks out, wondering if he'll have a job in the morning and not much caring.

He gets back to his office feeling pretty good. He laid it on the line to H. H. and the client, and kept his dignity reasonably intact. He lights a Camel and sits chain-smoking for almost an hour, reviewing what might be going down the next day, but unable to drag his mind away from the part Ingmar Laboris could be playing in this mishmash. A puzzlement . . .

When his phone rings, he stares at it for a moment, wondering whether he really wants to talk to anyone and maybe get leaned on again. Finally, sighing, he picks it up.

"Yeah?" he says.

"Davenport," the city detective says. "All right, I've cleaned up your mess. Everything's coordinated. We're hitting the art gallery and warehouse at eleven-thirty tomorrow morning."

"So early?" Cone says.

"It's New Year's Eve, you schmuck," the NYPD man says. "You want us to wait until late in the afternoon when everyone's gone home?"

"Oh, yeah, I didn't think about that."

"There's a lot you didn't think about, sherlock. MacEver says you're going with him."

"That's right. We're supposed to be brothers-in-law."

"God forbid," Davenport says. "Better he should have Godzilla for a relative. Anyway, he says to meet him fifteen minutes early across the street from the art gallery. Think you can remember that?"

"I'll remember," Cone says. "You're sore at me, aren't you?"

"Goddamn right I'm sore. I've had to spend all day on this Laboris thing. And it's not the only turnip on my plate, you know. But I had to push everything else aside while I got it organized."

"No one could have done it but you."

Davenport has to laugh. "What a bullshit artist you are!" he says. "Nah, I'm not sore at you. But next time be a little more up-front with me, will you?"

"Sure I will," Cone says. "Absolutely."

"Yeah," the city dick says, "I should live so long." And he hangs up.

Cone walks home through the violet twilight, still playing games occasionally to make sure he's not being tailed. He stops at a liquor store to pick up two bottles of Chianti Classico, figuring he'll buy the pizza on his way to Sam's place so it'll still be warm when he arrives.

Back in the loft, he feeds Cleo—some leftover breaded chicken nuggets he finds in the fridge. The omnivorous cat cleans up the plate, then sets to work grooming its whiskers. Cone strips and takes his ritual brush treatment under a hot shower, lacerating his skin with stiff bristles and rubbing on cornstarch after he's dried off.

He calls Samantha. She's home and waiting for him. So he dresses, checks his armament, and leaves the loft, not forgetting to take the wine. He feels excited and scary, like he's heading for the first date with a new woman. Nice feeling. Being young again.

It seems like a long time since they've been together, and seeing each other now is a little tight, stiff, confused. It takes them awhile to adjust—about two minutes. Then they slide into their comfortable roles, sit on the floor to chomp pizza and drink wine. Sam tells him everything that happened during her visit home, and he nods, smiling, stuffing his mouth, and realizing, as if for the first time, how complete she is.

She's wearing her long auburn hair up and pinned, and her sharp-featured face is devoid of makeup, washed and gleaming. Lots of jaw there, and steady blue-green eyes. Much woman, he thinks, and can see that stretched body under the jeans and turtleneck. He doesn't even want to imagine how empty his life would be without her. But, of course, he doesn't tell her that.

They demolish the pizza, clean up the mess, and open the second bottle of wine. They look at each other, and with no invitation from either, accepted or rejected, begin undressing lazily, still chattering about Samantha's trip and Cleo's new habit of sleeping under the kitchen sink.

It's only when their naked bodies are pressed does their gossip falter.

"Ah, Jesus," Sam says, sighing. "I thought of this a lot. Did you?"

"Yeah," Cone says.

"Do you know what I want to do right now?" she asks.

"What?"

She whispers in his ear.

"Well . . ." he says, "if you insist. If I don't enjoy it, I'll fake it."

"You louse!" she says, and sets to work.

They're possessed by demons that night, trying to make up for time lost. Their hard bodies are jangled with need, and sensation is not the answer. Neither knows what is, but they rend each other in a frantic effort to find relief. Not physical, for that is a mosquito bite compared to the hunger that gnaws at them.

Both prideful, they will not let go, unwilling to acknowledge that victory might lie in surrender. So they play their skin games, unable to yield to the heart's want, and settling for the satisfaction of greedy glands. Their lives are half-wins; they know it but cannot make the sacrifice total triumph demands. They show their naked bodies to each other, but will not present themselves flayed.

When their horizontal aerobics are concluded, they lie awhile, insensate and numb. Then Samantha stirs groggily to fetch the remainder of the chianti and their glasses. The wine, sipped slowly, revives them, and they look at each other with sappy smiles as if they had climbed Everest and returned intact.

And it is while they are in that loopy mood that Timothy Cone makes his Great Discovery.

"Where's Izzy?" Samantha demands. "You still have it, don't you?"

"Oh, sure. In the loft. I'd have brought it over tonight, but I had too much to carry. You can pick it up tomorrow night. You're coming over, aren't you?"

"Of course," she says. "It's New Year's Eve, isn't it? What are we eating?"

"I thought I'd pick up a roasted chicken and some odds and ends. And I suppose we'll have to drink champagne."

"What else? And do me a favor, will you: Change the sheets on that lumpy mattress of yours."

"Sure," he says equably. "I'll pick up my laundry tomorrow."

"Oh, boy," she says, "fresh laundry. A great way to start the New Year. Tim, why are you looking at me like that? Your face is all twisty."

"Laundry," he says wonderingly. "Jesus Christ, what a fucking moron I am!"

"So what else is new?" Samantha Whatley says.

He figures there's no point in going into the office at all on New Year's Eve. There will be a party. Guys will be nuzzling their secretaries, the secretaries will be goosing their bosses, and everyone will be drinking some lousy punch spiked with rotgut and decorated with slices of kiwi. Worst of all will be the forced jollity that Cone cannot endure.

So he spends the morning doing chores. Changes Cleo's litter. Goes out and picks up those bundles of laundry. Goes out again and returns with two bottles of Korbel champagne and puts them in the refrigerator. Goes out again to buy the largest roasted chicken he can find, some frozen yams in syrup, and salad stuff. Also a frozen apple pie and a package of sliced cheddar.

On one of his trips back to the loft, the phone shrills just as he's about to go out again. It's Samantha at the office.

"Why aren't you here?" she demands.

"I'm working," he says. "On the Laboris case."

"Bullshit," she says. "Are you going to show up at all today?"

"No."

"Well, you're going to miss one hell of an office party."

"Darn it," he says.

"Another thing," she says, "why didn't you tell me you had a hassle with H. H. about your expense account?"

"Oh, that," he says. "I left it on your desk, figuring you'd clean it up when you got back. But I guess he picked it up. Besides, it wasn't exactly a hassle. I explained every item."

"Oh, sure," she says. "He's still boiling."

"See you tonight," he says, and hangs up.

By 10:45 he's finished all his donkeywork. He tosses Cleo the tip of a chicken wing to gnaw on, checks his ankle holster, and heads uptown.

He finds Terry MacEver standing across Madison Avenue from the Laboris Gallery and about a block north. The sergeant, wearing his black bowler, has two plainclothesmen with him, a couple of Neanderthals who look like they dine on haunches of mammoth every night.

MacEver greets Cone with a grin. "Things almost go screwed up, didn't they?" he says.

"Almost doesn't count," the Wall Street dick says. "Everything's copacetic now."

"It is indeed," the sergeant agrees. "Here's the deal: My appointment with Erica Laboris is for eleven-thirty. You go in with me. That won't spook her. After all, I'm supposed to be your brother-in-law. When I get in the gallery, I take off my lid. Then she shows us the sword. Meanwhile, these two men have moved to the sidewalk in front of the gallery and are scoping the action through the window. If the sword is the real thing, I put my hat back on, and they come into the gallery like Gangbusters—just in case we have any problems with Erica. If the blade offered is junk, I keep my hat off and we leave the gallery with no harm done. How does that sound?"

"Simple and neat," Cone says. "It'll go like silk."

"Let us pray," MacEver says, glancing at his watch. "Okay, it's time. You guys," he tells the plainclothesmen, "don't stand in front of the window and gawk, but station yourselves where you can watch what's going on inside without being spotted."

"I gotta take a leak," one of them says.

"Tough," the sergeant says. "Clench your teeth."

MacEver and Cone cross Madison and walk south to the art gallery. They enter. MacEver removes his derby. Ingrid Laboris, the cream puff, comes swaying forward.

"Good morning, sirs," she says with the Laboris hiss. "How may I be of service?"

"J. Ransom Bailey to see Miss Erica Laboris," the sergeant says.

"Of course," Ingrid says. "I shall tell her you have arrived. And how are you today, Mr. Cone?"

"Surviving," he says. "Happy New Year."

"Likewise," she says. "Just a moment, sirs. Erica will be with you shortly."

They wait stolidly. Cone turns casually, as if to inspect a

crusty old pot on display, and glances out the front window.
He can't spot the two plainclothesmen. He doesn't know if
that's good or bad.

It's almost three minutes before Erica Laboris comes
stalking out of a back room. She's really a put-together
woman, Cone thinks admiringly, with her hair elaborately
coiffed and lacquered. She's wearing a black silk dress that
hints. Her fingernails are painted a jade green.

"Good morning, gentlemen," she says with her
mirthless smile. "So nice to see you again."

She's carrying a long box of rough wood with a hinged
lid. Cone notes that her clamping hands are white at the
knuckles, and her long talons dig into the wood.

"Over here, please," she says, leading the way to the
receptionist's desk. "I think you will be enchanted with
this, Mr. Bailey. Authentic, very old, very unusual."

Opens the long box. Lifts out a bundle of tissue paper.
Unwraps it carefully. Withdraws an ancient sword. Holds it
out to them.

To Cone, it looks like a piece of rusted iron that's been
reclaimed from a junkyard. But Terry MacEver, bending
low to inspect it, is impressed.

"Beautiful," he breathes. "A real museum piece."

"It is indeed," Erica Laboris says with her chilly smile.
"You wish to add it to your collection?"

She puts the blade down on the tissue paper. The sergeant
replaces his bowler atop his head. He reaches slowly inside
his coat and withdraws his ID wallet. He flips it open and
displays it to Erica.

"Sergeant Terry MacEver of the New York Police Department," he says. "You are under arrest for receiving and
possessing stolen property. I shall now read you your
rights."

She stares at him. Then turns her head to stare at the two
Neanderthals piling through the front door of the gallery.
Then she stares at Timothy Cone.

"You prick," she says.

"Yeah," Cone says, "I know."

It takes him almost twenty minutes to stop an empty cab, and by the time he gets over to the Laboris warehouse on Eleventh Avenue, there's not much to see. There are several empty cop cars parked outside, and a couple of blues wandering about, but otherwise things are quiet.

Cone marches up to the uniformed officer stationed at the warehouse door.

"Detective Neal Davenport around?" he asks. "I'm Timothy Cone. I'm supposed to meet him."

"Yeah?" the cop says. "I'll see. You wait here."

He goes inside, and the Wall Street dick waits, lighting a Camel and pacing up and down the driveway. A couple of plainclothesmen come out, their IDs clipped to their lapels. They take camera equipment from one of the cars and go back into the warehouse.

Cone has almost finished his second cigarette before Davenport appears. He looks a little bedraggled, but happy.

"Hey-hey," he says, "sherlock himself. How did things go at the art gallery?"

"MacEver cuffed Erica Laboris," Cone reports. "She was peddling a sword stolen from a Beirut museum. After she's booked, the sergeant is going back to the gallery to toss it. He figures he'll find more goodies. How are things going here?"

"Bingo," the city bull says. "So far we've found eight kilos of horse, a sweet arsenal of handguns and some small amounts of coke and pot."

"Much cash?" Cone asks.

"A few bucks. What's your interest in cash?"

"Something has come up I think you should know about."

"Oh, Jesus!" Davenport says despairingly. "Have you been holding out on me again?"

"I swear I haven't," Cone vows, holding up a palm. "I only got a line on it last night, by accident. It's about aboris Investments and where Ingmar fits into this whole chmear.''

"Yeah?" the NYPD man says. "Let's hear it.''

Cone talks rapidly for almost five minutes, as the two men walk up and down. Davenport listens intently, not interrupting. When the Wall Street dick finishes, the NYPD man looks at him narrowly and then slowly peels the wrapper from a fresh stick of Juicy Fruit.

"Could be," he says, frowning.

"Got to be," Cone says. "The entire Laboris clan are natural-born villains, and this puts Ingmar right in the middle of the picture.''

"But you've got no evidence?"

"No. Nothing.''

"So? What do you want from me?"

"Move in on Ingmar this afternoon. Take him for quesioning.''

"Whoa!" Davenport protests. "On what grounds? This is one for the DA. Or the SEC.''

"Can't you bring the DA in on it?"

"Hey, come on! It's New Year's Eve. Everyone will be partying. And tomorrow is New Year's Day. Maybe the next day.''

"Too late," Cone says desperately. "Ingmar will hear about the art gallery and warehouse by tonight. If we wait until the day after tomorrow, he'll be long gone. Listen, are you leaning on any of the cousins in the warehouse?''

"Yeah," the Department man says, "the shipping manager, a nerd named Edvard Laboris. We read him his rights and he started crying. I think he's ready to crack.''

"Why don't you brace him and see if he'll talk about what I just told you. If he does, then you'll have enough to get the DA's okay to take Ingmar.''

Davenport stares at him a long time. "Well, you gave us his package, so I can't complain. All right, I'll see if Edvard will break. You wait here.''

He goes back into the warehouse. Cone tramps up and

down, smoking furiously. A few minutes later, Petey A
varez comes bounding out of the warehouse, rushes over
Cone, embraces him.

"You crazy sonnenbitch!" he yells. "I love you, bab
Now we're up to ten kilos. What a score! Listen, you wa
to hear something nutty? This Laboris outfit brings in i
own brand of perfume, cologne, and after-shave lotion.

"I know," Cone says. *"Nuit de Fou."*

"Right. Well, half those cologne bottles are filled wi
high-grade shit. How do you like that? Isn't that beautifu
Look, I gotta go. We're still searching. Going for t
world's record. Thanks, bubbalah. I owe you one."

He runs back into the warehouse. Cone lights anoth
cigarette and resumes his pacing. It's a raw, biting day, b
he can feel the sweat dripping from his armpits. He wan
Ingmar. It's important to him, but for reasons he doesn
completely understand.

It's almost twenty minutes before Davenport comes o
again, accompanied by two uniformed officers. The dete
tive is pulling on a pair of gloves.

"Okay," he says, "I got enough out of Edvard to mak
me think you guessed right. I also got a good lead on t
Leonidas homicide. I've called the DA's office. There's a
assistant prosecutor I've done a few favors for. I spelled
out for him. He grumbled about leaving his office party, b
agreed to meet us at Laboris Investments in an hour. That'
give us time to pick up some burgers. I'm starved."

The man from the DA's office is a tall, skinny gink wearin
black horn-rimmed glasses. Davenport doesn't bother wit
introductions, and Cone figures the city detective doesn
want the assistant prosecutor to know that he's workin
with a lousy civilian.

The outer office of Laboris Investments is empty excep
for a blond receptionist filing her nails. The five men de
scend on her, the two uniformed officers moving close t
the desk. She isn't interested.

"Could we see Mr. Ingmar Laboris, please," Davenport
sks.

"Who shall I say is calling?"

The NYPD man looks at the two uniformed cops, then
ack at the blond. "The Salvation Army," he says. "On
econd thought, don't bother announcing us. Go back to
our nails, honey; we'll surprise him."

Cone leads the way to the inner office and opens the door.
ngmar Laboris is leaning back in his swivel chair, Gucci
oafers parked atop his huge mahogany desk. He's sucking
n a Louisville Slugger cigar and leafing through *Pent-
ouse*. He looks up when the five men come crowding in,
ut doesn't change his expression. A ballsy guy, Cone de-
ides.

"Ah, gentlemen," he says, "what can I do for you?"

"Ingmar Laboris?" Davenport asks.

"That is correct."

The detective and the man from the DA's office proffer
heir IDs. Laboris glances at them.

"So?" he says.

"We'd like you to come down to the office and answer a
ew questions," the prosecutor says.

"Now why should I do that?"

"Because it's more comfortable than the precinct
ouse," Davenport says.

Ingmar takes a long drag from his cigar. Then he sets it
arefully aside in the smoky quartz ashtray. He sits back
again, and regards the detective gravely.

"I must tell you," Laboris says in his sonorous voice, "I
would find it very inconvenient to accompany you gen-
lemen. At the moment, I am waiting for a very important
overseas call."

"I'm afraid it'll have to wait," the DA's man says.
"Let's not play games, Mr. Laboris. Do yourself a favor
and don't make trouble for us."

Ingmar reflects a moment. "May I call my attorney?" he
asks.

"If you feel it's necessary," the prosecutor says.

Laboris reaches for his phone, punches out a numbe "Ingmar Laboris calling," he says. "May I speak to M Bjorn Laboris, please." He looks up at the men standing front of his desk. "My cousin," he explains.

"What else?" Cone says.

Ingmar speaks rapidly into the phone in a low voic concealing his lips with a palm. Then he hangs up.

"Very well," he says briskly. "Bjorn will meet us at th district attorney's office. I presume this concerns Labor Investments?"

"That," Davenport says, "and other things. Can we g now?"

Ingmar rises, takes a cashmere overcoat and gray hom burg from a small closet. He carries the coat over his arm but dons the homburg, adjusting it to a rakish tilt.

"You stay here," Davenport says to one of the un formed officers. "No one in. Not a scrap of paper remove Got that? I'll make sure you get a relief in a couple hours."

"Oh, sure," the cop says bitterly. "On New Year Eve?"

On the way out the door, Ingmar Laboris pauses befor Cone. "I never did get that investment from your client, he says with a wan smile.

"The check is in the mail," Cone says.

Samantha Whatley comes directly to the loft from the o fice. She swears she's not swacked, but Cone can tell she got a nice mellow buzz on. That's okay; he's feeling no pai himself. After he returned from Wall Street, he had a coupl of stalwart vodkas while preparing the evening's festivitie

"The yams are thawed and baking," he tells her. "Th chicken is warming up on the stove. The salad is made We'll eat in about an hour. All right?"

"Fine with me."

"Meanwhile, why don't we crack a cold bottle of bub bles, just to get in the mood."

"Splendid idea," Sam says. "You missed a great office party, though I could have done without the Diet Pepsi in the punch. By the way, H. H. told me that Mrs. Hepplewaite paid her bill in full, your expenses included. And her daughter's fiancé got all his money back."

"That's nice," Cone says.

"How the hell did you manage that?" she asks, sipping her champagne.

"I didn't; you did."

"Me? What the hell are you talking about?"

"It's a long story."

"We've got all night," she says. "Come on, buster— *give*."

"Well, it started when you discovered Izzy came apart."

"I didn't discover it; it was an accident."

"Whatever. Anyway, that's what broke the whole thing."

He tells her about his purchase of the Kali statuettes, the traces of heroin found inside, and how Petey Alvarez, the narcotics cop, took over from there.

"They raided the Laboris Importers' warehouse this morning," he says, "and found kilos of the stuff. Petey should get a commendation at least. And all because you knocked Izzy off your bedside table."

"Crazy," Sam says, shaking her head. "Can we eat now? I'm famished."

While they're tearing the chicken apart—tossing scraps to a delighted Cleo—Cone tells her about Sergeant Terry MacEver and the sting operation.

"Another Laboris cousin," he says. "She was hawking stolen art smuggled in by the importing company. It probably traveled halfway around the world before it got to Manhattan. Anyway, Erica's in the clink."

"You *have* been a busy little boy," Sam says. "You want that last piece of yam?"

"No, you take it. Empty bottle? I'll open the other."

"I'll get smashed," Sam warns.

"That's okay; you're amongst friends."

"So keep talking," she says. "What's all this got to do with Mrs. Hepplewaite and Laboris Investments?"

Cone has already decided to tell her nothing about his run-in with Sidney Leonidas and the junkie's subsequent murder. Nor of the shoot-out on the night he and Petey Alvarez took the drug dealers. If he did, she'd just scream at him. Investigators for Haldering & Co. weren't supposed to get involved in such vulgar activities.

"Laboris Investments," Cone repeats. "I couldn't see the connection with drug dealing and art smuggling. I felt in my gonads that Ingmar was an A-Number-One wiseguy, but I couldn't figure his angle. He was paying a hefty return on investments, but that guy's no foreign-exchange dealer. He doesn't know a rand from a rupee. So it had to be something else—right?"

By this time the roasted chicken is destroyed, and Cleo is working on the carcass. The yams are gone, and so is most of the salad. They're deep into the second bottle of bubbly, and decide to save the apple pie and cheddar for a late-night snack. Or morning.

They're still at the desk, feet up on the littered newspaper tablecloth. They sip their champagne very, very slowly, eyes a mite glazed, movements slow and precise to prove their sobriety.

"What was I yakking about?" Cone asks.

"Laboris Investments. What Ingmar was up to."

"Oh, yeah. Well, here's where you come in again. You broke it."

"Now how the hell did I do that?" Samantha says.

"Last night you said you wanted me to put fresh sheets on the mattress and to be sure to pick up my laundry."

She stares at him a long moment before she gets it. "Laundry!" she yells. "Laboris Investments was laundering the cash from the dope dealing and art smuggling. Feeding it into their investment funds."

"Right," Cone says approvingly. "That's exactly what Ingmar was doing."

"But he was paying thirty percent. I can't see any villain cutting his profits like that."

"Ever hear of the Ponzi swindle?" he asks her.

"Vaguely," Samantha says. "It works like those pyramid clubs, doesn't it? You get a list of ten people, send five bucks to the name on top, add yours to the bottom, and send the chain letter to ten friends. When your name hits the top of the list, you're supposed to get a million dollars. Right?"

"Right. If you get in on the start, you might make a little. If you're down on the list, you're just out five bucks. The Ponzi scam, which was dreamed up by Charles Ponzi in the 1920s, works something like that. You promise investors a big return on their money. Ingmar Laboris started out paying thirty percent. But he was using the money coming in from new investors. He wasn't doing any foreign-exchange trading. He wasn't putting the money to work in *anything*. He was just paying off that thirty percent from funds coming in from fresh suckers. And pocketing the rest. The swindle will work if the pool of new investors is limitless. But of course it never is. As soon as the new money stops coming in, the whole con collapses. That's what was happening to Laboris Investments. Lucinda Hepplewaite's boyfriend got his shekels out just in time."

Samantha frowns. "You mean this Ponzi scheme was a cover?"

"Sure it was," Cone says. "For the laundering operation. All of Ingmar's cousins were putting in dirty money and then taking out clean cash. Ingmar knew it couldn't last, but the Laboris clan did okay while it was running. I reckon they planned to close up shop in the next month or so. Then Ingmar would retire to the French Riviera and spend his remaining years indulging in Havana cigars and nymphets."

"Where is he now?"

"In durance vile, I hope. The DA picked him up this afternoon."

"On your anonymous tip, no doubt," Sam says.

"Something like that."

"Tim," she says, staring at him, "how did you figure it all out?"

"I've got a criminal mind."

"I really think you have."

"Sure I do. Every cop in the world has a criminal mind. How else are we going to keep up with the bad guys?"

It's getting on as they finish the second bottle of Korbel, talking lazily of this and that. Samantha looks down at the clean sheets tucked around the mattress on the floor.

"You ready?" she asks.

"Not yet," Cone says. "Let's wait until after midnight. There's something about the first shtup of the new year."

"You're the most romantic man I've ever met," she says, kicking his shin.

But they're lying together on the clean sheets, fooling around, when they hear sirens, bells, firecrackers, and the crash of breaking glass. Samantha sits up and unpins her glorious hair. She touches Cone's face.

"Happy New Year, Tim," she says softly.

"Yeah," he says, "the same to you."

35 - 78 - 08 - 80

Joseph Assiz.